THE UNWELCOME CHILD

THE UNWELCOME CHILD

TERESE PAMPELLONNE

PINNACLE BOOKS
Kensington Publishing Corp.

For Bob

PINNACLE BOOKS are published by

Kensington Publishing Corp.
850 Third Avenue
New York, NY 10022

ISBN 0-7394-6215-6

No words can express the helplessness, the sense of personal desecration, the despair, which sinks into the heart of a woman when forced to submit to maternity under adverse circumstances, and when her own soul rejects it. It is no matter of wonder that abortions are purposely procured; it is to me a matter of wonder that a single child, undesignedly begotten and reluctantly conceived, is ever suffered to mature in the organism of the mother. Her whole nature repels it. How can she regard its ante-natal development but with sorrow and shrinking, since God, speaking through the body and soul of that mother, frowns on its conception, its development, and its birth.

Excerpt from: *The Unwelcome Child or The Crime of an Undesigned and Undesired Maternity,* by Henry Wright, published 1858.

PROLOGUE

Martha's Vineyard, winter of 1919

Sarah stood at the window that looked out over the ocean. The midwinter sun had set, and the grayish sky was slowly turning black. Her palms and forehead were resting against the icy glass, and the cold made her head throb and her hands ache. But no matter the discomfort, she willed herself to stay pressed against the pane.

"Don't take my baby."

Sarah rolled her forehead so she could see the pleading girl lying in the cot, and the tall grim figure of Sarah's mother towering over her. The girl's black hair was plastered against her white skin, and her eyes shone like wet stones as she clutched a fistful of Mrs. Clayton's black dress.

"Caryn, let go," she said in her deep, quiet voice. "This is doing you no good." As she pulled Caryn's hand from her dress and pressed it back against the girl's chest, she turned to Missy.

"I need her quiet."

"But ah giv'er what ah shood, mum," Missy answered in her thick Scots brogue.

Mrs. Clayton looked back down at Caryn, whose hands were now balled up under her chin, her eyes shimmering with fear. Mrs. Clayton reached out and caressed the girl's damp forehead.

"Just do as I say, Missy. Another tablespoon should do."

Caryn shuddered at her touch, just as she had on her arrival when Mrs. Clayton had taken her hand to help her down from the carriage. In just that momentary press of flesh, Caryn felt something deep inside recoil, as if the life growing in her belly had divined the purpose of those hands. She wasn't the only one to feel this way. She'd noticed whenever the tall, austere woman would enter a room conversation would cease, eyes would drop, and even the most boisterous girl would become as mute as a nun who'd taken a vow of silence. In spite of her feeling of loathing, she forced herself to take hold of Mrs. Clayton's rough hand in both of hers.

"Mrs. Clayton, I can work for my keep."

Mrs. Clayton pulled her hand away and placed it on Caryn's belly, already a small hill at four months.

"There's a lot more at stake here than a matter of money, Caryn." She looked into Caryn's anxious eyes. "A woman's corruption taints not only her own soul, but that of her child's as well."

Missy came over with a spoonful of medicine and held it to Caryn's mouth, but the girl knocked it away. The spoon went clattering across the wood floor as did the bottle, leaving a trail of dark liquid. Missy's forehead puckered in fury.

"Now look what ya dun!"

Caryn tried to get out of bed, but Mrs. Clayton easily pulled her back.

"Never mind, Missy. Hold her down on your side. Sarah," she called over her shoulder, "fetch us the ties."

Sarah hesitated. Caryn was struggling now, and hollering, but Sarah knew it was no good. She knew her mother's grip, and the girl's thigh flesh squeezed out between her mother's thick fingers like soft white dough.

"Sarah, now!"

Sarah grabbed the leather ties down from a hook on the wall and brought them over. She stood, as if unsure of what to do, as if she'd never done this before, as the girl screamed a piercing "No!"

"Ah, fer the luv of . . . Ya got to be quiet, Miss Caryn! Yu'll wake not oonly the babes in the nursery but the dead too!"

"Feet first, then the hands," Sarah's mother instructed before turning her face to the hysterical girl. "Caryn, if you don't take the medicine quietly, we'll give you an injection."

"It's not right! You have no right," the girl shouted back and then raised her head to see Sarah tying her feet to the bed railings.

"And your parents have the right to not have a whore for a daughter," Mrs. Clayton said, her tone calm and resolute.

Caryn stopped struggling, and her mouth slackened as she looked up at Mrs. Clayton's implacable face. "But . . . I'm not a whore, Mrs. Clayton. We were going to be married." Don't you see?" Mrs. Clayton moved out of the way so Sarah could tie her hand to the iron railing above her head. Caryn looked at Missy. "We were going to be married."

Missy's dull, heavy-lidded eyes showed her no compassion, either. With a baleful expression, she addressed Mrs. Clayton on the other side of the cot. "You want me ta prepare the other, mum?"

Mrs. Clayton nodded, and as Sarah tied the last tie, Caryn grasped her wrist. "Sarah?"

Sarah's fingers fumbled, and she had to retie the knot. She could feel the girl's hot breath on her neck, but she resisted looking at her face. When she

was done, she stepped away with her gaze trained
down onto the floor. Missy came over with the hypo-
dermic, and Caryn began to whimper. She struggled
once again with the ties, but Sarah had tied them well,
as her mother had taught her. Missy handed Mrs.
Clayton the shot.

"When it's all over and done with, you'll understand
it was for the best," Mrs. Clayton said, as she pierced
a pale blue vein in the crook of the girl's arm.

Caryn inhaled sharply, but a moment later her lids
began to droop, her muscles relaxed, and her head fell
slowly to the side. Her half-opened eyes seemed to rest
accusingly on Sarah, who stepped farther back into the
shadows. A gusty wind shook the windowpanes. She shivered and looked out, where the wind was whipping the
black ocean up into large swells. She felt something
brush against her skirts. It was their tabby, Patty. Sarah
picked the cat up and felt the comforting vibration of
Patty's purring against her chest.

"There you are, Miss Caryn," Missy said, bandaging
her arm. "It'll all be doon foor, and ya kin go back to
yer people holdin' yer head high."

Sarah turned away and hid her face in the cat's soft
fur. Her mother had warned her about keeping company with the guests: they were girls of "bad character." But Sarah had liked Caryn. She told Sarah she
had pretty hair, and enjoyed talking with Sarah about
babies. Her first day here she wanted to see the nursery, only it was against the rules. No one was allowed
to be near the babies except for Missy, Sarah, and her
mother—not even the real mothers, once they'd had
them. But last night Caryn had been so sad that Sarah
relented and took her up after the others had retired.
She thought maybe letting Caryn rock the Barnes boy
to sleep would make her happy, but it didn't. She only
cried harder than she had any other night before.

Sarah's mother left the bedside to scrub her hands

at a deep sink in the corner of the room. She glanced over at her daughter, huddling with the cat and shivering like a big ungainly bird.

"Why did I have to tell you twice to bring the ties, Daughter?"

Sarah swallowed hard as she watched her mother scrub with ferocious energy, as if she were trying to flay the very skin off her bones.

"I'm sorry, Mother."

Mrs. Clayton stood erect as she dried her hands. "You're nearly thirteen. You'd better start paying attention."

"Yes."

"Yes?"

"Yes, Mother."

"Look at me when you address me."

Sarah raised her eyes to meet her mother's, which seemed like two dark tunnels that no light could ever penetrate. Every time she looked into them, she saw her dreary future. She'd never be comely as the girls who came here, or as long-necked and straight-backed as Missy. Already Sarah had her mother's high, hunched shoulders, which gave all the Clayton women an almost vulturish physique.

"What we do here may be unpleasant, but the souls of the unborn are more important than your discomfort. If you're ever to carry on our work, you'll need to be strong."

"Yes, Mother."

Caryn called out a boy's name, weakly. Missy had rolled the cart with the hurricane lamp and instruments over to the bed. The yellowish light made the long needles and sharp-edged things, and something that made Sarah think of the scraper they used to gut pumpkins with, gleam like gold. A bucket rested at the foot of the bed. For now, that was all Sarah had to tend to. It was her duty to take it away once it was filled. Missy checked the girl's eyes.

"She's out, Mrs. Clayton. Yoo'll have na problem with har now."

Her mother pulled a chair up to the end of the cot, and Missy pulled back Caryn's nightgown, exposing her. Sarah turned away as her mother asked Missy for more light. It was pitch-black outside now, and the candles and hurricane light reflected her own face back at her from the window. She could hear the clicking of metal instruments against each other, and her mother's stern, efficient commands to Missy. When she heard something plop into the bucket, she squeezed Patty hard, who cried loudly in protest. The cat jumped from her arms and raced out of the room as her mother's chair scraped against the floor.

"Sarah. The bucket."

Sarah went over to the bed. She looked at the bloodstained sheets, and her mother's blood-covered hands. Then she looked at the girl's closed eyes, and willed them open. She wanted her to know she would take care of her baby. But the girl only groaned and her eyes remained closed. Missy sighed and wiped a frizzy red curl away from her forehead with the inside of her forearm.

"Yoo can go now, Sarah," she said, pushing her aside. "Ya're in the way here. Go now."

Sarah carried the bucket to the dumbwaiter, where a candle on the shelf was burning. It lit up the bucket's contents, and one perfectly round, black eye, still covered in milky membrane, stared up at her. Sarah cradled the bucket to her chest as if she could cradle the babe born of sin in her arms. A baby wailed.

"That'll be the Barnes boy, I'll stake ma life," Missy said as she undid the ties. Mrs. Clayton brought over a wheelchair, and then they both lifted Caryn out of the bed and into it. Her limbs were limp and her head hung heavy. She seemed as lifeless as Bettina, Sarah's favorite doll.

"Sarah," her mother said, wheeling Caryn out, "after you send it down, strip the cot and clean up."

Then they both left. Sarah placed the bucket in the dumbwaiter and set it going. She listened to the cables creak and knock together as the baby descended down through the three flights of the house to the basement, where her mother expected her to empty it into the sewer that led out to the ocean. But Sarah couldn't imagine the baby drifting out in that cold black water all by itself without ever having been held at least once.

When the dumbwaiter stopped, she shut its door and then went over and stuck her head out into the hallway. The Barnes baby was still crying, and she could hear Missy's and her mother's murmuring voices from the floor down below. She shut the door quietly and then hurried over to the cot where she took a long strip of gauze and pressed it into the wettest part of the sheet. Slowly the blood soaked through, and when the bandage was fully red, she rolled it up and carefully placed it inside her apron pocket. She'd make sure Caryn's baby was laid to rest in a shroud, stained with the still warm blood of its mother, just as she'd done with all the others.

Chapter 1

New York City, 1995

As I fiddled with my keys, he ground his pelvis into my ass, pinning me against the door and squeezing my breasts, in and so far up they almost reached my chin.

"You've got some tits," he whispered, blowing his hot breath, rank with bourbon and garlic peanuts, into my ear. I held my breath.

"Thanks . . ." I couldn't remember if his name was Chad or Brad. "You want to let me open the door?"

"Oh. Sure." He pulled away. "Cool."

I unlocked the door and gestured for him to enter. What was I thinking? Penny's orders. She was my co-victim on *Bloodfest IV, Corridor of Hell.* We'd just returned from a six-week shoot in the Catskills, and had been at the Dive bar on the Upper West Side having a drink before heading home. What was supposed to be *a* drink turned into five, so when this kid started hitting on me, I was game. "You haven't been laid in so long you probably have amnesia, but believe me, if anyone can bring your memory back, a twenty-two-year-old can," Penny had said.

As he stumbled past me into my apartment, I was

doubtful. Richie Cunningham in leather. I didn't think this faux punk could rock my world. Take away the nose stud and wild hair, the motorcycle jacket and storm trooper boots, he'd pass for any of the other clean-cut preppie kids from the suburbs who slummed in the city on the weekends. I let my bags slide off my shoulders onto the floor. He hadn't even offered to carry them.

"You live here alone?" he asked.

I flicked on a light. "Just me and the roaches."

My small studio was still the pigsty I'd left it in. Clothes all over the place, empty soda cans on the coffee table. A thick coat of dust made everything that much duller. He went to the couch and flopped down, plopped his boots up onto my coffee table.

"Hey, there you are," he said, pointing to a poster hanging over the fireplace.

There I was. Boobs popping out of a leather bustier, kneeling next to a mad scientist sitting on a throne while I stared out with the vacant gaze of the living dead. Above our heads, letters dripping in blood spelled out ZOMBIE LOVE. Chad, Brad, whatever, leered at me.

"I should tell you, I like my women brain-dead," he said, and then laughed. I hated it when people laughed at their own jokes, especially bad ones, but I was the host and made a halfhearted attempt to laugh with him.

"No, really," he said, reaching into his jacket pocket to pull out a bag of weed. "*Zombie Love* was one hot movie. I liked the idea of that crazy doctor dude turning all you CEO chicks into his sex slaves. *You* especially rocked." His face went serious. "Except the ending. That was a real downer."

I kicked off my shoes and shuffled past him to open the window that looked out onto Columbus Avenue.

"What's the matter, you didn't like the part where we rebel and castrate Dr. Love?"

"No way," he said, pouring weed out onto my coffee table. "That was way too cruel."

I pushed the window up and looked down onto the street. Summer in the city. One in the morning and the streets were still alive. A bunch of teenagers were hanging out in the courtyard of the housing project next door. Salsa blared from an open window, and a group of old men were sitting at a fold-up table underneath a streetlight playing dominos. Somewhere far off an ambulance wailed like a diva hanging on a note way too long. I sat on the windowsill facing the kid, who was intently sorting the seeds from the weed. Now that I had him here, I wanted him to go.

He sat up and looked at me, eyes hopeful. "Hey man, can I see it again?"

I cursed Penny to myself. All these *Bloodfest* fans were alike. I walked over to my duffel bag, reached in and pulled my souvenir out by its wild, black hair. In the movie there was a hot tub scene where Psycho Bob, serial killer extraordinaire, decapitated me. I held my severed head out in front of me. Its blue eyes were wide with surprise, and the full cheeks were pulled back into a silent scream. It had Styrofoam brains with a lead weight medulla to give it that dead *thud* sound when it hit the ground. We weren't supposed to take the props, in case any retakes were needed, but I didn't want to leave my head in anyone else's hands. I tossed it to Chad.

"Awesome," he said with a big grin on his face. "Fucking awesome. I can't believe I'm here with you. The guys are never going to believe it."

Then he placed the mouth to his crotch. "Hey Annie," he said, pumping his pelvis up and down. "I'll bet you give good head."

"Yeah, but I have this tendency to bite down."

The smile dropped off his face.

"Just kidding," I said, disappearing into the kitchen.

I took a bottle of Stoli out of the freezer, held it to the side of my face. Right now my idea of foreplay would be to rub it all over my body.

Chad joined me in the kitchen. "You think you might introduce me to Psycho Bob sometime?"

I looked at him, his eyes all bright with excitement, and wondered if he'd rather screw Bob than me. If they only knew. Underneath the mask Bob, a.k.a. Ralph, looked as harmless as Gomer Pile. He was married with five kids and lived on a farm in upstate New York where he bred hamsters as a hobby.

"Want a drink?" I was already pouring two shots into juice glasses.

"You know what I like about you?"

"Besides my tits, what?"

He took a drag on his joint, making his biceps grow into one large, veiny hump. "I never seen a girl slam back so many shots and still remain standing. You can really party."

"I'm a Pollack. Vodka's like milk to me." I handed him his drink. "Cheers."

I clicked my glass against his and knocked it back, savoring the oily burn down my throat. He set his glass down. "Open your mouth and close your eyes."

"Why?"

"You'll see," he said with a dopey smile that I think was meant to be seductive.

I closed them just enough to see through my eyelashes, and watched him take a huge hit off his joint. A second later his mouth clamped onto mine and he was blowing smoke down my throat. I began to cough like crazy as my head and focus went all fuzzy. I didn't find this sexy at all.

"Cool, huh?"

"I'm not much for pot," I wheezed, and then refilled my glass with vodka to clear my throat. Just as soon as I set my glass down he asked, "So, you want to fuck?"

Did I want to fuck. Not really, but like Penny said, it was time to get back on the horse.

I shrugged. "Yeah. Why—"

Chad clasped me behind my neck with one hand and shoved his tongue down my throat, while his other hand worked its way under my skirt and between my legs. I couldn't breathe and tried to push him away, but he was like a boa constrictor: the more you struggled, the tighter his grip got. Finally I pinched the inside skin of his thigh, a trick I learned in a self-defense class.

He squealed and pulled back. "Yo! That hurt."

"What the fuck!" I yelled, wiping his spit from my lips. That clueless look came over him again.

"What's the matter? I thought you wanted to get it on."

My hand was shaking. I dropped it so he couldn't see. "You know what?" I said, trying to steady my voice. "I've had too much to drink. You, I want you to go."

He stood there, rubbing the inside of his leg. "I can do it easy if you like," he said, breathing hard. "I just thought older chicks liked to get down to business."

Adrenaline had cleared my head enough to notice for the first time how completely he blocked the doorway to my kitchen. I tried to look sorry.

"It's not you, Chad," I said. "I just . . . had a long day."

He still wasn't moving. In my peripheral vision I could see his hand resting near the butcher block that held an assortment of carving knives.

"Maybe we can go out another time," I said, all the while calculating if I should throw the blender at him or the cast iron frying pan.

"Yeah, right," he said, sneering, and then backed out of the doorway. I swallowed hard and crushed out the butt of his joint, which was smoldering in a dirty plate.

In the living room, he whipped on his Harley jacket and smacked my dummy head to the side, which had been resting on his baggie of dope. Guess he was no longer a fan.

"You have my number," I said, only because I'd had the foresight to give him a bogus one.

He ignored me and stuffed the weed into his pocket before stomping to the door, only he couldn't figure out how to unlock all the dead bolts.

"Here, I'll do it. It's confusing."

I undid the locks and opened the door. He stood there frowning at me, and for a moment I conceded that maybe I had overreacted. He seemed more disappointed and hurt than mad. I tried to match his dejection, but couldn't, so I looked down.

He pushed past me. "And by the way, my name's not Chad. It's *Brad*."

I closed the door and listened for the sound of the elevator opening and shutting, and then the clanking of the ancient motor as it descended six flights down. I rebolted all the locks and went back into the kitchen. In the junk drawer I rummaged among the rubber bands, unused Nicoderm patches, and candle bits until I found my emergency packet of Camels. I'd been good for the last two months, but now my hands were shaking so bad from the nicotine heebie-jeebies I could barely open the pack. Soon as I got it lit I sucked in the smoke deep, as if my lungs were in my toes. When the shaking quieted to a tremor, I poured myself another shot to get his taste out of my mouth. I could still feel the touch of his tongue on my molars. Older chick my ass. My eyes rested on the Kitchen Aid blender I'd been ready to bash him over the head with.

I needed some air. I gathered up the vodka and cigarettes. On my way to the fire escape, I turned off all the lights and then climbed through the window, but instead of fresh air I was met with the stench of garbage from the alley below. I took a drag off my

cigarette and leaned my elbows on the railing. The
domino game had broken up and the cluster of
teens had gone home. The street was empty, and only
a few lights were on in the surrounding buildings.
I scanned the dark sky. No stars, no moon. I might
as well be on the bottom of the ocean.

I might as well have another drink.

I tipped the bottle to the glass and missed. I'd lied to
the kid. I had my limit, it just didn't show. Most people
didn't know I was shit-faced until I passed out. One
minute I could be perfectly lucid, and the next . . . Just
in case, I sat down on a step with the least amount of
pigeon shit. I'd worked too hard on this body to splat-
ter it like a watermelon. Besides, with my luck I'd survive, a cripple. I poured myself a shot and held my glass
up in a toast.

"Here's to dying intact."

I knocked the vodka back and closed my eyes. The
liquor seemed to burn through my veins. I felt them
expand, and imagined the vodka dissolving everything inside me until I was just a sack of skin filled with
hot liquid. Nice feeling. My cigarette had burned
down to the filter. I bent over to crush it out, but then
glimpsed a pile of colorful rags down below where the
streetlight partly illuminated the alleyway. Had to be
Tessa, a rag of a woman who sometimes camped out
there. Sometimes I stopped and talked to her, let
her bum a few cigarettes (when I used to smoke), and
a few bucks whenever I could spare it. Sad story, that
one. She told me she'd been a famous actress in her
day. I didn't believe it until she showed me the newspaper clippings of reviews she kept tucked in her
bra. They smelled like B.O. and were stained, but still
readable. I remember the words *promising* and *luminous beauty*. To think those words had once been
used to describe the toothless woman sleeping on the
garbage-strewn concrete below.

Luminous beauty had never been used to describe me, but promising had. And didn't I have a deal with myself that if I hadn't made it by thirty I'd either kill myself or get out? I brought the sweaty bottle to my sweaty forehead, too hard, and winced because it hurt and because I'm thirty-fucking-five and *still here.* Jan, friend numero uno, once reminded me there was a time I would have been insulted if an agent sent me to audition for the kind of films I now did. "You're a classically trained actress, Annie," she'd said. "You should be doing Shakespeare, not Schlock horror."

Fuck Shakespeare. I'd just be happy if I were doing a sitcom, but Jan has had faith in me ever since we were kids. Our families lived next door to each other in Fall River, Massachuesetts, and in our carport she and I would reenact the soap operas our mothers used to watch. Jan thought I was so good, she used to tell all the neighborhood kids to come and watch us. We billed our show *As the World Crashes and Dies.* A group of ten or so kids would sit around and watch as Jan and I screamed and threatened one another, usually over a fictional man. Jan was always the honest and true character, I the scheming devil. She'd always been my biggest fan, and used to joke that if I were ever discovered, she had a finder's fee coming her way.

Then came the *Bloodfest* series. She never saw I and II, her excuse being she didn't think she'd find it very entertaining to watch me being dismembered, but I finally talked her into coming to a screening for *Bloodfest III.* Most of them were shit, but number III, *Carnival of Blood,* was pretty good; there was actual character development. So she came, and sat poker-faced throughout the whole movie. Not one laugh, not one scream, not even when I was fed into the wheat thresher. Afterward in front of the theater I asked her what she thought, even though she looked like she was going to be sick. "When are you going to stop punishing yourself, Annie?" I asked her what the hell she was talking about. She shook her head and said, "Do you really think it's a coincidence you started doing these films soon after the rape?"

I slipped another cigarette out of the pack and glanced into my apartment, where light from the building next door streamed in, igniting the glass eyes of my prop head still resting on the couch. Thinking how that Chad had slapped her with the back of his hand made my blood pick up some speed.

"Fuck you," I'd almost spat at Jan, because I never used that word *rape*. I'd convinced myself that as long as I couldn't remember anything, I didn't have to deal with it. All I remember was sitting at a sleazy bar in Alphabet City talking to a man old enough to be my dad. Actually, he kind of reminded me of Dad. The kind of guy who called you a broad to your face and told off-color jokes. We were talking about the Super Bowl, and the next thing I know I'm waking up naked in my own bed with a headache so bad it felt like a concussion. I had the sense *something* had happened. I kept seeing his red, oily face over mine, but that was all. So I told myself that's what happens when you drink cheap vodka and tried to forget it. Only, one month later my pregnancy test came back positive.

I leaned my forehead against the railing and stared down into the alley below. As much as I tried to justify that it was better than waiting tables, I noticed I'd coast just a little bit longer after each movie. It had been ages since I'd been on an audition I actually had to prepare for, and last year I was disturbed to find I had a favorite in each category for the daytime Emmys. It wasn't like I was depressed or sad. Shit, I would have loved to be sad. I'd love to be able to wail the way my mother said I did when I was born. She said at first I didn't want to come and they had to use a forceps to pull me out, but once I was, they still had to slap my ass something like ten times to wake me up. Then all hell broke loose. I was told I screamed so hard I turned purple. "It wasn't a cry of surprise, it was a cry of fury," Mom said. Well, I'm not called the Queen of Scream for nothing. Who knew I'd put those lungs to such good use one day?

I let my unlit cigarette fall from my lips; it disappeared, a brief flash of white in the darkness. Then I emptied the whole pack because one day that could be me down there, clutching my *Zombie Love* poster in a dirty, tightfisted hand, the only remnant left of a burned-out life. I hoped they landed right on top of Tessa. Last time she tried to bum one off me I told her I'd quit, and she accused me of just being cheap.

"Sweet dreams, Tess," I said, and sat back to take a long swig from the bottle.

CHAPTER 2

The next morning I woke up feeling like a wet rag that had been left, twisted and caked with dirt, to dry in a hot sun. I squinted up at the clock on the wall. Eight o'clock and already my skin was clammy, my hair sticking to my scalp. Outside, the sun was evil; even the gray film on my windows couldn't dim its glare. I looked at my air conditioner. Normally she sounds like a terminal asthmatic, but now she was suspiciously quiet, as if her antifreeze soul had departed overnight. I sat up and held my hand in the path of the airstream—time to pull out the electric fans.

I flopped back down. The ceiling was slowly turning clockwise, leftover magic from the vodka. What to do now was the question. I could lie here all day and watch the lint coating my eyeballs float back and forth. There's something zenlike about tracking the lint in your eyes. It's there, but you don't see it until you really look for it. But I was in no mood for introspection. What I should do is go to the gym. Last August was hot like this, and I spent the month holed up in dark movie theaters scarfing a dozen Krispy Kremes at a time. By September my ass was lumpy as a tub of large-curd cottage cheese. It took me six months to smooth it back out.

The lint stopped floating. I blinked hard to set it back in motion. I should call Peggy, my agent, to see if she had anything for me, but lately that seemed to be an exercise in futility. Just thinking about her made me clutch my sheet in my fists. Last spring I had a long talk with her. I told her I wanted her to start sending me out for work that was more "elevated." Next audition she sent me out on was for a Raid commercial. "Young mom battles giant cockroach," was the breakdown. The entire audition consisted of looking terrified and screaming. I should have been a shoo-in, but I didn't get it because I was supposedly "too sexy" for a young mom. Will someone tell me why a woman with a kid can't be sexy? Ever since, there's been nothing, except for the occasional audition for "buxom victim." I needed to find a new agent.

I sat up and felt around for my eyeglasses. I found them, and as soon as everything came into focus I almost had a heart attack. Then I laughed. I'd left my head on the coffee table last night when I folded out the sofa bed, and it was staring right at me.

"Jesus. That's got to go." I said it, but I knew I wouldn't give it back. It would feel like a betrayal.

I showered, put my head in a box that held old LPs, and chugged down two glasses of strong iced coffee before calling the Leona Helmsley of agents. I sat in my kitchen nook and listened to her pitch a commercial for Dr. Scholl's orthopedic inserts.

"They want crippled waiters," she said. "Practice walking around like you have sore feet."

It wasn't the Public Theater, but it was something. She was almost on my good side until she reminded me to send her commission for *Corridor of Hell* to her address in the Hamptons.

"August in the city is for the flies, doll. You really should get out."

I wanted to say maybe if I were a blood-sucking leech like you I'd have the money to get out, but I wished her a lovely time instead, and hung up. It burned my ass because she had absolutely nothing to do with my getting cast in the *Bloodfest* series. Psycho Bob had been an old friend from acting class, *he* recommended me to the producers, but because she sent me out on the audition she still gets her lousy ten percent. I listened to the soft whir of the two little electric fans I'd dug out of my closet. Beads of sweat trickled down my chest and pooled in the crease of the tummy roll I'd developed from all the bagels, hot dogs, and pizza I'd been eating on the set for the last six weeks. What little money there was certainly didn't go toward keeping the actors healthy, though I'm convinced the real reason producers of low-budget movies served such shitty food was more out of a need for control than any monetary concerns: keep the actors on a carbo high and maybe it'll keep their minds off how below scale they're being paid.

I began to sort through the pile of mail on my kitchen table. Two Val-Paks, enough Chinese menus to wallpaper my entire kitchen, and the August issue of *Modern Maturity*. One of my friends had taken out a subscription for me as a joke when I turned thirty-five. I looked at Paul Newman's wrinkled face. It must be hard for old actors. Everyone compares you to how you looked when you were young. At one time, I actually used to worry I'd be one of those has-beens that people stop and stare at on the street and wonder, My God, she must have lived some hard life.

I threw Mr. Newman into the garbage. Next, there was a thin-papered envelope through which I could see what I thought was a chipmunk. It was that stationery you get whenever you donate five bucks to some charity, like the Humane Society or the Wildlife Fund. My dad. A month late and too cheap to buy an actual birthday card. I didn't need to open it. It always read the same: Happy Birthday, Dad. He should just get himself a rubber stamp. I tossed it off to the side and turned my attention to a light blue, pressed-paper envelope peppered with flecks of gold. By the return address, Provincetown, Massachuetts, I knew immediately it was from Jan's sister, Ryan. I tore it open.

You are cordially invited to a baby shower for Jan Marie Hostetter on Saturday, August 21st, 1995, at the home of Ryan Jones.
   P.S. Annie, it's a surprise! I hope you can make it.
Love, Ryan.

Isn't that terrific. The godmother misses the baby shower. Under ordinary circumstances missing a best friend's baby shower is disappointing enough, but this one would have been particularly special. Ever since I can remember, Jan has wanted a baby. In junior high we had to carry around a sack of flour for our sex ed class. It was supposed to give you an idea of the responsibility a baby would be. I left my sack in a dressing room at the mall the second day, but Jan held on to hers for two months, a record, until Richard LeClair dropkicked it out the window. She had even given it a name: Sackary.

I picked up the phone and dialed Jan's number. As it rang, I ran my fingertips over the raised calligraphy. Plus, this baby was considered a miracle. In her twenties, Jan had a bout of clamydia that left her sterile. She and her husband, Kevin, had spent a small fortune on in vitro, all for nothing. They were just beginning to entertain the idea of adopting when Jan got pregnant three months after moving into their new home up on Martha's Vineyard. I would have given anything to be there just to see her face as she opened up the baby presents: tiny booties, baby rattles, doll-sized pajamas . . .

"Hello."

"How dare you have a shower without the godmother-to-be?"

There was a clunk followed by the dial tone buzzing in my ear. I looked at the mouthpiece of the receiver. Did I say something wrong? I checked the number and dialed again.

This time when she picked up, I didn't fool around. "Jan it's Annie."

There was a short silence, as if she was mentally trying to put the voice with the face.

"Annie?

"What's the matter, you forget me already?" I'd left to shoot the movie in June and hadn't spoken to her since.

She groaned. "Annie . . ."

It took me a second to realize she was crying. "What's the matter?"

She sniffed. "I've just had the most hideous night-mare. Kevin took me to the hospital to deliver the baby, but once I got there they . . ." Her voice shrank to a whisper. "They gave me an abortion instead."

"Some dream."

"But it was so *real,* Annie. I'd never felt a dream be so real. I was in this dark room and they were hold-ing me down and I was screaming because I could feel my baby being torn from me—"

"Jan?"

"I could see it!"

"Jan, stop." On the other end she choked on a sob. "It was just a dream," I said. "It's over."

"But this isn't the first time I've had this night-mare, Annie," she rushed on. "And it's always the same. Same room, same woman, only it's never gone this far before. It must mean something. Don't you think it's significant I keep having the same dream over and over?"

I closed my eyes. At a cocktail party once, someone nicknamed Jan Princess of Doom because she'd discussed the threat of stray comets, serial killers, and mad cow disease all within the space of an hour. Right now I imagined her sitting with her eyes paralyzed wide from the horror show running through her imagination as she mindlessly nibbled off a bit of skin on each side of her fingernails, one after another.

"Stop chewing your cuticles, Janine."

"What? Oh. Yeah." She tsked. "Smart-ass."

"Do I know you or what?" I said as I got up and crossed into the living room. "Now look, these dreams do not mean anything. They're anxiety dreams."

I stood in front of the fan by the window and lifted my blouse to dry the sweat dripping between my tits. "In fact, I think I read somewhere once that it's common for pregnant mothers to have dreams about aborting their babies."

"Really?"

"Sure," I lied. It made sense to me. "Being pregnant can't all be hearts and roses."

"Ugh! Don't I know it. I can't seem to keep anything down, but then last night I ate an entire stick of butter. I haven't eaten butter in years!"

I tried to envision skinny Jan fat as I reached for my pack of cigarettes on the windowsill, but then remembered I'd thrown them out last night.

"Being pregnant must be like that movie *Invasion of the Body Snatchers*," I said, crumpling the packet. "Not only do they take over your body, they take over your mind. I'm warning you, once that kid's born you won't be able to communicate with adults any longer. They call it baby talk, but I know what's really going on. Please don't ask me to be around to witness it."

Jan burst out laughing. "Oh, Annie! You talk so tough. You know you'll be the biggest, blathering idiot of all."

I lifted my shirt once more. "Not me. By the way, I got back last night and just *now* opened the invite to your baby shower. I can't believe I missed it by one day."

"You didn't miss anything."

"I'll bet. Let me guess, Ryan hired a stripper."

Jan didn't laugh. "I mean it. You didn't miss anything, because there was no shower."

"How come?"

"I never asked for a baby shower."

"Since when is it up to the mother-to-be? Besides, it was supposed to be a surprise."

"Right now I don't need any surprises. Ryan knows I don't want to leave the house but she deliberately throws the shower in Provincetown."

I glanced out the window and dropped my shirt. A guy in the building next to mine was leaning on his balcony railing, smiling. He waved. I flicked him the bird and pulled the blinds down.

"Why don't you want to leave the house?"

"We had a huge fight. Ryan called me an ingrate and Kevin accused me of being insane. It's like everyone knows what's best for me. Well, you know what? *I* know what's best for me and if *I* don't want to travel all the way to Provincetown so everyone can gawk at me, then *I* don't have to. I'm sick of it!"

I paced patiently, in case she wanted to vent more, but she made a sound like she'd had enough of herself.

"I'm sorry. I never knew what a bitch I could be until I got pregnant."

I laughed. "Hey, now I know. Next baby, no shower."

"Yeah. Next baby."

The way she said that made me want to put my arms

around her. I walked over to my bookshelf, stuffed with paperbacks and framed pictures. One of them was of me and Jan, taken right after our high school commencement ceremony. We're standing in our graduation gowns next to the Virgin on the back lawn of the Sacred Heart Church. I'm making a goofy face while Jan smiles shyly out at the camera, oblivious of the fact I'm holding up two fingers behind her head.

"Seriously, is there anything I can do for you? You sound like you're having a hard time."

"I could use a friend," she said.

I sat down on the sofa with the picture in my hands. "Well, I better get up there before you make any more enemies. Promise me you look like a beached whale?"

She hesitated. "More like a pregnant ostrich."

"Figures. I'll bet even pregnant you still manage to fit into a size two. Thing is, I won't be able to come until next week. I have an audition for a Dr. Scholl's commercial on Monday. How's that sound?"

"It sounds great," she said, her voice soft and happy, as if she'd just been given a shot of morphine. "You know, Annie, I love you. I really do."

I blushed. I was always amazed Jan could say things like that without any embarrassment.

"Same here."

I hung up and stared down at the picture. Jan doesn't look any different today than she did back then. Tall but slouchy, with fine hair that's forever falling in her face, hiding her eyes. Kids in school used to call her Cousin It. Sometimes it was still hard for me to believe that she was going to have a baby. When she called to tell me she was pregnant, I was surprised at how I felt. It was like someone calling and telling you they'd won the lottery. You're happy, but at the same time realize that in one instant things have changed. After I congratulated her and Kevin, and accepted her offer of being made godmother, I hung up and sat at my kitchen table. Underneath the kitchen window there's a playground and over the years I'd learned to tune the mayhem out, but that night I listened to their voices as the day grew to dusk and the streetlights came on.

I got up, and as I set the picture back up on the bookshelf, I realized—she never did answer why she didn't want to leave the house.

CHAPTER 3

As I waited to be picked up at the ferry depot, my stomach began to settle and I sensed the greenish cast of my skin was finally draining to its normal complexion. The ferry ride on the *Island Queen* over from Falmouth had made me sick. I'd sat on the top deck in the hope that the sea air would steady my stomach but ended up heaving my breakfast over the railing anyway. Unfortunately, the wind must have shifted, because someone on the lower deck cried out. I ran to the ladies' room, mortified, and hid there till I was sure to be the last one off the boat.

The strong breeze had tangled my hair into a rat's nest. I twisted it to the front and tucked it under my bra strap. I checked my watch. Two-fifteen. Jan said she'd pick me up at two-thirty. I stretched my legs on top of my suitcase and adjusted my visor to cut the glare of the white sun. The Vineyard was packed. Across the street from the depot was a long square of green bordered by gingerbread homes. People were lazing about on their porches, and cyclists, like a swarm of colorful insects, buzzed past me up Sea View Avenue. From where I sat I could look down the street and see the Flying Horses Merry Go-Round, tucked in to the left. I used to be terrified of it as a kid. My dad would try to coax me on, but I had this idea that the poles running through the horses hurt them.

I should probably make a quick trip out to Fall River, just to make sure he's not dead. When Mom was in the hospital, she made me promise to look after him, but six months after she was in the grave he was already shacked up with some honey from one of his gin mill haunts. I was twelve when he brought her home. Her name was Dora and she smelled like sour milk. "Now Annie, you be a good girl for Dora because she's going to be like a mother to you from now on." She lasted five months. None of Dad's "girls" stayed long. He was charming up to six gin tonics, but after the seventh he came out swinging at whoever got in his way. His specialty was verbal assault. He must have had some power over women, though. I once asked my mom what made her fall in love with him. This was after one of their fights and he hadn't come home all night. She'd said, "The heart's like a magnet, Annie. Nothing you can do once you feel that pull." My mom actually said things like that. But I did promise her. And at least I'd have Jan to bring along. A green and white taxicab pulled up and the driver rolled down his window.

"Annie Wojtoko?"

"Yeah."

"You going to 450 Sea Thistle Road?"

I stood up. The driver, a grizzled old man, got out. "Here, I'll get your luggage. My name's James Green. Jan asked me to pick you up," he said, rounding the car, adjusting his golf cap. His muscle T-shirt showed off withered arms and sagging breasts, and from his neck hung a gold horseshoe medallion almost large enough to shoe a small pony.

"That's okay, I got it," I said, picking my suitcase up. "Is there anything wrong?"

"Nothing wrong." He took my suitcase from me, which almost toppled him at first, and tossed it into the trunk. He slammed down the hood and grinned. "Beautiful day, eh?"

We followed the main road that would take us to Aquinnah. I rolled down the window and the salt air whipped my hair around my face. Soon I found my eyes closing while Mr. Green carried on a one-way conversation, describing the travails of driving on the island—how he couldn't wait till the season was over and the roads were no longer jam-packed with mainland drivers and, if I wanted, he could take me to all the good party places. Eventually, he got onto the topic of driving for Ms. Hostetter, and that got my attention. He informed me that he did all the driving for the Hostetters—the shopping, errands, and such—when the mister was away.

"Well, I'm going to be here for a few days so I'll be shuttling Jan around," I muttered drowsily.

Mr. Green peered at me in his rearview mirror. "Don't think so. Ms. Hostetter won't leave the property, let alone step into a car."

He talked on, but I stopped listening. So she was serious. I'd just thought she was making a point. But knowing Jan, she must have gotten it into her head that car travel disturbed the embryonic fluid . . . made the kid seasick or something.

We turned onto Sea Thistle Lane, a sand-dusted road that bordered the shoreline of the Vineyard Sound. All around was a stubby jungle of wildflower, tall grass, and runtlike pine trees, but then at the top of a hill sat something out of a fairy tale. The other homes dotting the landscape had the traditional gray shingle and bay windows that were as common to the island as sand, but Jan's stood out like Cinderella among her stepsisters at the grand ball. It was a yellow, three-tiered cake with delicately carved trim. A widow's walk crowned the top and an enclosed porch circled the bottom. The lawn, so green and perfect it didn't seem right stepping on unless you wiped your feet first, rolled down the sloping hill until met by a line of regal, red rosebushes. A white picket fence was the only thing separating this prim paradise on the inside from the motley, multicolored vegetation on the outside.

"Wow," I said.

"Yep," Mr. Green said, turning off the motor. "Pretty as a picture. Ms. Hostetter's always working on her flower beds."

Just as I stepped out of the car, Jan appeared on the front porch. "Hey you!" she cried as she headed down the path leading from her house. I was too shocked to move. Instead of the jolly, filled-out face of a woman in her seventh month, Jan's was skeletal. Her legs had always been sleek and well muscled, but her loose shorts exposed them to be now pelican-like, fleshless and knobbed. A striped, scooped-neck shirt exposed the ridges of bone in her chest. They made a mockery of her swollen stomach; she didn't look capable of sustaining her own life, let alone another.

Mr. Green walked past me with my suitcase. "Which room will Ms. Wojtoko be staying in, Jan?" he asked.

"Third floor at the end of the hall. Thanks, Jimmy," she said, and then hugged me.

"Jan." I hugged back, trying to keep the shock out of my voice. Her shoulder blades felt like fragile bird wings under my hands. I understood why she might not want to be anywhere people could "gawk" at her.

She pulled away and smiled, her normally perfect teeth now too large for her too-thin face. "I know. I look awful. You don't have to make anything up."

"No! I'm just . . ." I stepped back and looked her over. ". . . pissed! Damn you!"

Her smile dropped. "Why? What'd I do?"

"Do you know how much I've been looking forward to seeing you *fat?*"

She laughed and pushed at my shoulder.

"I mean it. Fuck, you probably still look better in a bikini than I do."

"Yeah, well, think how disappointed I am—I was hoping I'd finally have bigger boobs than you," she said, taking my arm. As she led me up the path to the house, Mr. Green passed us on his way down to the car, yelling out to call if we needed anything else.

I stopped. "Wait." I shaded my eyes from the sun to look up at the house. When they'd bought the place, their intention had been to open a bed-and-breakfast. It had always been a dream of Jan's to have it look out onto the ocean. Her favorite movie of all time was *The Ghost and Mrs. Muir.* I squeezed her hand and pointed up to the widow's walk. "Now you can sit and watch for shipwrecks."

But Jan didn't look up. She kept her eyes down as she pulled me toward the house. "Come on," she said. "Let's get you settled."

She and Kevin had scoured antique shops all over New England, determined to restore the place to its original grandeur. Standing in the living room, it was clear they'd succeeded. Lace curtains billowed alongside tall windows that had been thrown wide open. The furniture reminded me of my grandmother's, the kind you were so afraid to sit on you unconsciously clenched your buttocks. It was all silk and embroidered, and so heavy-looking I'd hate to have to move it when vacuuming. From the high ceiling hung a chandelier, its crystal droplets tinkling in the breeze. That, coupled with the steady curve and roll of the surf outside, made me feel as if I'd stepped into a tranquil dream in a time long past.

"I'm blown away, Jan."

Then I noticed white fabric draped on an object

hanging over the fireplace. Same thing on the wall at the bottom of the staircase.

"Got something to hide?"

Jan blushed. "Mirrors. My appetite is bad enough without having to look at myself."

I hooked one arm around her frail neck and brought her cheek to mine. "So what if there are flies circling your head? Soon as you show me my room I'm going to call 911 and request an ambulance to Mad Martha's."

She smiled. "Mint chocolate chip and butter pecan are already in the freezer."

"Careful. I might not ever leave."

Jan pulled away and turned her back to me. I didn't think I'd said anything offensive. I touched her shoulder. "Hey, I was only joking. I promise not to be the houseguest from hell."

"It's not that. . . ." She shook her hair out of her eyes. "Come on," she said. "Let's get you unpacked."

I followed her up the narrow staircase and paused on the first landing to admire how a stained-glass skylight, three flights up, strained the sunlight into a kaleidoscope of colors onto the floor below.

"You don't see that kind of detail anymore," I murmured. The air seemed to vibrate as particles of dust swirled in the shafts of light.

"It just highlights the dust." Jan sighed as she leaned her elbows on the railing. "Did you know that dust is made up mainly of dead skin?"

I looked at her. "Is this something new to worry about?"

She shrugged. "No. But if you think about it, right now we're breathing in everyone who ever lived in this house."

I blew a puff of air out, making the cloud of dead epidermis eddy and disperse.

"Well, as long as they were Democrats I don't care.

I'd rather suffocate than breathe in anything Republican."

Jan continued up the stairs. "I'm going to tell Kevin you said that."

The second flight of stairs opened onto a small landing with a window. The breeze, warm as human breath, lifted white lace curtains into the air like two welcoming arms. I paused to look out at the ocean. A clipper, its sails stretched full in the wind, seemed like a toy boat in the immense ocean. I inhaled and held my breath to give my nicotine-lined lungs time to reacquaint themselves with the phenomenon of fresh air, but they mixed as well as a prom queen with the school slut, and I ended up having a coughing fit instead.

"Nothing like sea air," I rasped. Jan had already gone on to the third floor. She leaned over the banister.

"I put you in a room facing west so you can get a setting sun. I thought you'd like that. We've dubbed it the Queen Anne room."

She was referring to my long-running lament that I'd never yet been lucky enough to find an apartment in New York that faced west. I loved a sunset more than a sunrise, but in New York they were too expensive; seems the sun only sets for the rich. I followed her up to a room straight out of *Little Women*. The walls were papered with blue rosebuds and the polished wood floor glowed golden as spilt honey. A large bay window looked out onto the Sound. I went over and discovered the house had a split personality; the front was Jekyll, the back was Hyde. Gone was the civilizing presence of the rosebushes out front, and there was no picket fence to hold back the wild plant life that covered the rough land up until it dropped off sharply to the boulder-strewn beach below. I was turning to tell Jan I very much approved of the view when I noticed that the revolving mirror in the corner was set up to face the wall.

I pointed. "You know, you're going to give me a complex."

From Jan's look, I again felt like I'd said something I shouldn't have. After an awkward moment, she picked up a dish from a table next to an iron-framed bed.

"See?" she said, holding it out to me. "I even set you out a chocolate. I make them myself." As I took the candy, I noticed her hand was trembling. She set the dish back down. "And look." She crossed over to an armoire. "There's this woman in Brewster who makes these flower stencils? Supposedly no two patterns are alike," she said, running her hand over a pattern of blue peonies and yellow daffodils. "I had to repaint the darn thing twice because I kept messing it up."

I stretched my legs out on the settee underneath the window and unwrapped my candy, a white chocolate rose.

"Man, if Martha Stewart weren't still alive I'd say you were possessed and send for a priest."

"What did you say?"

I looked up at her. "What?"

I thought I saw alarm in her eyes, but she turned away. "So you, you think it's too much?"

"Jan, I was joking." I felt a little exasperated. Of all people, Jan should know when I'm joking.

She began to pace. "I wanted this place to make people feel as if they'd stepped back into a quieter, gentler time. It sounds corny, but I wanted it to be magical and . . ." She stopped pacing and dropped onto the queen-sized bed. "Annie, there's not going to be any inn."

"Why not?"

She looked down at her stomach. "We didn't expect to get pregnant."

I went over and sat beside her. "For now maybe, but soon as you're settled with the baby and everything—"

"No." She rested back onto her elbows and her

eyes flickered over the room. "To be honest, sometimes I think it would be best if it burned down."

I must have been looking at her queerly, because her face reddened.

"I just meant the place is heavily insured. Kevin's parents are furious. They had to cosign, you know."

"Fuck 'em. So the old bat will have to go a year without redecorating one of her homes."

Kevin's parents convinced me the only good in-laws were dead in-laws. They hadn't been exactly pleased he married a working-class girl from Fall River. They were old money, obsessed with keeping their lineage up to a "certain standard." When Kevin and Jan talked of adopting, they threatened to cut him out of their will. Jan lay back and stared up into the blades of a ceiling fan above. It wobbled and made a ticking sound.

"I once heard a person was decapitated when one of the blades from his ceiling fan flew off. Do you think that's possible?" she asked.

I rested on my elbow next to her. The upper rims of her cheekbones stood out sharply. A wisp of hair was attached to an eyelash. I brushed it aside and let my fingers drag through her hair, which had thinned out; I could see the white scalp showing through.

"What's troubling you?"

A high-pitched screeching erupted. I looked out the window where two seagulls circled each other.

"Our beach is a mating ground," Jan said, as she caressed her stomach with her ragged fingertips. "Sometimes the males attack each other and it can sound like a screaming baby. I'll have plenty of that soon, I guess."

"Hey Jan, what's the real reason you wouldn't go to the baby shower?"

She closed her eyes. "Why are you asking that now?"

"The cabdriver mentioned you never leave the house. I'd thought you were just exaggerating."

Her hands stopped moving. She took one of mine and pressed it to her stomach. "Feel."

The expression on her face made me think of a kid on a roller coaster, waiting at the top of the steepest hill just before the plunge. Her eyes remained closed as if to savor the sensation. Through the soft cotton of her smock I thought I felt two faint—very faint— thumps against my hand.

"Isn't it great, Annie?" she whispered. When I didn't answer, she opened her eyes and looked at me, her eyes again with a hint of alarm. "Please tell me you felt it."

My hand slid off her belly and I cupped it in my other hand. "How could I not? Kid's got quite a kick."

She patted her stomach. "Strong, huh?"

"She's either going to be a Rockette or a black belt."

"So you think it's a girl?"

I paused, a little surprised at my presumption. "Well, it better be; I just know you're going to make the poor kid take ballet lessons. What, you've decided to keep it a surprise?"

Her smile evaporated as she curled up onto her side and cradled her stomach with her arms. "I don't care what it is, as long as it's real."

I laughed. "What other kind is there?"

She stayed in some remote region of her mind for a moment more before finally smiling up at me drowsily. "I'm so happy you're here, Ann," she said, giving my hand a squeeze. "Thanks for coming up."

I shrugged. "I just came to gloat. Your stomach's finally bigger than mine."

"Your turn next."

I withdrew my hand and sat up. The birds were gone and it was quiet now, except for the rushing of the waves up onto the beach.

"Some lucky gull's wing's been won," I said, and looked back at Jan. Her eyes were closing. "You're tired."

She yawned. "Mmm. Sometimes I feel like I could just sleep forever."

"Then sleep."

She pressed both hands into a prayer position, then rested the side of her head on them.

"Would you mind? There's tea in the fridge, and chicken wings . . ." Her voice slid into a drowsy mumble. "I know how much you like chicken wings. . . ."

Her lips parted, and she was out. I pulled the end of the coverlet over her and returned to the window. The sun glinted here and there off the waves, and some dark birds were pecking at the tiny mussels that clung to the grass-skirted boulders on the beach.

My turn. I didn't want a turn. I didn't even want to be in the game, but lately it seemed inevitable. Like a plague, all my friends were being struck with baby fever. Some had babies, but the ones who didn't were acting like they were part of some cult. Sex had become a ritual and ovulation a sacred cycle. As soon as her temperature was right, Lindy confided in me, she pulled out her lucky sheet and lit up her special fertility incense, and Sarah and Roger admitted they'd taken to chanting as they fucked. I found them a riot, and sincerely hoped the Fertility Goddess would smile down on them, but it was the ones that already had kids I found really overbearing. "Annie, this is something you don't want to miss out on," one said as she held her kid under my nose, as if she were offering me a tempting dish. I smiled and shook the little morsel's hand, but inside I was thinking, *Misery loves company.*

The sound of breaking glass came from above. In the quiet of the house, it sounded like a small explosion. I walked over to the door and looked down the hallway toward a stairwell leading to the top floor. It was dark up there, as if the day had suddenly gone cloudy.

"Hello?" I listened, then glanced back at Jan. It was silly to wake her; probably just a lamp blown over by the wind. A scene from *Bloodfest I* came to mind. Scantily clad girl is in house alone. Strange sound is heard. Girl investigates. Girl gets throat slashed by psycho killer but not, of course, until most of girl's clothes are first slashed off. I headed toward the stairs. Jan would flip if I suggested she rent her house out as a movie location. But hey, it would be a good way to make money.

At the top of the stairs I discovered the reason for the gloom. The windows on either end of the hall had been covered with tar paper while the doors to all the rooms were shut, except for one down at the end where a sliver of sunlight strayed. They hadn't finished renovating up here. Plastic sheeting covered planks of wood, and slabs of Sheetrock were leaning all along the walls. The floorboards creaked as I walked down the hallway. A sudden breeze puffed up the plastic before it floated back down with the steadiness of a long, drawn-out sigh. I pushed the door open.

A green vase lay in shards underneath a wide-open window. As I looked around, I began to have an even deeper appreciation of how much work Jan and Kevin had to do to get this place in shape. The plaster ceiling was crumbling, the wood floor had warped in spots, and the wallpaper, once blue but now a water-stained gray, was peeling away from the walls, exposing yellowed, snotlike glue underneath. A broken shade hung from the ceiling over an old box spring. The only other fixture in the room was a porcelain basin. I held my breath. It smelled as if animals had nested up here. There was a strong odor of decay—something.

I went over to shut the window but leaned against the casement a moment, and tried to imagine living here. I wondered if I'd get bored, gazing out day after day on a horizon so empty of buildings, things, people. I'd probably go crazy. When things are too calm and quiet, it makes your inner demons that much easier to hear. Maybe that was Jan's problem. She just needed to get away, spend a few weeks in the city with me. I closed the window, which was so heavy and stiff I was surprised that the gentle breeze blowing today could have nudged it open so wide. I walked over to the basin. It was a grand old sink, except that the porcelain was stained a reddish brown. I turned one of the spigots. The pipes shuddered and groaned until finally mud-colored water came first sputtering, then dribbling out. I turned the faucet off.

Across the room hanging on the wall was what could only be another mirror; a sheet was hanging over it. Now why would she need one up here? This room didn't look like it was visited regularly. I went over and grabbed a handful of fabric.

"Mirror, mirror on the wall, who's the fairest of them all? . . ." I gave the sheet a listless tug and my own face stared back at me. Most of the mirror's silver patina had worn off, but there was still enough to see a red swelling over my eyebrow.

"Certainly not you."

Bordering on middle-aged and still getting acne. My dermatologist said that it would diminish as I got older, but by that time I'd have wrinkles to contend with. I didn't find that funny. You never think of yourself as aging—that's for others to worry about—but then there you are one day, staring into a mirror in a light brighter than usual. For the first time you notice the lines, fine as spider silk radiating out like a web from the corner of your eyes, along with the furrows crossing your forehead and along the sides of your mouth, as clearly defined as the creases in an old leather boot.

I was about to cover the mirror back up but when

I'd pulled the cover off it had tilted, exposing the frame of what appeared to be a cabinet behind it. I lifted the mirror off the wall and saw that it was a small door. Obviously the mirror had been here a long time; the wallpaper behind it was bright and fresh. I set it down and tried to lift the latch of the door, but it was jammed. Since this upper floor hadn't been renovated, I had the sensational feeling that I'd discovered something secret. Perhaps something valuable? My imagination took off: Annie Wojtoko, well-intentioned busybody, finds cache of gold, gems . . . whatever, and saves the Hostetters' marriage from being sunk in abysmal debt to avaricious in-laws. I looked around for something to pry it open. A metal rod was resting in the corner. I took it and jimmied it underneath the latch until the door swung open and a puff of cold, foul air rushed out at me. I pulled back. That hint of decay I'd smelled was now a full-blown assault. I covered my nose and mouth with the bottom of my shirt as I peered down into what seemed to be the opening to a shaft. Something had died down there all right. Not recently, though. It wasn't fresh enough to make me gag.

Right inside the door was a chain. I tugged on it, and felt something give way from below. Holding my breath, I pulled on the chain, one hand over the other. It required some serious muscle, and from the way it jerked and squeaked it likely hadn't been used in years. Then the pulley got stuck, like it was snagged on something. I leaned in and looked down into the darkness. Maybe three feet below I thought I could see what looked to be a bucket on top of a carriage.

"Annie?"

I straightened up and bumped my head. "Fuck!"

With my hand on my head I turned to see Kevin, standing in the doorway, so tall his head almost touched the top of the frame. He was handsome in a perverse, Howdy Doody way. His ears didn't stick out and he didn't have a goofy smile, but he did have the red wavy hair and freckles as fine as paprika. The face itself was broad and rounded, not a sharp angle anywhere except for his upwardly slanting eyes.

"Kevin," I said, rubbing the back of my head. "What are you doing?"

He came over to give me a hug, but I took his arm and guided him to the little doorway instead.

"I came up here because the wind broke a vase, but then I found a dumbwaiter behind this mirror. I think something died down there." I tugged on the chain. "I was trying to pull it up, but it's stuck."

Kevin peered down into the shaft and scowled. "I didn't even know this was here. We were just about to renovate this floor when we found out Jan was pregnant."

I moved out of the way. He tugged on the pulley a few times. When it still wouldn't give, he took off his jacket.

"Hold this, will you?" he asked, handing it to me. Then he rolled up his shirtsleeves and pulled a small key-ring flashlight out of his pants pocket, which he turned on before reaching into the shaft so far his upper body disappeared.

"Careful, Kevin," I said, grabbing on to his belt, just in case.

I could hear something knock against the inside of the wall, a hollow, disembodied sound. A second later he backed out. He looked sickened as he rested his hands on the edge of the doorjamb.

"What?" I asked.

Cobwebs were clinging to his shirt. He set the key ring aside and lifted the sheet off the floor to wipe the dirt from his hands. "It's Butterball."

"What's a butterball?"

"Jan's cat. She got caught behind the walls." He

threw the sheet back down and reached into the shaft again. This time when he came out, he had a large metal bucket in his hands. I covered my nose and mouth back up as Kevin carried it over to the other side of the room. He opened the window.

"I'll be damned." He looked up at me. "Annie, come here and look at this." I didn't particularly want to see a decaying cat. I stayed where I was.

"What?" I asked through the cloth of my shirt.

He tilted the bucket into the light. "Tell me what you see."

I crossed the room and looked in. It was a dead cat all right. Her skin was rotting away, but some fur was still intact. Her legs were stiff straight, as if she'd been pushing away from something when she'd died. The sockets of her eyes were empty, like two dark caves over sharp fangs, bared in an eternal hiss. Then I noticed what looked like fine needles with downlike fluff clinging to them, scattered around the bottom of the bucket.

"Looks like bones," I said.

He shook his head incredulously. "She must have crawled in here to have her litter. Look at that." He reached in and pulled something out. It looked like the spine of a sardine, but it was actually a tiny tail.

"Oh, how sad," I whispered. Kevin threw the tail back into the bucket and stared down at it.

"We could hear her crying, but whenever I broke through to where I thought she was, there was nothing. She couldn't have been pregnant. She was spayed," he said. "I took her myself."

"Obviously it didn't take."

We were silent another moment. He set the bucket down and shoved his hands into his pockets; his expression had changed from bewilderment to worry. "Listen, Annie," he said, still staring down into the bucket. "I'd appreciate if you didn't mention this to Jan."

I took my shirt from my mouth. "But I think it would be a relief to her to know what happened to her cat."

He turned away. "Normally, yeah," he said, heading back to the dumbwaiter. "But as you'll see, things aren't exactly normal around here."

I waited for him to explain as he shut the small door, closed the latch, and then lifted the mirror back up onto the wall. "Are you talking about all the covered mirrors?"

"Oh. That." He bent down and wiped his hands on the sheet one last time. "She thinks it's bad luck for a pregnant woman to see herself in a mirror."

"Really?" I said, thinking she'd told me something different. Also, was I hearing disdain in his voice, or was I imagining it?

He brought the sheet over and covered the bucket. "I'll bury her later."

"Aren't you afraid Jan will find it?"

"Jan doesn't come up here," he said brusquely as he unrolled his sleeves. "This place used to be a home for good girls gone bad, and supposedly they used to do the abortions in this room. I wanted to use it as our nursery, as it has the best light in the house, but"— he gave each cuff an angry pull—"Jan wouldn't hear of it." When he looked up at me, the tenseness around his mouth relaxed.

"Hey, I didn't get my hug," he said, pulling me into him. I could feel his collarbone pressing into my temple and his heart pounding against my ear. I wasn't sure what was making me more uncomfortable: his asking me not to tell Jan about her cat or the way his hand was slowly rubbing up and down my spine, as if he were counting off the vertebrae.

I pulled away and knelt down to pick up the larger pieces of glass. "Maybe we can glue it back together."

"Don't bother. Nothing up here is of any value." He glanced at his watch. "Shit." He whipped his jacket up off the box spring where I had laid it and slipped the key ring back into his pocket. "I'm supposed to be on a conference call right now."

At the door he blew me a kiss. "Annie, we'll talk later. I'm making my famous paella tonight," he called out before disappearing down the hall.

I stood there, staring after him, wondering if I'd just imagined it. Either he missed me very much or he was extremely horny. But something else bothered me more. Something in his manner when talking about Jan. The mirrors. Silly, yes, but Kevin used to find Jan's idiosyncrasies endearing. Now there was an impatience there.

Something thumped against the window. It was a huge, black-green horsefly and it charged the window, bumping its fleshy body against the glass again and again as if it were trying to break through to get at the decomposing cat. I looked down at the sheet-covered bucket and I felt the smell of the decaying cat was seeping through my pores. The acid in my stomach rose to the base of my throat. I placed the shards of glass on the windowsill and hurried out of the room, sure I was about to throw up.

CHAPTER 4

That night we ate Kevin's paella in the kitchen in honor of tradition. Jan and I had been roommates up until the time she and Kevin married. We lived in a one-bedroom, and every other month I got the bed while she slept on the couch, and vice versa. Kevin lived in Westchester and worked in a law firm in the city, and whenever he stayed over he'd bribe me with his grandmother's "famous paella recipe" so they could have the bedroom. It was the worst paella I ever had, and after a few meals I struck a deal that I'd sleep on the couch only so long as he never cooked for me again. From then on he ordered in, and we'd stay up all hours drinking beer or red wine, fuel for our fights over politics, race, and class.

"You think Guiliani's a racist," Kevin said once. "What about Dinkins? If it had been whites rioting in Crown Heights, no way would he have let it go as long as it did."

"Don't even try and put Dinkins on the same planet with Guiliani," I shouted back. "He was a lousy mayor, but at least the city didn't feel like a Disneyfied Stalag Thirteen!"

These debates typically arose close to election time,

with the objective being to win Jan over to Kevin's or my candidate. Jan, in her typically fence-straddling fashion, had no particular allegiance and was usually still undecided right up until the election. Whether she ended up voting Democrat or Republican depended upon which of us was the more convincing in our debates. Of course, she almost always ended up voting Republican, but I think that was because Kevin did most of his persuading in bed.

Good times. But tonight we might as well have eaten in their formal dining room at the mahogany table that seated twelve. All through dinner I noticed Jan avoided eye contact with Kevin. Kevin on the other hand was being so polite I couldn't even get him to rise to my bait.

"So, Kevin, what's it like living in the enemy camp?" I asked.

He was watching Jan. She'd been nudging the same shrimp around her plate as if to wake it from a deep sleep.

"Kevin?"

He looked up at me. "I'm sorry, Annie, what did you say?"

"I asked how you liked living in the land of the Democrats."

His eyes rested on Jan again, and he sighed. "Well, you know, the things you do for love."

Jan glanced up and then back down, her head bowed even lower over her plate as she continued to toy with her food.

"Love?" he said. "The shrimp's been stripped and boiled—why don't you just put it out of its misery and eat it?"

I smiled at Jan, nervously. She'd pulled her hair back into a tight knot on top of her head, giving her eyes a slant that was beyond Asian. The Tiffany lamp overhead highlighted the sharper angles of her face, deepening the shadows in her sunken cheeks and eye sockets, making her head skull-like. She forked the shrimp.

"I'm sorry but . . . it's not deveined. See the black line running up its back?" she said, holding it up to me. "That's the shrimp's crap. If you don't devein, you're ingesting all the PCPs, mercury . . . whatever the shrimp has ingested. That's not good for you. Especially pregnant women." She delicately scraped the shrimp off her fork onto the side of her plate.

The tension in here was pulling at our collective nerves as tautly as Jan's hairdo was threatening to pull her scalp from her skull. I was afraid our reunion dinner was going to split up prematurely if I didn't do something to loosen things up.

"So that's why it tasted edible." I laughed as I stabbed her shrimp with my fork and popped it into my mouth. "Kevin, I think we finally found your grandmother's secret ingredient."

His eyes narrowed at Jan. "I think our baby would be *grateful*, Janine, for even toxic shrimp rather than starve."

Jan twisted her napkin in her hands. "Kevin, I ate as much as I could."

He tore off a piece of roll he'd been eating and threw it down in disgust. "You took one bite of chicken."

Her eyes pleaded with him. "My stomach is upset."

I turned to Kevin. "The paella was spicy."

"A boiled potato would be too spicy for her," he said, and then drained his glass of wine.

Jan moved her chair back. "If you'll excuse me."

I grabbed her wrist. "Jan, you don't feel like eating right now, don't."

"Thanks, Annie," Kevin said, refilling his glass. "You're a big help."

"And neither are you by making her feel like a criminal."

I was still holding Jan's wrist and gave it a small tug. "Pull your chair up."

She did, reluctantly. It was raining lightly, and we could hear the patter of water falling on water outside. The humidity was making my thighs stick to the wooden chair. I looked at Kevin, his lips pressed together into a mean thin line, and then at Jan, who was now gnawing at her fingertips. No way this was over a canceled baby shower.

"Jan, why don't you tell me about the house? While we were preparing dinner your husband gave me a little run down on its history," I said, glancing at Kevin.

She looked back down at her full plate. "I just think that the house is special, that's all."

"Whoever lives here supposedly gets pregnant. Sometimes I think my wife gives the house more credit for our baby than me," he said, swirling his wine in his glass. "Hope you brought protection, Annie."

I looked at Jan. "Is that true?"

She leaned into me and gripped the edge of the table with both hands. "My friend Gail told me one woman who lived here was *fifty-five* when she got pregnant, and she'd been through menopause one year earlier."

"Gail," Kevin said sneeringly. "What does that old dyke know about conception anyway? Christ, she wouldn't know what to do with a dick if it slapped her in the face."

It was a comment so uncharacteristic of Kevin I almost laughed out loud until I saw Jan's face—pure outrage. He reddened slightly as he took a sip of wine. "Anyway," he continued, "menopause can take years to go through."

"And what about me, Kevin? I was sterile," Jan said, still vibrating with indignation.

"So said that *quack* in Boston!" He'd set his glass down so hard wine sloshed over the edge. "Who I will be suing for the thirty grand we'd spent on fertility treatments, thank you very much."

Jan dropped her eyes to her stomach, stroking it, as if to calm the baby inside down. "We don't need to sue anybody. We should just be happy it worked out fine."

"Yeah. Everything's worked out just beautifully," he muttered.

I turned my face to the window where a clammy breeze was streaming in. The rain had tapered off, but the clouds still blocked out the stars and moon. Only the sound of the surf and a dinging buoy gave away that there was any ocean at all.

"Maybe it's the sea air," I suggested. "You know, that may be something you could use to your advantage. Advertise the house as a type of Lourdes for barren women."

"Don't make fun, Annie," Jan said.

"I'm not. Actually, I think there is something to what you say."

Kevin threw his napkin down and got up. "Yes, it's called magical thinking. I'll make some coffee."

"It's not," Jan said under her breath, like a child to its parent rather than a wife to her husband.

"I have to tell you about this chiropractor in the city I went to," I continued. "You know how my back is always going out. Anyway, a friend recommended this 'holistic' chiropractor. Man was he a trip. He has you lie down and hold out your arms, and then he throws a packet of sugar onto your stomach. If he can push your arms down, it means you have an intolerance to sugar. It weakens you. He said that's why my back kept going out."

"You need a degree for that?" Kevin asked as he filled a coffee carafe with water from the sink.

I hooked my arm around the back of my chair to look at him. "Listen, I thought it was a load too, but why I brought it up was because before I went, my friend warned me that I'd better make sure I was on birth control because this doctor gets women pregnant."

Kevin hooted. "I'll bet."

I turned back to Jan. "Supposedly, he releases psychic resistance. He stands over you and moves his fingers around like . . . like they're antennae picking up ESP waves. He told me I was hanging on to the past, and if I didn't let go my back would do it for me."

Jan nodded her head in solemn approval. "He sounds like a smart man."

"It's just power of suggestion, Jan, but a lot women believe it and actually go there thinking he's going to unblock their maternal aura or whatever."

"So," Kevin said, smiling slyly over his shoulder, "did you take your friend's advice about the birth control?"

"Unless he could induce immaculate conception, I had nothing to worry about. For me it was a waste. I guess I'm resistant to suggestion because my back went out again a week later."

"Maybe he's right, Annie," Jan said. "I think you do hang on to . . . unfortunate things that have happened in the past."

What she was referring to didn't need to be acknowledged; I pushed my plate away. "Speaking of unfortunate things, I know this goes beyond the call of friendship, but would you ride out with me to my dad's one day?"

Kevin slapped the cupboard shut. "Fat chance."

I swiveled around. "Okay, Kevin, what bug crawled up your ass tonight?"

He pointed at Jan. "Didn't she tell you why she wouldn't go to her baby shower?"

"Kevin . . . don't," Jan stammered.

"The one her sister spent two months planning and her friend Nadia flew all the way from California to be at?"

She lifted her head, her jaw so tight the ligaments in her neck stood out like vines on a tree trunk. "I couldn't," she choked out. "I was having cramps . . . I was afraid I was going to lose the baby."

He stood over her. "All the more reason to go to the hospital, right? But then that would mean tests—maybe an amniocentesis? What's the matter, Jan, afraid they'll find our baby has a tail and cloven hooves, or something worse?"

A tear ran down her face as her mouth worked soundlessly, struggling for the words. "I just wanted you all to leave me alone. Why won't you leave me *alone*?"

"Because that baby is half *me*, and we know what that means, don't we?"

She crunched over her stomach with balled fists pressed to the side of her head. "Stop it."

"Hell, a tail and hooves would be the least of our worries," he said, still staring down at her.

"Kevin, I don't know what the hell you're talking about, but you need to chill out," I said.

His eyes snapped up at me. "Don't tell me to chill out, Annie."

Jan covered her face with both hands.

"Jan, don't cry," I said, reaching for her. I glared at Kevin. "Why are you being such a prick?"

"Because what she's doing is child abuse!"

Jan's head snapped up. "Why don't you tell Annie how you'd abort our baby if you could? Go on, tell her!"

"What was the agreement Jan?" he asked. She got up from the table. "What was the agreement?" he half shouted, his face so red the freckles had disappeared.

Jan looked at him as if he were someone she loathed rather than loved. "And he wonders why I've lost my appetite," she said, her voice a harsh whisper. "I'm sorry, Annie. But I've had enough for one night."

Then she pushed through the swinging kitchen doors so hard they banged off the walls.

I sat, stunned, listening to her pad up the stairs. After I heard a door shut, I turned back to Kevin. "What agreement?"

He leaned back against the counter, rubbing his eyes for a moment before dropping his hands. The weary sagginess of his face made him look old. "I have a brother. He was born severely retarded and has been in an institution since he was ten."

"I didn't know this."

"One thing Jan and I always agreed on was that if she ever did get pregnant, we'd go for genetic counseling. There's a very high chance our baby could be born with Down's. Jan and I agreed, we *agreed*," he said, jabbing the air with his forefinger, "that if her amnio came back positive, we'd have an abortion."

I sat there, disconcerted. For years all I heard about was breakthrough fertility treatments, side effects of the hormones and the indignity of the procedures, yet never once did Jan mention this. "She never said anything to me," I said, more to myself than Kevin.

He focused up at a spot on the ceiling as if he could see Jan through two floors. "She doesn't know what it's like to raise a severely disabled child. It practically destroyed my parents' marriage. I do not want to condemn an innocent soul to a life of hell," he said, then turned back to finish preparing the coffee.

"So you think that's why she won't go to the doctor?"

"It's too late now anyway. Right now, all I want is to find out either way so we can prepare, but thanks to that . . ." His back was to me, but the contraction of his shoulder blades made his disdain palpable. "Gail told Jan that all the women who conceived in this house, once they moved away, their babies died."

He brought over two cups of coffee and set them down onto the table.

"How creepy."

"It's not creepy. It's crazy." He went to the freezer and pulled out a bottle of Sambuca. "My wife is convinced if she leaves, even steps off the property, our baby will die." He poured a shot into my coffee. "The day of the shower she was hysterical. She accused me of deliberately trying to cause a miscarriage."

"But if she was having cramps . . ."

"We're talking about Jan, Annie," he said. "It's the same thing that caused her career to go down the drain."

I rested my chin in my hands, unable to say anything. Jan had been discovered by an agent for a top modeling agency while selling clams on a Provincetown beach. She had the body, the face, everything but the desire. They flew her out to New York where she lived in a penthouse apartment with five other hopefuls. Her big break was a *Sports Illustrated* spread. It was the type of opportunity that came around once in a model's career—a crossroad between Macy's catalogue work and *Vogue*—but the day before the shoot Jan broke out in hives so bad she showed up on the set looking like a giant strawberry. They canceled her contract and she never modeled again.

Kevin shook his head in frustration. "This Gail has taken a series of unfortunate coincidences and made them into some sinister legend."

"So the women's babies did die."

"The fifty-five-year-old and her infant died in a car crash. Another baby was stillborn and the third I couldn't track down."

"And her baby?"

Kevin hesitated. "I don't know."

There was a pause, in which I wavered between believing it or not. "Well," I said, "even if it is psychosomatic, the way you're treating her certainly isn't going to help."

He folded his hands in front of his mouth, and the red-gold hairs on his hands glistened in the overhead light. "Sometimes I think it would be best if I just left until the baby arrives. You know she hasn't touched me since she's gotten pregnant?"

I shifted uncomfortably, remembering the intimate way his hand worked up and down my back. "I think that might be common. Especially with first pregnancies."

He stared down into his coffee. I could feel his hopelessness. I stretched my hand out to put it on his, but couldn't reach. I rested it on the edge of the table instead.

"You know, Annie, when I met Jan and found out she couldn't have children I was relieved?"

I sat back, dismayed. "If you didn't want a baby, why did you go to all that trouble?"

He looked up at me with very tired eyes. "Because." He sighed and then shrugged. "She did."

Kevin made an excuse he had some work to do, so I went upstairs to check on Jan. The door to their bedroom was open; I stuck my head in. It was much larger than mine, and was furnished with heavy mahogany antiques. The room glowed wherever the moonlight touched. A path of light led out to an open balcony where a planter was swinging in the wind.

"Jan?"

Since she wasn't there, I was about to head to my own room when a light clicked on behind me. I turned around. There was a door, kitty-corner to Jan's, opened just enough to let out a sliver of yellowish light.

"Jan, you in there?"

I pushed the door open. The room was empty, but an elaborate mobile above a crib was dancing in the air, as if someone had tugged on it, setting the figurines bobbing up and down and spinning at the same time. I walked over to the crib and reached for one of the dangling figures, a tin clown. I was thinking it was kind of eerie that the light had gone on by itself, until I noticed the timer at its base. I let go of the clown and looked around the gloomy room, trying to figure out why Jan would prefer this one to the one upstairs. Granted it would take a lot of work to get it into shape, but it had an abundance of light and air as compared to this room with its one small window, oppressively dark paneling, and heavy moldings. It didn't feel light and playful as a nursery should, in spite of all the dolls, which were everywhere—lined up on shelves, posed around a child's table set up for tea, in a play crib and on top of a toy chest. Dolls, dolls, dolls. Only they weren't the modern kind. They didn't pee their pants or cry mama; there were no strings to pull whenever you wanted to hear "I love you." These were antiques, and some looked more human than a lot of people I've known.

Restoring dolls was Jan's passion. She treated them as if they were battered children and she wouldn't stop working on them until they were rehabilitated to pristine condition. When we lived together there were always tiny disarticulated arms and legs, disembodied heads, and glass eyes lying around the apartment. I preferred the dolls dismembered to when they were whole. Until they were sold they'd just sit there, staring at me with those eyes that seemed to follow me wherever I went—like now.

I took a step and something sharp jabbed my foot. I hopped back. "Shit!"

I'd stepped on one. It was facedown, next to the table set up for tea, as if it had been booted out by the three prissy-looking dolls posed there. Its legs were tangled and one arm was twisted around its back. I picked it up. It had a rag body with pillowed felt feet and was dressed in a checkered pinafore. Its dusty black wig was in good condition, but its pink enameled skin had flaked away in places and some of the fingers had broken off. But what really creeped me out was behind its red lips you could see every single space between its teeth. They were so real- looking I imagined if I put my finger too close, it would bite down. I noticed a needle, woven into its right arm. It was being repaired. The arm had a small tear in its shoulder, where a bit of its stringlike stuffing protruded.

I turned on a lamp to see the damage to my foot. In the middle of the arch a pinpoint of blood was welling up.

"Assassin," I hissed, and threw her into an oversized rocking chair. Then I looked closely at what I'd first thought was just ugly wallpaper. It had been too dim to see clearly, but with the extra light I could now see it was a fairy-tale landscape covering the entire length of the wall. It took me a minute to get it, until I recognized the one-legged soldier sailing down a blue stream, a girl with red shoes dancing across a bridge.

"Do you like it?"

Jan stood in the doorway, wearing a black nightgown. She'd let her hair down from its S&M bun and her eyes were no longer orientalized, just red and puffy from crying.

"It's great. I came in here because the light was on and—are you okay?"

She came over and stood in front of the mural. "My friend Gail painted this for me. I'd mentioned in passing that Hans Christian Andersen was my favorite author as a child, and one day she showed up with paint, brushes . . . really special, isn't it?"

My eyes roamed the mural, a forest of cottages, castles, and windmills. I spotted the Match Girl, my favorite, cupping her hands around a match as she huddled against a curling wind whipped up by the Snow Queen whizzing down a mountain in her sleigh. I moved down the wall looking for others I recognized, but then one stood out from the charm of the others: a pleading woman, kneeling in front of a tombstone with a hooded figure standing behind her.

"Which one is this?" I asked.

"The Dead Child."

I looked at Jan, incredulous. "Dead Child? Kind of morbid for a nursery, isn't it?"

A funny look came over her face. "It's in honor of what happened here. Five children were smothered by Sybil Clayton, the woman who ran the place."

"God." I looked back at the pleading mother. "Why?"

Jan licked her lips and took a breath. "She had a daughter who drowned. At least that's what they assumed. They never found her body, but they did find her doll out on the rocks out back." She turned and glanced around. "This one as a matter of fact," she said, picking up the doll I'd stepped on. "Her mother performed the abortions, and leading up to the killings they say she heard babies' cries even when there weren't any in the house."

She held the doll up. "We've met," I said. "Not only does it look like it has leprosy, it stabbed my foot."

"You and your doll phobia," she said, sitting down in the rocker. She held the doll out in front of her and in a motherly coo said, "Don't listen to her. When I'm through with you, you're going to be just as beautiful as the others."

"Jan, you're weird," I said, turning my focus back to the Goya-esque image—the mother's gaping mouth, her pleading, upturned palms as Death stands faceless behind her. I thought about the room upstairs, and was about to ask why a room where five infants were murdered was any better than one where abortions took place, but remembered my promise to Kevin. I looked over my shoulder at Jan. She was searching through a red sewing basket. I thought it was odd she wasn't more upset about what had happened downstairs. Whenever they'd have a fight in the past, which was rare, Jan would be inconsolable. For her, a quarrel was a portent of divorce. Now she was behaving as if we'd had the most pleasant dinner. I picked one of the tea-partying dolls up by the head and moved her aside so I could sit; a good portion of my butt hung over each side of the child-sized chair. I gestured around to my companions at the table. "You might want to think about getting a few GI Joes just in case it's a boy."

Jan's head was lowered, but she peered up at me. "Can you keep a secret?"

"Not if money's offered."

She leaned forward. "I already know it's going to be a girl," she whispered, then rocked back away with a pleased-as-punch smile on her face. I waited for her to explain, but she seemed to be waiting for me to ask.

"What, you just have a feeling or something?"

She shook her head. "Not me." She stopped rocking and glanced toward the doorway. "Gail. She has second sight," she said in a hushed, exhilarated voice. "The first day we moved in she came over to welcome us and . . ." Jan took my hand in both of hers. "She holds my hand like this, and just keeps on holding it with the strangest look on her face, like she's in some kind of trance, right? And I swear, Annie, the electricity that came off this woman could have lit up this whole house, but she looks me straight in the eye and in this voice—she has the most amazing voice— says to me, 'Within three months, you are going to be pregnant with a healthy baby girl.'"

She let go of my hand and rocked back, both hands on her stomach. "Three months later, I was."

I nodded and forced myself to smile with her, while

at the same time thinking how much I already disliked this woman. "So. You're pretty close to this Gail, huh?"

"Annie," she sighed, pulling the needle out of the doll's arm. "I don't know how I would have gotten through the last few months without her."

"Really?" I could feel my smile growing stale.

"Yeah." She gazed down at the doll in her lap. "She's been like a mother to me, even though no one can ever replace Mom."

Not even close, I thought. When Mrs. Kiley died in a car accident two years ago, it was like losing my own mother all over again. After Mom died, Mrs. Kiley knew my dad had no idea what to do with a twelve-year-old girl. She went shopping with me for my first bra, and helped me with my Girl Scout activities so I could earn just as many badges on my sash as Jan. When I got my period, my dad turned white and muttered, "Oh, Christ," and then sent me off next door to Mrs. Kiley so she could explain to me what was happening.

"Kevin thinks she's just a kook, but she's not," Jan said as she guided black thread through the eye of a needle. "He's always been such a linear thinker. He can't understand sometimes things happen that are outside of our normal experience. Some things just can't be explained. He thinks it's all in my head, but it's not." Her focus shifted from her threading down to the burgundy carpeting. "I felt something happening the day of the shower when I tried to leave. It was real." She returned her attention back to the doll. "Like I said, it can't be explained."

"Kevin said this Gail told you that if you left the house your baby would die. You really believe that?"

She glanced up, just long enough for me to see her lips and brows pinch together before she bowed her head back over her sewing.

"I really cannot stand it when people discuss me behind my back," she said.

"What did you expect after that scene downstairs? I asked him what was going on."

I watched her hand move up and down, her fingertips pressed white against the needle. I waited for her to offer a rational explanation, but getting things out of Jan can be like prying open a sealed pistachio shell with nothing but a blunt fingernail.

"*Did* she actually tell you that? Because if she did, I have to agree with Kevin, the woman sounds like she's either crazy or she's running some type of scam."

She flicked her hair out of her eyes. "I have absolute confidence in Gail. If I didn't, I wouldn't be having her deliver my baby."

When she snipped the thread and knotted it, I had this runaway fantasy of Gail, her likeness inspired via the cronish mother of the Dead Child in the mural, standing over Jan's baby and laughing maniacally as she snipped its umbilical cord with a pair of bloody scissors.

"I thought Ryan was delivering your baby."

Slowly she wound the thread around the spool. "Gail's a licensed midwife."

"But Ryan's your sister!"

She hesitated. Her eyes flickered up at me and then back down. "Ryan . . . she works at a clinic where they do abortions. I can't have her deliver my baby."

I stared at her in shock. "Since when are you pro-life?"

She looked annoyed, her brows knitted together. "It's not just that. Gail and I are more . . . in tune with each other. She doesn't believe in amnios and all those other tests." She dropped her hands in her lap. "We both agree, it's a strange time to be a mother. Women practically having litters thanks to fertility drugs, young girls giving their eggs away for money . . . it's getting so there's not much difference between a free-range hen and a woman."

"Does Kevin know this?"

She bit her bottom lip. "Not yet," she said, and began to fuss with the doll again.

I watched her adjust its dress, smooth back its hair, until I couldn't keep it in any longer. "Jan, why didn't you tell me there might be a problem with the baby?"

The crease in her brow deepened even further. "There is no problem," she said.

"But what if there is?"

"There *isn't!*" She thrust the doll into the sewing basket. "And even if there were, it still wouldn't make a difference."

She pushed herself out of the rocking chair, crossed the room to rearrange a doll-heavy shelf on the opposite wall. "You know what this is really all about, Annie? It's not about 'condemning an innocent soul to a life of hell,' it's about the great Hostetter bloodline. His parents just can't face the possibility that the only heir to their throne might be . . ." She turned around and brought her hand to her head. "Now how did Kevin's mother describe Ronnie? Oh yeah. A mistake. They called him a *mistake*, Annie." She grabbed a clown with an unhinged grin from the shelf as she sat down on the toy box. "How can you say that about your own child?" she almost cried, stroking the orange hair that made the doll's white head look as if it were on fire.

"What's so surprising? We knew they were assholes when they boycotted your wedding."

"They're not just assholes, they're evil." She stood up and pointed in the general direction I assumed Kevin's parents lived. "Those people have the money to keep Ronnie home, but instead they keep him tucked away in some institution. It's this big family secret. They're so ashamed of him they won't even bring him home on the holidays! I'm surprised they didn't put a pillow over his face a long time ago," she said red-faced, spit flying.

"Jan, calm down."

"Well you know what?" She went to the door and leaned out, shaking the clown in her fist as she yelled toward the stairs. "A baby's not a piece of pottery that can be scratched and started over if you're not happy with the form!"

I waited for her to face me again. "Come on. Sit down. Let's just talk about this calmly, okay?"

"I never would have agreed to something so horrible knowing what I know now," she said, leaning back against the wall with both hands on top of her stomach. "That's why I'm having those terrible dreams, Annie. If I'd had the amnio and it had come back positive for Down's, Kevin would have insisted I have an abortion."

"But it's too late for that now. He just wants to know so you two are prepared. What's wrong with that?"

She looked at me in disbelief. "Are you taking his side?"

"No! I just think your responsibility to your baby should override some . . . *crackpot's* premonition!"

"You are," she said, tossing the clown into the crib. "You're taking his side. I can't believe it."

"There are no sides! But Kevin is right, Jan, a handicapped baby is a huge commitment. You need to be prepared for—"

"Excuse me," she said, holding up her hands. "But since you're more an expert on ending a pregnancy than keeping one going, I think I'll forgo the advice."

Right after she said it, she looked away. I was more surprised than hurt, but when she kept her head down, hidden behind that curtain of hair of hers, I realized it wasn't just a thoughtless outburst. I felt like I was witnessing a chasm tear open between us, caused not so much by what she'd said as by the almost imperceptible fissures of doubt that sometimes nagged at me about Jan. Could she have been judging me all along, holding me in some secret contempt? She swept her hair back with both hands until they gripped the base of her neck, leaving her long forearms to rest against her chest like folded wings.

"It's been a long day," I said, turning for the door. "I think I'll just go to bed."

"Annie?" I paused, and looked at her over my shoulder. "I didn't mean to hurt your feelings."

I shrugged. "How could you? I have no regrets."

Back in my room, I undressed and flopped into bed thinking I was going to pass right out. Instead, I stared up at the unsteady ceiling fan. In the daylight its wobbling and ticking hadn't seemed nearly so menacing, but now I wondered if Jan's fear wasn't so far off base—if I should be worried that any moment now the blades were going to fly off and decapitate me.

I turned onto my stomach and reached under the bed where I'd stashed my one pack of cigarettes in a sneaker. It wasn't there. I checked the other, then turned on the lamp to see if it somehow fell out, but there wasn't even a dust ball let alone an errant cigarette. I threw my sneaker across the room in the direction of Jan's bedroom. Somehow Mother Hubbard down the hall always knew where my stash was.

I listened to the fan: *tsk-tsk-tsk-tsk-tsk-tsk-tsk*. Hot as it was, I couldn't stand it any longer. I grabbed the remote and aimed it at the fan until it went silent. Everything was quiet, except for the ocean. Down below, the waves lapped at the beach. I tried to concentrate on their rhythm, but just as I began to feel drowsy I heard voices flare up from down the hallway and then a door open and slam, followed by footsteps hurrying down the stairs. I couldn't tell if they were Jan's or Kevin's.

No regrets. I didn't have any because I never thought about it. It's not like I'm a sociopath, it's just that you have to move on. If I fell apart every time I did something that made my conscience squirm, I'd still be in fucking Fall River. And shit happens. Especially to a dumb fifteen-year-old whose boobs were the size of cantaloupes by the time she was thirteen. There wasn't a guy in school that didn't want to get into my pants. Who wouldn't like the attention, even if it was only ten minutes at a time?

After I left my flour sack baby at the mall, I flunked sex ed, and the only heart-to-heart with my dad about birth control consisted of, "You ever come home knocked up I'll knock the shit and anything else right out of you." Not the kind of guy you ask for help from. Jan's sister, Ryan, was in college at the time, and set it up for me at a Planned Parenthood. It was all over and done with on a Saturday morning. When I came home, I told my dad I thought I was coming down with the flu and stayed in bed the rest of the weekend. It didn't occur to me to worry over whether or not I'd just destroyed anything. I was too relieved, and so grateful that I swore off boys forever. Until Carl.

He was my first real boyfriend; we met at Boston U. He was studying business, I was there on a drama scholarship. We both worked at a place called Bowl World, where I rented out the shoes and he worked the register. On our breaks we used to go down underneath the alleys where the machines reset the pins. Our breaks were short, so we did it as if we were going for a record. Any outbursts were covered up by the crashing sounds of spares and strikes above and the grinding machinery below. Carl loved me, but I was only fond of him. Okay, maybe it was more than just fondness. It was hard not to fall in love with someone who believed you were nice enough to plan a life around.

After work, he'd drive me home in his Pinto and go on about what we'd be doing next year, and the year after that, even though he knew I was leaving as soon as I got the money together. Jan was already in New York and the longer I stayed in Massachusetts, the further I felt left behind. He pretended to accept my plans, but on the night he claimed to have forgotten his condoms I should have known better. As usual, we'd been drinking peach schnapps. It dulled the sound of crashing pins, and helped stomach the smell of rosin and other people's stinking feet on my hands. I said okay, just promise to pull out before you come, and he swore he would. But he didn't. He shot everything he had up inside me and I just lay there, feeling trapped under his heavy body.

I didn't tell him until it was done. "It was our baby, Annie," he cried in Bowl World's parking lot at two in the morning. "I would have taken care of it. You still could have gone to New York." But like hell was I going to get saddled with a rug rat at twenty and settle into his pathetic little Ozzie and Harriet daydream. "Go to hell, Carl," I screamed back. "When I want to have a baby, it'll be *my* choice!" Six months later, I was in New York.

Sometimes I wonder how things would have turned out if I'd had it, if I'd stayed and married Carl. Once, while visiting my dad in Fall River, I saw Carl at an A&P. He'd turned into a cliché. His hair had thinned and he had the flaccid, grayish skin of someone who works in a fluorescently lit environment. He was pushing a cart full of groceries—a toddler in the seat, two identical little girls hanging off the front—and I could just picture him driving a minivan home to a three-bedroom ranch somewhere in a comfortable suburb. I didn't want him to see me, so I followed close behind.

I was fascinated at the patience he displayed when the toddler tore open a bag of nuts, spraying cashews and peanuts all over the floor, and the way he negotiated with the twins in the candy aisle. He actually finessed them into a bag of dried fruit over gummy bears. It was clear he liked being a dad. He was good at it. Until then, I didn't believe he was serious when he said he would have taken care of my baby.

The last one? No way would I ever have any regrets over that one. The nurse who processed my paperwork noted it was my third, looked at me, and said, "This isn't a form of birth control, you know." I'd just read an article on cell harvesting from aborted fetuses, so I looked at her and said, "Science needs fetuses. I'm just doing my part."

I think I've always known that Jan resented me. In a way, I couldn't blame her; she couldn't conceive while I seemed to be as fertile as a midwestern cornfield. But it's not as if I went tra-la-la-ing on my way afterward. The guilt's like a pilot light—it never goes out, which is one of the reasons why I've decided never to have a kid. Plus, every time I think of the possibility, I remember the sickening dread of it all. The missed period, the swollen breasts, the double pink line in the urine-soaked circle. The "oh, fuck" feeling, the feeling my body had betrayed me. It had its own agenda whether I liked it or not. Men don't have that. The thing that comes closest is maybe an inconvenient erection. And of course, nobody looks at a childless man with pity. When he decides he doesn't want one, he's not considered a callous monster, a baby killer, which is what those lunatics outside the clinic called me on my way in this last time.

And it was the last time. Three strikes, you're out. I meant it when I told Jan I didn't have any regrets, but as I've gotten older, I did think about it more. I reached for the remote and turned the fan back on. Soon as it was up to speed, it continued its mantra. *Tsk-tsk-tsk-tsk-tsk-tsk-tsk-tsk.*

As much as I missed my mother, I was sometimes glad she wasn't around. She wouldn't like the movies, or the fact that I wasn't married, had no kids. She especially wouldn't understand three abortions. She'd been very Catholic; in her eyes, just one would have condemned me to hell. I wondered if the dead could see and hear, if they stood beside us and watched what we did.

My pity party was interrupted by a gust of wind so strong the blinds lifted up high into the air and clattered back down against the window. Another gust blew in and knocked over my can of mousse on top of the bureau. I ran to hoist up the blinds before they cracked the glass, and a second later thunder boomed and the sky opened up. Or more like a piggy bank had been broken and emptied out—it sounded as if the house were being pelted with quarters.

I shut the window and sat on the settee, staring out into the dark and listening to the rain as the lightning flashed every so often, illuminating the landscape outside. Gradually, the rhythm of the raindrops drummed me into a sleepy metaconsciousness. I wasn't aware I was nodding off until my forehead dropped against the windowpane. Not wanting to disturb what I could feel promised to be a deep, dreamless sleep, I curled up on the settee and closed my eyes.

I woke up too alert to have been asleep for very long. It was still raining and the wind was still blowing, but everything had been taken down a notch, just enough to hear something else. I sat up. It was barely detectable. Underneath the cacophony of rain, wind, and the ceiling fan overhead, it was like trying to hear a lone cricket in a pond of toads. I reached for the remote and turned off the fan. I think I'd known what it was when I'd first heard it, but it didn't make sense. A baby, somewhere far off, was crying. The sounds of the storm made it hard to pin down the direction it was coming from. Perhaps a car parked by the road? I walked to the door, but as soon as I stuck my head out into the hallway, the crying stopped. If that's what it was. The ears play tricks in unfamiliar surroundings. I closed the door. It was probably just babies on the brain, my imagination stirred up from all the talk tonight.

I climbed back into bed and thought about the house. Some people believe that the energy of a house's occupants penetrates its walls the way blood will a garment, not unlike Jan believing the dust in this house was made up of everyone who ever lived here. If that were true, then the air I was now breathing should choke me with despair. Abortions conducted upstairs, infants murdered down the hall—I could only imagine how many unhappy women spent sleepless nights in this very room. Having a baby was supposed to be a happy, exciting experience, but so far all I'd witnessed between Jan and Kevin was anger and fear. Was it really this baby that was tearing them apart, or something else? I shut my eyes and told myself the house was just old, with plenty of cracks and warped windows for the wind to skinny through during a storm. It was bound to complain and whine as loudly as an old woman, or even a crying baby.

CHAPTER 5

The morning arrived with a dull cramp on the right side of my pelvis, but when I pulled the elastic waistband of my pajamas away from my body, there was no blood. That was odd. Not only was I overdue, I'd just had my usual premenstrual nightmare. I always dream about blood the night before my period, and what this one was inspired by was no surprise. I was in the doll-infested nursery. A baby was crying, and I was trying to get to it, but there were row after row of cribs and in each crib was a smiling doll. I'd toss the doll out and push the crib aside. It seemed endless, as if the nursery, the cribs, the crying went on into infinity. Finally, I turned around and saw the dolls on the floor where I'd thrown them, except they were no longer dolls. They were infants. Bleeding, dying. No, not dying—dead.

As I was coming out of the bathroom, Jan stuck her head in through the door.

"Morning." She entered carrying a tray covered with a red-checked napkin and set it on my nightstand. "Voila," she said, whipping off the napkin.

The bacon, the fruit-topped waffle, the glass of fresh-squeezed orange juice, and a coffeepot in the shape of a red rooster left me unimpressed. "What did you do with my cigarettes?"

"Breakfast in bed was one of the amenities we were going to offer," she went on, ignoring my icy look. "I think it's nice for the proprietor to be hands-on, make the guests feel like they're special. Do you feel special?" she asked, smiling, looking like one of her oversized dolls in her white sailor smock, blue shorts, and red Keds sneakers. Her ponytail was drawn up almost to the crown of her head, making it look like a hair-spouting fountain.

"I feel bitchy, bloated, and I want my friggin' cigarettes."

Her smile dimmed, but she walked over to the dresser, pulled out my Camels from a porcelain canister, and handed them to me. "I'm sorry. You know me—big fat busybody. After all these years you still hide them in your left sneaker."

I stretched out on the settee, lit up a cigarette and inhaled deeply. I exhaled out the window. Outside was a blur—I didn't have my contacts in—but I could make out white figures swooping down to the boulders below.

"It's going to be a beautiful day. High eighties. Great for lying out on the beach," Jan said in a voice too high, too phonily bright.

"Since when have you ever lain out on a beach?"

"Kevin made me a type of tent," she said, bringing the tray over. "I like it because it makes me feel like an Arabian princess sitting underneath it."

I kept my eyes focused on my blurry landscape. "I'm not hungry, Jan."

"Oh. Sure. I just wanted you to see . . ." I heard her sigh and felt her slump, like a jacket that's slipped off the back of a chair. Grudgingly, I looked at her.

"Annie," she said in a shaky voice, "about what I said

last night. I was angry at Kevin and . . ." She looked down at her thumb and pulled at a nib of bloody cuticle. "There's no excuse. If you want to leave, I'd understand."

"Do you *want* me to leave?"

She shook her head no and hiccuped, which sent a tear splatting onto her stomach. I resisted her for a few moments, but finally gave up.

"Stop that. Look . . ." I snubbed my cigarette out in the candy dish and put my arm around her shoulder. "If I wanted a trouble-free vacation I'd go to Club Med. The last place I'd come is here because you're *always* a pain in the ass."

She laughed, and snorted a stream of snot onto my thigh.

"Oh my God!" she exclaimed.

I looked down at the streak of mucus, and then looked back up at her, her face as red as her Keds. "Now I really feel special."

She grabbed the napkin and frantically wiped it from my leg, a stream of apologies coming from her while I was laughing so hard I began to wheeze. She joined in, and we didn't stop until my abs were quivering and Jan was sweating. When we finally caught our breath, she placed her hand on mine.

"Thanks, Annie."

"Thanks for what?"

"No one makes me laugh like you. God, do I miss that! Laughing . . ."

"And I miss laughing at you."

We sat quiet a moment, smiling at each other. I've never been friendless. I have so many friends I wouldn't mind getting rid of a few, but all of them put together couldn't make up one Jan.

I sprang up. "I brought you something."

I went over to my suitcase. From an inside pocket

I pulled out a locket and held it up by its gold chain. A bittersweet pang pinched the back of my throat, a momentary reservation.

"My mother's," I said, bringing it over. I set it down in the palm of her hand. "I want you to have it."

She ran her finger over the face of the Virgin Mary, carved in ivory on the front. "Oh, Annie. It's beautiful. It must be very valuable."

"According to my mother the real treasure's inside."

I unsnapped the latch and it sprang open, revealing a bundled wisp of light brown hair.

"It's the only thing left of me that's sin-free. When my aunt Elaine visited the Vatican, Mom gave her a lock of my hair for the pope to bless."

Jan looked up at me. "I can't take this."

"Yes, you can," I said, fastening it around her neck. "When I was a kid I used to sneak into her jewelry box just to look at it. She promised it would be mine when I could add my own baby's hair to it, but since that's not going to happen . . ."

"You don't know that."

I stood back to see how it looked, resting against the upraised grille of her chest bones. I took her arm and pulled her to the mirror. "Come take a look."

She resisted. "I can't take this."

"You have to." The mirror was still facing the wall. I rotated it around to face us. "The Virgin Mary suits you much better than it does me."

"No."

I stood her in front of the mirror and put my hands on her shoulders. She kept her eyes down, almost as if she were afraid to look. I shook her, gently.

"Would you stop? You look beautiful as ever." She raised her eyes and then touched the locket with her fingertips. "You should have it since this baby is a miracle, right?"

She didn't answer. Her eyes were now transfixed on her reflection.

"Jan?" I couldn't tell if she was overwhelmed by the gesture, or trying to figure out a nice way to tell me it wasn't her style.

"Don't feel like you have to wear it. I know it's a little grandmotherly."

Slowly she lifted her hand to her face and caressed her cheek, then her fingertips traced the cliff of her chin down the slope of her throat until they reached her shallow cleavage, where the locket was resting. She placed her other hand on top of the hand resting on the locket, and they both slid apart to follow the bottom curve of each breast. They lingered there while a look of rapt fascination spread across her face, as if she were just discovering she had breasts. Finally, her hands glided over the curve of her belly.

"My baby," she murmured. "Nothing's ever going to happen to you."

I crossed my arms, pleased that she thought the locket would protect her baby, even though I didn't believe in divine intervention. But then she began to twist back and forth in a rocking motion, her head tilted to the side and downward like a wilting flower. Although her eyes were half closed, they remained tightly focused on the mirror as her hand circled the globe of her stomach. The lack of self-consciousness made me feel like I was watching something very private. She began to hum. It sounded unlike anything I'd ever heard. Half dirge, half lullaby, it was soothing, and yet haunting. Sometimes, a song touches something in you, like a bow to a violin string, and it sets off an emotional vibration that awakens so many things at once—memories you can't put into images but can only feel, a longing for something intangible. Or something lost.

"That's beautiful," I said. "I've never heard anything like it."

My voice broke the spell. She stopped humming, her body went still, and she looked at me in the mirror's reflection.

"It puts the little ones right to sleep," she said in a flat voice. "I'll go into the nursery at night and sit in the rocker and rock them to sleep, one by one. They like that, the rocking . . ."

"The dolls? Are you kidding?"

She was looking at me, but clearly seeing something or someone else. "Mother'd be angry if she knew. She doesn't like me around the babies." She raised herself taller and in a different, mimicking voice said, "A child born of sin is a child damned."

"Is this a joke?"

For the first time since she started to sing that song, she connected with me. Her eyes narrowed, almost as if studying me, and then blinked with the unnatural slowness of a cold-blooded creature. "I don't want you here," she said firmly. "I want you to go."

I looked at the mirror, then back at her, then reached out and turned the mirror back over to face the wall just as the screen door banged downstairs.

"Anyone home?"

Jan brought her hand to her forehead. "Ryan! I forgot she was coming today!" She rolled her eyes and dropped her hands to her sides. "You're in for a treat. You finally get to meet *Sherry*." Before I could say anything, not that I could, she hurried out the door.

"Be right down," she called out.

I stared after her, and a few moments later I heard Jan pleasantly welcoming them downstairs, an exchange of greetings, and then Ryan's husky voice.

"Still in bed! Hey Annie! Get your movie-star ass dressed and down here!"

"A minute," I yelled, then reached out and turned the long oval glass back over. I stared hard at myself, as if somehow my reflection held the clue to what the hell had just happened.

I peeked through the swinging doors to the kitchen. Ryan was sitting on the counter next to Jan, who was cutting up something. At the table was a sharp-faced, spiky-haired redhead sucking on a sucker, who had to be Sherry, and across from her sat Ryan's nine-year-old daughter, Grace.

Jan laughed at something Ryan said, then playfully punched her sister. She lifted up the locket for Ryan to see. "Can you believe this? Annie's just the best."

I stepped back, still confused. Upstairs she'd told me she wanted me out. Now, I was the best. Could I have embarrassed her in some way? She did strange things when embarrassed. Like the time her mother came to visit us in our first apartment and she'd left her diaphragm on the coffee table. Instead of just discreetly picking it up and putting it away, she chucked it out the window. The next day we found a panhandler selling it out on the street for two bucks. Maybe that was it. Or maybe when you're pregnant your sense of humor becomes strange. It was probably a joke. I didn't really believe it, but at least that explanation was better than the other, which was none.

I fixed a smile on my face and pushed through the doors. "Hey, hey, hey!"

"Annie!" Ryan hopped off the counter and came toward me with extended arms. Ryan could bench-press 150 easy, and almost lifted me off the ground. "Man, it's good to see you!"

After kissing each other on the cheek, I held her at arm's length to check her out. She had the bulging

thighs and shrink-wrapped skin of a competitive body-
builder, and was wearing her signature ass-hugging
leather shorts and muscle T-shirt. But even when she
was in her nurse's whites, she was still someone you
wouldn't want to tussle with over a parking space. Tall
and bleached blond, she was the hammer-wielding
Brunhild tattooed on her left shoulder, insignia of the
Iron Maidens, a lesbian motorcycle club. On her
other shoulder was a small sleeping angel, done when
her daughter, Grace, was born. There'd been a tribute to her ex-husband somewhere on her ass, but
Jan told me that had been burned off and replaced
with something for Sherry.

I whistled in appreciation. "I see you're still doing
your calisthenics."

Ryan crooked her arm, causing her biceps to mushroom up into a lump the size of a shot put. "Sweetheart,
you are looking at the runner-up for Ms. Provincetown."

"She's beginning to look like the Incredible Hulk,"
Jan tossed over her shoulder.

"She looks *fabulous*," Sherry said, drawing her lips
over the purple ball of her sucker. She was a petite
woman, with a body as sinewy and striated as a tennis
racket. Her cutoff T-shirt read *Fuck Newt Gingrich*,
and I noticed she had the same Iron Maiden tattoo
on her shoulder. Her eyes did a once-over my body
as she said, "If it hadn't been for that transsexual
and her fake tits, you would have come in first."

"I don't believe that," Ryan said, straddling a chair.

"Please. She could have floated across the Atlantic
with those things. And how many women do you know
have razor burns on their ass?"

For some reason she'd addressed this question to
me, but I didn't think transsexuals and fake tits were

appropriate topics around a nine-year-old kid. I extended my hand. "Hi. I don't believe we've met."

Sherry pulled the sucker out of her mouth before taking my outstretched hand. "I'm Sherry. Ryan's partner and personal trainer."

"Nice to meet you. I'm—"

"Annie Wojtoko. Ryan rents your films all the time," she said with a thin smile.

During this whole time, Grace had been staring at me as if she were afraid I was going to disappear. I tousled her hair. "How are ya, sweet pea?"

"Fine," she whispered, her face flushing to a sunburned red. I was never much of a kid person, but for this one I had a spot as soft as a Junior Mint. She was awkward-ugly—big ears sticking out from lax hair and frog-eyed from her bottle-thick glasses—but she was lanky and already had Ryan's and Jan's chiseled cheekbones. Plus, she always let me win at putt-putt golf.

Jan came over and placed a platter of finger sandwiches and crudités down on the table. As she introduced the variety of sandwiches, she aimed a stiff forefinger at each one as if she was going to shoot it off the plate with an imaginary gun.

"There's cucumber with pesto almond butter, sundried tomato with olive tapenade, and mango chutney with maple honey ham. They're all my recipes. Except for the piccalilli. That's Gail's," she said proudly.

At the mention of Gail's name, I saw Sherry and Ryan exchange looks. "I think I'll pass on the piccalilli," Ryan muttered as she reached for the sun-dried tomato.

Sherry slid the platter out of her reach. "You'll pass on all of it. You're competing next week. You want to bloat up like a zeppelin?"

Jan turned to me, obviously annoyed. "How about you, Annie, are you afraid of bloating also?"

I took one. "Bloating's a natural condition for me."

Sherry lifted one of the sandwiches to her nose and sniffed, then tossed it back down onto the plate. "Speaking of bloat, we ran into Gail last week while on escort duty, and hey!" She hiked her leg up protectively and looked at Ryan as if she were crazy. "Why'd you—"

"Oh, Annie," Ryan said, turning to me, "would you please explain to Grace that the pigs in *Blood Fever* didn't really explode? Ever since she went on a field trip to a farm with her school, she's had this thing for pigs."

She'd switched tracks so fast it took me a minute to get caught up. "Pigs? Oh yeah. The pigs."

Jan was cracking ice into a pitcher. "Ryan, you let her watch those movies?"

"My sentiments exactly," Sherry said, rubbing her shin.

Ryan flicked her hair out of her eyes, a cousin gesture to Jan's. "She sneaks them! She was up all night crying before I finally got out of her what she was so upset about."

I crossed my arms. "Nice, Grace. I got impaled with a curtain rod in that one, but you're more upset over a bunch of exploded pigs."

Grace sat up, earnest-eyed. "But you're always getting killed in your movies."

Sherry snorted. "Misogynistic filmmaking at its best."

"I know. PETA hates us too. Listen," I said, leaning in closer to Grace, "the pigs didn't explode."

"But there was blood and guts everywhere."

I nodded. "The guts were raw chicken, and the blood cherry syrup. Believe me, those pigs were a lot safer on that movie set than on any farm." Grace was almost about to smile when I added, "At least they were until the barbecue at our wrap party." She stared at me and I winked. "The pigs were fine."

I looked over at Jan, who was watching me. She smiled before turning back to the counter. Seeing my mom's locket on her made me feel good that I'd given it to her, and I decided to just chalk whatever happened upstairs to hormones. But the good feeling went away when Sherry, an inquisitorial look on her face, shifted in her chair and said, "You make it sound *so* harmless."

Ryan pointed a carrot stick at her. "Sherry, don't start."

"What, you going to *kick* me again? No offense, Annie, but those movies are a form of pornography. They kill you off in every movie, but then you show up in the next one. If that's not objectification, I don't know what is."

I pretended to consider her point while I was really thinking how much she reminded me of a woodpecker, with her pointy nose, spiky red hair, and jackhammer personality.

"Sherry, I've heard all this before. I'm not responsible for what goes on in guys' heads. I once had a boyfriend who got"—I glanced at Grace—"*stiff* with happiness over Mary Poppins, for Christ's sake."

Woody leaned in and aimed her lollipop at me. "Now there you're wrong. We do have a responsibility for what goes on in their heads, and if more women realized that, especially in the film industry, then maybe a woman wouldn't be raped every two minutes in this country."

"That's *not* Annie's fault."

We all turned to Jan, who looked like a stick figure drawn angry. "She's the best damn thing in those movies," she said, pointing a wooden spoon at me.

It occurred to me that there had been a lot of

pointing going on. I smiled at her in grateful surprise, because even though she hated the films more than anyone else, my bud was standing up for me.

Sherry crunched her candy in half and placed the stick down on the crudités plate. "All I was saying, Jan, is—"

"Sweetie," Ryan interrupted. "Put a sock in it, okay?" She'd said it with a smile, but her eyes were saying something else.

Sherry's upper lip curled. "Sure, *honey*. Whatever you say."

Then she turned away. We all sat there, listening to the ice cubes clink against the glass pitcher as Jan stirred the iced tea. Finally, Ryan nudged Grace, who had been happily forming one of the sandwiches into a doughy ball.

"Hey, Gracey, why don't you get up and show Annie and your aunt Jan your roundhouse kick?"

The kid's face crumpled like an empty bag of potato chips. "*Why?*"

"Because. I want you to show everyone how hard you and Sherry've been working to get your blue belt." She tried to catch Sherry's eye. "Isn't that right, Sher?"

Sherry shrugged sullenly. "She could have a yellow belt by now, but she doesn't want it bad enough."

"I hate karate," Grace mumbled.

"Since when?" Ryan said. "Now get up."

Kids aren't dumb. Grace hunched into herself further, like a turtle into its shell. "Mom, I don't *want* to."

"I'll take your word for it, Ryan," I said. But Ryan was already pulling her out of her chair. "Kids pick on her all the time at school, so Sherry and I thought karate would toughen her up."

Jan placed the pitcher of iced tea down on the table. "Toughen her up? She's nine years old."

"Yeah," Sherry retorted, "and at her school there's

a nine-year-old boy who's always pushing her down, pulling her hair . . ."

I laughed. "From what I remember, that's usually how boys showed you they liked you, right Jan?"

But Jan wasn't laughing, she was staring at Sherry with a defeated look instead. She still thought of Sherry as just a bad reaction to a nightmare marriage, and was hoping Ryan would return to her heterosexual senses one day. I never had the heart to shatter her delusion, but Ryan was gay way before she was ever married—she'd made a pass at me the night of Jan's bridal shower.

"I just want my daughter to be able to stand up for herself," Ryan said.

I looked at Grace, in her oversized Tweety Bird T-shirt, with sympathy. Ryan's ex used her as a punching bag until she met Sherry at a battered women's center. Not long after, Ryan tried to run him over with a car, her way of letting him know she wanted a divorce, and since then she's turned herself into a one-woman commando team: kickboxing, karate, weight lifting. No man was ever going to fuck with her again, she'd said. I could only imagine the therapy bills Grace was going to have later in life.

"Keep it up, Ryan," Jan said, "and one day your little girl is going to get seriously hurt."

"So she's supposed to go around being afraid?" Sherry asked. It was more a challenge than a question. "Jan, it's the ones that are afraid that get hurt. Men can smell fear like they smell sex," she said, picking up a celery spear and biting a piece off.

Just then, Grace let out an earsplitting scream Jackie Chan would have been proud of as she whipped one spindly leg out so hard I thought she was going to take Sherry's head off. But she stopped within maybe a quarter of an inch of Sherry's pointed nose.

We were all stunned, Sherry especially, who had the anxious stillness of someone who'd just shit her pants. Her eyes were straining to see sideways without turning her head. If she had, her nose would have been pouring blood now.

Ryan reached over to grab Grace's foot, kissed her ankle, and held it up even higher in the air. "Is my kid awesome or what!"

"Yeah," I said, actually a bit wary. "Grace, will you come to New York and be my bodyguard?"

Ryan let her leg drop and she and Grace high-fived one another. I looked at Jan to see what she thought of this little display, but she just rolled her eyes and turned away. Grace broke from her mother and announced she was going downstairs to see Kevin's ant farm, then skipped out of the kitchen, happy because life was good again; not only had she made her mother proud, she almost bashed her mom's girlfriend's face in.

As soon as she was gone, Ryan took Sherry's hand and kissed it. "You okay? Hey, you should be proud. I've never seen her—"

Sherry pulled her hand away and stood up. "She almost takes my face off and you congratulate her!"

"Aw, Sher-bear, she was only playing—"

"No, she wasn't! And if you think it's bad now, just wait till I have this baby!"

She left, letting the screen door bang behind her. I don't know about Jan, but I was too stupefied to say anything. Ryan looked at the platter of sandwiches. "Ah, fuck it," she said, and then stuffed one in her mouth. I hadn't realized I was staring until she swallowed and smiled sheepishly.

"Artificial insemination. We thought it would make us all more of a family."

"The father?"

"A friend."

"Oh. Well. Congratulations." I looked at Jan. "Ain't that something, Jan?"

Ryan turned in her chair to see Jan better, who was standing at the sink, her mouth squeezed into a small button of disapproval. Ryan turned back around and grabbed another sandwich off the plate. "See, Jan, I didn't want to tell you because of that *exact* look on your face."

"Annie, do you mind checking on Grace? I don't like her down there alone," Jan said, her eyes still locked on her sister.

I got up. "Sure," I said, and slipped out of the kitchen. As soon as the cellar door shut behind me, I heard, "Ryan, don't you think Grace has been through enough? Talk about being irresponsible."

"You know what? Stop worrying about my kid and worry about your own!"

Downstairs I found Grace entranced in front of a large, dirt-filled case on a table, lit by an overhead lamp. Jan had her dolls, Kevin had his ant farm. I guess you'd call him a gentleman ant-farmer. Their soil was imported, their atmosphere perfectly controlled, and they were fed only live insects. He claimed watching the ants was better than TV, and would have had it set up in their living room if Jan had allowed it.

I came up beside her. "Hey." The cellar was deep, two flights of stairs to get down there, and except for the hum of a freezer, it was quiet. Through the glass wall we watched the ants make their way through their tunnels, crawling over each other, clearing the dirt away grain by grain. The toil of keeping their world from collapsing in on them seemed sad and pointless, especially since all I had to do was reach out

and push it over. Nothing like an ant farm to make
you feel omnipotent.

"Reminds me of rush hour," I murmured. I heard
voices rise above us, but they were indistinct. I glanced
at Grace, and could only imagine how she felt about
this new baby she would probably be expected to see
as a sister. If it were me, I think I'd want to do a lot
more damage than a roundhouse kick.

"Look." Grace pointed to a cavity near the bottom,
where the queen was surrounded by white pellets.
There was a magnifying glass attached to the case by
a movable arm. I positioned it over the nest so we
could watch the pellets slip out of her, one by one, as
easily as if she were giving birth to pearls. As they came
out, tiny ants scurried around like frantic midwives,
gathering them up and then pushing them together
into one white mass. I wondered how Jan was ever
going to get up the nerve to tell Ryan that Gail would
be delivering her baby instead of her.

"Ants are cool," Grace said.

"Hmmm. Can you imagine giving birth until the
end of your life? Thank God for menopause."

"What's that?"

I straightened up and moved the magnifier aside.
"Something you're not going to have to worry about
for a very long time."

I looked around the dungeonlike cellar. I could appreciate why Jan didn't want Grace to be running
around down here alone. This was the real house, not
the remodeled showpiece with its handpicked antiques up above. Plaster had cracked off the walls here
and there, exposing mottled, pitted brickwork underneath. Thick stone columns were spaced every ten
feet or so and the floor was made up of erratically
shaped flagstones. A few naked lightbulbs were lit, but
the place was so huge they created more shadow than

light. The only modern feature seemed to be a furnace in the corner, its two armlike ducts holding up the ceiling. Across from it was a washbasin where old sheets were hung from a clothesline, creating a curtain that stretched from one side of the room to the other. Beyond that, it was total darkness.

"You like hanging out down here?"

"Yeah. Uncle Kevin and me played hide-and-seek down here once, but we had to use flashlights because not all the lights work. You want to play?"

"Uh . . ." I shivered. "I don't know. Wouldn't you rather play somewhere upstairs?"

"Don't be scared," she said, staring up at me, those huge eyes shining like twin moons.

"Scared? We'll see who gets scared. Go get the flashlights."

She yelled a "Hurray" as she ran off toward the stairs. When she came back, she informed me that I would be *it*. "You count to fifty. Really slow because it's really big down here, okay?"

I sighed, taking the flashlight. "I don't have to worry about mice, do I?"

"And keep your eyes closed really tight," she said, pushing me into a corner.

"Yeah, yeah." I turned around and closed my eyes as Grace took off. I could hear her footsteps against the gritty floor as I began to count to myself.

"Out loud, Aunt Annie!"

"One, two, three . . ." At five I turned around and peeked. The sheets were swaying. Why couldn't she just hide under the stairs? *"Six, seven, eight . . .* I thought I heard the cellar door shut at twenty. "Grace, you have to stay in the cellar." I peered up the stairwell, then sat down on the bottom step and continued counting, skipping the thirties, until I reached fifty.

I turned my flashlight on. "Ready or not, here I come!"

I got up and slipped through the curtain of sheets. The space had to be huge because my light stretched pretty far, but it still didn't reach the end of the room. It just got swallowed up into the dark, as if the cellar went on forever.

I walked on. I recognized the canoe from Kevin's outdoorsman phase, the skis they used to take with them to Vail, Colorado, where Jan broke her ankle, and the ostentatious Louis Vuitton luggage some rich friend of Kevin's had bought them for their honeymoon trip to Europe. My light rested on a Ping-Pong table. That was new. How come as soon as people moved to the suburbs or country they inevitably got a Ping-Pong table? It was as if a latent Ping-Pong gene manifested itself as soon as they moved to large homes. Just beyond it was a wicker steamer trunk that seemed a likely hiding place.

I crept up and flipped back the lid. "Aha!"

Empty. I shut the lid and walked on. "Grace . . . oh, Gra-a-a-a-ce. I'm coming to get you, Grace. . . ." I cackled evilly, which always sent her into giggling fits. But she was good. She wasn't giving herself away. I walked on, whistling aimlessly as I tried to ignore the uneasiness in my stomach. I never liked cellars. Something about being underground, surrounded by earth. In my will it's specified that I be cremated. It's a ridiculous precaution, because before you're buried you're embalmed, but after a bad experience in *The Dead Must Rise*, I wasn't about to take any chances.

I was, of course, the dead that just won't stay that way, and in the climactic scene my boyfriend dug me up with the intent of thrusting the sharpened-down end of a tire iron through my heart, but the spring mechanism in the coffin got jammed and it took almost two hours for them to get me out. I had oxygen, that wasn't the problem. The problem was being in a dark, small space. I became so frantic they had to drill a hole and slip me three Valiums. When they finally got the coffin open, the director, an opportunistic prick, took close-up shots of me because my dazed, half-crazed state was just "too authentic" to let go to waste.

I came to a long freezer near the wall and opened it up. It was filled with parcels of meat, neatly wrapped in brown paper. In *House on Hell Street* I was dismembered, packaged, and frozen in just this way. I lifted one package listing the portion as *rump* and yelled out, "Hey, Grace, look what I found. Frozen body parts!"

I tossed the meat back in, and then heard a creaking sound come from behind me. Dead-on sound effect, as we'd say in the horror industry. I lowered the freezer door and pointed my flashlight in the direction it had come from. My beam landed on a heavy wood door across the room.

"Come out, come out, wherever you are," I sang, heading over.

I pushed the door in and felt around for a light switch. A light flickered on, only to be followed by the *plink* of a bulb blowing.

"Grace?"

I scanned the room with my flashlight. It appeared to be full of stuff left over from when the house was a lying-in hospital. An ancient wheelchair, lopsided from missing a wheel, was leaning against a battered medical cabinet, and against the opposite wall were a number of cribs. Something moved across the room.

I spun around. "Grace?"

My light illuminated a row of freestanding shelves lined with what looked like more pre–Planned Parenthood artifacts. I walked over. In a rusted bedpan I lifted out a long metal and glass tube with a pump at one end and a rubber hose at the other. Left to my own wits, I would have guessed sex toy or bicycle pump, but if I understood the engraved inscription, *Mattson's Irrigator—No. 4 Intrauterine Syringe,* correctly, it was probably an old-fashioned douche. I set it back, and noticed a black doctor's bag. It caught my attention mainly because affixed to the cracked leather was a sticker reading PROPERTY OF GAIL RUSKER. Just the overemphasized way it was printed annoyed me. Fuck if it was hers.

I unsnapped the clasp and as I pulled the mouth apart the case cleverly folded out into two horizontal ledges—I suppose so the doctor could have everything at hand instead of having to dig. They were lined with blue velvet sleeves tied shut with string. I untied the string and found tucked into the individual pockets a chilling array of antique obstetrical instruments: gleaming metal forceps shaped like the mandibles of an insect, a speculum that could have doubled as a shoe tree, and a corkscrewlike contraption, which I pulled out.

It was metal, with three long rods that swelled in the middle and then narrowed to a point at the end, like the tentacles of a squid. Twisting the knob at the top caused them to expand in creaky increments, like the fingers of an arthritic hand. My inner thighs instinctively squeezed together as I tried to imagine what it would be like, lying on a bed, legs spread and having this come at me. Or Jan. If these were in fact Gail's, I sincerely hoped she wasn't intending on using these instruments to deliver Jan's baby.

I slipped it back into its cocoon. The only other thing in the case was a long red leather-bound box. Across the top the name *Sybil Clayton* was embossed in gold lettering. It reminded me of something you'd keep a family heirloom in, but judging from the goodies I'd already found, I didn't anticipate finding a sapphire necklace with matching earrings, and I was right. I didn't know much about medical instruments, but the moment I opened the box I knew these were in a different class from the others. They were used to extract babies, not deliver them. Hooks of various lengths, long gripping things with ridged teeth. All of them were ivory handled and made of highly polished steel. One particularly ominous object had a curved, spoonlike handle at one end and was shaped into a pointed arrowhead at the other. This gruesome thing was meant to puncture, to impale—to scrape the insides of the uterus as cleanly as the inside of a pumpkin.

A soft swishing sound came from somewhere in the back of the room. I moved the bag so I could look through to the other side. More rows. It was either mice or Grace back there. The floor was a raised platform made of wooden slats. I stamped one foot down, hoping to startle her. The clamor set off a symphony of calamity at the back of the room. Something came crashing down. Metal clanged, three glass bombs exploded, and an object *thump, thump, thumped* across the hollow floor. I watched as a can of condensed milk rolled past my feet and hit the door with a dull thud. If that didn't send the kid scurrying out, she wasn't in here. I placed the baby harpoon back into the box and went to find what had broken.

A steel bucket had overturned and three jars of baby food had shattered. However, the whole shelf could have come crashing down and Jan *still* would have enough pureed beef stew and strained peas to last the kid well into adulthood. Three rows alone were devoted to baby food, and there was more lined up against the wall in unopened boxes. This stockpiling should be a poignant sight. Instead, it made my heart shrink. Even though it implied the joyful anticipation of a healthy baby, anyone could see just by looking at Jan that wasn't likely to happen. Not even if she stockpiled all the baby food in the world.

I kneeled down to clean the mess up, and was about to use the bucket to put the broken pieces of glass in when I realized it already had something in it: Jan's doll. Staring down into the bucket, I thought it had to be a practical joke of some sort. But when I lifted her out and aimed my flashlight on her, I realized it wasn't the kind of joke Jan would have found funny. The arm she'd sewn on last night was now hanging by a thread, and her midsection appeared emptied out. I lifted her dress. A mass of tangled pink string trailed out from a ragged tear between her legs. Something was caught up in it. I set my flashlight on the shelf so I could disentangle it from the string.

The object was small, no bigger than my thumb and wrapped up in stiff brown cloth with the ends tucked in, like a stuffed cabbage. I set the doll on the shelf, and untucked the ends and unrolled the cloth until it revealed a reddish piece of wood. Its shape resembled that of a shrimp, no bigger than the one Jan had chased around her plate last night, but when I turned it over with my forefinger, I made out a pair of arms and legs, barely the width of a string of thread. It was a fetus, its form mummified to such a degree that these tiny limbs were the only recognizably human feature. If it hadn't been wrapped in the brown-colored cloth, which I now concluded was dried blood, I might even still have thought it was a piece of wood. I looked up at the doll, its stringy entrails hanging over the edge of the shelf. Although it was unquestionably gruesome, it was also intriguing. A little thrilling, actually. I felt as if I'd found a secret treasure, buried by a little girl long dead. A little girl raised in a place where women came to have unwanted babies. Or not. You couldn't help but wonder at the intention, what was going on in the mind of her, or whomever, while she sewed this grisly memento of what had to be an unhappy event into the belly of a favorite doll. What did it mean?

"Aunt Annie, you're supposed to try and *find* me." I whirled around. I'd been so caught up in the doll I hadn't noticed Grace had come up behind me.

"What's that in your hand?" she asked.

"Just a candy I spit out," I said, slightly turning away to fold the little fossil back up in its shroud. I slid it into my front pocket and reached down for the bucket. "Be careful. I broke a few jars of baby food. Sorry about the game, hon, but I thought you'd come in here and . . ."

When I stood up, Grace was looking down in disgust at the doll in her hands. "What happened to her?"

"Oh, I think maybe a rat or something got to it," I said, taking it from her and placing it back up on the shelf. I realized it was the wrong explanation as her eyes froze behind her thick-glassed lenses. "I meant mouse. A tiny mouse."

Luckily, Ryan called down that they were leaving. "Go on," I said. Usually Grace hated parting from my company, but after my inciting her imagination with cannibalistic rodents, she seemed more than happy to get out of there.

She had just reached the door when I thought of something. "Hey, Grace." She turned around, one foot out the door. "Were you playing in here earlier?"

She shook her head. "Aunt Jan told me not to come in here."

"Why?"

"I don't know." She shrugged. "She just said not to."

She glanced down at the floor and shuffled her feet nervously. I told her to tell them I'd be up in a minute.

After she was gone, I took the doll back down from the shelf. As angry as she might be about Sherry and her mother having a baby, I didn't believe Grace did this. But if she didn't, then who did? Jan certainly didn't. She was as likely to trash one of her dolls as she was to let a coat of dust cover her furniture, and Kevin wasn't the vindictive type. I began to push the string stuffing back into the doll. Even though my rat theory had been spun off the top of my head, it was probably accurate. Jan must have come down here for something, accidentally left the doll behind, and a rat had somehow sniffed out the dried blood on the bandage.

I held it closer to the light. Now that the string was pushed all the way in, I could see, from the tattered material and tiny ragged holes where thread had been ripped out, that it had been torn open many times. It sent a chill through me, and made me wonder what had the little girl been playing at.

CHAPTER 6

When I came out of the house, Ryan and company were already climbing onto their Harleys in the driveway. Sherry's was a glittering cherry red, so outsized for her punkish body it seemed she needed training wheels. Ryan on the other hand straddled her black-and-orange flamed bike with no problem. As I walked toward them, Jan was helping Grace with her helmet. She hugged her niece, then left without saying good-bye to either Ryan or Sherry.

"Jan, what you're doing is really stupid," Ryan yelled out, just as the porch door shut. She looked at me, nostrils quivering.

"Don't worry," I said, coming up beside her. "She'll get used to the idea."

"I could give a fuck if she does or doesn't."

Grace tapped her mom on the shoulder. "Hey Mom, you said you weren't going to use the F word anymore."

"Sorry," she said, glancing over her shoulder. "Keep reminding me." Ryan leaned forward. "My sister just informed me she won't let one of the doctors I work for, someone who is very busy and was doing me a huge favor, come out here and examine her. Why? Because that asshole Gail Rusker told her Dr. Sherman volunteers at a women's health clinic one day a week. She tells me she can't bring herself to 'trust hands that are used to taking life.' Next she'll be telling me I'm morally unacceptable to deliver her baby."

I was tempted to tell her right then that was exactly what was going to happen, but I didn't want to get between two sisters.

"She tell you about her new friend?"

"A little," I said, glancing at the house, feeling like we were gossiping.

"Did she tell you she founded the Guardian Angels?"

The only guardian angels I'd ever heard of were the red-bereted crime-busters that roamed the subways in the eighties, but somehow I couldn't see dainty, pregnant Jan running with a bunch of vigilantes. "What's a Guardian Angel?"

"Pro-life fascists," Sherry hissed.

"The guy that killed that doctor in Vermont was one of them," Ryan said, squeezing her handlebars so tightly the veins in her arms pushed against her skin, round and plump as worms struggling out of the earth after a strong rain.

"Man, you should see this womb-Nazi in action," Sherry said as she wheeled her bike on tiptoe up alongside Ryan's. "Ryan and I were on escort duty at this Planned Parenthood—it just opened in Hyannis, right? So I'm escortin' this lady when Gail comes up and shoves this fetus right in our faces! It looked like it had been preserved or something. 'Is this what you want to do to your unborn child?' she's yelling. Meanwhile, the poor woman isn't even pregnant. She didn't have insurance and just wanted a fucking pap smear, for Christ's sake!"

Ryan huffed. "Could you not use the F word *please*? And why were you going to bring it up around Jan anyway? You knew it was just going to cause trouble!"

Sherry huffed back. "Your sister's not made of glass. Maybe if she hears what her friend is *really* like, she might think twice about having her around. Anyway, I told Gail if she ever shoved a fetus in my face again I'd knock the shit right out of her," Sherry said as she pointed her finger in my face.

I took one step back from the quivering appendage while at the same time reaching into my pocket to touch the stiff package with the tip of my finger, as if I had to make sure it was still there.

"She actually said Dr. Sherman's hands were covered in blood," Ryan said, shaking her head, staring down at the blacktop driveway in disbelief. Then she yanked her helmet over her head. "I told her, bloody hands or not, if she expected me to deliver her baby at home she at least needed to get a sonogram. Without it, it's like swimming underwater at night. You don't know what you're going to run into."

I couldn't keep up the pretense any longer. "Ryan," I said, "there's something you should know—"

"Mom don't forget I have kickbox class."

Ryan glanced at her watch. "Listen, Annie, we have to go," she said, turning the key in the ignition. Her bike roared to life and Sherry's followed. Ryan reached out to hug me. Over the engines she yelled, "Be prepared. Once Kevin hears she won't see Dr. Sherman, all hell's going to break out. I'll give you a call later, okay? Grace, both arms."

I watched them ease out of the driveway. Once they were on the road, they gunned their engines and tore off. As soon as they were no longer distinguishable from all the other specks of color off in the distance, I felt my shoulder drop. When I'm tense, my left shoulder hitches up higher than the right. It's almost imperceptible, and I never know I'm doing it until it releases.

I went back into the house and stood in the living

room. Yesterday its quiet tranquility seemed like a tonic for my city-racked nerves, but now? The windows had been shut overnight and everything was still. No billowing curtains, or tinkling chandelier. Even the sound of the ocean was muffled. I could feel that suffocating sensation I'd had in the upstairs room return, and proceeded to crank all the windows open. The effect was as if the house had been holding its breath and was now exhaling. The curtains swayed, the glass droplets on the chandelier clinked together in a toast to the good life.

I sat down at a rolltop desk by one of the windows and gazed out. On the other side of Sea Thistle Lane there was a large pond in the middle of a grassy field, and beyond that a hilly landscape dense with prickly underbrush and tufted trees. The blunt roundness of a black and white lighthouse stood out from the gray uniformity of the other homes. Most of them seemed content to snuggle down into the wild, scrubby vegetation. I wondered if they saw Jan's property, with its manicured lawn and bushes trimmed to perfect uniformity, as an affront. I knew how she would view theirs. She'd see the undomesticated landscape across the road as messy, and messy things made her uncomfortable. She liked order, so it was really not such a surprise that she'd be drawn to an organization such as the Guardian Angels. To them, a complex issue such as abortion had only two sides: right or wrong. Messy or neat. Plus, Jan had a malleable turn of mind that fanatics love.

When we were fourteen she got saved. We'd been roped into attending an Assembly of God youth revival. We just went along for the free ice cream afterward, but they showed a film about the rapture called *In the Blink of an Eye*. Its basic message was that God was going to take all the *true* Christians, i.e., born-agains, up into heaven while the rest of us would be left behind with the Antichrist. To survive, we had to have the number 666 stamped on our foreheads, which was like a bar code for the damned, but eventually we'd be destroyed by the rains of fire, disease, and general chaos that one would expect to come with the end of the world.

Its production value was low and the acting so pitiful I found it a goof, but Jan? When they asked if anyone wanted to come up to the altar to "give their heart to Jesus," she practically knocked down an old lady to get there. For a month afterward she acted as if she'd had a lobotomy, affecting this creepy, homecoming-queen smile while telling anyone who'd listen how much Jesus loved them. Then she'd hand them these tracts with colorful pictures of tormented sinners burning in lakes of fire. They reminded me of small comic books, except the devil was the evil genius and the superhero God. I couldn't stand her. No one could. But the final straw was when she told Sister Hunsworth that all Catholics were going to hell because they prayed to statues. Her father grounded her until she decided to be a Catholic again; after two weeks sans TV she renounced her new religion and went to confession. The only good thing to come out of that whole episode was that during it the nervous habits that had plagued her for as long as I'd known her—the biting of her cuticles, the neurotic worrying, even her shyness—had disappeared. It was as if she needed something to believe in, no matter how ridiculous, to be confident in her own skin.

I looked down at a stack of old books on the desk and was struck by the irony of their titles. *Satan in Society, Penitent Female's Refuge, Secret Sins of Society*. Just a little recreational reading for the fallen woman. One was particularly promising. I picked up *The Unwelcome Child or The Crime of an Undesigned and Undesired Maternity*, and flipped through the pages until I

came to one with a folded-back corner and an underlined passage:

No words can express the helplessness, the
sense of personal desecration, the despair, which
sinks into the heart of a woman when forced to
submit to maternity under adverse circumstances,
and when her own soul rejects it. It is no matter
of wonder that abortions are purposely procured;
it is to me a matter of wonder that a single child,
undesignedly begotten and reluctantly conceived,
is ever suffered to mature in the organism of the
mother. Her whole nature repels it. How can
she regard its ante-natal development but with
sorrow and shrinking, since God, speaking
through the body and soul of that mother, frowns
on its conception, its development, and its birth.

In a spidery scrawl next to this last line someone had
written *Born of sin and so would be damned.* I leaned back
into my chair with a sense of déjà vu.
Jan peeked her head through the swinging doors
of the kitchen. "I heard them leave."
"Yes."
She trundled into the living room and lowered
herself into the easy chair until she was slumped so
far down her bony arms hung off the high armrests
at awkward angles, making her sharp shoulders jut up
to her ears. With her legs stretched out onto the ottoman at different lengths—one knee protruding
up, the other splayed out—and her grimacing skin-
stretched face, she looked like a an angry science
lab skeleton, pissed off that someone had taken her
down from her hook and tossed her into an undigni-
fied jumble.
"What they're doing is so immoral."
I glanced back at the book before swiveling around

to face her. "A child born of sin and so would be damned, right?"

Her thin brows furrowed. "What did you say?"

"*You* said it, not me," I said as I walked over, book in hand. "You quoted it verbatim from . . ." I perched on the arm of her chair and read the cover, "*The Unwelcome Child or The Crime of an Undesigned and Undesired Maternity.* Here." I held the book out to her and pointed to the writing next to the underlined text. "Why did that passage in particular make such an impression on you?"

Jan shook her head, mystified, unable to tear her eyes away from the page. "This is one of Gail's books. I've never read one page of it."

"Well, you quoted from it."

She looked up at me. "*Why* would I advocate something I don't believe?"

I tossed the book onto the coffee table. "I don't know, but you did," I said, shifting to the ottoman she'd been resting her feet on so I could face her directly.

"Oh really, and I suppose I danced the cha-cha too."

"No. But you did sing."

"Singing," she scoffed, throwing her head back. "When have you ever known me to sing?"

"It was more like humming, actually, and it was after I put the necklace around your neck."

An uncertainty replaced the mockery. I could tell by the serious stillness of her eyes, and the way she began to twirl a damp strand of hair between her fingers. Jan knew that although I might be a smart-ass, I wasn't one for playing jokes.

"What did it sound like?"

"It went like . . ." I was about to hum it for her, but it was as if the melody had evaporated from my memory. What I did remember was that it was sad, and almost as discordant as the music created by the pinging crystals of the chandelier above our heads.

"Huh. Can't remember now. Except that it wasn't anything contemporary. You told me you sang it as you rocked the little ones to sleep. I thought you were talking about your dolls, but you said something like . . . your mother would be angry if she knew. She didn't like you to be around babies. That I found really weird, because as we both know your mother was a baby freak just like you. Then after that you told me to leave, you didn't want me here, but then not five minutes later you're downstairs telling Ryan I'm just the *best.*"

I recited the above with a deliberately easy equanimity, yet I noticed her gripping the armrests and pressing herself deeper into her chair. "Please, Annie," she said. "If this is some joke I'm not getting it. I mean, I know I offended you last night. . . ."

I leaned forward, resting my elbows on my knees. "Jan, I'm not offended, I'm worried. Not only because you did say and do these things, but because you don't seem to have a recollection of any of it."

She pulled the necklace out of her shirt and stared down at the Madonna's face, carved in ivory. "You gave me the necklace," she said slowly. "Then you put it on me. . . ." I could feel her straining, willing the synapses in her brain to put it all together for her. Finally she let the locket drop against her chest and looked back up at me, her eyes round with distress.

I went over and knelt down beside her. "You really don't have the faintest idea what I'm talking about, do you?"

She placed her hands on either side of her stomach, and formed a triangle with the tips of her forefingers and thumbs. Like a fortune-teller trying to see the future in the depths of a crystal ball, she gazed down with a penetrating intensity.

"For a while, I thought I might have a brain tumor. Or I was going crazy. Chunks of time were disappearing. I'd be doing one thing, and the next thing I knew I'd find myself doing something else, totally not knowing or remembering what happened in between." She paused to look out toward the ocean. It was eerily quiet out there. Not a sound from the seagulls. Just the lazy rush and retreat of the surf.

"What are you thinking?"

She opened her mouth as if to speak, but clamped it shut along with her eyes. A silent laugh started from somewhere deep inside her, and worked its way up her body, shaking her frame, mottling her pale skin red. Tears began to run down her cheeks.

"I'm thinking how funny . . . that my sister is sharing her baby with a live woman while I'm sharing mine with one that's dead."

I brought Jan a glass of water from the kitchen. "Here, drink this."

I sat down beside her. She looked like a prizefighter who had gone one too many rounds; her puffed-up face made her pig-eyed, her nose was swollen and red. I hadn't seen her cry like that since her mother died. I had to think carefully how best to approach this. When she said she was sharing a baby with a dead woman, she could have meant a variety of things. On a talk show once, one of those know-it-alls-for-hire was explaining how women, pregnant for the first time, sometimes fear that their identity will be completely subsumed by the baby. As I'd joked to Jan a few days earlier, *Invasion of the Body Snatchers*. But what impressed me was the idea that this fear can cause erratic behavior. It's the root of postpartum depression when a woman may unconsciously try to hurt herself, or her baby.

"Now, when you say dead woman, you mean figuratively, right? Like, you feel dead inside?"

Jan looked up at me warily. "You won't believe me. You're going to make fun or tell me I'm crazy."

I sat forward with clasped hands. "First of all, I don't think any of this is funny. And as far as being crazy goes, just you bringing it up tells me you're kind of scared of that possibility yourself."

"I think I'd prefer it to the other."

"And that would be what?"

Jan lifted her chin to see something behind me. I looked over my shoulder at the covered mirror above the fireplace, then back at her.

"Jan, tell me the real reason why the mirrors are covered."

She stared at me a second, as if fighting a decision, then stood up and slowly walked over to the fire-place, which was large enough for her to lie down in if she were so inclined. But she kept her distance, as if she were afraid she might be sucked up the chimney. I joined her, and I had the feeling something was going to happen; so much static electricity was coming off her I could feel the hair on my arms rise up. With one quick action she reached up and tugged the sheet down, and then just as quickly stepped behind me, just like when we were kids standing in front of my bureau mirror at the stroke of midnight to test whether or not the devil's tail really would dart out and strangle us.

The only unusual thing about the mirror was that the glass was tinted, just enough to make everything in its reflection look like an old, sepia-tinted photo-graph. Through the window behind us, the beach and sky were a dull beige and the ocean a liverish brown. I touched the glass frame, wondering why anyone would want a mirror that reflected a dead, colorless world. There was something else peculiar. Perhaps it was the lack of color, but the mirror did give the illu-sion that the ocean was moving very slowly. It seemed to undulate, like the gel in one of those handheld polyurethane blocks that you tilt back and forth to simulate waves. Jan was still peering over my shoulder at the mirror.

"Are you okay?"

"I am," she said, obviously relieved. "I am." Then she edged around me, still clutching the sheet to her chest. "The first time I saw her, I was taking a bath."

"Saw who?"

With a trembling hand she touched her lips in the reflection. "Sarah Clayton, the drowned girl I was telling you about last night. At first I thought it was just the steam, but it didn't go away when I wiped it. It was her face, superimposed over my own, like in a photograph, or a mask. There was something wrong with one of her eyes," she said, touching the glass where her own eye was reflected. "And it made her look sad." She dropped her hand. "The next thing I know, it's hours later and I'm sitting at the table with Kevin."

"It was probably a play of light or something," I said. "And anyway, how do you know it's her? How do you even know what she looks like?"

Jan was still staring at her reflection. "Because I went to the library and saw her picture for myself. It was the same blond braid, same lazy eye . . ."

I sighed. "Jan, remember what I was saying last night about the power of suggestion? Remember?"

Jan shook her head slowly but firmly. "No. This was after I saw her. After Gail told me I'd be pregnant in a month."

Gail. I was beginning to hate that name. "Oh, that's right. She has second sight," I said, not even bothering to keep the sarcasm out of my voice.

Jan draped the sheet back over the mirror. "I wasn't completely honest about that. Gail is an amazingly insightful woman, but the real reason she knew I would be pregnant was that that's the way it happened with the other women. All of them saw the girl first before they got pregnant."

I leaned in to catch her eye. "What are you saying?"

"Women get pregnant here, Annie. Barren women. I shouldn't be pregnant but I am!"

The image of the cat in the bucket upstairs, surrounded by the bones of a litter that shouldn't have been, popped up in my mind. It wasn't possible. "Janine, you are not making sense."

"I'm *trying* to explain."

"Explain what! That you're the Virgin Mary?" I pointed at her stomach. "That's a flesh-and-blood baby made by you and Kevin."

She took both my hands and led me back to the couch, walking backward. "Listen, Annie. Just listen. Please." She sat down and pulled me onto the couch next her. Her eyes were jittery and I could feel her soft, sweaty hands trembling as they held mine.

"Remember when I was telling you about the dust in the air? How it's made up of all the people who ever lived here? It's like that. Except instead of dead skin what's been left behind here are the memories, the feelings. All those aborted babies . . ." Her attention had drifted down to our hands, but then her focus snapped back up, as if in response to something I'd said. "Just because a baby doesn't live to take a breath on its own doesn't mean it doesn't have a soul, now does it? You can tear it out, but it leaves something behind whether *you* like it or not."

She'd snapped the last words out, her pupils two burning points of accusation. That "you" made me pull my hands from hers and stand up.

"Ryan's right," I said, taking a cigarette out from my upper shirt pocket as I maneuvered myself to the sofa on the other side of the coffee table. "You've gone pro-life."

As I lit my cigarette with the crystal lighter from the table, I realized my hands were shaking.

"That has nothing to do with what I'm talking about," she said.

I fell back onto the sofa and blew a plume of smoke out of the side of my mouth. "Look, Jan, Ryan told me all about your friend. You're entitled to believe whatever you want, but please don't tell me this isn't some Guardian Angel–inspired propaganda."

"It's not!"

"Then how come *you*," I said, jabbing my finger in her direction, "get this opportunity to have a doctor examine you here in your home but won't because why? He volunteers at a women's clinic once a week!"

Jan sat back, placing her own hands underneath her thighs. "You wouldn't understand."

"Well, you're right. That, I don't. But I would think taking care of your baby would be more important than some pro-life zealot's agenda."

"You said the baby is flesh and blood, made by me and Kevin, but it's not. It's like the dust we saw in the shaft of light yesterday. Outside, it would dissipate, but in here, it has a shape. That's why I have to stay *here*, Annie. That's why I can never, ever leave once I have this baby."

I stared at her, still unable to grasp what I'd just been told. This was Jan, not some attention-seeking schmuck on daytime TV. Far as I knew, she'd never been one to peruse the *National Enquirer* in checkout lines, and had never called Dionne Warwick for psychic advice, so I thought of three possibilities of what was happening here: One, Jan was having a nervous breakdown. Two, Gail was setting this all up for some twisted reason. Three, this place really was possessed by the spirit of a dead child, and somehow she caused the particles of all the children who were aborted here to coalesce into flesh and blood.

Number three I outright rejected. Things like this didn't happen in real life, they happened in B movies and paperback novels. Even in *Rosemary's Baby* there was intercourse. It had to be Gail. For what purpose, I had no idea, but I was definitely going to find out. It was a loathsome thing to do, playing some game with a desperate woman's desire to have a child, and that brought me to reason number one. If Jan wasn't having a nervous breakdown exactly, it was a way of coping with what, in my opinion, was far more scary than anything I'd heard so far this afternoon.

"Annie, say something."

I reached out to crush my cigarette in the ashtray. "Jan, I'm no psychotherapist, but I can't help but think all this is your not being able to face the possibility that the baby might not be okay."

"No."

"It's easier to think of it as a product of a supernatural force than damaged genes."

She shifted over to her hip and turned away, the heel of her hand pressed into her forehead, making it impossible for me to see her face.

"I think you need to take that sonogram, if for no other reason than to put your mind at ease. I really think that if you do that, all this fear, this dread, is going to go away." I waited, hoping for some reaction. "We'll get another doctor. Have this Gail find you one if you got a problem with Ryan's."

Suddenly she stood up.

"Jan?"

"It's time for my nap."

She smoothed down her smock and was about to walk away but then hesitated. "Everything I've told you is just between me and you, right? You won't say anything to Kevin or Ryan or anyone. Promise me, Annie."

I felt too defeated to argue. "I promise." She stood

there, as if waiting for more reassurance. "I am not going to say anything."

"Good." She hesitated. "Kevin won't be home until late. Is leftover paella okay?"

I stared at her, bewildered how she could worry about dinner plans after what we'd just discussed, then shrugged. "Sure. Whatever."

"Fine," she nodded, and headed for the stairs. Halfway up she turned around. "Oh, Annie, you haven't seen Bettina, have you?"

"Bettina?"

"The doll I was working on last night. I could have sworn I left her in the nursery and she wasn't there this morning."

"No," I said, shaking my head, feigning ignorance. "I haven't."

"Oh. I wonder where she's at," she said as she turned back around and continued up the stairs, past the skylight, which was radiating its rainbow of color-streaked light down onto the floor. The late afternoon sun wasn't strong enough or at the right angle to show up the dust that Jan believed was made up of everyone who had ever lived, and died, in this house. For the longest time I sat there and stared up at the landing, waiting for her to reappear any moment with a goofy, triumphant smile on her face and announce that it was all a joke. Just one big joke.

CHAPTER 7

Jan slept through dinner. After I ate what was left of the paella and drank a whole bottle of wine, I decided to open another and lie out on the back porch in Jan and Kevin's immense hammock to watch the sun melt into the horizon like a blob of orange wax. Normally I don't like to drink alone, but after Jan had gone upstairs, I'd decided to read the *Unwelcome Child*. It was a very slim volume, published in the mid-1800s, and I breezed right through it in spite of its melodramatic rhetoric. I had been hoping it would give some hint into what was going on with Jan. However, after finishing it I was inclined to believe that she was telling the truth about not reading it. To someone who loved babies and believed that being a mother was the end-all, it would make for queasy reading.

Its thesis wasn't far from the argument that today's pro-choice advocates make concerning abortion, or "feticide," as the book calls it, which is basically that an unwanted baby is going to be born a fuckup. Only instead of becoming a murderer, crack addict, or politician, like today's "undesigned" babies, back then they worried they'd become slaveholders, pirates, or, God forbid, misers. The author labors extensively to convince the reader that a war is being waged in the womb, between a child's desire to live against the mother's desire for it to die, and this discord is supposedly bred into the very bones, "organized into every fibre of its being." He concludes that the child, like some demon from hell, needs to be destroyed in order to protect the woman from further "evil."

That didn't get me upset. I actually found myself agreeing with most of his rhetoric, except for the idea that abortion was a righteous thing, something that God approves. What got me all wound up was I started thinking about my last feticide. If it hadn't been legal, I would have torn my womb inside out myself, that's how much I hated it. I didn't feel any part of it was me; it was all *him*. The book got me in touch with those violent, ugly feelings. So much so I wanted to go get that thing in the storage room, the one that looked like it could scrape the stringy, seedy guts out of even the toughest melon, and use it on myself just to make sure nothing of *it* was left. The rage turned into pain, and I don't like pain. Cowards generally don't, so that's when I decided to drink myself back to a happy state of denial. Ever since I'd gotten here, it seemed all I'd talked and thought about was abortion. It occurred to me how much I wanted to leave. I didn't know how to help Jan. She needed a psychiatrist, not a friend. Besides, she already had a friend. One that she was obviously more "in tune" with.

I refilled my glass. I was feeling sufficiently inebriated to call my dad. I reached for my cell phone in my shirt pocket but instead pulled out the calcified fetus. I unwrapped it and held it up. I wasn't sure what I intended to do with it. In light of everything that had happened this afternoon, showing it to Jan didn't seem such a good idea. She'd probably deny doing it, wouldn't remember tearing the doll up. One thing I knew, it wasn't that implausible she could have done something this weird and not remember.

When I was twenty, I'd given my dad the book *Jonathan Livingston Seagull* as a gift for Christmas. I gave it to him in the hope that it would help him, if not accept my dream of becoming an actress, then at least understand it. Twenty is a delusional age. The one and only time he opened it up was that Christmas morning. I remember him pulling the wrapping away, looking at the cover, and then opening it. The first words that came out of his mouth were, "What the hell is this?" I knew he'd be baffled, because my dad wasn't the kind of guy you buy books for, but I didn't think he'd be angry.

"It's a *book*. A great book, but I should have known—"

"Someone didn't think so," he said, cutting me off as he showed me the black Magic Marker scribblings on the inside flap, expletives written in an almost childish hand.

Fuck you, bastard, I hope you rot in hell. Stuff like that. I stared at it in shock because it was a brand-new book and I'd thumbed through it before I'd bought it, a habit. There was no way I would have missed the markings, but then who else had done it? I told my dad I'd bought the book in a secondhand bookstore, and they must have already been there. He believed it, but I was shaken up. Not because I never thought those things about him, but if I could do something like that with absolutely no memory of it, what else was I capable of?

I wrapped the grotesque chatchka back up and shoved it back into my pocket. Time to call Dad. I found I wasn't dreading it so much as I thought. Maybe because right now, I wanted to connect with something familiar. If there was one thing I could count on, it was that there would be no surprises with my dad. He was always the same. I punched him in on my cell phone and waited for him to pick up, listening to the ringing in my ear until I felt myself begin to doze off. Then on the eighth ring his growl startled me awake.

"Yeah, what is it?"

Ever since Dad had turned sixty-five three years ago, he'd been plagued by telemarketers trying to sell him everything from time-shares in the Everglades to burial insurance. In response he'd developed this method of greeting as a way of discouragement.

"It's Annie."

"Annie?"

"Your daughter."

"I know who you are, I jus . . . What time is it?"

"Eight."

"Eight? Ah, shit. Hang on, I'm lookin' for my cigarettes. . . ." He sounded groggy, not drunk, which was a relief. It was always a disaster if both of us were drinking. I pictured him in his natty, brown-and-tan-checked Lazy-Boy looking around for his cigarettes, patting his chest pockets.

"Ah. There they are. Annie. You get my card?"

"Huh? Oh yeah. Cute chipmunk."

I heard the click of his lighter, the one with the red dice floating in water on the top that he'd won at a casino on some Indian reservation in Canada.

"Made me think of that chipmunk you brought home that one time."

"It was a squirrel."

He paused. "A squirrel? You sure?"

"Long as I lived in Fall River I never saw a chipmunk."

"Awful big for a squirrel. You sure?"

"I'm sure." I sat up and straddled the hammock and rested my forehead in my hand. I'd given up trying to understand the way my dad's brain was wired ages ago. Why he'd send me a card that reminded him of a mauled squirrel I once brought home and had been inconsolable over for days afterward when it died the next morning, and for my birthday no less, I'll never know.

"Listen, I'm up here visiting Jan. Are you going to be around this weekend?"

"So to what do I owe the honor?"

"Just thought I'd stop by." He was silent. "You there?"

"Don't do me any favors. You came up to visit your friend, visit her."

"Are you saying you don't want me to come?" I asked, trying to keep the hopefulness out of my voice.

"I'm not sayin' anything. Do what you want."

"Why are *you* pissed?"

"I'm not pissed. Just don't expect me to set out the fancy nuts just because Ms. Hotshot movie star decides to stop by like her home is some truck stop. Tell you what, you don't even have to slow down. Just honk and wave as you drive by."

Was that the sound of a hurt feeling in my dad's gravel-lined voice? It had to be the wine; I was hearing things that weren't there.

"Look, I'm supposed to be in the city rehearsing a play right now, but Jan had an emergency. This wasn't planned."

He mumbled something.

"What?"

"What's wrong with Jan?"

"She's . . . pregnant."

"What's the emergency about that?"

There was a forsythia bush in front of the porch. I reached out and tore off a handful of leaves. "I don't know. She's nervous."

"What's she got to be nervous about? Women been havin' babies since we were draggin' our knuckles."

Of course, the ultimate exploiter of women would have such a sympathetic viewpoint.

"If I come by Saturday will you be there?" I asked.

"This play you're in—you at least keep your clothes on?"

I tossed the leaves over the porch railing. "I'll call before I come," I said, and then hung up. Even in a four-minute conversation, he had to stick it to me. My dad's never admitted to watching any of my movies, but one time when I'd taken him shopping for some clothes at the mall he saw a poster for *Zombie Love*. The poster is tame in comparison to some of them, but Dad stopped so suddenly I thought he'd had a stroke until he turned to me with a look of unreserved disgust on his face and said, "Christ, Annie. What decent guy is gonna have you now?"

I stretched back out onto the hammock. His getting bent out of shape because I came up on account of Jan and not him was a new thing altogether. Maybe he was at that age where it was finally sinking in that he was going to die, and was beginning to admit to himself what a shitty father he'd been. But then, I guess I hadn't been such a hot daughter.

A buoy was ringing. I looked out to the horizon, which reminded me of one of those three-in-one Jell-O desserts: The bottom layer the dark blue sea, a band of light blue clouds floating above, topped off by the glimmering crest of the setting sun. Stars were just beginning to bud. Living in the city, I tended to forget about stars. It was so insulated sometimes it felt as if I were living on a giant soundstage. But even with all the crime and craziness of New York, I felt safer there than out here. Ambulance sirens and car alarms were like a lullaby to me; they assured me life was going on, either for the good or the bad. Mayhem was preferable to the singular, steady thumping of my heart, which in all this quiet

made me feel as alone as that bouy ringing somewhere
out there in the darkening night.

*My mother is standing by my bedside in the dumbwaiter
room. She's wearing the white dress she was buried in. I smile,
because for one impossible moment, she's not dead. "Here,
Annie," she says and holds out the locket she'd been clutching to her chest.*
"It'll be yours when your baby is born."
*I reach out to take it, but someone's tied one wrist to the
bed railing above my head. A nurse in a white surgical mask
appears at my other side. She takes my other wrist.*
*"It'll be all over before you know it," she says as she ties it
to the railing, too. I look at my mother, but she's backing away,
shaking her head sadly.*
*"Mom!" Then I look down, and for the first time, I real-
ize a woman is sitting at the end of the bed. She's dressed in
black with a white kerchief around her head. Her face looks
like a death mask, white as a moon floating between my upraised knees.*
*"What are you doing?" The woman murmurs something
I can't hear. "What did you say?" I turn my head to the nurse.
"What did she say?"*
*Then the woman lifts up her hands and in them is my womb,
quivering like a frightened animal, my two gray ovaries dangling like ugly ornaments. She takes them both in one hand
and rips them off as easily as if they were leaves on a plant,
then drops everything into a bucket by her side.*

I sat up. My heart was racing. It took a moment for
my eyes to adjust, and I realized I was still on the
porch. It was night, and the orange tip of a lit cigarette
floated ahead of me in the dark. A light clicked on
overhead. Kevin was sitting on the railing, cigarette
in one hand, glass of wine in the other.

"You okay?" he asked.

"Yeah," I said with a shaky laugh. "Just a bad dream." I felt myself wavering with grogginess and too much wine. I swung my legs to the side of the hammock and held my head in my hands a second. Looking down, I noticed the bottle I'd started was standing by his foot. Something was wrong. Not only because he looked haggard and tired, but because he was drinking out of a jelly jar and smoking. Usually Kevin won't drink red wine out of a white wineglass, let alone a jelly jar, and it took him ten years to finally stop smoking. He regressed only in times of extreme stress.

"Are *you* okay?"

He took another drag, and when he spoke, his throat was hoarse. "I've been sitting here, thinking how I've handled everything so far. If I hadn't been so wrapped up in my goddamn work, things might not have gotten to this point." He stopped speaking and stared off into the night, as if he were going over in his head all the things he could have done and didn't. He leaned back against a support beam. "Ryan called me at work to tell me about Jan refusing to see the doctor, and now I got a tough decision to make. Something that if I go ahead with, I'm pretty sure will destroy our marriage."

He took another drag off his cigarette and was about to offer it to me, but then hesitated. "Sorry. I forgot you're trying to quit."

"No," I said, extending my hand. "After today, I need it more than ever." Right away I regretted saying that.

"What happened today?" he asked.

I inhaled deeply, burning the cigarette down to gain time to come up with something. "Uh, nothing really. Just that Jan was pretty upset about Sherry being pregnant." I handed him back the cigarette. "What's the decision you have to make?"

He crossed his wrists on top of his right thigh, jelly

jar still in hand, cigarette in the other. "I have to leave on a month-long business trip—"

"A month? You can't leave Jan now!"

"You know what it cost to fix this place up?" he exploded, half his wine flying out of the glass as he pointed toward the house. "We put everything we had into it thinking it would eventually pay for itself, but as you can see, that doesn't seem likely to happen! It might've been different if I'd made partner, but I didn't, or if Jan hadn't gotten pregnant, but she did. I may not be able to stop her from losing her mind, but at least I can make sure she's damn comfortable while she's doing it."

He sat back against the beam with such force it seemed like he wanted to hurt himself, then turned his eyes away from the light. I stared at him, unsure of what I was hearing. "What do you mean?"

With a heavy sigh, his chin dropped to his chest. "There's this place near Hyannis. Eloise. It used to be an insane asylum, but now it's more a spa for the neurotic. I went up to see it. It's beautiful. Lot of trees and bike paths . . ." His voice kind of died, as if for the first time he was wondering how a lot of trees and riding a bike was going to help Jan. He drew himself up and shook off whatever doubts he was having. "Anyway, since I'm going to be gone for so long, I'm thinking it might be best for Jan to sit the rest of her pregnancy out in a place where, you know, she could be looked after."

"You mean have her committed."

His eyes roamed the porch, thinking of a gentler way to put it, I suppose, but then he flicked the ashes off the tip of the cigarette. "Yeah, I guess that *is* what I mean."

I sat inert, not knowing what to say, or if I should say anything. When I first came up here, all I thought I'd be dealing with was a case of first-baby jitters.

They'd been so happy! Or so I'd thought. Maybe I'd just been nearsighted about their marriage all this time. Things just don't go this bad this fast. When I looked up, Kevin was eyeing me warily. "What do you think about that?" he asked.

I struggled out of the hammock and went over to the railing. A soft, cool breeze blew the hair from my face. A lone boat's mooring lights stood out in all that dark water, like the lighthouse on the hill. "I think you're right," I said. "She'll never forgive you."

He crushed the cigarette out on the wood railing. "What am I supposed to do? Just let her live in this psycho world she's concocted for herself? Shit!"

Before I could answer he flung his glass out into the yard with such a fury it shattered against something hard. After a few moments, his shoulders sagged.

"Feel better now?"

"I'm sorry. I'm really sorry. It's just that . . . Annie, I don't want to lose her, but I am and I don't know how to stop it. Something's happening here that's . . ." He gestured helplessly before letting his hand drop. I felt for him. Here was a man who had always had the answers. He was a lawyer, and used to problems being solved logically. Methodically.

"Maybe we should just cut our losses and put the house up for sale. My parents would never talk to us again, but that would suit Jan just fine."

A sound came from above. We both looked up at the porch ceiling over our heads. Jan and Kevin's window was directly above it. Even though it was doubtful she could hear us clearly, I lowered my voice.

"Kevin, before you do anything, let me see if I can somehow help."

He looked at me doubtfully. "What are you going to do that I can't?"

I shrugged, because earlier this evening I'd asked

myself that very question. "Maybe right now she needs a friend more than a husband, you know what I mean?"

He studied me a few moments before looking away. "Yeah, I think I do."

"It sounds to me that a lot of this stuff she believes about the house is inspired by pro-life rhetoric, and it's hitting home with her because the baby might be . . ."

I hesitated to search for the right word.

"You can say it," he said. "Retarded. Defective. Damaged. So many adjectives it's hard to choose, isn't it?"

Hearing him speak this way, I could understand why Jan might feel embattled. "You really couldn't love a child that wasn't perfect?"

"Love?" He smiled cynically. "How can I love someone I've never met? Maybe once it's in my arms, looking up at me with, hopefully, two eyes, I'll feel some fatherly love flow from me. But frankly right now, I wish it didn't exist. I wish it would miscarry, so Jan and I could get the hell out of here and start all over somewhere else."

Up above us a window shut. Kevin glanced upward and then stood. He shoved his hands in his pockets and looked down at the black burn mark where he'd stubbed his cigarette out. "I better go bury that cat," he said, ashamed, I could tell.

"So what is your decision?"

His right hand began to jiggle his keys in his pocket, a nervous tic I knew annoyed Jan to no end. He looked up at me. "How long can you stay?"

I'd planned on staying a week. "Um, I think I could stay a month," I said. "Depends on what happens with this commercial I auditioned for, but I'm pretty sure I'm not going to get it."

As he thought about it, he rubbed his chin. I could hear the bristling of his five o'clock shadow against his hand. Then his face relaxed, slightly. "Okay. When I come back, if she's not any better we'll take it from there."

My shoulder dropped, and I felt a surge of blood rush up my neck that the last tense ten minutes had choked off. Perhaps there was a way to bring everything back down to earth here.

Kevin was almost through the screen door when he looked back. "Hey, Annie, what I just said about the baby . . ."

"I understand, Kevin."

He hesitated. "You do? In what way?"

"Because I feel like I've been displaced too."

Our eyes locked on each other in full understanding. Finally, he nodded. "Thanks, Annie."

He disappeared into the dark kitchen. I brushed the ashes and cigarette butt from the railing, picked up the empty bottle and turned out the lamp before following him in.

I pushed the kitchen curtain aside to look out onto the predawn, pearly-gray sky. The ocean was choppy, and a few seagulls were floating atop the waves as easily as bars of soap. I'd just missed Kevin leaving for the airport. Usually an early rising for me was ten o'clock, but around four I woke up convinced someone was standing at the foot of my bed. I was too afraid to move and stayed frozen as I listened hard for a breathing pattern other than my own, or movement of any kind. But as my eyes gradually adjusted to the dark and saw that nothing was there, I turned on my light to find the only other human form in the room was my reflection, staring back at me from the full-length mirror.

After that, I couldn't sleep. Not only was the feeling that someone had been in my room still lingering, but I worried if I'd been hasty in offering to stay with Jan. Maybe the best thing would be for her to get away from this house. I should have told Kevin about everything that had happened earlier in the day—the weird behavior in front of the mirror, finding the mutilated doll in the cellar—both proof that she was having these blackouts, but I didn't. Why? Because she made me promise not to? It wasn't the same as when we were in the fifth grade and she'd sworn me to secrecy that I wouldn't tell anyone she had a crush on Larry Baker. Perhaps I was deluding myself in the power of my friendship: she didn't need a doctor, all she needed was me. These doubts kept circling around my brain pan like a marble in a roulette wheel until finally I heard a taxi honk and Kevin leaving the house. By the time I got down the stairs, he was already gone.

A humid, warm breeze wafted in through the window screen. It promised to be a hot day. The thing to do now was to just keep things relaxed. I'd suggest to Jan we set up her tent, have a picnic on the beach—wade in the water, or just play Parchese. Anything to get her mind off phantom fetuses, and my mind off my well-meant but possibly misguided intentions.

I opened the cellar door and flipped the switch that ignited the meager light at the bottom of the stairs. I didn't relish coming down here by myself, but I didn't want to pretend any longer that I had no idea what happened to Jan's doll. After I fixed the damn thing up, I was going to put it back in the nursery so she'd think she'd just missed it or something. It would be one less thing for her to worry about.

At the bottom step I grabbed one of the flashlights Grace and I had used yesterday to take into the storeroom with me. I was about to pass through the curtain of sheets when I saw a glittering mess of shattered glass, dirt, and debris where Kevin's ant farm had once stood. The table it had rested on was upended, and the frame of the farm had been broken apart. I crouched down to where the ants were scrambling all over the destruction, like dazed victims after an earthquake. A number of them had clustered around something. The magnifying glass that had been trained over the queen's nest was lying nearby. I picked it up and held it over a glistening white and black mass, all that was left of her and her larvae.

Jan came down as I was pouring my second cup of coffee. With the belt of her flowered robe tied into a big bow in front, her stomach looked like a present ready to be opened. But it was the only thing about her that looked festive. Her face was puffy and underneath her eyes were dark circles, like two thumbprints pressed into an overripe peach. As she lowered herself into a seat at the table her hair, plaited into a braid, swung forward. As long as I'd known her I'd never seen her hair braided. She rested her chin in the heel of her hand and smiled weakly.

"Hi," she said in a tiny voice.

"Hi." I watched her carefully, looking for any sign of anxiety or upset. "You look exhausted."

She blinked slowly and placed a hand on top of her stomach. "I swear she was doing somersaults all night," she said, her smile turning rueful. "Do you think babies have nightmares?"

"I don't know. Maybe they experience their mother's."

Her brow creased. "Funny, last night was the first time I didn't. Except for her waking me up with a good kick in the ribs every now and then, I slept soundly. My muscles ache though," she said, kneading her right arm with her left hand.

"Are you sure?"

Her head was hanging to the side. She tilted her head up. "Yes I'm sure. Why?"

"Because someone destroyed Kevin's ant farm."

She stopped kneading her arm and straightened up in her chair. "What?"

"The table was tipped over. There's shattered glass and dirt everywhere."

"W-well," she stuttered as her fingers began to nervously play with her braid. "It probably fell over."

I shook my head no. "Nothing heavy fell on the queen or her larvae . . . someone deliberately crushed them."

Jan pushed up out of her chair and flew over to the open cellar door but went no farther. Instead she stood at the threshold, staring down the dimly lit stairwell. I got up.

"Come on," I said, taking her by her arm. "I'll show you."

When we reached the bottom, Jan stared at the chaos with an open mouth and horror-stricken eyes.

"If you look closer you can see this wasn't any accident," I said, walking over and picking up a piece of the wooden frame.

"I don't need to come closer." She sat down on a step with her elbows on her knees and fists balled up in front of her mouth. "Kevin will be heartbroken."

I wondered if she had overheard Kevin and me talking last night, the things he said about the baby— if that could make her angry enough to do this.

"Jan, did you two have a fight last night?"

It took her a second to register what I was suggesting. She moved her hands from her mouth. The shallow light showed her cheeks wet. "What are you saying?"

I tossed the piece of wood down. "I just thought . . . maybe you had one of those, you know, blackout episodes."

She shook her head, blinking back tears. "No," she whimpered. "No. How could I? Why?"

I walked back over and sat down on the step below

her and looked up into her shocked-white face. "Did you overhear us talking last night on the porch?"

Her hands were cupped loosely, suspended halfway between her face and knees. She stared into them for a second. "N-no. I mean, I heard you talking but I wasn't listening. In fact I shut the window because I was trying to sleep. Why?" she said, gripping her knees. "What were you saying?"

"Kevin was upset about you not seeing that doctor. He's really reached the end of his rope, Jan. You have to compromise, or do something. I mean, look!" I said, flinging my arm out toward the debris.

"What do you mean he's reached the end of his rope? What's he going to do?"

Her voice had risen an anxious notch. I stared at her a second, debating whether or not I should tell her. What good would it do, except exacerbate the situation between them? But then, it just might force her into getting some help.

"He's considering having you sit out the rest of your pregnancy somewhere else."

She reared back, incredulous. "He can't do that. How can he? He has no right."

"Jan, he does. And if he can prove it to the courts that you're unfit to make decisions concerning your baby's welfare, then . . . what do you expect him to do? Especially after this? What if you'd tripped coming down here?"

She swallowed hard and shook her head. "She, she wouldn't let anything happen to me, Annie. She needs me. Why would she—"

I grabbed her shoulders and gave her a shake. "Not she, you! It's you, Jan. And you need help."

Jan searched my face anxiously. "How do you know Kevin didn't do this?"

"What? Why would he destroy something he's loved for years?"

"Isn't that what he's doing to me?" she cried.

I let go of her and sat back against the wall. "Jan."

"Maybe, maybe he's setting me up. Making it look like I'm crazy so he can make me leave and I'll miscarry. That's what he said he wants, isn't it?"

"I thought you said you didn't hear our conversation last night."

Suddenly, her supercharged expression crumpled and she shrank away from me, her arms encircling her stomach protectively. "He said that?" she whispered, and that's when I realized she'd been fishing. I started to say something, but she cut me off.

"It's okay," she said, smiling bitterly. "I didn't need to hear him say it to know it. I can feel it." She looked down at the destroyed ant farm, where the dirt itself seemed alive because of the frantic activity of the ants. "He hasn't even asked to listen to our baby's heartbeat."

I debated telling her about the doll. It hadn't been in the storage room when I'd looked, and I worried that if she could convince herself he'd destroyed his own ant farm, then she could believe he was playing hide-and-seek with her doll. She stood up.

"What are you going to do?" I asked.

"I'm going to call him in Texas and tell him to stay there," she said, climbing the stairs, holding the rail with one hand, the hem of her robe up with the other. "I'm going to tell him I don't want him to come home. Ever."

After she was gone, I got a broom and dustpan and began to sweep up the glass, wood, and dirt with gentle strokes, trying not to kill any more ants. The crushed queen I left alone. Out of respect, I guess. There was still a small band of ants clustered around her, and when I knelt down I held the magnifying glass over what seemed to me a tiny funeral procession. They were covering her with dirt, one grain at a time.

CHAPTER 8

A few hours later, I was pedaling out onto the road. It was still early. There were no cars yet and it would have been peaceful hearing just the sound of my wheels glide along the asphalt, the gentle click of the shifting gears every time I went up a hill, except that my mind was gummed up with one disturbing image after another—the glistening, crushed body of the queen ant, Jan's face the moment she deduced what Kevin had said about the baby. Whether or not he really meant it, he did say it, and whether or not she really heard it for herself, or just understood by the look on my face, she believed it. I felt as if I had my own troublesome baby inside, kicking me for telling her about his wanting to send her away.

A vehicle honked and I moved over to let a Vineyard tour bus pass me on the narrow road. As I watched it grow smaller and then slip from view over a tree-canopied hill, I realized I had no idea where I was. Vast green fields with cattle grazing on the other side of fences made of boulders stretched out on either side of the road. I didn't think a drugstore would be in such a remote area. I'd forgotten to pack my tampons, and even though my period was late, I hoped just the act of buying a box would remind my ovaries of their job—kind of like showing an amnesiac pictures of people they once knew in hopes of stimulating their memory. I had a fear of early menopause, not just because I already had a tendency for facial hair, but because my mother's stopped when she was thirty-seven and shortly after that she was diagnosed with the cancer.

It was weird. In all my egg-producing days, I'd been late only three times. Perhaps it was just the phenomenon that sometimes happens when women live together where their cycles adjust so everyone is on the same schedule, except this was the reverse. Maybe mine had stopped in sympathy with Jan's pregnant state, or I was succumbing to the house's charm and a ghost child was now incubating in me. In that case, I suppose an exorcism would be required instead of an abortion.

I pulled over to the side of the road and took out the directions to the drugstore Jan had written out for me. As I studied it, a black steer with curved horns came over to the stone fence and stared at me. After I concluded I'd missed my turnoff a few miles back, I stuck the slip back into my pocket. "Sorry. You're not my type." He merely snorted, which was comparatively civil to some of the responses I'd received whenever I'd used that excuse in a bar.

An hour later, I stepped out of Carson's Drug Den with a bottle of Aleve, a box of tampons, and a carton of cigarettes. As I tied the bag to the handlebars, I noticed a single-storied house at the end of a wide dirt driveway across the street. Its sides were weathered brown, the roof an iron gray. If it hadn't been for a small white sign tacked to the bark of a large fluffy tree, I would have mistaken it for just another Cape Cod home instead of the public library.

Remembering that Jan had said she'd seen a picture

of Sarah Clayton at the library, I rode my bike over, parked it by a clump of bushes out front, and climbed the sloping ramp that served as its entrance.

Inside, it was mostly empty, except for a senior citizen reading group in the corner. An old man wearing a beret and a monocle was reading poetry out loud in a voice shaking with a mixture of age and dramatic fervor, while the others had their heads buried in their own books. Either they couldn't see the print or had nodded off, I couldn't tell. I went up to the checkout desk, where an obese fiftyish woman wearing a man's checkered shirt was hunched over reading a newspaper.

"Hi," I said. She looked up at me and her face made me think of an overcrowded salad. A nose as round as a crimini mushroom and black eyes the size of small black olives stared out of a bunched-up, overly fleshy face. A collar of fat bulged out from underneath her broad jaw and her arms kind of rested on the sides of her body, as if she were wearing an inner tube underneath her clothes. Her hair was shellacked to such petrified perfection it probably didn't require more than a mild dusting every once in a while by way of upkeep.

"Can I help you?" she asked in a gruff voice.

"I was wondering if you might have some archival material on the Clayton House."

She looked off to the side in thought. "Clayton House?"

"It uh, used to be a lying-in hospital and was at the center of a tragedy around the 1920s. The midwife who ran the place killed five newborns?"

The woman's chin disappeared into her neck as she looked down at the floor a second. "Oh yeah. Her. Crazy Sybil. Smothered them, I think," she said, and then held her fist to her mouth to smother a burp. "I'm sure we got stuff on microfiche. I'll show you where to look it up."

I followed her to a back room, and she set me down at a table in front of a viewer. "Be back in a minute." Twenty minutes later she came back with some cartridges and the strong smell of liverwurst and onions on her breath.

"These are all I could find. We had a fire some years ago. A lot of material was burned up. All we have left is an article from the *Vineyard Vine*, which is no longer in circulation."

She set them down and waited. I looked up at her. "Thank you," I said, and was about to slide one in, but then realized she seemed to be waiting for something. Were you supposed to tip librarians? "You've been very helpful."

"I'm trying to picture where I've seen your face," she said.

"I'm an actress."

She snapped her fingers, but they were too plump to made anything but a ploppy noise. "That's it! You do those films. My son has a poster of you in his bedroom."

She crossed her arms and pulled her face back reprovingly, making a frame of fat around the lower half of her head. She'd probably caught him whacking off to my image.

"They grow out of it," I said, and turned back to the viewer.

"He's thirty-one." There was a long pause. "He's got weird hobbies."

"Don't we all," I said. Even though she seemed to be focusing on my face, I knew she was taking measure of my chest. I could imagine her calling him and telling him "they're fake." I sighed. "Well, better get on this before someone else wants to use the viewer."

"Name's Anita if you need anything," she said, and then left.

It didn't take me long to find what I was looking

for. The *Vineyard Vine* did not have much local news to report on in those days, aside from a runaway cow cutting through town and a two-headed fish turning up in a local fisherman's catch (general consensus was that it had something to do with all the poison that had been released during the war). Then I came to a front-page, tabloid-worthy headline dated August 21, 1922. Below it were two photographs, one of a very plain, light-haired girl, no more than fourteen or so. A braid trailed down one side of her body, and her eyes had an emptiness in them that could be interpreted as either nothing going on behind them or too much. And as Jan described, her left eye did appear to be lazy. The photo next to her was that of an older woman. The grainy softness of the photo did nothing to dispel her harsh aura. Grim mouth, the eyes of a snapping turtle, and her hair parted down the center and pulled back at the nape of her neck. I went on to read the article.

FOUNDLING HOSPITAL HORROR
by Jay O'Rourke

On the morning of August 20, the gruesome discovery of five newborn infants, all smothered in their cribs, was made by the attending nurse, Missy Tungston. "I knew something was wrong the moment I woke up," Ms. Tungston informed the Vineyard Vine. "Usually I'm wakened by their cries. Once one starts, it no sooner starts off the others, but today it was unusually quiet. We'd stopped taking on boarders recently, because of the madam not being up to it, but still had some charges. When I went in, I found them, all peaceful looking, excepting they was blue as the early morning sky." Miss Tungston went on to say that her mistress, Sybil

Clayton (pictured above), was sitting by the window with the pillow she'd used, still on her lap. The only child to survive the massacre was a baby girl who'd been colicky that night and slept in the nurse's room.

Mrs. Clayton, a midwife by trade, has run the mansion on Sea Thistle Hill as a home for unfortunate women since 1900, after the death of her husband, Dr. Seward Clayton. Speculation was rampant as to the cause of Mrs. Clayton's heinous deed. However, according to several sources closest to her, she had not been the same after the disappearance of her daughter (also pictured above), who has been missing since May 16 of this year. It is believed the girl had been washed out to sea, as her doll was found on the jetty behind the home where the young lady was fond of walking. Her body has never been found. Lissa Parks, the kitchen maid, claimed that since that time, Mrs. Clayton's behavior had turned very strange. "She began to hear things, like a crying baby, even when the little ones were fast asleep, and seeing things too. Mrs. Clayton abhorred vanity, but she began to hang mirrors all over the house. Sometimes I'd wake late at night to find her, just staring at herself like she was in a trance. It was grief that did it," the maid said. Whatever the reason, or lack thereof, one thing is certain: Mrs. Clayton will remain in custody without bail until her hearing. As for the slaughtered lambs, a memorial service will be held in their honor at St. Justine's this Saturday. Their cries may have been silenced forever, but the memory of them will live on.

I sat back, and thought about the storm, my first night here. The wind had sounded almost human. A crying baby, I'd thought at first, which was understandable since I'd gone to sleep with babies on the brain. It wasn't hard to imagine how a grief-stricken mother might not be able to rationalize such a natural phenomenon. It was crazy to make excuses for a woman who murdered five newborns, but I guess I could see how Sybil Clayton might hear the wind's wailing as her own child's, drowning somewhere out in the ocean. An unhinged mind would want to smother those cries, even if they were only in her head.

The librarian stuck her head in with a big grin. "Everything okay in here?"

"Everything's hunky-dory," I said, grinning back.

She moved aside and a giant stepped shyly into view. He was wearing shorts, sandals, and a shirt that read *Mike's Bikes*. Right away I knew it was her son. Not only did he have the same mushroom nose and eyes, set as deeply into his fat face as buttons in an overstuffed chair, he was clutching a rolled-up poster in his right hand.

"This is my son, Carl," Anita said with a proud pat on his back.

"Oh. Hi," I said.

The blush already coloring his face flushed up to his shaved scalp, where beads of sweat trimmed his hairline like jewels in a crown. "Hi," he said, twisting the poster in his hands.

"It's such a coincidence, after you telling me who you are, and then Carl just happens to stop by," Anita said.

I nodded with my smile still intact. Coincidence. Right. He always traveled around with one of my posters, too.

"Carl rescues bikers who've gone out too far and can't make it back. Everyone thinks they're Lance Armstrong or something. Anyway, if it's not too much of an imposition, he was wondering if you could autograph one of your posters for him."

"Had it in the van," he said, holding it up.

He hadn't taken his eyes off me once since he stepped into the doorway. Probably disappointed. I looked much different in real life, for which I was extremely grateful. "Well, sure," I said, holding my hand out to take the poster. He leaned in, keeping his feet just on the other side of the doorway, as if he were reaching over a fence. Either I had body odor or he was afraid I might bite. I unrolled it on the table and wasn't surprised to see it was *Zombie Love*. Anita handed me a marker.

"Is this your favorite movie?" I asked, as I began to sign underneath my brain-zapped, kneeling alter ego.

"It's my favorite poster, but to tell you the truth I liked *Carnival of Horror* best. It had real character development, and I thought the special effects were top-notch."

A noxious smell filled the room. One of them had cut a silent one. My bet was on Anita given the liverwurst and onions I'd smelled on her breath earlier. I held my own breath as I handed the poster back to Carl, which he reached out over his imaginary boundary to accept.

"I always hate it when you get killed," he said, rolling the poster up without taking his eyes off me.

"Eh, it pays the bills. Anita, if I wanted to find out more about Sybil Clayton, where should I go?"

Anita scrunched up her face. "Hmmm," she said, crossing her arms as she rocked back onto her heels. "Your best bet would be Ginny Hershel. She's kind of like our local historian."

"And where would I find her?"

"The Little Brown Schoolhouse. It's kept just the way it was in the 1800s, and run like it too. Teachers like to send their students there to get a taste of what it was like to go to school back then. Ginny is the school-marm."

"Great," I said, glancing at my watch. I stood up. If I didn't get a breath of fresh air I was going to pass out.

"Gosh, I gotta run. I have a friend waiting for me."

"I can drive you," Carl said. "I got my van right out front. Where do you live?"

"Not far," I said with a frozen smile. "But thanks anyway." Carl looked like a harmless oaf, but I'd learned the hard way not to trust *anyone*. They moved aside to let me through and I called out my thanks to Anita as I ran for the door. It wasn't till I was outside that I was able to exhale the fart-tinged air still wafting through my nasal passages.

Eloise Asylum, Truro, 1939

The winter sun streamed through the bars on the window of the high-ceilinged dayroom, alternating bands of light and dark shadow across the girl's face sitting in the straight-backed chair near a metal table. Dust swirling in a shaft of light held her attention steadily, so that she didn't notice the old man shuffling back and forth as he talked to himself, the woman with wild hair singing "Jingle Bells," or the trio of older women sitting at a card table playing checkers, their Thorazine-dulled eyes following the plastic disk as one slowly pushed it from a black square to red.

A nurse in a starched white uniform came into the room holding a tray with paper cups filled with pills and water. She went around, offering the tray to the patients like a hostess serving hors d'oeuvres at a party. Most were compliant. They took their medicine and washed it down with the water, then returned to whatever it was they were doing: singing, playing checkers, muttering, or staring. She brought the last one over to the girl and stood there. Even though the girl wasn't on strong medication, she sat inert. Her hands were lying in her lap, palms up, the only comfortable way to hold them since her wrists were heavily bandaged. The nurse thought, *What a shame. So young.* And pretty too, with her blond hair long enough to sit on.

"How are we doing today? It's time for your medicine," she said, handing the cup out for the girl to take. The girl slowly turned her head and looked at what was being offered to her. Then she looked up at the nurse. Her bright red lips surrounded by her powdered white skin reminded her of the bloody gaping wounds she'd made in her wrists, before they were sewn up. The girl took the cup and tilted her head back so the pills fell out of the cup into her open mouth. It hurt too much to twist or bend her wrists. She did the same with the water, and the nurse watched to see if she swallowed. She did.

"Good. You know, you'd enjoy yourself much more if you tried to interact with the other patients. Your doctor wants you not to isolate yourself. It's not good for you to be so alone all the time."

The girl's eyes dropped to her wrists, and she waited for the nurse to go. It was a relief when the nurse's rubber shoes squeaked against the gray linoleum as she pivoted away, but she remained like this as she listened to the voices that seemed to hang in the air, as diffuse and ephemeral as the dust in the sunlight. Some voices whispered, others spoke loudly. Someone was weeping. A heavy metal door slammed shut somewhere else. A tear dropped onto her bandages. It was her fault Isabelle was dead. The tea her mother had given her was too dark, it tasted too bitter, but she drank it anyway and soon after came the awful pain. She had prayed for it to stop, and when it seemed her prayers were finally answered she looked down into the toilet bowl and saw her Isabelle, no bigger than her fist, floating in the bloody water. That's when she took a razor and opened up her wrists.

"Sarah?"

The girl looked up to see a very old, misshapen woman leaning on a cane. She'd once been a tall woman, but her back had rounded over the years so that now her head seemed to shrink into her shoulders. Her thin gray hair was parted down the middle and unlike the other inmates, she was dressed in normal clothing: a long black skirt, a plain white blouse, and a black sweater tied around her shoulders. The skin hung loose around her eyes, showing the pink membrane underneath, but the eyes themselves were bright and alert.

"Sarah," the woman repeated, this time as if it were a fact.

"No," the girl said, shaking her head. "I'm not Sarah. I'm Gail."

As the woman's sharp eyes roamed Gail's face, a smile of wonder stretched her thin lips until her gaze rested on her long blond hair.

"Sarah, why isn't your hair braided? How many times have I told you, it will be cut if it's not pulled back. It's unsanitary."

Gail turned her head slowly, already feeling the affects of the medicine, to see if the nurse was anywhere.

Then the woman's eyes dropped to Gail's bandaged wrists. "Oh, child, what have you done?"

With one shaking hand, the woman lifted Gail's left wrist, gently. Gail was afraid if she pulled away, the woman would hurt her, but when the woman looked back up at Gail, her eyes were full of sympathy.

"Dear girl, you shouldn't have despaired so. It was born of sin and would have been an unhappy child.

But she's up in heaven now. They all go to heaven when they come to my home."

Gail stared at the woman, wide-eyed, not understanding except that the woman was saying what she wanted to hear. What she needed to believe. Isabelle was in heaven.

CHAPTER 9

By the time I reached Sea Thistle Road, it was midafternoon. A late-model green station wagon was parked in Jan's driveway. I got off my bike and walked it up the steep hill. When I was close enough, I could see an angel stenciled on the back window. It was wielding a sword and had an infant under a winged arm. On the bumper was a sticker: HONK IF YOU BELIEVE ABORTION IS MURDER. Well, I guess I was about to meet the womb-Nazi herself. I had to admit, I was nervous. Knowing what I did about her was going to make it difficult to be cordial, but being antagonistic would only alienate Jan. So in the meantime I'd just pretend this was one of my horror flicks and take satisfaction that Gail, cast as the villain, would most certainly get it in the end.

As I rolled Jan's bike into the garage I was met with a barrage of grisly posters, lined up against the walls. I climbed off to better survey the aborted fetuses, one posed carefully in front of a blue background like some twisted parody of a Kmart baby portrait, and slogans that screamed: THE SUPREME COURT MURDERS BABIES! and YOUR ABORTIONIST IS IN HELL! One had EIGHTH WEEK OF LIFE over one of the few intact fetuses in the group. Looking at these brought back the memory of entering the Planned Parenthood on East Thirty-third Street, all those furious faces shouting at me and waving their homemade posters. "It's not too late," a middle-aged woman pleaded. "Please don't kill your baby." I told her it wasn't mine, it was the bastard's who raped me, so fuck off. If I had any guts I'd mark these posters up right now.

On the tool bench was something that on first glance made me avert my eyes. I'd thought it was a skinned animal, but that didn't make sense. Cautiously, I looked in that direction once more and then sighed with relief. It was a papier-mâché fetus, realistic enough to be a prop in one of my movies. The red paint was the proper hue of blood (amateurs tend to use too bright a red) and there was a faint webbing between the fingers. I lifted it up and looked at its lidless, bulging eyes.

My cell phone rang. I pulled it out of its belt clip, checked the number, and flipped the cover up. "Hey, Ryan."

"What's all this about Jan getting a divorce because Kevin smashed his ant farm up?"

"It's a long story." I set the fetus down. "She thinks Kevin wants her to miscarry."

"What's new about that? She's been saying that all along."

"She thinks he did it to make her look crazy."

"Maybe it just fell over."

"If you saw it, you'd know that wasn't possible. Thing is, she overheard a conversation he and I had, but he was just, you know, blowing off some steam. He'd had too much to drink and said some things. Crazy things, like putting her in an insane asylum."

"Eloise is no longer an insane asylum and it would be the best thing for her."

"He discussed this with you?"

"I suggested it to him. I have a friend who works there and . . . Fill this out. Make sure you put the date of your last period," she said, her voice growing distant as if she'd moved the receiver from her mouth. "Sorry, I'm at work," she said, loud and clear again.

"I can't believe you're in on this."

"You make it sound like we were going to hide behind the couch and throw a net over her. Don't worry. It ain't gonna happen. Problem is it's easy to get in, not so easy to get out. If you don't know the exact date, just approximate. Hang on, Annie," she said with an exasperated sigh, and the next moment I was listening to Olivia Newton John singing "Xanadu."

The sight of the posters was making me sick, so I walked out of the macabre gallery and down the sloping lawn toward the rosebushes Jan had so lovingly nurtured. A plane droned on somewhere up above the clouds. I kicked off my sneakers and plopped down onto the grass, firm as a bed of nails. I wondered how much Ryan knew, or how much I should say. It seemed she was ready to send her sister off to the looney bin as it was; what would she do if I told her Jan believed she was possessed?

"Annie, it's hard to talk right now. I'm going to come over later, see if I can straighten this out because tomorrow Sherry and I are leaving for the Fiji Islands."

"Fiji Islands?"

"Yeah. I'm going for the Ms. Pacific Island title. Grace is staying with her dad. The fuck."

"Well, just a heads-up, I think her friend Gail is here. The garage is filled up with all sorts of goodies. Tell Sherry the fetus she had waved in her face is made of papier-mâché."

"Shit. Sounds like the Guardian Angels are setting up a welcoming party for Dr. Haine."

"Who's that?"

"A replacement for one of the ob/gyns that got

scared off from a new clinic we're opening up. I swear, I love my sister, but sometimes I think the baby has taken all her brain cells."

We said our good-byes and I tucked my phone into its holster. I sat a moment, admiring a rose that was such a fiery red it blistered the eye just to look at. It was perfect in its symmetry, each petal softly waved and cupped behind another. On impulse, I reached out and placed the centermost tender part of my thumb up against a thorn and pressed until I felt a sharp jab of pain. When I pulled it back, a bud of blood swelled, and I watched as it grew to a teardrop, trailing down to the base of my thumb. A stupid, senseless thing to do. Something I can't even explain except that somehow I felt better for doing it.

They were sitting at the end of the back porch around a table in two high-backed wicker chairs. Jan was facing away from me, but the other chair was positioned so I could see a large woman, maybe early seventies, whom I assumed was Gail. She was simply dressed. Just a purple cotton shift, and the only jewelry she had on were two Wonder Woman–like cuffs on her wrists. The most striking thing about her was her hair. It had the texture of fiberglass, and was spun into a braid so long it disappeared beneath the edge of the table.

As I walked toward them, the woman lifted her head, eyes squinting.

Jan craned her head around the back of her chair. "Annie, I was starting to get worried you got lost."

"I did," I said, coming up to the table.

"Did you get what you needed?"

"Yeah." I was a little taken aback. Jan looked great. Her skin was glowing, and her loose, diaphanous dress with fluted sleeves and the flowered headband holding back her hair made her look a little like a Renaissance Madonna. The dark circles under her eyes had faded, and she was even wearing lipstick. I glanced at the table, which was set up with a pitcher of iced tea, glasses, and a milk-white bottle with a stopper. An empty glass with a thick green residue was in front of Jan. Also, an open tackle box, which I knew Jan used as her doll repair kit.

"Gail," she said, extending her arm to pull me over. "This is Annie. Annie, Gail."

"Hi," I said with the sincerest smile I could manage. I was about to give her my right hand, but exchanged it for the other. "Sorry," I said. "I pricked my thumb on a rosebush out front."

"Do you need a bandage?" Jan asked.

"No," I said, pressing my forefinger to my thumb. "It's almost stopped."

"So good to meet you, Annie," Gail said, shaking my hand with both of hers. "I've heard so much about you."

"Me too. I mean, and I . . . you."

I was surprised she had such a strong, hearty voice for someone her age. But then, I guess it was regularly strengthened by harassing and shouting at women. We let go of each other's hands, and I felt my hand pulse slightly with a surge of blood. Not only did she have a strong voice, she had the grip of a lumberjack. Jan lifted the doll from her lap and held it up.

"You found it." I was astonished at its pristine condition.

"Gail did. Downstairs. Grace must have been playing with her."

I looked at Gail in bewilderment. How was that possible? I'd looked all over for it. I held out my hand.

"Can I see?" I asked.

She handed it to me. "I'm giving her a facelift."

The arm was sewn back perfectly. It would look like I was some kind of doll pervert if I lifted the skirt up, so I turned her over instead and gave her middle an imperceptible squeeze. Not only did Gail sew it up, she'd replaced its secret surprise. I wondered what with. I couldn't very well ask what she was doing downstairs.

"You know, it's funny, because I looked for it in the storage room and didn't see it."

"How did you know she was in the storage room?" Jan asked with a puzzled frown.

"Well . . ." I fumbled for an excuse. "I didn't really. It's just that Grace and I were playing hide-and-seek and I found *her* in the storage room. I guess I just thought maybe she'd been playing with it and left it there."

I felt a trickle of sweat run down the back of my neck.

Jan sighed and shook her head. "I specifically told Grace I did not want her in there."

"Why not?"

They shared a look, and I sensed Jan was checking with Gail on what to say.

"Jan's just being overly protective," Gail said laughingly. "You see, a good deal stored down there is mine. I have a very small house with not much storage space, and Jan is sweet enough to lend me the use of her basement."

I wondered if she had a key to the house, too.

"Annie," Gail said, reaching for the pitcher, "would you like some iced tea?"

I pulled up a chair. "Actually, I'll have whatever Jan's having. It smells . . ." I held the glass to my nose and sniffed. ". . . healthy."

"Oh no," Gail exclaimed, taking the glass from me. "Not unless you want to gain weight. My girl here needs to put some fat on those bones, but . . ." She paused to place it on the other side of the table. "You're fine just the way you are."

Did I ask your opinion? I thought as I stared at the white bottle. "What is it exactly?"

"Oh, just this and that from my garden," she said, pouring me a glass of iced tea. "Some herbs and different oils."

"It tastes how you'd imagine mildewed grout to taste," Jan said dryly.

"Now, Jan," Gail murmured with a slightly bemused smile.

"Doesn't sound like a good way to build up your appetite by drinking something that makes you want to gag."

Jan leaned forward and dipped a tiny brush into a small mound of grayish white paint, then touched it with great delicacy to the tip of the doll's chipped nose.

"Did you talk to Kevin?" I asked.

She held the doll out to Gail. "I think this pigment matches her tone best. What do you think?"

Gail took the doll from her. Thick-lensed glasses were hanging from her neck, and she slid them on. The loving way she looked down at the ugly doll you'd think it was a pink rubber replica of a newborn instead of a chipped, grisly-toothed rag stuffed with string.

"I think Sarah would be very happy to know her doll is in such good, careful hands."

Jan was blushing. I looked down at my thumb, which was still bleeding slightly.

"How do you know it's this Sarah Clayton's doll anyway?" I asked, sucking my thumb.

"Because Mrs. Clayton gave it to me," Gail answered, her smile fading as she absentmindedly stroked the doll's black hair. "Because I reminded her of her little girl."

Her eyes hadn't left the doll, but she'd stopped stroking it, and that crinkle-eyed warmth she seemed to exude was replaced with an unnerving blankness, as if her soul had flat-lined. Then she handed the doll back to Jan with an embarrassed laugh. "You see, my mother worked as a nurse at the asylum where Mrs. Clayton was incarcerated, and they became great friends."

I tried to catch Jan's eye, but she was blowing on the doll's nose. Didn't she think this was a little creepy? How many mothers made friends with mass murderers, let alone let their daughters socialize with them? As if reading my mind, she continued, "Mrs. Clayton never spoke about the murders. My mother said she didn't even remember them, but in her remaining years she repented of the way she'd run the house. It was her dying wish for this place to be reincarnated from a place of holocaust for the unborn into a refuge for young women without means to have their babies."

With her hands draped off the wicker armrests, Gail settled back and sighed. Her blue eyes grew misty as they roamed the grand porch, the tall beams and latticed trim.

"Her wish turned into my dream. Years ago I put a bid on this house, but it wasn't enough."

I looked at Jan. "Her dream isn't that far from yours, Jan. Except instead of serving breakfast you'd be delivering babies," I said, pressing my thumb to my mouth again.

Jan set the doll and brush down. "That's still bleeding. Let me get you a bandage," she said, getting up. Before I could protest she was gone. I turned to Gail, who was gazing out at the tree-covered hill that separated Jan's house from her neighbors. She was rubbing the palms of her large, boxer hands against each other, making a papery sound that set my nerves on edge. They seemed better suited for throwing a pass than delivering a baby.

"So. Jan says you're a midwife."

"I'm more or less retired these days. But I suppose you could say I'm still in the same field. I used to deliver babies into life, and now I deliver them from death." She smiled at what I guess she considered a witticism. "I'm president of the Guardian Angels' local chapter."

"Oh. So those posters in the garage are yours."

"I'll be distributing them at our meeting here Saturday."

"Meeting?"

"Didn't Jan tell you? It will be a rather large group, and knowing my limited space, she graciously offered to hold it here. I hope you will be able to attend."

"Hmmm," I said, looking down as if I were mentally calculating my time frame. I looked back up with feigned regret. "Darn. I can't. I was planning on driving to the mainland to see my dad. But if any of them are obstetricians, make sure Jan gets their number."

Gail looked puzzled. "Now what would Jan want with an obstetrician?"

"Maybe because she's pregnant?" I laughed. She didn't. I cleared my throat. "Actually I think it's because her husband is upset that she's yet to have a sonogram."

Gail raised an eyebrow as a fly landed on Jan's plate. "I don't believe in sonograms," she said as she took Jan's empty glass and held it above the insect, which appeared to have just stopped off for a second of grooming. It was rubbing its two front legs together and didn't seem to notice the threat from above. "Turning a woman's body into a television set. Not only is it used as a tool to deem a child worthy or not of life, it's an invasion of something sacred. The creation of life is not for man's eyes," she said, before pressing the glass down and crushing the oblivious insect. Her face remained as smooth as a fitted sheet as she twisted the glass back and forth, slowly grinding the insect beyond pulp. Just like the queen ant and her larvae.

"Annie, have you ever been a mother?"

I was still mesmerized by her exacting calm, the overkill. "Excuse me?"

She smiled up at me and began to wipe the bottom of the jar off with a napkin. "Have you ever carried life in your womb?"

Was this a trick question? But if Gail wanted a debate, I'd give her one. I crossed my arms on the table. "What makes you think being a mother and carrying 'life' in your womb is the same thing?"

"Motherhood begins with conception," Gail said firmly.

"I don't think two cells dividing in my uterus makes me a mother. As far as I'm concerned, at that point I'm more a human petri dish than anything else."

Gail almost hiccuped. "A petri dish? My Lord, girl, the human body isn't a science project." She half laughed. Then she straightened up and with hands clasped together on the table, regarded me as if I were a clogged drain she was determined to flush out. "Tell me, Annie," she said, leaning forward, "when *do* you feel motherhood begins?"

I shrugged innocently. "I've never been a mother, so I really don't know. But I'd say it's when you have a mutually beneficial relationship with the child rather than a parasitical one."

"You think of a fetus as a parasite?"

"It's feeding off you, isn't it?"

Gail shook her head sadly. "Oh, my dear girl. Not at all. Not at *all*. Don't you know a woman is never more powerful than when she's pregnant? You see, it's the power of two souls intermingled in one body," she said, clasping her hands together, fingers entwined in an attempt to demonstrate this blessed intermingling. "That's why I feel that when a woman decides to have an abortion, not only is she killing her baby, she's killing a part of herself."

Her mind seemed to drift off somewhere as her eyes

shimmered with a beatific reverie. "One mind, one blood. It's almost impossible to describe the feeling of such completeness. The only word that comes to mind is . . . sublime." Suddenly she grasped my wrist. "Right now, Jan has the intuition of *two* beings, and that's why we shouldn't interfere. Only she can know what's right, and if it's her decision not to want modern medicine to interfere with what is a totally natural process, then we have to respect that."

I noticed that as she'd reached for my hand, the gold cuff on her right wrist had moved up her arm, exposing a pink, jagged scar. When she realized what I was seeing, she removed her hand and shook the cuff back in place while I surreptitiously wiped my own wrist under the table where I still felt her touch.

"Annie, it's a shame you can't make it to our meeting on Saturday. We want to save women just as much as we want to save babies."

"See, Gail, that's the problem with groups like the Guardian Angels. It's not up to you to decide who needs to be saved and who doesn't."

Jan pushed through the screen door, and as she walked toward us she kept her eyes on the floor, as if deep in thought. "Here you are," she said, tearing the bandage open.

I held my blood-smeared thumb up for her to wrap. "Thanks, Mom." When I looked up at her, she was staring at me with the oddest expression on her face. "Are you okay?"

"I'm fine," she said, taking her seat. "I just want to apologize that I haven't been replacing your chocolate in the morning."

"Chocolate?"

"In the candy dish in your room."

"Oh, the chocolate," I said, it now dawning on me what she was talking about. "It makes me break out anyway. Jan, Gail was just telling me about the Guardian Angels meeting you're having here Saturday."

Her one shoulder lifted in a defensive hunch. "Yes," she murmured as she picked up the brush once again.

"Unfortunately, Annie can't be here, Jan," Gail said. "I feel just terrible I'm imposing on your friend's visit."

Jan looked up sharply. "Why can't you?"

"I'm supposed to see my dad on Saturday. Remember?"

"But you can see him anytime."

Ordinarily, I would have thought she was being provocative. She had to know I had about as much interest in attending a meeting for the Guardian Angels as I did for the Aryan Brotherhood, but there was something insistent in her voice. An anxiety. My cell phone rang. I checked the number and turned off the ringer. It was Peggy, my agent.

I slid my chair back. "Excuse me, but I have to return this call."

Upstairs in my room, I called my agent back. "Hey, Peggy."

"Where the hell you been? You don't check your messages?"

A small cramp pinched my side. I went over to the settee and sat. "I'm sorry. I've been kind of caught up with personal matters. What's up?"

"They want to see you again for the Dr. Scholl's," she sang in a childishly high voice.

"When?"

"Well," she sniffed. "You don't sound exactly overjoyed. It's a national, you know."

"I'm doing the mambo with a tray on my shoulder, Peggy. How overjoyed should I be?"

"Well, excuuuuse me. When the Public calls asking for your availability I'll let you know."

What could I say? She was right. "When do they want to see me?"

"Friday."

"I can't."

"Excuse me?"

"I said I can't. My friend is having a crisis up here. She can't be left alone right now."

"Not even for a *day?*"

I imagined Peggy's badly lined lips quivering with disappointment, her eyebrows, thick and black as licorice, pointing up into a tragic arch. I really couldn't afford to pass this up. It was only a day. If I had to, I could leave here in the morning, do the audition, and be back by late evening.

"There's no way I can be there in the morning. Can you get them to see me around two?"

"I'll tell them you're auditioning all over the city that day—make it sound like they should be grateful you're fitting *them* in. You'd be surprised how accommodating people can be if they think you're in demand," Peggy said, once again pleasant and accommodating herself. "Oh, and they want someone with a world-weary look. If I were you, I wouldn't even wear under-eye concealer."

After I hung up with her, I went over to the full-length mirror and looked at myself. I should be a shoo-in. There was certainly no sparkle in my eye. My face looked drawn and colorless. But it would be okay. If I got this commercial, I could take time to just . . . what? What comes next for a B-level actress in her midthirties? *Don't go there.* Most actors would be shittin' their pants with happiness over the prospect of a nationally run commercial. *Be happy. Be grateful. Be . . .* I turned away from the mirror, ashamed of myself for being angry.

* * *

I stayed up in my room, listening to David Bowie's greatest hits on my portable CD player. I'd just passed his Ziggy Stardust phase when Jan showed up in my doorway. She moved her lips, and I took my headphones off.

"Huh?"

"I asked what Peggy had to say."

I sat up and swung my legs around to the side of the bed. "I have to go to the city tomorrow for an audition, but I promise I'll be back in the evening."

She shrugged. "You don't have to rush back. Gail can stay the night with me."

"That's what I'm afraid of."

Jan tried to place her hands on her hips, but as she forgot she no longer had any, they slid off. She crossed her arms on her belly instead, looking like an aggravated genie none too happy to grant a wish. "Okay. Why don't you just get it off your chest and tell me what you *really* think of Gail?"

I hung my head to think a moment, unsure how I was going to get my fears across without sounding as crazy as Jan. Then I sat up. My inspirational lightbulb may have dimmed over the years to an almost undetectable brightness, but every once in a while it could still flare up to klieg-grade wattage.

"You ever see the movie *Gaslight*?"

"No," she said, a little too sharply to let me know she wasn't even going to try to recall if she had.

"Ingmar Bergman and Charles Boyer."

She looked puzzled. "Isn't Ingmar Bergman a Swedish director?"

I hesitated. "If I said Ingmar I meant Ingrid. Anyway, they're married, and at first you think Charles Boyer is the perfect husband, except after they move into the home where her aunt was murdered ten years before, weird things start to happen that indicate that Ingmar—"

"Ingrid."

"Whatever. As I was saying, bizarre things begin to happen that only Ingrid . . ." I paused. "The actress, *not* the director, seems to be responsible for. Objects keep disappearing and showing up in places only she could know about. Like, a painting on the wall ends up behind a potted plant, or Charles's pocket watch is missing but turns up in Ingrid's purse. And I think there's a brooch that goes missing altogether. . . ."

Jan sighed and let her arms flop to her sides. "What does any of this have to do with Gail?"

"I'm getting to that. The point is, she does things that she has no memory of doing, and it gets so bad she doesn't even trust herself to leave the house because it appears she might be losing her mind."

I'd handled the last three words as if they were pieces of broken glass, but Jan tsked loudly. "I think everyone around here already thinks I'm crazy, so what's—"

I held my hand up. "Let me finish. The thing is, she is *not* crazy. Charles Boyer is trying to make her *think* she's crazy," I said, tapping the air with my finger. "He's been doing it all—the picture, the brooch, the watch. Plus, he's the one behind the dimming of the gaslights, which I didn't go into. See, it turns out that he murdered her aunt ten years ago because he was trying to steal some jewels hidden somewhere in the house—"

"Annie, *please* get to the point," Jan moaned. "I'm just not in the mood to reminisce about old movies, okay?"

"Okay, okay. Abridged version? He's driving her insane so he can commit her and have absolute control over the house."

Her eyes suddenly widened and her hands flew up to her mouth. "Omigod! So you *do* think Kevin destroyed the ant farm."

"No!" I jumped up, exasperated because I should have foreseen that's where she'd go. "Gail did!"

Her hands dropped from her mouth to her chest. "Gail?"

"Ten to one she has a key to the house, doesn't she?"

Her expression changed from one of surprise to one of wariness. "She stays with me when Kevin's gone on business. So what?"

"So, she didn't 'find' that doll in the storage room today. I did, yesterday."

Jan stared at me a moment as the fan above caused wispy tendrils of hair to flutter over her forehead. "You knew I was looking for it and you didn't tell me?"

I shoved my hands into the pockets of my shorts. "I didn't think it was a good idea. Especially after what you'd told me yesterday. And plus, it was kind of . . . damaged."

"What?" she said, coming toward me. "What do you mean? Bettina's in perfect condition."

"That's because Gail sewed her up."

"Why would she do that?"

"Just listen first," I said, trying to keep the impatience out of my voice. "After I discovered Kevin's ant farm, I went into the storage room to get her. I remember specifically leaving her on a shelf, but she wasn't there. Now I looked all over that room so when Gail shows up with it today, all patched up, it suggests to me someone's playing games."

Instead of arguing, Jan floated over to the settee. With her gown trailing behind her, she would have looked like an apparition from the Renaissance if not for chewing the side of her thumb like a cannibal nibbling an hor d'oeuvre. She sat down. The late afternoon sun had begun to stretch and distort the shadows of the furniture and bric-a-brac around the room into unrecognizable shapes. Finally, she released her tortured thumb from her teeth. "How was she damaged?" she said, keeping her eyes down.

"What does it matter?"

Her head snapped up. "It matters to me!"

I thought a moment. What was I going to tell her that wouldn't inspire any ominous foreboding? "She was torn a little and . . . well, some of the stuffing was kind of hanging out."

"Where? Where was she torn?"

I groaned. "Oh, for Christ's sake!"

"Tell me, Annie," she cried, balling her fists.

"The crotch, okay?" I yelled. "She was torn in the crotch!"

She turned her head to look out the window, and swallowed so deeply her already thin neck stretched thinner. "An abortion," she said, which was exactly why I didn't want to tell her in the first place. As she sat, this time nibbling on a fresh cuticle, I hoped her mind was beginning to spin clockwise, but then she looked back at me with her head tilted defiantly.

"Okay, if I'm to understand this correctly, Gail, in an effort to drive me crazy, snuck into the house the night before, hid my doll in the cellar, came back last night to sew her up, and for good measure knocked over Kevin's ant farm, all while we were sleeping."

I found it absurd that we'd switched roles from yesterday, where I was now in the position of defending myself while she was the skeptic. I pointed at her. "It's not as far-fetched as thinking you're carrying a . . . a *dust* ball instead of a baby!"

Jan placed her hands on her stomach as if I'd just kicked her. "Annie! I was using a *metaphor*," she said, her voice lowered to an offended hush.

I turned around on myself and then fell onto the bed. "I'm sorry. It's just upsetting that you'd rather believe that your husband is trying to harm you more than Gail, whom you've known for less than a year."

I'd been lying on my back, talking to the ceiling, but now sat up. "Jan, it's just too coincidental. The way she was talking about her vision for this place you'd think she was describing the second coming. The place is already set up for guests, you got your nursery across the hall, a midwife in the house, a—"

A zippingly loud clatter interrupted me as Jan pulled the blind cord as if it were an emergency brake. The blinds compacted and in an instant the black and white pattern of shadow streaking her face disappeared.

"Just answer one thing," she said, in an overly temperate manner, as if the cord she was still hanging on to allowed her some kind of moral authority. "Why would she tear apart a doll that is very, very special to her, only to sew it back up? If she's guilty of playing *Gaslight* as you're suggesting, you'd think she'd want me to see it."

She had me there. What *was* the point of tearing the doll apart if Jan didn't see it? Then it came to me in such a rush of triumph I almost couldn't stop myself from snapping my fingers and shouting "Aha!" I walked over to the little table next to the bed with the confidence of a prosecutor about to show the jury crucial evidence that will send the villain to the electric chair. "Because, my doubting friend, tangled up in the stuffing I'd found a little dried-up fetus. At first I didn't know what it was, but there was no mistaking . . . hey . . ."

I'd opened the drawer, but except for a number of silver-wrapped chocolates, it was empty. I pushed the candies aside. "It was here last night."

Jan had joined me at the table. "Annie—"

"I'm telling you, it was here! She must have come in here and taken it. Somehow she knew."

"Annie," she said, placing her hand on my shoulder, "I already know about it. It wasn't a fetus. It was a pit."

I looked at her. "What?"

"Gail told me. In those days when a little girl was nearing puberty, a pit was sewn into the stomach of her favorite doll. It was kind of like a totem to ensure fertility."

I shut the drawer. "Jan, I think I can tell the difference between a plum pit and a fetus."

She shook her head as she returned to the settee. "It doesn't even matter." She sighed. "I shouldn't have told you what I did. Gail warned me not to, but I thought . . . Listen, if it makes you feel better to believe Gail is doing all this, then fine, but it doesn't change the fact that I have *seen* Sarah Clayton."

I went over and sat next to her. "Jan, she's *talked* you into seeing her. I may not be able to explain everything, yet, but there's enough here to at least be suspicious. Jesus, we don't even know what's in that drink she's been giving you."

"It's just a health drink," she said, stretching her legs out and sitting back.

"Then why wouldn't she let me have any?"

"She told you why, you don't need to gain weight."

"As if she should talk." I leaned forward on my hands. "I'll bet you can't even name one ingredient in it."

"Of course I know. Let's see," she said, placing her forefinger to her chin as she looked up at the ceiling. "First, she grinds up a peyote tablet into some strychnine, and then I believe a liberal sprinkling of angel dust follows—"

"Cut it out," I snapped. "It's not funny."

Her hand dropped and she shook her head as she gazed out at the waves, bubbling up onto the beach with each pass at the shore. "I was hoping you two would be friends," she said in a quiet, dispirited voice. "But I can see that's not going to happen."

I almost choked. "Are you for real? The woman is a fanatical *loon*. You should have heard her talking about the 'blessed mingling of the two souls,'" I said in a breathy voice, twisting my hands in mockery of Gail's attempt to enlighten me. "She doesn't believe in sonograms. Why? Because 'The creation of life is not meant for man's eyes.' Not only is she arrogant, pompous, crazy," I said, ticking off all three qualities one finger at a time, "I don't *trust* her. She wants something from you, and I think it's the house, so she's set up this elaborate bullshit story to worm her way into your confidence."

I'd practically been yelling, but Jan never once looked at me. The whole time she'd been gazing outside. I pushed the curtain aside to see what had been drawing her attention away from my tirade: a crooked jetty, pointing out to the horizon like an arthritic finger.

"They found her doll down on those rocks," she said softly.

I let the curtain go and looked at her. "Jan, did you hear anything I just said?"

"I heard. And I'm sorry because Gail is going to be a part of my life from now on, and if you can't make room for her, then it's going to feel very crowded for you as my friend."

I cocked my right ear forward, unsure if I misheard or misunderstood what she'd just said. "Are you saying it's either me or her?"

Jan's mouth hardened as she looked down at her hands, fingers interlaced like tightly drawn shoestrings. "It's not because I love her better than you. But I *need* her, Annie." She looked at me. "Can you understand that? Whatever she's doing or does, she's the reason I'm having this baby, and as for having to make a choice between you and Gail, then yes, I'll have to choose Gail. Not because I like her better, but because I love this baby more than anything else in the world."

I felt a jealous burn, as if a hot branding iron had

been pressed to my heart. Ironically, it was toward the baby rather than Gail. I couldn't believe I was actually jealous of a baby. "Does this go for Kevin and Ryan too?"

"If they get in my way of what I feel I need to do, then yes."

We stared at each other a moment. She swung her legs off the settee. "I'm going for a walk on the beach," she said. "I'd love you to come with me, but I understand if you don't want to." At the door, she turned around. "I'll even understand if you want to leave."

I was still speechless. Yet even though she spoke tough, I could see by her outline she was trembling. "Jan. I came up here because you said you needed a friend."

"Yes," she said, a tear escaping down her cheek. "And I still do."

After she left, I went over to the little table to look for the fetus one more time. I opened the drawer so abruptly the chocolates all came tumbling to the front and the candy dish would have slipped off if I hadn't stilled it with my hand. But as my fingers touched on the rose-shaped chocolates resting in it, something else tumbled to the forefront of my mind: the odd way Jan looked at me downstairs after she'd come back with the Band-Aid, and her strange apology that she hadn't been refilling my candy dish.

CHAPTER 10

The next morning I was sitting in the beige hallway outside Sommes Casting, waiting for my turn to be seen. I was wearing a white shirt and black pants, standard waitress wear. I'd put my hair up in an attractive French twist and stuck a pencil behind my ear for effect. Even though they didn't expect you to dress the part, it was supposed to give you that edge. Except that five of the women sitting outside with me and the two that had already come out had dressed like waitresses too. I glanced around at my competition. World-weary? As usual, Peggy didn't know what she was talking about. They were all as fresh and sweet-looking as just-baked donuts. Except for the one sitting across from me. She had the hard look of a seasoned waitress. She even had on a pink uniform, complete with a white apron, a cap and badge that said MADGE. She was cracking her gum and reading a magazine, but must have sensed me staring, because she shot me a mind-your-own-business look. I returned a sour smile and checked my watch.

Two o'clock. At this rate, I'd be here the rest of the day. Especially if they asked me to stick around. Not that it mattered. After Jan found out what Ryan and

I had done last night, I was sure she'd be FedExing the rest of my stuff back to New York anyway. It all started when Ryan showed up, furious because the clinic she worked at had received a bomb threat. It was taken for granted that the Guardian Angels were behind it since they'd been threatening reprisals ever since it was announced that Dr. Haine, the Dr. Hyde of obstetricians, would be practicing at their new clinic. That, in addition to my telling her Jan's garage had been turned into Guardian Angel Central earlier in the day, caused her to take the ferry straight over from work.

I was upstairs packing and had my earphones on, so I hadn't heard them arguing until Jan came up the stairs with Ryan following behind her, yelling, "You are actually going to let that fat-assed fanatic deliver your baby? Are you insane?"

I'd taken off my earphones and had stepped into the hallway just as Jan whirled around at the top of the steps to shout down, "Apparently so, since both my sister and husband are trying to have me put away!"

She pivoted and went into her room and slammed the door behind herself, which Ryan flung back open with equal force. She was still wearing her nurse's whites from work, but this was no Florence Nightingale. I had no doubt that when she told patients to pull their pants down and bend over, not too many disobeyed.

"Guess what? If I could I'd call the rubber wagon tonight! Tell me," she said, crossing her arms, leaning into one hip. "Does Kevin know about this? Because you *know* it's going to be over his dead body that Gail delivers his baby."

I crept up behind her, not wanting to get too close, unsure if I should interfere.

"Kevin has no say in this," Jan said.

Over Ryan's shoulder I saw her sitting on the edge of her canopied bed, arms cradling her belly as she looked in the direction of the French windows. The day had taken a turn and the wind coming through them had set the whole room in motion, undulating the gauzy white curtains, ruffling the trim of the canopy above Jan's still body. Ryan fell against the doorway in a hapless pose, arms hanging limp, shoulders slumped.

"Jan," she said in a calmer voice, "you don't know what you're dealing with here. This woman is part of an organization that has *killed* people."

"No, you don't know what you're dealing with," Jan said, snapping around, her small face almost feral as her rage pinched all her features together. Until she saw me over Ryan's shoulder. Then she got up and went over to a planter of flowers near the windows. Ryan twisted around to look at me.

"Did you know about this?" I leaned back against the wall with my hands behind me and hung my head. "And you didn't say anything?"

"I made her promise not to," Jan said.

"And just when were you going to tell me, Jan?"

I looked back up just as Jan shrugged and stepped through the windows onto the balcony.

"Okay. Fine. As far as I'm concerned, you're on your own now. You want to destroy yourself, your marriage, then you go right ahead and let that bitch deliver your baby. Hopefully she'll be able to fit it in between planning assassinations and phoning in bomb threats."

Ryan turned and stalked off down the hall toward the stairs. A second later Jan ran to her door to yell down.

"You're the murderer, Ryan. Working at that abortion camp you call a clinic!"

When she realized I was staring at her, she stepped back and shut her door.

The monitor sitting at the desk outside the audition room called for a Cassy Lake, and the pink-uniformed woman stood up, pulled a pencil out of her apron, and stuck it behind her ear before entering the room. I took my pencil from my ear and shoved it in my bag. Fuck. Might as well just leave now. The tall, lithe girl with coal-black eyes and thick eyebrows sitting next to me leaned in and held up the sides. She was the only one dressed normally.

"Excuse me," she said in a British accent. "I've never been to one of these before. Is the material always so . . . thin?"

I smiled. "Pretty much. You want thick, you have to go for the feminine protection ads."

She sat back and looked down at the sides, dismayed. "But how do they determine if you are a competent actress or not?"

I wasn't sure if she was serious, but the rigid way she held herself, her spine stubbornly refusing to conform to the curved bucket-seat chairs the rest of us were slouched in, told me she was.

"I think they're more interested if you can sell their shoe inserts than act. "

Now her caterpillar eyebrows were all over her forehead, one lifted, the other down, as if they were being pulled in opposite directions. "Yes, I suppose that is true, but I really want them to see what I can do. Do you think there's any chance of them asking me to perform a monologue?"

I shrugged. "In my experience, probably not. But, you never know."

"Hmmm," she said, her face drawn down in great consternation. "I've been doing Shakespeare for so long, I'm afraid my more contemporary ones have gone a bit rusty."

"Well, if I were you, I'd stay away from the classics. Keep it light. After all, we're talking Dr. Scholl's here."

She seemed to be pondering my wisdom a moment before nodding her head.

"True. Very true." Then she tittered and leaned into me as if we were conspirators. "Normally I wouldn't be caught *dead* auditioning for a commercial, but things have been rather slow and one must pay the bills, mustn't one?"

I shook my head. "I am right there with you. Excuse me," I said, shifting in my seat, "but I just want to, you know, kind of prepare before I go in."

"Oh, of course. I'm so sorry. May I ask what technique you use for such . . . fare?" she said, glancing down at the script with distaste.

I really did understand where she was coming from, but her pretentious accent, which I suspected was fake, and my own nervousness were wearing on me.

"Oh, there are a few, but my favorite is to just sit back and think of Mel Gibson's ass."

The girl's eyebrows shot up to her hairline. "Hey," I said, "don't knock it till you try it. It puts one in a very favorable state of mind. Good luck."

I sat back and closed my eyes and felt her move one chair over. I had no intention of thinking about Mel Gibson's ass, mainly because I was a pec woman myself. I thought of Ryan instead, now flying over the Pacific Ocean on her way to Fiji. After the fight with Jan, I found her standing at the tool bench in the garage, holding herself, looking at everything and nothing.

I went up to her and put my arm around her shoulder. "I'm sorry, Ryan."

She bit her lip. Most of her blond hair had slipped

out of the clasp she used to pull it back, and it hung in silky strands around her face.

"We should have put a stop to this earlier," she muttered.

I gave her a little shake. "Come on. It'll work out."

She looked at me with a shattered face. "You know, if this woman weren't filling her head with such shit I could handle it, but she's talked Jan into having zero medical attention even though there's obviously something wrong with her. My guess is diabetes, and if she doesn't have that treated, her baby's not the only thing she's going to lose," she said, her eyes intensely locked onto me, as if she were waiting for me to tell her something. At this point, I didn't think it mattered if I told her or not.

I leaned back against the tool bench. "She thinks she's possessed, that the baby is some kind of manifestation of the house, and that Gail is the only one who can deliver it safely."

Ryan squinted in disbelief. "What?"

I took a breath. "She thinks she's a surrogate for a ghost."

She turned her head one way, then another, as if a different head position would make sense of what I'd just told her. Finally she settled on straight forward. "Tell me you're joking."

The papier-mâché fetus was at my elbow. I nudged it to the side. "No. Unfortunately not."

"And how long have you known this?"

I looked down, feeling the hot flush of guilt singe my face like a fresh razor burn. "Just today," I lied.

She looked down at the fetus. "If Kevin had known this he never would have left. I should have pushed him harder. We could have gotten her into Eloise within a week, maybe less if—"

"Ryan, you're not really just going to give up on her, are you?" I asked, changing the subject before I told her it was all my fault and ended up on the other side of her wrath.

She seemed calm as she grabbed the fetus by the leg, threw it up, somersaulting it in the air and then catching it with one hand. But I could see by the way her neck thickened and how the vein in her temple was pulsing visibly that she was anything but. "Annie," she said, tossing it again, even higher, "I've been kicking ass on my sister's behalf since grade school. What do you think?"

She tossed the fetus again but this time let it drop to the cement floor. Then she looked at me, her eyes filled with an evil glint as she lifted her white nurse's shoe and brought it down on its fragile head, which made a sharp *pop*.

"Oops," she said with a crazy smile. I just stood there, looking down at the caved-in face with my hands on my hips. Then I turned around and opened a cupboard above the work bench and said, "I think these posters could use some touching up, don't you? Let's see if we can find some spray paint."

"Ann Wojtoko," the monitor called, just as "Madge" came out, looking as satisfied as a cat who just ate the pet canary. I gathered up my bag and as I walked toward the audition room, I decided not to even try and compete with my cute and perky competition. My strategy would be to stick with the world-weary air of the perennially defeated instead. Not only would I stand out among the Sandy Duncans of the world, but I looked better grimacing than smiling anyway.

Later that night, I kicked back on my couch and cracked open a beer with my friend Penny. She was a petite redhead with a pixie-cut hairstyle and small but intensely sexy eyes. Penny and I went way back. Her boyfriend, Chester, was a major *Bloodfest* investor, and she'd worked her way up from being a background zombie on *Zombie Love* to co-victim in the one we'd just finished shooting in the Poconos. She gets almost, but not quite, equal snuff time in the film. The movie we were watching tonight was a comedy, in the genre of *Porky's*, which meant a lot of frat boy antics and shower room scenes. Chester had invested heavily in this one also, and Penny got cast as a cheerleader.

Now she was chopping up a line of coke on a mirror. I snorted with her every once in a while just to be social. She offered me the mirror and a straw. I set my beer down and aimed the straw at one end of the white line and inhaled all the way to the other before handing it back to her.

"So how did the audition go?" she said in her flat, Midwestern twang.

I shrugged and took a swig of beer. "They laughed. And they asked if I had any conflict with the hold dates."

"That's great!"

I rolled my eyes at her enthusiasm. "Penny, there's still a long way to go. I'll probably have to go in a few more times still."

"But you're great, Annie," she said, wiping the coke from her nose. "How could they not pick you?"

"You're right. I'm just so amazingly wonderful, how could they not?"

"All right, smart-ass, go ahead and be pessimistic. But let me tell you, the only reason I got the part in *Bloodfest IV* was because I stayed positive. I said my affirmations, day and night."

"Sure it didn't have something to do with Chester putting a couple hundred grand in?"

Penny suppressed a smile as she shrugged a coy shoulder. "Maybe. Maybe not. Are we going to watch this masterpiece or what?" she said, wiping the residue from the mirror with her finger and then rubbing it against her gums.

"Yeah." I picked up the remote but then let my hand drop in my lap. "Penny, you think you ever want to have a kid?"

She looked at me in surprise as she wiped her finger on her jeans. "Where did *that* come from?"

I sank a little lower into the couch. "I just came back from visiting my friend Jan. She's seven months pregnant and it's like, I don't even know her anymore. Completely changed. This is a woman who has stronger convictions about color schemes than the crisis in the Middle East, but now she's involved with this crackpot from the Guardian Angels and has gone totally pro-life."

Penny's forehead crinkled in puzzlement. "I thought those guys hung out on the subways to stop muggings."

"Not them. These Guardian Angels hang out in front of abortion clinics. But if you asked them, I guess they'd consider themselves to be doing pretty much the same thing."

"Well," she said, squiggling back into her corner of the sofa, "to answer your question, a few years ago I did get that baby craving, but Chester wouldn't stand for it. He said he didn't put twenty thousand dollars into this body just to have me blow it out."

My eyes dropped to Penny's chest. When I first knew her, she was a nice B, but Chester was obsessed with big boobs and like a mad scientist who had gone over the edge he'd had hers pumped up to a D, to the point her breasts now hovered over her chest like twin zeppelins ready to lift her small body up into the atmosphere. The poor girl practically needed crutches to walk, but Penny put up with the smarmy middle-aged prick because she was convinced he was going to make her a star. What she didn't realize, even though I tried to tell her, was that with a chest that size, no one was going to take her seriously. And it was too bad, because Penny was a decent actress.

"Chester's a dick," I said.

She nodded as she looked down into her deep cleavage, and I remembered she'd once told me that he liked to snort lines of coke off her tits. "Yes." She sighed. "But he's a rich dick." She looked up and crossed her legs as she slid her hands between her thighs, prayerlike. "And you, Annie? You think you want a baby?"

I shook my head as vigorously as an epileptic. "God no! After seeing what it's done to my friend."

"That so? What's it done?"

I tried to laugh. "She's . . . possessed! Or at least she thinks she is."

Penny leaned forward, her small eyes now large. "Really?"

"No, not really. She's having emotional problems. It's a long story, but it seems like ever since she's turned pregnant everything's gotten fucked up, her marriage, her relationship with her sister, our friendship. She and I have been like this," I said, crossing my fingers, "but now it's like nothing matters except this baby. I mean, I understand that once you're pregnant the baby takes precedence, but at the expense of everyone else?"

Penny shook her head in empathy. "But you know, that's just the way it is. As much as Chester says he hates his kids—he refers to the oldest as a turd—I know that if we were in a lifeboat in the middle of the ocean and dead weight had to go, guess who'd be doin' the backstroke?" She smiled and lifted her breasts up with both hands. "Or at least the dead man's float."

We both laughed, and Penny scooted forward to the edge of the couch to tap some more coke out onto the mirror from a glass vial. "Look, as soon as she has the kid, things will go back to normal. Right now she's in the baby-love phase, but once the kid turns two it'll be a different story."

I thought of Jan's skeletal frame, the desperate sadness in her eyes. Whatever phase she was in, it certainly wasn't baby-love. "I hope so," I said quietly. "I really hope so."

I lifted the remote from my lap and clicked the TV on. "Anyway, let's get watching . . ." I glanced at the video cover on the table. "*Blowhard Boys I?*"

Penny smiled impishly. "Chester's hopeful there'll be a Two."

Penny left at one, and I passed out by two. I was in a buzzy sleep when my machine picked up. I lifted my head off the pillow to hear who it was, but they were speaking so softly, or the ringing in my ears was so loud, I had to pick up the phone.

"Who is this?"

"It's Jan. Jan Hostetter."

"As opposed to all the other Jans I know." I squinted to see the alarm clock. "It's three o'clock. What's wrong?"

She sobbed and said something, but it was mangled in a choked-up whisper.

"Jan, speak up, I can barely hear you."

"Gail found Butterball!"

Now I sat up and fumbled for the light in the dark; when I turned it on it was like an explosion to my eyes. "She what?"

"She was in a bucket in a room upstairs."

I had to think; I was sure Kevin had said he was going to bury her before he left.

"I don't understand," I murmured, rubbing my eyes. "What was Gail doing up there?"

"Nothing but bones. Tiny little bones scattered

everywhere. Annie, she had a litter but Butterball was spayed! That cat was spayed! See, this proves I'm not crazy. I'm not going out of my mind!"

Little breaths punctuated her words like hyphens. "Jan, calm down. It doesn't prove anything. Sometimes those things don't take."

"No," she whimpered. "I don't think I really accepted it until now. Some part of me just hoped I was crazy, but I feel the realness of it now. I feel it in my bones."

The Unwelcome Child spoke of bones. Ingratitude, hatred, bred into a child's bones, as if emotion were the equivalent of an amino acid.

"Jan—"

"Annie I want my *own* baby, I don't want hers! God, I want to die. I just want to . . ."

She sobbed again, and I heard the receiver drop. I called her name over and over, but her crying grew increasingly distant as she moved away from the phone.

CHAPTER 11

"Like I told you earlier, Ms. Wojtoko, Ms. Hostetter was fine. A little put out 'cause she claimed she'd been having a real sound sleep, but other than that, fine."

It was nine in the morning, and I'd just stepped off the ferry and was back in Mr. Green's taxi. As soon as I'd hung the phone up last night, I called the number of Kevin's hotel where his schedule said he'd be staying for at least the rest of the week. He was in Dallas, only one hour behind, so it was somewhat disconcerting to hear a woman's voice answer the phone.

"I told you already," she said groggily. "He's sleeping."

I hung up, stunned, my hand gripping the receiver. It had to be a mistake, but I couldn't make myself call back. I was too confused. She'd told me already? Unless Ryan had called Kevin from the air on her way to Fiji, Jan was the only one who would phone him in the middle of the night. My heart contracted not just a little at the idea of Jan, scared and reaching out to Kevin, only to be met by this sleepy bitch's voice. As the lesser of two evils, I prayed it was just a hooker, then frantically rummaged around in my bag for Mr. Green's card. I reached him at an all-night poker game and asked him to go check on Jan, then got packed and drove back up to the Vineyard, sweating all the way with worry about what was happening to her—what she might do. I looked at Mr. Green's weathered face in the rearview mirror.

"I can't thank you enough. If you'd heard how scared she sounded. Her husband's away and her friend Gail stayed over."

He shook his head. "Having her for a friend, who wouldn't be scared?"

I scooched forward and rested my arms on top of the front seat. "You know Gail?" I asked, speaking into his hair-filled ear.

Mr. Green pulled a pack of gum out of the pocket of his red satin windbreaker. "Went to school with her," he said, unwrapping a stick. "Had a crush on her once, too. Until she went weird in the head." He offered me the packet and I shook my head no.

"What do you mean?"

We stopped at a red light, and he turned to face me. "Tried to kill herself twice in high school. There was a rumor that she got pregnant, but who knows?" He shrugged with one shoulder. "If I had a mother like Mrs. Rusker, I'd probably want to kill myself too. Worked as a waitress down at one of the bars on the mainland, serving drinks and something else too, if you get my meaning." He ducked his head to see if the light was still red.

"A waitress?" I asked. "Are you sure she wasn't a nurse at Eloise Asylum?"

The light turned green and he turned back around to shift into drive. "The only nursing her mother ever did was on a bottle. Now Gail, *she* spent some considerable time at Eloise. In their guest room. The kind where the mattresses are on the walls," he said, and winked at me in the mirror.

He swerved to avoid a small animal darting out onto the sandy road and I gripped the seat, almost toppling over. I decided no matter how compelling this information was, I'd better sit back and buckle my seat belt. Mr. Green lifted and then reset his plaid golf cap on top of his head.

"I told Jan to be careful around that woman. Cozies up to anyone who moves in there. Got a weird fixation on the house after she sued the Clayton estate for ownership."

"Sued? She told Jan and me she tried to buy the house."

"Ha. More like tried to steal it. When the old girl who killed those babies kicked off, Gail claimed she left her the house—supposedly wrote it down on her hand right before she died—but the coroner washed it off. Now you tell me, who's going to buy such a cock-and-bull story?"

Jan, I thought. He leaned his head out the window to spit out his gum. When he pulled his head back in, he looked at me in the rearview mirror.

"Anyway, the Claytons won, not that it did them any good. House had been sitting empty for years 'cause people were too spooked. Plus, the animals and weather had done so much damage it was no longer habitable."

I gazed out my window at the phlegmy sky and gray ocean laid out like a slab of granite beyond the dunes on the side of the road. Gail's story sounded like something out of a Gothic novel. Girl from a troubled home gets pregnant, tries to commit suicide, ends up in a loony bin where she finds the mother figure she's always craved in the person of Sybil Clayton, baby murderer. In some twisted way I guess it explained her fixation with saving the unborn. After all, she couldn't save her own. Or did she?

"Mr. Green, did Gail Rusker ever have any children?"

He was now turning the car onto Sea Thistle Road. "Like I said, that was a rumor, but I know she's never been married. The only kin she's got is Ginny Hershel, and I'm not sure in what way they're related."

Ginny Hershel. I remembered that name. "She runs the Little Brown Schoolhouse."

"That's right. Looks like Jan's having a party."

I looked up at the tiered house on the hill. Cars filled the driveway and were parked along the street.

"Yeah," I said as he pulled up at the bottom of the hill to let me out. "Some party."

I entered the house, and was met with a crowd that, on first sight at least, certainly didn't resemble your typical Vineyard crowd. Sitting and chatting quietly on the sofa and easy chair were a trio of dainty, elderly women dressed in their Sunday best. Looking at them you'd think they'd gathered here to sew a quilt instead of plan their strategy for their next antiabortion demonstration. But I'd seen them in action, and they were a powerful presence at protests. All they had to do was stand there looking heartbroken. They might touch a woman's arm as she reached for the door. Who's going to shake off an old woman, or be rude to someone who could be your grandmother? They were comforting instead of confrontational, empathetic instead of judgmental. Not many women, especially the vulnerable and confused, could resist their pull.

I didn't see Jan anywhere, but I was curious to see what kind of people a group like the Guardian Angels recruited, so I poured myself a cup of tea from the silver samovar set up on a lace-covered table and sat down on the stairs to observe. Standing in front of the window was a group of husbands and wives. From their dress I could tell they were from the mainland— inexpensive and lacking style. The men were a mix of Bermuda shorts and short-sleeved dress shirts,

sneakers with tube socks, and one pair of white poly-
ester pants. As for the women, they were WASP versions of the Orthodox Jews in New York, except
instead of bad wigs and dowdy suits they wore the type
of dresses you might find in Wal-Marts for $30.95:
nightmarish flower prints with matching cardboard
belts, shiny, low-heeled vinyl shoes. I dubbed them the
Surrendered Wives club when one of the men handed
his wife his empty plate and cup to be refilled (she did
without a complaint or cross look), and another
joked that her Al was so fussy the cubes of beef in her
beef stew had to be perfectly symmetrical; otherwise
he wouldn't touch it. Ha ha ha.

A young couple joined me on the stairs. I talked to
them a bit. The girl was hugely pregnant, couldn't be
more than nineteen, and her pale skin and sluggish
manner reminded me of warm paste. She stayed
quiet as her companion, a shaggy-haired kid with
peach fuzz on his chin, went on about how they
wanted to move to Canada when their baby was born.
The Army of God had a compound up there, and
were training recruits for the upcoming civil war.

"Civil war?" I asked, incredulous.

"Sure," he said, his eyes firing up. "Abortion is already destroying this country, and people sooner or
later are going to have to take sides, good against evil."

It was hot and muggy. I kind of drifted off as he
spoke. I stared at his nose where there was a ghost of
a hole. Other faint indents were above his brows and
lips, too. I was wondering if he still had a tongue
stud when he said, "Becky and I were really messed
up until we met Gail Rusker. Living on the streets of
New York, doing drugs. Becky'd been hooking to
support the both of us. Then we came across Gail at
a Planned Parenthood. She got us a place to stay,
got us off the meth." He looked down at Becky's

stomach. "Don't even know whose baby it is, but it doesn't matter."

"God's baby," Becky said with a laugh. Then Jan entered, carrying a ceramic Mexican hat filled with guacamole. She was wearing a knee-length, sleeveless blue smock with a lace collar and black clogs; they made her stick-thin ankles look like twiglike seedlings stuck into oversized planters. Her hair was loose, pushed back behind her ears. She set the guacamole hat on the coffee table, and as she exchanged pleasantries with the ladies her face betrayed none of the despair I'd heard the night before. It gave me hope that she hadn't called Kevin after all. Perhaps I'd mistaken what the woman had said.

Then Gail entered carrying a music stand, and all eyes turned to her. She was wearing a black dress, belted at the waist. In a more tight-fitting dress you could see how enormous she was. Her huge breasts rested on top of her stomach and the flesh on her arms hung like sloppy garland as she held the stand out in front of her. Her long braid hung down her back, its tail nestling in the crack of her ass. Right away the "Angels" began to settle themselves around the living room. Chairs had been brought in from the dining area. Jan was busy restacking the teacups into a symmetrical pyramid and didn't see me. I moved to the bottom stair so I wouldn't be too noticeable behind a wall of folding chairs and upright backs. I felt like a mole, a secret agent trying to pass myself off as one of the enemy.

"All right everyone." Gail's voice lifted above the babble effortlessly. The defender of the fetus was standing behind the couch, her hands held up for quiet. She was still wearing those gold wrist-cuffs, and I imagined her flinging a golden lasso around a villainous abortionist, hunkered down between the stirruped legs of an unconscious woman, and then dragging him off up into the sky as a cheering crowd below shouted, "Thank you, Wonder Mother! Thank you!"

"Thank you for coming," Gail said as everyone quieted down. "As always, your dedication is only surpassed by your passion for our work."

I made a disparaging sound, which I hadn't meant for anyone else to hear, but a tall, bald man glared at me over his shoulder.

"Unfortunately, I'll be requiring a bit more than usual as some vandals broke into Jan's garage and all the posters will have to be redone. The brutes also crushed Baby Jane's head in. . . ." She paused to let the murmur of shock and outrage riffle through the room before continuing. "In a moment you'll see the irony of her destruction, but first I'd like to thank our host, Janine Hostetter, for so generously allowing us the use of her wonderful home. And providing such great food! Jan?"

Heads turned in the direction of the swinging doors of the kitchen, which Jan was just about to enter. She blushed and smiled.

"Hear, hear!" someone said. Others began to applaud. Jan ducked her head in acknowledgment, and then retreated into the kitchen.

"First order of business," Gail continued on. "An abortion mill will be opening in Chatham this September tenth. Its attending physician will be Dr. Sidney Haine, who as you know has the distinction of being one of the country's leading practitioners of partial-birth abortion."

A disapproving murmur bubbled through the crowd. The beef cubist woman yelled out, "I'd like to see a partial-birth abortion performed on that SOB!" A hail of clapping ensued, some whistles too. Gail just kept her watery blue eyes down until everyone was finished, before addressing the woman.

"I understand your sentiments, Kathy, but without these women Haine wouldn't exist. This country has fostered such an anti–mother/child culture, American women have been brainwashed into believing that the issue of *choice* empowers them more than a child ever can. They're the ones we need to focus on, not Haine, and if we do our job right, I guarantee we'll have the Chatham Women's Health Center closed down before winter is out."

There was applause and more cheers. Gail held up a videotape.

"I have here in my hand a training video. It's used to teach doctors how to perform a partial-birth abortion. Since it's a teaching tool, it's of course being presented in a very matter-of- fact, ordinary way. By the tone of the voice-over, you'd think they were demonstrating how to cook an omelet. Peter, please slip this into the VCR and, Dora and Samantha, would you mind closing the blinds?"

The living room dimmed and became quiet enough to hear the click and whir of the VCR starting up. I craned my neck so I could see. All faces were tensely trained on the TV camouflaged in the credenza. *Training video IV for Intrauterine Cranial Decompression, Cambridge Obstetric Medical College* showed up in blurred white letters across the black screen. A voice came next, introducing the procedure as the black screen was replaced with a white operating room. On a table a pregnant woman lay prone, with her feet in stirrups and an anesthesia mask obscuring her face. A team of residents in blue stood around the table, at the bottom of which sat, between the patient's legs, a female doctor in white.

"This form of abortion should only be performed in extreme cases, such as when the woman's life is in danger, or there is a dire genetic defect in which the fetus will not survive outside the womb. In this particular case, the child, a female, has no eyes and has developed only the right hemisphere of its brain, resulting in partial cranial collapse."

A voice from behind one of the white masks asked a question, but it was inaudible. The doctor glanced up and said, "Forty-three. This would have been her first pregnancy." The camera closed in on the space between the woman's legs, where forceps were inserted into her vagina. Something in me told me to *look away, once it's in your head it's there forever,* but I was transfixed as two feet, no bigger than my thumbs, were pulled out. There were a few gasps, heads turned away as the narrator went on to describe the puncturing of the fetus's cranium.

"We insert the suction curette, which will extract brain matter and spinal fluid from the skull, allowing for total collapse."

My sinuses began to swell, my throat was aching, but I forbade myself to let the dam break. That was exactly what they would be counting on. Still, I couldn't look anymore. I focused on the softly gleaming bald head in front of me and instead tried to imagine why in God's name anyone would allow her abortion to be videotaped. Maybe she did it to convince herself this was the way to go. Half a brain, it wouldn't live very long, even though that hasn't stopped some people I know. I looked up just in time to see the bluish body of the fetus extracted from its dark, watery cave. One loose tear trickled down my cheek and settled into the corner of my mouth. Poor baby. It had no idea it was an atrocity of nature, better off dead than alive. All it had ever known was the safe haven of its mother's uterus.

Gail turned to the group. "It will be very important on your part to explain to people that in the eyes of the law, a distance of perhaps five inches distinguishes this procedure from infanticide. If this baby's head were allowed to emerge from the birth canal, this would be considered a live birth."

I got up to find Jan. She was in the kitchen, sitting at the table looking down at folded hands.

"You're missing the entertainment."

She looked up, surprised. "Annie."

"Personally I can't watch a movie without popcorn."

"Don't. They'll hear!" I sat down across from her. "When did you get here?" she whispered.

"A while ago." Up close, she looked like she was the one who'd stayed up all night snorting coke. Her eyes were feverish; bluish rings circled under them like dark half-moons. "Are you okay?"

"You didn't have to call Mr. Green," she said in an angry whisper. "He's the island gossip. The last thing I want is everyone knowing my business."

"Excuse me, but you left the phone off the hook after telling me you wanted to die." She looked down at the table, shamefaced. "Jan, you scared the shit out of me."

She lifted her head, and looked over her shoulder to the window where gray clouds clotted the sky. "Gail buried Butterball for me this morning. Back there by the fence."

I dreaded asking the next question, but I had to know. "So . . . did you speak to Kevin at all?"

She continued to stare out the window. "Gail said she had to have eaten her litter to survive for as long as she did. Can you imagine?"

To me this gruesome tidbit was just another indication that Gail was pursuing her own agenda here; even if it were true, why mention it to Jan?

"Jan—"

"No, I didn't speak to him." A tear fell down her cheek and she wiped it away with a rough swipe of her hand while still keeping her eyes in the direction of

Butterball's grave. "But I did call. Sounds like some business trip he's having." Her lips trembled. "The woman who answered told me he was sleeping."

I'd been holding my breath and exhaled. "Jan, it might not be what you think. Maybe it was just, you know, one of those things. . . ."

She gripped her belly with both hands and looked down. "My girl here is very selfish, Annie. She wants me all to herself and she's getting it. Aren't you, sweetheart?"

I reached out and grabbed her wrists. "You're not alone. I'm here. Ryan's ticked off, but she's here." I faltered. "Kevin . . . I can't say, but you're right about one thing . . . things are being orchestrated all right, but not by your baby, and not by some dead girl."

With urgency I repeated to her the conversation I'd had with Mr. Green in the car. Gail's lies about her mother, her suicide attempts, and her attempt to sue for ownership of the house. When I was done, Jan didn't say anything. She just got up and went to the refrigerator and took a bowl out that on first glance appeared to be filled with peaches in syrup.

"I want to show you something," she said, taking a spoon out of a dish rack before coming back over to the table. "I haven't been able to stomach eggs since I've been pregnant, but this morning I had the most intense craving for them."

She set the bowl down in front of me, which I could now see was filled with eggs, their yellow yolks separated from their whites. In the center was a red and white blob. With great gentleness, Jan spooned it up and held it over the bowl as the yoke drained from it, slowly revealing the beak, the black round eyes, and the veiny body of a chick.

"It's a baby chick," I said.

Jan set the spoon and the unfortunate creature back into the bowl. "It's a warning."

"What do you mean, it's a warning?"

She sat down, eyes concentrated on the bowl. "After I called you last night I began to imagine what life would be like once the baby was born. Kevin gone, never leaving this place. I felt like I was in a straightjacket. I just had to get out so . . . I did. I just started walking . . . out of the house, down the driveway. When I reached the street, I was beginning to think I could do it, you know?" she said, turning her eyes back up to me, half hopeful. "But then halfway down the street I began to feel the pain, and it was nothing like I'd felt before." She crossed her arms and shrank into herself, as if she were right now trussed up in a straightjacket. "Next thing I know, Gail is helping me up the driveway. She'd woke up, sure something was wrong. If she hadn't, I would have killed my baby."

She took the spoon once again and lifted the chick up at an angle until all the yolk had drained from it. "So whatever you have to say about Gail, I don't care. All I care about is that she saved my baby."

When I entered Fall River I pulled over at a Mobil station to fill Jan's Mercedes with gas. After my talk with Jan, I was actually looking forward to seeing my dad. As the attendant filled up the car, I walked out to the curb to get a better look at Durfee's Mill, where my dad used to work before they laid him off. It was a huge stone building with endless rows of windows and a giant watchtower peaking up out of its center. It looked more like a mental institution or prison than a factory. The benches, now marked up with graffiti, were still there in front where my mom and I used to wait for my dad with his paper bag lunch. The shuttles from the hundreds of looms inside would rattle and thunder so loud I used to have to cover my ears. Then Dad would come out, red-faced and soaked with sweat from the 120-degree heat of the dye rooms. He used to say you didn't know hell until you worked in a textile mill.

Now it sat silent. Most of the mills were, and the ones that weren't had been reincarnated into health clubs, furniture outlets, or car dealerships. Next to Durfee's was Pagerson's Mill, where Jan's father had worked. The huge smokestack that used to chug out dark gray smoke now had a Wendy's logo and an arrow showing the way to Grease City. They'd built the Wendy's right in the middle of its parking lot where the mill executives used to park their fancy cars. It would have been better if they'd just torn it all down. Leaving the old mills standing was a mockery to all the families that had been destroyed when the industry moved south. With the textile mills gone, there was nothing left, but people still had rent to pay and kids to feed. Families broke up and fathers began to drink. Mine especially.

I paid the attendant and took off up Bedford, past the blue VFW Dad used to belong to. Some windows were broken, others boarded up. At least when that was open he had some semblance of a social life, but now I was pretty sure he just stayed home and drank. I was driving slowly, in no hurry to get there, but before I knew it I was passing by the taupe and brown Borden house, now a bed-and-breakfast. A few years ago I had my picture taken on the couch where Mr. Borden was murdered. The legend had always been a favorite of mine, ever since I was seven and Dad first told it to me as a bedtime story. After that, I couldn't have cared less about Winnie the Pooh or Peter Cottontail. I only had ears for Lizzie, and how she hacked her stepmother and father to death. It terrified and thrilled me at the same time. I was constantly asking questions, like what did the heads look like, or how much blood was there. Dad thought it was funny, but my mother never forgave him. She accused him of turning me into a morbid kid.

I pulled up alongside the faded, sea-green, three-story clapboard house I grew up in. We rented the second floor, and Jan's family rented the second floor of the brown box next door. They were built, like most of the homes in Fall River, to warehouse the textile workers and their families, so space wasn't a consideration. Jan and I used to be able to whisper to each other across the alleyway that separated our houses at night when we were supposed to be in bed. As I got out of the car I couldn't help but feel strange coming from such an elegant mansion with an endless view of the sea to this—it felt as if my whole world had instantly contracted.

I pushed open the rusted gate that enclosed the minuscule yard. When our landlady, Mrs. Peeley, had been alive it had been real nice, but now it had gone to seed. The green lawn had worn away to dirt, the path leading to the front door was weed-choked, and her flower beds had long since turned to dust. The old oak, though, the one that shaded my bedroom window from the rising sun, was still hanging in there. Underneath it was a tipped-over tricycle. That must mean someone with kids was now living on one of the other floors. Dad must love that.

I stepped onto the porch and stood in front of the screen door, its metal netting ripped and curled outward. As usual, my dad's mailbox was jammed full. He only bothered checking it at the end of the month when he expected his Social Security check. I took the mail out and unlocked the door with my spare key. Inside I was met with a toddler in a dirty pink bathing suit sitting in the open doorway of Mrs. Peeley's old apartment, surrounded by empty cans that had spilled out from a paper bag. From inside I could hear the hootin' and hollering audience specific to daytime TV. The little girl held out a Budweiser can to me.

"A little early for that, isn't it?" I asked, taking it from her. A young, plump woman in tight shorts and a loose halter top stepped into the doorway.

"Bonnie, how many times I tell you, *stay* outta the garbage! Look at this shit," she said as she began to throw the cans back into the bag.

I handed her the can the tot had given me. "Here."

She looked at me as if I'd appeared out of thin air. "Who are you?"

"John Wojtoko's daughter."

She was chewing on a wad of gum and glowered at me suspiciously as a huge pink bubble mushroomed from her lips. Just before it was large enough to obscure the lower half of her face, she sucked it back in and exclaimed, "Johnny never tol' me he had a daughter," in that tough New England accent, where all the t's were d's. It cost me a lot of time and money in vocal coaches to get rid of it, and if I stayed in the area too long it inevitably crept its way back into my o's and a's.

"That's okay," I said, climbing the stairs. "I don't tell many people I have a dad."

"'Ey," she called out again, waiting for me to look down at her. "He's good people, your dad."

I looked down at the bloated moon face glowing up at me, and wondered if this sentiment was inspired by the free beer my dad probably gave her. He was a sucker for big breasts, and hers jiggled in their sling like twin Jell-O molds with every move. Nice to know his Social Security checks were being put to good use.

"Yeah. He's swell," I said.

Upstairs, after knocking a few times, I let myself in. I found "Johnny" conked out in front of the TV in his patched-up Lazy-boy, snoring. A game show was on and empty beer cans, same brand as Miss White Trash's downstairs, littered the small table my mom used to keep her crocheting in. The place was dark and stifling. He liked it that way, and never opened the drapes or windows no matter how hot. I think he'd built up a tolerance to heat from all those years working in the dye rooms. I looked down at him a moment. My dad was only sixty-eight, but he looked eighty. Over the years his drinking had cauliflowered his nose and the skin on his face hung loose, as if all the times he'd bloated himself up over a lifetime of benders had worn out its elasticity. It didn't help that the white hair on his head was as sparse as the grass outside, and . . . *shit*, he was thin. That meant one thing: gin diet. I could smell it. And see it—an empty bottle, tipped over onto its side, rested against his chair.

I walked over to the TV and was about to turn it off when I noticed the video box cover for *Zombie Love* on top of the VCR. The box was empty and the video was sticking out of the VCR slot. I pulled it out. Either the tape hadn't been rewound all the way or he couldn't bear to watch it to the end. I looked back at my dad, his jaw hanging so low it seemed unhinged, and wondered if he'd finished the bottle before or after he watched the tape. I pushed the tape back in and turned the TV off. Like a reverse alarm, the break in noise woke him up.

"Alice," he sputtered. It surprised me, him calling out my mother's name. So he still must dream of her. After she died, I remember he used to call out her name in his sleep almost every night. Other than that, he never mentioned her. I'd always assumed it was out of guilt.

"It's me, Dad. Annie," I said, going over to the drapes. I pulled them open.

"Shut that, Annie," he growled. "I don't like the light."

"I know," I said as I pried the window up. "It's bad for hangovers."

He looked confused, as if he didn't know where he was. Predictably, he patted the front pocket of his flannel shirt, the same shirt he wore year-round. "Where are my damn smokes?" he mumbled. I glanced around and saw his Lucky Strikes on the floor, next to a spilled ashtray. Gray ash and butts littered the worn blue carpet. I gave him his cigarettes and carried the ashtray into the kitchen.

"Damn it, Dad! What if one of these had been lit?"

"So I'll save you the cost of a cremation."

I was going to put the ashtray in the sink but it was full with dirty dishes. I'd offered several times to pay for a housecleaner to come at least once a month, but he wouldn't have it. He didn't like anyone "muckin'" around, as he put it. I came back into the living room. As soon as I sat down on the sofa, he said, "Annie, be a good girl, will ya?"

I knew what was coming. "No, Dad. Buy your own liquor."

His bleary eyes tried to focus. "I was going to ask you to buy some groceries so I could offer you lunch, but since you mentioned it, here." He pulled two twenties out of his pocket—the effort seemed to exhaust him—and he held them out to me. "Just one bottle. I'm tryin' to cut down." I stared at the money, torn between doing the right thing and making life easy for myself. He wouldn't give it a rest until I got it for him. I snatched the money out of his hand.

When I came back, I walked past him with an armful of groceries and a plastic bottle of gin. My dad liked cheap gin. To his way of thinking, you got more for your money. I told myself I'd make him lunch, then head back to the island before an argument broke out, which almost always did.

Like a dog knowing he was in for a treat he followed me into the kitchen. "You get it?"

"Yeah. I got it," I said, opening the refrigerator. It

was empty, of course, except for some ancient hot dog buns and a crusted jar of yellow mustard. Dad lived on cold hot dogs and Spaghetti-Os most of the time. I glanced out of the corner of my eye. He was already digging through the grocery bag for the gin.

"Can't you at least wait until I make you something to eat?"

"I always have a cocktail, five o'clock on the dot," he said, pulling out the bottle.

I glanced up at the wall clock that advertised Miller beer. It was three. "What happens if you're late, your blood turn to powder or something?"

"You always were a smart-ass kid, Annie."

As he made himself his cocktail, warm gin straight up, I put the groceries into the refrigerator. I'd bought him two packages of hot dogs, fresh buns, coffee, and apples for roughage. Anything else I figured would rot.

"Just open me up some Spaghetti-Os, will you? I'll eat it out of a can so you can go. I know you don't want to be here."

"You can't eat Spaghetti-Os cold," I said as I scraped the orange gunk out of its can into a pot with half the Teflon flaked off. "It's bad enough warm, it's got to be disgusting cold." I dumped a few dogs in and turned the burner on.

"Hey," he said, pouring himself another. "Sit down and have a drink with your dad."

"I'm driving."

As soon as I sat down I could feel him scrutinizing me, like he used to do when I'd come home after a date, trying to see in my eyes if I was still a virgin or not. I looked down at the yellowed linoleum. The whole apartment, the walls, the ceiling, even the furniture seemed to be tinted a jaundiced yellow. I was just waiting for him to bring up *Zombie Love*. Not that I cared what he thought. I wondered if his watching the tape set him off on this binge. I glanced at his pack of cigarettes, dying for a smoke, but then that would make me a hypocrite since I was always lecturing him about stopping. He slurped his gin slowly, unlike the old days when he used to knock shots back as if he were popping peanuts.

"I know you didn't come all the way up here just to heat me up some hot dogs," he said.

I got up to check the Spaghetti-Os because he really didn't like his food hot.

"Remember? I told you I had to come up and see Jan. She's pregnant." I said, twisting the burner off, annoyed. Drinking wiped out his short-term memory, too.

"Pregnant?"

"Yeah. Pregnant."

"Ain't she too old for that?"

I forked the dogs and stuck them in two stiff buns. "Women have babies later in life these days."

He scowled. "That's what I hear. In my opinion it ain't right. Women have no business having babies after thirty. They dry up. You got to be fresh for that."

"She's not a loaf of bread."

I placed his hot dogs on a paper plate, dumped the runny Spaghetti-Os into a coffee mug, the only clean container in the cupboard, and set them in front of him.

He looked up at me. "So what about you? You waitin' till you're old enough to be a grandmother?"

"Fortunately, this branch of the Wojtoko family is going to end with me."

"Oh, and why's that?"

I was about to sit down, but as soon as my ass touched the seat he said, "Mustard," and I got back up, exasperated. He's done this for as long as I can remember. Just as you were about to sit, he'd remember something else he wanted. I can still picture my mother popping up and down from the table like a jack-in-the-box every meal. After she'd died, it was my turn.

"Let's just say I don't have much faith in the Woj-toko gene pool," I said, swinging the fridge door open. "I figure we should quit while we're ahead."

My father grimaced. "Now that's an asinine thing to say. If anything we're the good end of things. Look at my brother Charley's kids. They reproduce like weeds and every one of them is choking the life out of 'im. Hank is up for assault, Julie's on her fifth kid with her third husband, and the little one, Jakey? You know what that kid did? He decapitated the Sacred Heart Virgin. Little bastard stowed the head away in his tree house. Never would have known if it hadn't 'a fell and killed the neighbor's cat."

I opened the crusty jar and stuck a knife into the yellow muck and slathered it on the hot dog, which had turned orange from soaking in the Spaghetti-Os.

He looked down at his food glumly. "No onions?"

If you didn't know him, you'd think this was a joke. "Sorry, but the closest thing to the vegetable family in that refrigerator is mold."

He sighed and pushed his food away. He wasn't fooling me. He couldn't care less about onions, it was just an excuse so the food wouldn't soak up the gin in his stomach. He brought his glass to his lips with an exaggerated slowness, as if it were filled with nitro. When he set it back down, he said, "You're like me. I was never the family man type. If it hadn't 'a been for your mother, I wouldn't 'a bothered. Who knows how different things would' a been had she lived?"

"I got news for you, Dad. We weren't exactly the American dream while she was alive."

His tongue ran around his lips, sweeping up any gin he might have missed. "Won't argue with that, but at least you would have had a what do you call it . . . a role model. I guarantee you wouldn't be living the life you are now. What man would take you now with all the men you've had?"

I closed my eyes. *Here we go.* My father believed the only women that should be unmarried were nuns, and if you weren't, it meant you were a whore.

"Your mother would have seen to it you had a man to take care of you a long time ago."

I opened my eyes and glared at him. "Like you took care of Mom? No thanks."

He looked down into his glass sadly. "Your mother deserved better, that's for sure," he said in a quiet voice. We sat in silence, like two strangers after the small talk has been exhausted. An ice cream truck somewhere in the neighborhood was playing "Pop Goes the Weasel." I felt as if I were suffocating.

I sprang up and went over to the kitchen window. "Christ it's hot in here."

I opened it and stood looking out at the concrete backyard down below where a child's pool, full of dirty water, sat out under the sunless sky. A game of hop-scotch had been chalked in on the grease-stained drive-way, right where the carport Jan and I used to hold our little dramas in had once been. I heard the cellophane of my father's cigarette pack crinkle behind me.

"Listen, who you going to have once I'm gone? You ever think about that? At least I got you to spit on my grave."

I turned around just in time to see him blow smoke onto his food. "Where's all this fatherly concern coming from?" I asked.

"Whattya mean?"

"I mean it's a little late in the day to play Fred Mc-Murray. Since when do you care about anything other than where your next drink is coming from?"

He pointed his finger at me. "You watch your mouth, sis. I may be old, but I can still knock the stars out of the sky for you."

Our eyes locked. When I was small, yeah, but I wasn't a kid anymore. I was a grown woman, he was now an old man; he needed me more than I needed him.

"You do that, Dad," I said. "You just do that."

He was still pointing his finger at me. Then as if some director shouted *cut,* his shoulders slumped, his face dropped—his thirty-second-tough-guy routine had sapped all his strength and he was done for the day. He sighed and shook his head. "Like I said, I know I was a shit father, but I ain't got long. I don't want to fight with you no more."

I rolled my eyes at this old tune. I had no doubt the man would outlive me. On his side they didn't grow old and die, they just fossilized. "Dad, you're only sixty-eight, but if you're so worried about it, stop smoking and drinking."

"What the hell for? I'm ready. I'm tired." His voice shook as he spoke, and now his head was hanging. I had to look away not to laugh. "Anyway," he said, "I want you to know I plan on making things up to you when I'm dead. I got some money put aside."

I stared at him. As far as I knew, all he had was his Social Security. His last job, a security guard at Sears, hadn't even offered him a pension.

"How much?"

He cocked one eyebrow. "That, you won't know till I'm dead and buried."

"Oh yeah? Well, in that case, have another cigarette," I said, pushing the pack toward him. "I need new head shots."

"I'm serious now, so pay attention."

He'd raised his voice. I checked the time. Three-thirty. I had to catch the five-fifteen ferry.

"All right, all right. I'm just having a hard time believing we have some secret fortune stashed away somewhere."

He shook his head. "It ain't no fortune, but it's

enough so I can die in peace knowin' you won't have to end up a fat old tart on the street somewhere."

I got up and snatched his food away. "You know what, Dad? For your information I'm doing just fine. People recognize me on the street. I get *fan* mail!"

"So what? So did Marilyn Chambers."

"Hey, I may not be at the level where I'm discussing script changes over a cappuccino with Scorcese, but I am making a living in what I was trained for and that's good enough for me!"

"Ah, come on, Annie. If you was gonna make it you would' a done it by now."

"Maybe if I'd had a little support from the beginning I might be farther along," I yelled, banging the cup furiously against the side of the garbage can to get every last slimy O out. "Where the hell was all this money when I needed it?"

"I told you then, and I'll tell it to you again, I wasn't gonna give you one red cent to subsidize that actin' crap! You should have gone into something respectable, like teaching. Or nursing."

"Oh, please! If I'd been a missionary you still wouldn't have helped me out!"

"What you gettin' so angry for? I'm just tryin' to do right by you."

"You wanted ta do right by me ya should' a done it a long time ago! I don't want your money. Give it to your welfare witch girlfriend downstairs!"

I was losing it. Whenever I was losing it, I reverted to my Fall River accent. My dad banged his hand on the table. "Listen, ya little shit, you're gettin' it and that's that!"

"I don't want it!"

"You're takin' it!"

We stared at each other, fuming. Finally I plopped down into the chair across from him and took out a cigarette, lit it up.

Dad slid the ashtray in my direction. "I don't know how to talk to you, Annie. I never did."

I blew some smoke toward the open window. "Why'd you watch my video?"

He shifted in his chair. "Glenda rented it."

I looked at him in disbelief. "Are you really seeing that girl?"

He shrugged. "I take her out for some fish and chips every Friday. She's got a nice little girl. Sometimes, I babysit."

"You? You're babysitting a *toddler*?"

He scowled indignantly. "I'm not an asshole. I don't drink around her." He paused to refill his glass. "You know, I think I would' a made a better grandfather. I didn't enjoy you the way I should've. This kid is real sweet."

I never knew if my dad was just so fucking stupid and insensitive he didn't know he was hurting me, or if he knew exactly what he was doing. Either way, how I felt toward him right then, the thoughts I was having, his head should have exploded into a thousand pieces.

I got up. "I have to catch the ferry. It fills up fast."

A pained look appeared on his face. "I was thinkin' . . . maybe you'd wanna see your mom."

I looked at him to see if he meant it. Every time I had suggested it in the past, he had an excuse. Sometimes, he didn't even have that. He just didn't want to go, claiming there was more of her in this house than that grave. And I had to agree. But I still liked her having fresh flowers.

"Dad, I want to ask you something," I said, taking a seat. He looked at me, but I couldn't look at him back. I pinched the plastic tablecloth between my forefinger and thumb as I asked him what had been on my mind ever since I'd spoken to Jan this morning. "Did Mom . . . after she had me, did she ever feel like her life was over?"

He pulled back, with a face as if I'd asked him if they'd had strange sex. "Come on, you gotta ask a thing like that?"

I shifted uncomfortably. He rested his elbows on the table and leaned so close I could smell his breath, see the tiny veins in his eyes. "Annie, you were that woman's life. The only reason she hung on as long as she did was 'cause of you," He patted my hand. "Come on now. Let's go visit your mom."

As we were walking out to the car, the little girl in the pink bathing suit came out from the back riding her tricycle. As soon as she saw my dad, she yelled out, "Papa John!" and came tearing over.

"'Eyyy! How's my girl?" My dad lowered and opened his arms so the kid could run right into them. He picked her up and tossed her into the air. She squealed and giggled. I'd forgotten, it seems unbelievable now, but he used to do the same thing with me when my mom and I would meet him with his lunch. I used to get so impatient waiting for him, as soon as I saw him I'd run up and he'd toss me in the air the same way. My dad wiped away some crusted food underneath her nose with his dye-stained fingers.

"How many times I tell you, you eat with your mouth, not your nose."

"Take me to the playground later?"

He glanced at me. "Not today, kid. Hey, Bonnie, this is my kid. *My* little girl."

I'd been watching this tender little scene, iron-faced. The little girl looked at me warily. "But she's big," she said.

My dad laughed, and even I smiled. He set her back down and told her not to bite any dogs, and she got back onto her bike and rode away. Dad watched her, smiling, with hands in his pockets like a proud father.

"So, is that my half-sister?"

His smile turned into a scowl. "You got a perverted mind, you know that?"

It wasn't often I felt like I was on the wrong side of things with my dad, but now I did. I felt ashamed for ruining a happy moment. Especially since he'd reassured me about my mom. She loved me. I wasn't something that had sucked the life out of her. I had given her something to live for. Maybe I'd been cruel because now I felt so cheated of it. Love, that is. It was hard seeing my dad, who had been so niggardly with it growing up, now giving it away so freely, as if it were money and he were the richest man in the world.

"Come on," I mumbled. "I want to get to the cemetery before it closes."

When I pulled up the driveway to Jan's house, I noticed the window in the dumbwaiter room was wide open. Gail must have left it open when she found Butterball. That was something I meant to find out; what was she doing up there anyway? As I got out of the car I made a mental note to go up and close it.

In the kitchen, a corner of a white frosted cake was wrapped in plastic on the counter. I called out for Jan, but there was no answer. I cut myself a piece of cake, and ate it while looking out the kitchen window that had a view of the ocean. The day was on the verge of dusk. With the sun just a hint on the horizon, the fading light gave the normally cheery kitchen a gloomy aspect.

Or maybe it was just me. I couldn't get my dad out of my mind. I'd never minded being what at the very best could be said was estranged. It was convenient. But that was when I thought his life was empty. Now I was entertaining absurd fantasies of having someone who was fifteen years younger, maybe even more, be my stepmom. The irony that his life was filling up while mine seemed to be emptying out was about as hard to swallow as this overly sweet cake.

I found them standing by the window in the nursery, their silhouettes outlined by the navy blue sky. They didn't see me, and I held back from entering.

"Gail, I'm scared."

"Haven't I taken care of everything so far?"

Jan hung her head, and the older woman lifted her chin with her fingertips. "Janine, you just have to be strong for a little while longer."

I held my breath, waiting to hear anything else that might explain what they were talking about, but then Gail kneeled down as Jan lifted her smock and exposed her bare stomach. Just the thought of that woman's lips so close to Jan's flesh made me shudder, but all she did was stare at Jan's belly for the longest time, as if she were examining her womb with X-ray vision. Then she placed her ear and hands on it too, à la Spock from the *Star Trek* series. When she took her ear away she looked up at Jan and said, "Our girl's fine, Janine. Just fine."

Our girl. I stepped into the room. "Hello."

"Oh!" Jan stepped back from Gail, startled. "Annie," she said, smoothing down the front of her smock. "I didn't expect you back so early."

Gail was lifting her elephantine body up with the help of the windowsill.

"I hope I haven't interrupted anything," I said, pleased that I had.

"Not at all. Not at all," Gail said as she brushed the lint from her dress. "I was just determining the position of the baby."

"Oh?" I sauntered over to the doll's table and took a seat as Jan sat in her rocking chair. "I didn't think you could do that without a sonogram."

Gail rested her hands on her prodigious hips and

laughed. "Well now, what do you think they did before the introduction of such a medical marvel?"

I shrugged. "I think they must have at least used a stethoscope." I crossed my legs and leaned my elbow on the table in an effort to appear nonchalant. "So how'd the meeting go?"

"I'm sorry if it upset you," Gail said, reaching out to touch my arm. "I saw you get up and leave. The video *is* graphic, I know. Believe me, if we didn't feel we had to take such drastic measures . . ."

I itched my nose to escape her touch. "If you knew me better, you'd know I would have found a live birth just as hard to watch." I looked at Jan, who was going through her sewing basket, pretending to be busy so she could avoid meeting my eye.

"My dad and I went to my mom's grave. We checked on your mom and dad's, Jan. Ryan must have been there recently. There were fresh flowers."

As I spoke, Gail had maneuvered herself behind Jan's chair, where she hovered like a prison guard. Her gold wrist-cuffs shimmered softly in the waning light.

"We had a fine time here," Gail said, touching Jan's shoulders, smoothing her hair to the back of her nape. "One of our members had a birthday."

"Mom's birthday is soon." Jan was speaking directly to me. Her eyes softened, and for an instant, we connected.

I leaned forward and placed a hand on her knee. "September first. Two days before my mom's." I glanced up at Gail. "Too bad we can't drive out."

Gail leaned over slightly and placed her hand on her shoulder. "Janine, I'll go for you."

Jan smiled up at Gail as she patted her hand, and I knew that whatever connection we'd just had was gone. I sat back.

"Well, that's kind of defeating the point, isn't it? I mean, I can do that."

Gail began to massage her neck, and Jan's head fell forward. A ventriloquist with her dummy.

Jan moaned. "That feels great."

"Perhaps we could go together," Gail said, peering at me over the tops of her glasses.

"That's an idea," Jan mumbled, chin on chest.

There was no way out of it without being rude. I stood up. "I almost forgot. The window in the room upstairs is wide open. I'd better go shut it."

Gail's head shot up. "No!"

Jan flinched. "Ow! Gail, that hurt," she said, pulling away. Gail gave her shoulders an apologetic squeeze. "I'm sorry, it's just that after I found Butterball I locked the door after myself and unfortunately, I left the key at home."

"Why would you lock the door?"

"The floorboards up there are in danger of collapsing. I didn't think it was safe—I know Jan's young niece sometimes visits."

I remembered the floor was warped, but certainly in no danger of collapsing. For some reason Gail didn't want anyone up there. Ergo, I intended to go look for myself as soon as she left.

"Well," I said, "let's just hope it doesn't rain tonight."

"I'll bring it back tomorrow. Take it from me, girls. Start taking your ginkgo biloba now. It's frightful how forgetful I've become in my old age."

"Forgetting a key is okay. It's time to worry when you start leaving your shoes in the refrigerator," Jan said.

Or forget who your *real* friends are, I thought, moving across the room to the doll-covered toy box. I moved a Pippy Longstocking out of the way to make room and sat. Gail had resumed her massage, but there was something disconcerting in the way she was putting her whole body into it, as if Jan had the neck of a wrestler. I lifted Pippy up by stretching her braids out in opposite directions so I'd have something else to focus on.

"That must have been upsetting finding Butter-ball. You'd think eating your litter would go against maternal instinct."

"Are we talking feline, or human?"

I glanced up, a little surprised at the jump in species, and began to twirl the doll between her braids. "I was talking about Jan's cat."

"The reason I ask is that it makes all the differ-ence in how I answer. Butterball is an animal, and her prime objective is to survive, not necessarily ensure the survival of her offspring. But you see, as humans, we expect our mothers to protect their children, and when they don't, then they're really not much differ-ent than Jan's cat, are they?"

I dropped my hands. "Wait a minute. You're equat-ing a woman who ends a pregnancy to a cat who has eaten her *litter*?" I asked in disbelief.

Gail's eyes widened innocently. "They both put their survival before their offspring's, don't they?"

"Yeah, because no mother, no offspring."

She rested her hands on Jan's shoulders. "Of course the mother is important. But when she puts herself before her child's welfare, or life? That is a disgrace. Isn't that right, Jan," she asked, looking down at the crown of Jan's head. Jan was frowning down at the floor, her mind obviously somewhere else.

"Jan?" Gail prompted.

"Of course," Jan murmured. "A good mother always puts her child's welfare first," she said, like a child who'd learned a lesson by rote. Gail took up her mas-sage again, and Jan's head fell forward.

"Even if that baby has no brain or eyes?"

Gail made a sound as if a gas bubble had burst somewhere deep in her colon. "No matter how many times I see that partial-birth abortion video, I am still amazed at a mother's capacity to sacrifice her child for her own comfort."

"*Comfort?* Why don't you show a video of what life would be like if that baby lived?"

Gail shook her head sadly. "Humans are the only creatures on this earth arrogant enough to think they have the right to decide when another human being may live or die. It's that type of arrogance that to me is the true essence of evil."

I picked the Pippy Longstocking doll back up and twirled her with a vengeance, which was what I wanted to do with Gail right then. "No, what's arrogant is to decide for others what they can or cannot do with their own bodies."

Jan shot me a warning look, which quickly turned to indignation as she realized I was twirling her doll between my hands.

"Annie, what are you doing to Pippy? Stop that!"

I shrugged sheepishly and stuffed her among the other dolls. "I'm sorry."

"You have no respect for my dolls. You never have."

"All right already," I said, holding up my hands. "I said I was sorry."

Jan held my eyes a moment longer before shaking her head in disgust. Once she bowed her head for Gail to continue, I rolled my eyes.

Gail laughed, obviously tickled by our little exchange. "Jan's extraordinarily protective of her dolls."

"Yeah, I know. Her kid'll be lucky to handle them before she's eighteen."

"She'll be taught to respect and love them," Jan said, head hanging so low she was talking into her belly. "Unlike some people. Annie has a fear of dolls, Gail. Absolutely hates them."

Gail smiled. "That's unfortunate. They say how a girl treats her dolls is an indication of how she'll treat her children."

"Well, if Annie ever has children, God help them. Her dolls were always the filthiest things," Jan said. "Hair uncombed, mismatched outfits." She began to snicker. "Only Annie could turn Barbie into an absolute slattern."

"What are you talking about? I bought her that way." She peered up at me. "Oh, really?"

"Really. You never heard of White Trash Barbie? Instead of a rhinestone clutch, she came with a six-pack of Rhinebeck."

We both laughed, harder than the joke deserved, but Gail didn't join in. Instead, her face hardened and she took her hands from Jan's shoulders. Jan began to sober up, and there was an uncomfortable silence until I said, "As you can see, I'll probably never be a charter member of the Guardian Angels," and then Jan and I broke out into sniggers again.

"I don't feel what I do is a laughing matter. Saving unborn babies from slaughter doesn't exactly strike my funny bone the right way."

Jan was curled into herself, fiddling nervously with the bow on her dress. "We're sorry, Gail. I'm sure Annie meant no offense. Right, Annie?"

She looked at me entreatingly. I nodded. "Oh. Sure. No offense was meant on my part at all."

Gail turned away and looked out the window, where the moon was still a ghost in the sky. "I know I can sound . . . self-righteous sometimes. It's just that the work I do with the Guardian Angels is extremely close to my heart," she said, fingering the drapes.

Jan twisted around in the rocker. "Gail, Annie was really impressed by the mural."

I hated kowtowing to this moose, but Jan was gnawing away at her fingertips with a nervous zeal, anxious for things to be okay. "Yeah. It, uh, it's really cool. I was especially intrigued by *The Dead Child*."

Jan reached out and placed her hand on Gail's forearm. "I told her it was your favorite."

"What's it about?" I asked, trying to affect an earnest, friendly tone.

Gail looked over her shoulder at the mural. "It's about the particular grief of losing a child," she said. "The inconsolability of it." She walked over with her chin held high, hands clasped behind her back. Once there, she stood regarding the scene with a reverence more fitting for a Renoir than a fairy-tale mural on a nursery room wall. "The scene here represents the part of the story where Death takes the mother down to the Underworld. You see, she'd rather be with her child there than up above among the living without him."

I walked over. "So this is a tribute to Sybil Clayton then."

Gail turned her head to me and drew her chin in, as if my question were an affront. "It's a tribute to all women who have known this grief."

She turned her focus back to Death and the mother, and began to twist her right bracelet with her left hand, back and forth as she spoke, conjuring up for me the memory of her scar.

"When I was young I miscarried, and was so sad I tell you I just wanted to die. Until one day I met a woman who told me that the souls of unborn babies don't die, and that they're actually around us, as numerous as specks of dust hanging in the air, waiting for the chance to be born again. Now every time I stop a woman from aborting her child I tell myself, I'm saving Isabelle. Her soul could be in any one of these babies." She dropped her hands by her sides. "And that's how the mother in this story finds the courage to go on. By realizing her child lives on." She turned to Jan with a queer, enigmatic expression. "Unfortunately, sometimes it takes a very, very long time."

Jan had come up beside her. "I can't imagine such

grief," she almost whispered, circling her arm around Gail's large waist. Gail drew her in close. "And I'll make sure that you never do."

I looked at Jan, incredulous. "What do you mean you can't imagine such grief? I just visited the graves of your mother and father."

Gail shook her head with a resolute smugness. "It's not the same. Until you've experienced such a thing, you can't understand. Losing a child is the most unspeakable grief there is."

"Oh, I see. The childless are on a much lower spiritual plane."

Jan glanced up at Gail, who was taller. "That's not what she's saying, Annie."

"But it is no doubt *the* most special bond," Gail said.

"You don't know what love is until you have a child, is that it?" I asked, crossing my arms.

"Annie," Jan said, "why are you getting so defensive?"

"Because as far as I'm concerned, grief is grief, it just depends on how deeply you loved the thing you're grieving for."

"Well," Gail said with a condescending tilt of her head, "like I said, until you've experienced carrying a child—"

"Excuse me, but I have experienced it! Three times as a matter of fact!"

My words hung in the air, ringing like gunshots on a quiet morning. I was stunned that I'd blurted that out. Perhaps it was the stress of having to be so solicitous of Gail, something akin to making a mongoose play nice with a snake. Jan looked away, embarrassed, and Gail was staring at me in pitying triumph. I whirled around and hurried from the room.

At my doorway, I slowed down and looked back over my shoulder at the nursery. I could hear them talking quietly. Stupid, stupid, stupid! What was wrong with me? But it was typical of me, having to one-up

Gail as if there were an award for the most-wounded womb. I rested my forehead against the door, feeling as if I'd just engaged in a game of tug-of-war for Jan's affection and had lost. Dragged through the mud. Then I heard Gail say something and they both laughed, just as Jan and I had laughed earlier, and I decided I wasn't going to wait to find out why Gail didn't want anyone in that upstairs room.

Dusk had darkened into night and I had to feel my way through the hallway leading to the room. I expected the door to be locked, but when I turned the knob it opened. She'd lied, and I wasn't surprised. When I turned on the light switch, I saw the sheet Kevin had used to cover Butterball with was balled up in the sink, and the mirror covering the dumbwaiter door had been taken down and was leaning against the wall. That meant Gail must have known about the dumbwaiter, because I distinctly remember Kevin hanging it back up.

My walk across the room reaffirmed to me that Gail was lying. Yes, the floors were warped, but they were hardly in danger of collapsing. So far I couldn't see why she wouldn't want anyone up here, but after I'd shut the window and turned around, I noticed a cardboard box sticking halfway out from underneath the box spring. I went over and kneeled down next to it. In black magic marker was written PROPERTY OF GAIL RUSKER, but underneath, a label had been crossed out: CLAYTON HOME PHARMACEUTICALS. Her penchant for labeling things around this house was so out of control I was surprised she hadn't yet stamped her name on Jan's forehead. I pulled the box out and opened the flaps. Inside were antique-looking bottles, labeled with strange names such as oil of savin, rue, ergot. I took one out, uncorked the stopper, and held the mouth of the bottle to my nose. It smelled a little like the green stuff Jan had been drinking the other day.

I stoppered it up and put it back, then turned my attention to some plain, utilitarian-looking boxes. DR. BRONSON'S FEMALE PILLS, read one antique-lettered label. Another, BELCHEM'S FEMALE CURE. Huh. So there was a cure after all. I opened that one up; inside were little pink pills. I checked the list of ingredients on the outside of the box. They weren't very illuminating as to how they effected a cure, except that whatever they did they must have the same objective as the contents of the bottles. Savin, rue, and ergot were listed among them—probably a precursor to Pamperin. I was wondering if there might be something in here to start menstruation since mine was still on hiatus, when I noticed some printing on the underside of the lid. *Supplement with tansy tea twice daily until obstruction is removed.*

Obstruction removed. What kind of obstruction?

Then I heard a noise, as if something were falling. At first I couldn't tell where it was coming from, but as soon as my senses homed in on the dumbwaiter door, it stopped. It sounded as if the carriage had slipped a ways down the shaft before its fall had been broken. I walked over and placed my ear against the small door and listened to something—perhaps the chain bumping against the interior. I stepped back and opened the door to find the cables were still swaying slightly, and the chain dancing in the air. I leaned over to look down into the shaft, but unlike the day Kevin discovered Butterball, the top of the carriage could no longer be seen. It was just a deep pit of darkness. When we tried to pull it up the other day we must have loosened something up.

I placed both hands on the chain and pulled, but once again it was stuck. Then it occurred to me that there must be some kind of switch. Otherwise, what was the point of having a dumbwaiter if it demanded as much physical exertion as climbing four flights of stairs? I felt around the inside of the shaft, but there was nothing but rough stone. I closed the door again, and examined the area surrounding it, running my hands up and down the smooth wallpaper. Then I knelt down, and underneath the frame I noticed a swatch of wallpaper where the pattern was different. Looking closer, I realized it wasn't different, just faded. Someone had taken a piece of paper from the surrounding walls to camouflage whatever was underneath it. I ripped the paper off and there it was, one of those modern mechanisms that separates man from his primitive ancestors: a button.

I pushed it, and immediately the pulley began to groan at the strain of bringing the carriage up from what sounded like the very depths of the shaft. I scooted back across the floor and stared at the closed door. As the carriage rose the noise increased, along with my growing anxiety. Even though I kept telling myself the scariest thing I'd find was perhaps a forgotten dinner, rotted away after all these years, my intuition was telling me to go. But it was more than that. I had the feeling that I didn't belong here. Bizarre as it sounds, I felt like a thief about to loot a poorhouse box, or a whore at a baby's christening. Finally, the mechanical straining ceased and I got to my feet. All I had to do was open the door to see what was inside. My hand was shaking like someone with Parkinson's as I reached out and opened the door once more.

As soon as it swung open I felt a mixture of relief and disappointment at the same time, because only the top three inches of the carriage had made it into the opening. It was almost as if the dumbwaiter were an animate thing that resisted being pulled from the dark, inner space of the shaft out into the open air and light. I pulled on the chain, but it was still a no-go. A musty odor wafted out from it, along with something else I couldn't identify. If I really wanted to see what was inside, all I had to do was put my face close to those three inches. With not just a little apprehension, I crouched down so I was eye level with the opening. Sweat was pouring down my face. That sense of being an invader was still with me, but my curiosity was stronger than any misgivings. I was sure that whatever was in this dumbwaiter was behind Gail's lame lie, so I made myself press my forehead against the metal and cupped my hands around my eyes.

Something was in there, but it was too dark to see what. I pulled away slightly, and then cautiously slipped my fingers through the narrow opening. My hand couldn't go in any farther than just above my knuckles. I slid my hand along, feeling the cold stone of the shaft against my skin until something tickled the tip of my fingertips. I wiggled my fingers around trying to get hold of it, but it proved frustratingly elusive. After a few more seconds of this, I finally caught whatever it was between my thumb and forefinger, gave it a tug, and extracted my prize: Three strands of very long, blond hair.

Suddenly I felt a painful cramp. I looked down, and saw that blood was flowing down my leg. For a moment I was relieved. Finally I was getting my period! But when another cramp doubled me over, this time so bad it was like something inside me was being pulled apart, that relief turned to panic. Especially when I saw that the blood running down my leg was now flowing so heavy and fast it had already begun to pool in my sneakers.

CHAPTER 12

I opened my eyes to see Ryan's worried face hovering over mine. "Ryan?"

She smiled and caressed my cheek. "Welcome back. How you feel?"

I licked my lips, wondered why they were so cracked, and why Ryan was in her nurse uniform. Then I saw the institutional furniture, the fluorescent light above, the TV in the corner near the ceiling. And the flowers. So many flowers!

I looked down at the IV needle tucked into the crook of my arm and then back up at Ryan. "Am I at Eloise?"

"No." She laughed. "You're at the Vineyard Hospital. You've had an emergency, but you're going to be okay."

My heart hiccuped. I tried to sit up, but my right side hurt too much.

Ryan pressed me back down. "Sweetheart, lie back down."

"What do you mean lie back down! What happened to me?"

"You were hemorrhaging, badly. Do you remember that?"

Hemorrhaging? I tried to remember, and I think I remembered *something*. . . but it was like trying to close my hands around a small fish that would swim away just as it was about to get caught. I shook my head no.

"Four days ago you went into septic shock."

"Four days? I've been unconscious for *four days?*"

She nodded. "In and out. You were one sick girl. Your body just shut down. But everything's fine now."

I tried to speak, but she shushed me as she brushed aside a clump of stiff, greasy hair that had fallen in my eyes.

"You had a cyst on your right ovary and it ruptured." She squeezed my wrist. "They had to remove the ovary."

I felt as if I were watching a foreign movie, one in which the white subtitles were blending in with a light background. "What?"

"The fallopian tube had twisted. Sometimes when that happens the blood supply is cut off and . . . it had become necrotic. They couldn't save it."

I slid my hand under the sheet down to my pelvis, and felt a small prickly line of stitches on the right side of it.

"I have cancer?"

Ryan's big hands waved off the thought. "No, no, no. It was benign as a boiled egg. It was really the sepsis that sent you into a tailspin."

As she smoothed out my sheets, I thought of my mother. My age when she died, her insides eaten up by cancer. A doctor once suggested that if I was sure I didn't want to have children, I might want to have a radical hysterectomy. I didn't want to. I had this belief that without the female plumbing I'd no longer be a woman. Now nature was doing it for me.

"How did I get here?"

"Gail. She found you at the foot of the stairs."

A few images came to the surface. Gail and Jan laughing, me standing at the door to the room upstairs, and even though I couldn't see myself in the room, I felt *sure* that I had been inside. There was something frightening about it.

"Not in a room upstairs?"

"No. Why?"

"What about Jan?"

Ryan's face wavered like a TV picture that had lost momentary control as she adjusted my IV. "It's thanks to her you got here in time. Dumb-ass Gail wanted to drive you herself. Can you imagine her dragging you down three flights? Talk about poor judgment. And this woman's delivering my sister's baby," she said, shaking her head in disgust as she brought over a vase with red, white, and blue carnations and a light pink balloon with a silver *Get Well* on it.

"These are from Grace," she said, setting them down on the table next to my bed. "She's going to be so happy when I tell her you finally woke up."

I looked at the pink balloon, and I thought the color reminded me of something, but a wave of nausea swept it away. "Why can't I remember anything?"

"Your memory's going to be poor for a while. Happens even with short-term comas," she said as she adjusted the stake the balloon was tethered to.

"Ryan, I think Gail is dangerous."

"I agree. Stupidity combined with insanity is dangerous. Since you've been in the hospital they had this ridiculous demonstration in front of our clinic. They set up a double row of TVs, each one showing a partial-birth abortion so that anyone coming in to the clinic had to pass through it, like some film festival from hell. But"— she paused to snigger—"their stupid setup backfired. It upset people so much this one guy took a baseball bat to the TV's. The cops came and hauled them all away, Gail included!"

"I'm not talking about that. I meant . . . I think . . ." I gestured for her to come closer. She rested her hands on the rail. I tried to lift my head, but it was too heavy and I let it drop back onto the pillow.

"Don't strain." She brought her face close to mine. "Now tell me."

"Gail *did* something to me."

The lines around her eyes contracted. "Like what?"

"This," I whispered, tapping the suture through the sheet with my forefinger.

Her face relaxed and she straightened up. "Annie," she said, shaking her head, "the woman's guilty for a lot of things, but your cyst ain't one of them. This is something that's been there for a long time. You know what a Teratoma cyst is? We used to call them tumbleweed tumors in nursing school because you find everything in them—hair, teeth, skin, bone—you want to see yours? Your doctor saved it for you. Some people like to see."

She brought down a jar from a shelf above my head. "Grace thought it looked like a monster so she gave it a name, Fester. If she asks if she can take it to school for show-and-tell, please tell her no."

I took the jar from her hands and looked at the purplish gray glob, fuzzy with hair and studded with small white orbs. When I looked closer, I could see the orbs were perfectly formed molars, staring back at me like two white, pupilless eyes.

"You should have seen your dad," Ryan continued. "He threatened to sue if they touched anything else."

"My dad," I said, still mesmerized by the nightmare they'd preserved for me.

"Oh yeah. They won't forget him for a while. Thing is, he's right. Sometimes these doctors can be a little overzealous. So what if you got one less ovary, that kind of thinking, you know? Funny how they're not so cavalier when it comes to testicles. But believe me, this one had to go."

I tipped the jar and Fester turned on his side, and

I did too. At least that's the way the morphine or whatever it was they had me doped up on made me feel. As if the room were rolling. Ryan checked her watch.

"Shit. I gotta go. Since Gail's video demonstration we've had a lot of threats and I have to work overtime 'cause some of the staff are too spooked to come to work. I'll try and stop by tomorrow."

She reached over and picked up her motorcycle helmet from a green Naugahyde chair.

"Annie, you're going to be fine," she said as she leaned in to kiss me on the cheek. "Right now, just worry about getting well."

After she left, I placed the jar on the side table and watched this ovary-eating id of mine bob and turn in its liquid universe. Fester. How does such a thing come into being? I had a crazy, probably drug-induced idea: What if somehow the three babies I'd once had inside me had each left a little of themselves behind—skin, hair, teeth, and bone—and somehow they'd bonded and grown into . . . this? Why not? It was only fair; I had killed them, why shouldn't they return the favor?

My dad's eyes, gray and watery as oysters, were fixed on me with a Billy Graham gaze—soft with sorrow yet grim with determination to save the sinner. He'd had that same look in his eyes when I woke up in the hospital a year or so after the rape. Memories had been coming back, flashbacks. Flashes of light, as if a camera were going off, a sweaty, blurred face close to mine and breathing hard. A therapist I was seeing at the time had said they weren't reliable; a Ruffee totally wipes out short-term memory, and my imagination was filling in the blanks with scenarios I feared the most: a video of the event being sold over the Internet, being raped not just by one guy but many. I'd heard of these things happening on programs like *20/20*, and the myriad of sickening possibilities haunted me until one night I got so drunk I took a fistful of my antidepressants and ended up in Bellevue. Even though I assured them it had been just a stupid accident, they kept me for observation and didn't let me go until my father came down. He never asked what was wrong, why I was drinking so much, why I'd taken the pills. The look in his eyes said it all: *It's finally happened. Just as I always knew it would.*

I cleared my throat. "Daddy." I hadn't called him that since I was eight.

He patted my hand and smiled. "How ya doin', kid?"

I looked toward my table for Fester, but it was gone. "Did you see what they took out of me?"

A look of disgust flitted over his face. "You don't need somethin' like that around."

"Where is it?"

"I don't know. They want to do tests on it. 'Cause of the way you reacted."

It felt as if a heavy foot were pressing down on my pelvis. I warbled a moan. My dad held up a contraption with a button. "Here. Nurse said push this if you got any pain."

I did, and a few seconds later it felt as if I were being slowly lowered into the softest down-filled bed in the world. I looked back up at him. "Tell them I want it back," I mumbled.

My dad waved his hand at me. "You don't want that."

"I want it."

"You're too doped up to know what you want."

"I want it!" I said with the vehemence of a mother whose newborn has just been spirited away forever. My dad looked at me as if I'd lost my mind.

"All right, all right. I'll ask," he said, and then

groused, "It's not something you put under your pillow for the tooth fairy, you know." He reached for some magazines at the foot of my bed. "I brought you *People,* and some of Glenda's fashion magazines."

Dad's face creased in disapproval as he looked down at the *Cosmo* on top with its bold question: ORGASMS: HOW MANY IS TOO MANY? He surreptitiously slipped it to the bottom when he set them back down. The tears in my eyes began to soften the lines in his face.

He shook my hand roughly. "Come on now. You're a tough girl. Don't do that."

I wiped the tears away with the back of my hand. "Ryan said you raised hell."

He shrugged. "Your mother's quack cut her up like a pie and what good did it do, 'cept pay for his time-share in Florida?"

My dad still blamed the doctor who took care of my mother, though not even Ben Casey could have saved her. He kept his hand on mine. "So, what do you want to do after here?"

My mind was a fuzzy blank. "I don't know. Lie somewhere else."

"Whyn't you do it at home?"

I tried to imagine staying at my dad's. He couldn't take care of himself, let alone me, but there was a look on his face and a tone in his voice that seemed to be asking: let me try. I was just about to say maybe when his chubby girlfriend carried in her little girl, Bonnie, on her hip. Glenda was wearing cutoff jean shorts, a Betty Boop T-shirt, and a rainbow of eyeshadow. Bonnie had on the same shade of glittery lip gloss.

"'Ey Johnny, this one here wants a Happy Meal. Can we stop off on the way home?" When she saw I was awake, she said, "Oh, hiya."

"Hi," I said, and pushed the pain button, but the thing must have been on time-release—no fresh infusion of that soft downy feeling when I needed it most.

"Papa John," the kid squeaked, "can I have a Happy Meal?"

"What you got to be so happy about?" he asked her. I noticed her clothes were filthy.

She seemed to be thinking seriously about it, then shrugged. "I don't know."

Glenda, the good welfare witch, set her progeny down and then took a magazine off my bed before plopping down in the pea-green visitor's chair.

Bonnie came over and looked up at me through the bed rail. "Are you sick?"

"I'm just pretending."

"'Cause you don't want to go to school?"

I nodded.

"I had a tumor once," Glenda said as she leafed through her magazine. "It kept movin' around. Sometimes it was near my elbow, sometimes my wrist. Real annoyin'. Then one day it disappeared and now I gotta say, I kinda miss it."

At that, I closed my eyes and pretended to drop off into a coma. I heard my dad say, "Whyn't you two go wait outside?"

"Hope ya feel betta, Annie," Glenda said. When they were gone, he nudged me, but I didn't show any sign of life. I felt him adjust my sheet, and only when I was sure he was gone did I open my eyes. They'd just left, but already I could picture them, squeezed into the front seat of my dad's run-down truck, happily eating their Happy Meals. There was no way I'd be staying with my dad.

The next day the druggy fog was beginning to clear. They'd replaced the hard stuff with a Junior League painkiller, and I was reasonably lucid when Jan called in the morning. She was upset and sorry she couldn't come visit, and hoped I would understand.

I let that one pass, and asked her how they found me. She confirmed what Ryan had told me: Gail did, she didn't. She'd gone downstairs to make some tea when surprise, surprise, it turned out the key to the dangerous room with the floor ready to cave in had been in Gail's purse all along. She was just on her way to close that window—after all, you never knew when the island was going to be hit with a monsoon—when she found me at the foot of the stairs. Not a word of it sat right with me, but I let Jan run on, waiting to see when she was going to mention Kevin. She didn't. I had to ask, and when I did, I was met with a long silence. "That part of my life is over," she said flatly.

There was a long silence in which I was too drained to argue with her, but then I realized she was weeping. "Jan, don't worry. You and Kevin will work this out. I know you two—"

"Annie," she cut in with a harsh whisper, "why didn't you just *leave* the baby in Bettina? Why did you take her out?"

"Baby," I repeated, confused. Who was Bettina and what baby? Then I realized. "Are you talking about that friggin' doll?"

She sobbed. "I knew something bad was going to happen to you. You had no right to take it!"

My grasp tightened around the phone. "Oh, now it's a baby? I thought it was a pit."

She gasped. "I didn't want to scare you. I hoped if I just put it back, everything would be fine," she said, then disintegrated into another crying jag.

"What, am I too *unclean* to have even touched it? I can't believe you lied to me. What was the point of that stupid charade?"

"What was the point? What was the point!" I could hear her almost choking, as if her rage were a chicken bone. "You never even *tried* to believe me, Annie! Right from the start, all I got from you was the same condescending attitude you've had toward me since we were kids. Oh, it's just *Jan!* Crazy, hysterical Jan who has never had a thought in her brain that hasn't been put there by someone else. I thought maybe you'd cut me a break this time and at least listen, but you're just like Kevin and Ryan. This is really happening, Annie. It's not a movie! It's not fucking *Gaslight!*" Her breath caught slightly. "Gail just drove up," she whispered, like a grounded teenager who was in danger of being caught using the phone. "I got to go."

She hung up, and I sat there with the receiver still pressed to my ear in shock. Jan had said the word *fuck*. In my whole life I've never heard her use that word. It was a sign of how badly she felt I'd failed her. She nailed me good, I thought as I put the receiver down in its cradle, because how often had I dismissed Jan's beliefs as being misguided or sometimes even downright stupid? I made fun of her love of dolls, her fear of alien abduction, her feng shui phase when the toilet seat in our apartment was never allowed to be left open lest some evil spirit bite us in the ass. Her aches and pains I almost always wrote off as being in her head (they usually were), and I considered her quest to have a baby bordering on the pathological—all that money wasted on fertility treatments when there were so many kids out there who needed a mom!

Jan had always taken the teasing, the mocking, in her usual good-natured manner. And I wasn't the only one. Everyone liked to kid Jan, and I have to admit I never gave much thought as to its affect on her. Except one time. We were still living together, and she wasn't working, so when I saw her mooning over *The Hand That Rocks the Cradle*, a magazine dedicated to nursery design, I commented perhaps she might make better use of her time browsing the help-wanted section instead. It was mean and unwarranted, because she wasn't even behind in her share of the rent yet, but instead of defending herself Jan put her magazine down and asked me if I considered her a frivolous person. I was somewhat taken aback because I could see in her eyes it was something she feared herself. However, I didn't even have to think before I answered and told her I'd never met a more sincere person in my life. And I meant it too, because Jan had faith. Not only in the things she believed, but in the people she loved. I have no doubt that if the current situation were reversed, she would have sent for a priest by now.

For a moment, I tried to just be open to the possibility that a supernatural force was active in the house, that Gail was some kind of "psychic guide" leading Jan safely through the outer bounds of reality, but it was like slipping into a dress two sizes too small. I just couldn't believe in ghosts. Once you were dead, you were dead, and it was wishful thinking to believe you continued on in some way, or that you were allowed to come back and complete unfinished business. If it turned out I was wrong, then serve me right if everyone else's souls floated up to heaven while mine remained here on earth, my lack of faith weighting me down like a cement block holding a corpse underwater.

My eyes rested on the pink balloon that had come tethered to Grace's flowers, and these thoughts bobbing around in the upper reaches of my consciousness, which admittedly had the loftiness of a mobile home, came back down to a more solid plane. Ever since I'd first laid eyes on the balloon it had been nudging my memory into giving up what had happened in that room. The pink color, the shape, meant something to me. I closed my eyes and saw myself standing in the hallway . . . I'd gone up there because Gail didn't want me to, and when I opened the door, I saw that the mirror was off the wall. Or had I taken it off? It all became vague and elusive after that, like something you've eaten a while ago but the taste is still lingering on your tongue. Then I opened my eyes and saw Gail standing in the doorway of my room, and whatever chance I had of recapturing that night was gone.

She looked like a jolly green giantess, dressed in a flowing green shift and pants, and wearing a large green sun hat decorated with daisies. In her right hand she was carrying a shopping bag. Enormous sunflowers were sticking out, bobbing their grotesque heads like captives wearied from a long journey, and I noticed the thick bracelets were gone. Instead, she was wearing green leather gloves, long enough to cover up her thick scars.

"Annie," Gail's voice sang out in a velvety salvo. The room rolled and she seemed to surf a transparent wave over to my side. In an instant she was looming over me.

"I've brought sustenance and sunshine," she said, pulling the sunflowers from the bag and placing them on my lap. Their brown centers stared up at me like greedy eyes and I felt a nauseous flutter in my stomach. I loathed sunflowers. All those seeds. Too fecund. I tried not to look at them as Gail chattered on.

"My prize-winning blueberry preserves," she said, setting a blue-ribboned jar down on the bedside table, next to Fester. Fester! Dad must have got him back for me. I smiled.

"I knew my preserves would bring a smile to your face," she said. "Those little containers of jelly they give you in here are absolutely in-di-gestible. And these are from Jan." She pulled out a Tupperware bowl from the bag and placed it on the table too. "Chocolate chip," she said, overly loud. Or maybe it was the drugs in my system, amplifying sound. Then she gasped. She'd just noticed the cyst in the jar.

"Oh my," she said, crouching so she could look at Fester, eye to tooth. "Is this it?" she asked in a hushed, awed voice as she lifted it up. I didn't like seeing him in her hands. I reached for him, but Gail moved past me, over to the window.

"How bizarre. How . . . sad," she mused while I struggled to speak. The insides of my throat felt stuck together. "The teeth, the hair . . . poor child," she whispered. "Poor, poor child."

"Give it to me," I finally exclaimed. Gail turned around, a pitying look on her face. She brought it over. I took it from her and held it to my chest. I could feel the thick liquid slosh, and Fester bumping gently against the glass. My stomach burbled again, sending a small geyser of bile up my throat. I swallowed it back. "It's *not* a child."

Gail sighed. "Of course it isn't, dear," she said as she extracted a hat pin the size of a shish kebab skewer from her bonnet. She hung the hat from my IV stand. Her hairdo was unfortunate in that it made her look like an aging Swiss Miss, but I couldn't stop staring at the long white braids looping back and forth across the top of her head.

"It's ironic, though, isn't it?" she said, pulling up a chair to the bed. "I mean, from just the short time I've known you, I can sense in you a strong ambivalence toward motherhood—childbearing."

I was unconsciously holding my breath. There was a strange smell about her, as if something had crawled underneath that nest of braids and died.

"Sometimes women support abortion rights out of fear. They insist their position is ideologically based— a woman's right to reproductive freedom. But from my experience, and I've been fighting on the side of pro-life for many years now, I know more often than not their beliefs, their position, have grown out of self-loathing. They hate being women. They hate their bodies. What better way to manifest this hatred than destroy the essential thing that makes them female?"

I gasped for air and looked away. The room began to rotate, slowly. Something was happening to me. Either I was having a reaction to the new medication, or I was having some kind of allergic reaction to Gail. She reached through the railing and grabbed my empty hand.

"I know you've had opportunities to bear a child, but for whatever your reasons, you decided not to, even though perhaps some small part of you wanted to, but the self-hating part was stronger. And this," she said, tapping the jar, "is the result."

I pulled my hand away from her and placed Fester on the table. When I looked back at her, the pink balloon was positioned just to the right of her head, and it all came back. The strands of long blond hair I'd taken from the dumbwaiter, the little pink pills in the box.

"You lied."

Gail tilted her head, puzzled. "I'm sorry?"

"The room wasn't locked. It was open."

She seemed to think a moment, but then leaned forward and in a concerned whisper said, "My dear, you're mistaken. The room was definitely locked. I found you at the foot of the stairs."

"No," I said, shaking my head. "There's something in that dumbwaiter that you're hiding. I pulled out strands of long blond hair."

Gail's expression of concern didn't change. "Dumbwaiter? I wasn't even aware there was a dumbwaiter up there."

"And the pills and bottles in that box—they cause miscarriages, don't they?"

Her brow creased as if she had to strain to think, and then it relaxed and she laughed. "Oh my. Annie, dear, those are from a long time ago when the house was a hospital. I'd brought them down from the attic. They're meant to be part of an exhibit the Guardian Angels are curating at the Hyannis Civic League. It's called 'the Abortion Holocaust.' In fact, that's how I found Butterball. On my way down, I noticed this really *nasty* smell coming from that room," she said, wrinkling her nose.

She seemed to have an answer for everything. I looked down at the flowers and pushed them away, because I was now sure the really nasty smell was coming from them.

Gail sighed. "Annie, I know what it's like to be ill for a long time. Even the most innocuous things begin to take on ominous meanings."

"At Eloise, right? Is that where you were sick?"

The patronizing look in her eyes disappeared. She sat back and looked down at her gloved hands, her head atilt to a melancholy angle as she began to rub the scar on her right wrist with her left thumb, as if she were trying to smooth away the scar tissue underneath the green leather.

"When I was sixteen my mother gave me some tea to drink. I hadn't told her I was pregnant, but somehow she knew. I suppose she'd been through it enough times to know the signs," she said bitterly. She looked up, and her faded blue eyes looked almost white through a film of tears. "Do you remember me telling you about Isabelle?" Gail had whispered the name through a trembling smile. I looked down, determined not to feel sorry for her. I was sure this was just another manipulation of hers.

She wiped her tears and laughed sadly. "Anyway, yes. I am very well acquainted with Eloise. But the good thing about it was that it got me away from my mother, who needless to say was having a toxic affect on my state of mind, and body, and that's the very reason why I'm here today."

She sniffed loudly as she drew herself up tall. "I would very much like to offer you the use of my house while you recuperate. I have a lovely little cottage, not far from Jan's—very peaceful, with a garden out back and lots of trees. Often the women we rescue need a place to stay and live until they have their baby, so I have a nice room set up with its own bath."

"I don't need a place to recuperate."

"Annie, I know for some reason you see me as the enemy. Perhaps it's my politics, or you resent my closeness with Jan, but please believe me when I tell you I only want to help. Staying in that house is no good for you." She leaned in closer. "And as you must know by now, dear, she doesn't want you there."

She'd said the last very quietly. So quietly I wasn't sure I'd heard right. I noticed that her expression, usually as benign as a cow's, was now as intense as a day trader's five minutes before the close of the bell.

"Who doesn't, Jan?"

Gail stared at me steadily another moment. A cold drop of sweat ran down my face.

The nurse came in. "Visiting hours are over," she shouted. "And that's an IV stand, not a hat rack, do you mind?"

Gail apologized, and then smiled at me as if we'd just spent the last fifteen minutes exchanging inane pleasantries.

"I do hope you enjoy the goodies, Annie. Oh, nurse, could you possibly find something to put these flowers in?" she asked, thrusting them at her before she had a chance to answer.

The nurse looked at the flowers crossly as she headed toward the door. "As if I don't have enough to do without playing florist," she muttered.

Gail reached to squeeze my hand, but I shoved it under the covers, and she had to settle for my biceps instead. "Annie, I'll be sure to give Jan your love and please, think about my offer."

As soon as she was gone the nurse came back with the flowers in one of those plastic pee bottles. She was about to put it on the table when she stopped and looked at me. "Your color was good this morning. What happened?"

I lifted a shaking hand to my slick forehead.

"You got a fever?" she asked, reaching to touch my forehead, bringing the flowers closer to me.

"Please," I said, pushing her hand away. "Please throw those away!"

The nurse looked at me queerly. "Done," she said, pulling them out of the bottle, then folding them in half. She threw them into the wastebasket. "They got some kind of mold all over them anyway. I'll be right back to take your vitals."

I stared at the broken stems sticking out of the basket, shivered, then leaned over the side of the bed and heaved.

"Stop handling that, Grace."

"But I want to look at it."

"If you break it, I don't think Aunt Annie will be too happy to replace it."

I opened my eyes just enough to see Ryan sitting on the green Naugahyde chair, one leg draped over the armrest, while Sherry was perched on the heating unit near the window. They must have been out riding with their motorcycle club, the Iron Maidens; both were dressed in black leather pants, motorcycle jackets, and Frye biker boots. Grace was standing at my bedside, her face a portrait of longing as she stared at Fester. She was also dressed in leather pants and jacket. I thought how cool it would be to have a biker club the equivalent of the Iron Maidens for children, except they'd be called the Iron Maidenettes and drive Schwinns instead of Harleys.

Grace rested her chin on the railing. "Hey, Mom, I think she's waking up."

I opened my eyes all the way.

"Hi, Aunt Annie. Can I take Fester to school to show my friends?"

"You got friends?" I croaked. My fever had broken during the night, and I'd stopped vomiting sometime this morning, but it had left behind a pounding headache and a rough voice. Behind her Ryan was waving her hands and shaking her head no. I rubbed my eyes. "Sweat pea, I don't mind being responsible for adult's nightmares, but kids are a different matter."

Grace looked over her shoulder at her mom. "I know my mom told you to say no."

"How are you feeling?" Ryan asked, coming up behind her.

"Aside from trying to throw my entire digestive track up, fine." I placed a hand on my throat, which was scratchy and sore. "What the hell hit me?"

"The sunflowers were contaminated with some kind of mold. The nurse got sick too, but not as bad. Normally it wouldn't be such a big deal, but with your weakened immune system it can knock you on your ass."

"She did it on purpose," I muttered, looking over at the now empty wastebasket.

"Who did what on purpose?"

I looked up at Ryan. "Gail. She brought those sunflowers and she was wearing gloves."

"Are you talking about the fat lady who Mom calls the womb-Nazi?" Grace asked. I wondered if she even knew what a womb was, but didn't think it prudent to discuss it in front of her. "Yeah." I threw the covers aside. "The fat womb-Nazi. Can you believe I want a cigarette?"

"It's not allowed, you know," Ryan said, helping me sit up.

I pointed to the top drawer of the table stand. "Grace, get my cigarettes out of there, will you?"

She opened the drawer and handed them to me. Then she pulled the Tupperware container out of the drawer and opened it. "Hey, cookies," she exclaimed. "Can I have one?"

"No!" Both she and Ryan looked at me in surprise. I gave Ryan a meaningful look. "Gail brought those too," I said, shuffling off to the window.

"Oh." Ryan put the cookies back into the drawer and shut it. "Grace, those cookies aren't for kids."

Grace whined. "Why not?"

I had a feeling after today I would no longer be her favorite aunt. First I deny her a prize subject for show-and-tell, now cookies.

"Because. They make you go to the bathroom."

"Hi, Sherry," I said, lighting up. I'd forgotten if they told me how far along she was, but already her stomach was bulging enough to push out the waistband of her leather pants.

"Welcome back from the dead," she said, making room by moving to the chair. I inhaled, and immediately broke into a choking, hacking fit.

"See?" Ryan said, moving around to the other side of the bed. I shot her a drop-dead look, feeling as evil as I was sure I looked. I felt my hair, which was now stiff as a greasy Brillo pad. I looked down at the driveway underneath the window, where a man was pushing an elderly woman in a wheelchair up a ramp into the back of his pickup truck. She was small, but he still had to brace his back up against the back of her chair, much the way I imagined Sisyphus struggled with his boulder up the mountain. Since my room was only one flight up, I could make out the woman's face clearly. She didn't seem the least put out by the man's struggling on her behalf. In fact, she had an almost queenly serenity to her, with her face tilted up to the sun, a self-satisfied smile on her lips.

Selfish old bitch, I thought, seeing her but thinking of Gail. Had she meant to do more than make me sick? What balls! But then she didn't become head of an outfit like the Guardian Angels by being fainthearted. The man was now threading a rope between the spokes of the wheels, the arms of the chair, and then around the woman's waist, and all the while the serene smile never once left her lips.

I turned around. "You have to make Kevin come home."

"He already was."

"And?"

Ryan turned to Grace, who was leaning half her body on my bed, staring at Fester so close her nose was about to touch the glass. Ryan grabbed the glass jar out of her hands. "What did I say!" She set Fester back on the table, and Grace pushed away from the bed angrily.

Ryan pulled a five out of her pocket and held it out to her. "Here. Go to the cafeteria and buy yourself an ice cream."

"You just don't want me to hear things."

"That's right, now go."

Grace snatched the money from her mom and stalked off. "I'll go, but I'm *not* getting an ice cream." At the door, she turned around to glare at her mother. "*I'm* getting a coffee."

"No, you are not." But Grace left and Ryan shouted after her. "You come back with coffee breath, no TV tonight!"

An old man walking by with an IV on wheels paused in front of our door, unsure if Ryan was yelling at him. Ryan smiled and waved. He waved back and wheeled on. During this exchange, I tried to think if I'd ever seen Grace act so bratty. She was usually such a shy, sweet kid that I had to wonder how much it had to do with Sherry having a baby with her mom.

Ryan turned back around and stuck her thumbs through her belt loops. "I called him the day after you went into the hospital and he came home, but she refused to see him. Supposedly she called him in the middle of the night and a woman answered. He says she was mistaken. I don't know what to believe."

I batted the smoke away from my eyes. "She's not mistaken. I called him myself and a woman did answer."

"I told you, Ryan," Sherry said as she fiddled with her belly ring. "Republican jerk."

"Jerk or not, he has to come back home," I said. "You have to make him, Ryan."

She slapped both hands on her leather-clad thighs. "Annie, I don't like it any better than you do, but my sister is a grown woman. She does not want Kevin anywhere near her and I got to be honest, I don't blame her! Christ, my sister's having his baby and he's getting his dick sucked in Dallas? And to think I was going to help him put her in Eloise!"

"I don't care. She can't be alone with Gail. That woman is dangerous!" I turned around to throw my cigarette out the window, because I had to work up courage for what I was going to say next. When I turned back to face them, I crossed my arms. "Listen, I remember being in that upstairs room the night I passed out."

Sherry unwrapped a sucker she'd pulled from her jacket pocket. "I thought you didn't have any memory of that night."

"It came back."

"Just like that?"

"Yeah," I said, growing annoyed. "Just like that."

"Then how did you get to the bottom of the stairs?"

Ryan sighed. "Sherry, would you quit with the cross-examination and let her speak?"

Sherry shrugged and stuck the sucker in her mouth before slumping down into the chair. Ryan gestured with her chin for me to continue.

I sneered at Sherry. "Because Gail put me there. She didn't want anyone seeing what I saw."

"What?" Ryan asked. "What did you see?"

I hesitated, because when it came down to it, I didn't exactly see anything except for three strands of hair and a box of old medicine. "Well, to be honest, I can't really see for sure, but . . . I think Gail's hiding a body in a dumbwaiter in that room."

Sherry dropped her head to hide a smile. "Annie—" Ryan started.

I held my hands up. "Just hear me out. The only reason I went up there was that the window was open, but when I mentioned this in front of Gail, you should have seen the way she reacted—the woman practically had a stroke. Then she makes up some lame excuse that she'd locked it after herself and left the key at home, supposedly because the floorboards were in danger of collapsing."

"Sounds believable to me," Sherry said. "She weighs more than an SUV."

"The floors were fine! She lied because she didn't want anyone up in that room. What she didn't know was that Kevin and I already knew about the dumbwaiter because that's where we found Butterball."

Sherry yawned. "Now what did this body in the dumbwaiter look like?"

"I told you, I didn't exactly *see* a body. The carriage wouldn't come all the way up, but I did pull out some hair."

"Hair," Ryan repeated.

"Yes. Three strands of very long blond hair."

They looked at each other, and then Ryan looked back at me. "I'm sorry, Annie, I'm not getting it."

Neither was I. It had seemed so clear in my mind before, but the way they were looking at me, as if I were crazy, made me doubt myself. "Ryan, remember me telling you Jan thinks she's possessed by a girl in the house? Well, this little girl happens to have long blond hair."

She snorted in contempt. "So what, you're saying you believe my sister?"

"No! I don't. I . . ." I moved away because their skeptical looks were too much and because suddenly I wasn't so sure what I believed anymore. When I reached the opposite wall, I decided to use the same tactic I'd used with Jan, and started in on my *Gaslight* theory. I told them the plot of the movie, and then went on to compare it with the strange incidents concerning the doll, Gail's designs on the house, her trying to keep me from staying with Jan. I tried to make it as coherent as possible, but when I finished Ryan was blinking quickly, which meant she was having trouble processing, while Sherry was staring at me with great amusement.

"You think this is funny?"

She took her sucker out of her mouth and pointed it at me. "What I think is that you, my friend, have been in one too many horror movies."

"Screw you." I flicked my hand out at Ryan. "Ryan, you know me. I'm not a person who goes on flights of fancy.

"It's not that, Annie. . . ." Ryan said.

"Then what?"

"It's just that . . ." She pulled the lobe of her ear as she looked down and to the side. "You kind of sound like Jan."

"You think I'm crazy?"

"No. Just a little . . . overstimulated."

"I'm not a fucking ovary, Ryan." I took a deep breath; I could see I wasn't getting anywhere. I was just making myself look paranoid. "Okay, never mind the dumbwaiter, never mind Charles Boyer or Ingrid Bergman or even that miserable doll, but at least check out the box I found up there full of medicine. They all had ingredients that are supposed to 'remove obstructions.'"

"What kind of ingredients?"

I thought a moment. "Savin, something like ergo, I think . . . She's been having Jan drink this green stuff that smelled like one of the liquids in the bottles."

Ryan looked at Sherry with concern. "Ergot's a fungus that causes contractions. Maybe we should check it out."

Sherry took the sucker from her mouth and now pointed it at Ryan. "No. Not only is your sister kicking you in the teeth by letting a woman who stands for the antithesis of everything we believe in deliver her baby, she insults us by calling *our* baby a moral outrage. How much more do you need to get it that she wants you to stay out of her life? You've done all you can do. Plus, you have a daughter to think about, and another on the way."

During her harangue, she'd been wagging the sucker at Ryan like a finger. "Sherry, she's my sister. I have to see what's going on."

Sherry stood up, a red-haired imp compared to Ryan's Brunhild-ish dimensions. She pointed her sucker at Ryan's chest. "Well, get this. I'm not playing Trixie Belden to your Nancy Drew. You go out there, you go alone. I've had it with your crazy sister." She glared at me. "And her crazy friends."

She whipped her helmet off the coat hook on the wall and stormed out, pausing to hurl what was left of her sucker in the garbage but missing. We could hear her boots clunking heavily all the way down the hall, the chain belt rattling on her hips. Ryan stood there, looking down with the defeated look of a henpecked husband.

"Don't worry. I'll check it out," she said, swiping hers and Grace's helmets off the floor. "I think it's time I had a talk with Gail anyway." She gave me a quick kiss on the cheek. "I got to go get Grace before she ODs on caffeine. And don't listen to Sherry. It's just hormones talking."

She was almost out the door when I called her name. She turned around, half in, half out. "Ryan, don't go alone," I said.

"Believe me, I'm more nervous about facing Sherry than I am Gail. See you."

She left, and a nurse came in, holding a blood pressure kit. She stopped in her tracks and sniffed. "Has someone been smoking in here?"

CHAPTER 13

The taxi eased through the congestion of Commercial Street, the main thoroughfare in Province-town. Window-shopping tourists clogged the narrow street, gawking at stores offering everything from seashell-trimmed dog leashes to fine art, not to mention the same-sex couples holding hands and making out. Of all the tourist attractions, observing the openly gay culture of P-town was probably the most popular.

We stopped behind the trolley that drove tourists through the town and then out to the National Seashore Park. It was parked in front of the white clapboard building that served as the town hall and public toilet. Ryan's street was just the other side of it, so I paid the driver his fare and got out. All I had with me was an overnight tote. Mr. Green had been supposed to drive me to Jan's, but I changed my mind and headed out here instead, and had him take my suitcase to the house with a message for Jan where I would be. It was a beautiful, Indian summer day. End of September and it felt as if it were still the middle of August. The sun blazed in the blue sky. I slipped my sunglasses on; it had been a while since my eyes had seen real daylight. It was hard to believe two weeks had passed, most of which had been spent in a hospital. I still felt weak, but that was from not doing anything but lying in bed and worrying. I hadn't heard from Ryan since her last visit. I'd called a few times, until finally Grace picked up the phone and explained that Sherry'd had a miscarriage.

I turned onto Maple Crock Way, Ryan's street. All the homes were from the last century, and stood side by side with barely shoulder space between. Ryan and Sherry's was a red and white row house. They actually lived on the top two floors, and rented out the bottom floor to summer guests. I knocked on the door—there was no front lawn or anything, it opened onto the sidewalk, but planters of wildflowers hung under the two ground-floor windows. Grace answered the door, looking glum and dirty. Her white T-shirt was wrinkled and stained with what looked like mustard, and her light blond hair hung stringy and dark from not being washed. She smiled with chocolate-smeared lips and tackled me.

"How are you, sweet pea?"

She didn't let go. I smoothed her messy hair. The poor kid must have been going through some shit. Stuff she only half understood.

She looked up at me with her arms still circled around my waist. "Are you going to stay?"

"I'm just visiting, hon. I plan on going back to Aunt Jan's."

"Oh," she said, her face shading over with disappointment.

"Where's your mom?"

"She's not feeling well."

"Is she sick?"

She shrugged one shoulder. "Yeah. Kind of. I guess."

"Where is she?"

"Upstairs."

She moved aside to let me pass. A hallway led to the

back of the house and a small sitting room opened onto the left of a narrow stairway. Two mousy women were sitting at a table playing cards. They glanced up and gave us a tepid greeting. As Grace led me up the stairs, I noticed the seat of her pants were filthy. Either Ryan was too busy to do laundry or the kid was being neglected. She led me into a tiny garret. It was too small for anything other than boxes and an old lamp, but there was a rolled-up sleeping bag and alarm clock on the floor, and two nurse uniforms hung from a rafter. Grace pointed to a tall window that opened onto a balcony where Ryan was dozing in a lawn chair. Grace peered up at me, hopefully.

"Aunt Annie, did you bring him?"

I thought it was kind of creepy that she was so fixated on this thing, but then, so was I. I opened my tote and pulled out the jar. Grace eagerly eyed Fester as I handed it to her. A big grin broke out on her face.

"Can I show my best friend, Robin? She just lives down the street."

I sensed she hadn't smiled like that in a while; I didn't want it to go away. "Yeah. But don't let your mom know. And don't open the jar. He bites."

"I promise."

Then she ran out, probably worried I might change my mind. I had to duck to step out onto the balcony, which had a view of the crowded harbor where sail masts were as numerous as TV antennae in a third-world country. Ryan's head was resting to the side, her hands folded on her stomach. A number of empty beer bottles lay at her feet. She'd lost weight and her tan had faded to an ashy gray. Her long blond hair, half covering her face, looked as unkempt as Grace's. I pushed it aside, and saw a long scratch running down her neck. It was scabbed over at one end, so it had been deep enough to bleed. She made a groaning sound and

her head rolled toward me. Slowly, her eyes opened.
"Annie."

I swallowed. "Please tell me Gail didn't do that."

She sneered drowsily as she sat up. "That fat old
cow? Hardly. No," she said, picking up a beer bottle and
shaking it to see if any beer was left. "Your friend did.
I say your friend because she is no longer my sister."

She swigged down the dregs of the beer and let it
drop clumsily to the floor. She was drunk.

I sat down in the chair behind me. "What do you
mean?"

She looked up, cockeyed. "I mean . . ." She lifted
her hand and made a clawing action along with a
scratching sound, just above the scar on her neck. "We
had ourselves an honest-to-goodness knock-down,
drag-out catfight. At least she did. Lucky I've had
practice working with deranged patients and showed
restraint. Otherwise I would have killed her."

"My God, Ryan. She's your sister."

"She's not," she yelled, her face contorted into an ugly
snarl. "I don't know who the *fuck* she is, but she's not
my sister. Especially not as long as that . . . *Cunt* is playing nursemaid, midwife, whatever the fuck, to her."

I despised that word, but no one despised it more
than Ryan, who once kicked a man in the balls for calling her one. She'd been pointing at me, and now let
her arm drop along with her head. It hung there.
When she lifted it back up, she pressed the knuckles
of her fist into her eyes.

"I'm sorry. I'm wasted. I can't believe I drank so
much. And I'm supposed to go into work. If I call in
sick one more time, I'm going to get canned. No,
that's not true. I'm the only one stupid enough to
show up with all the bomb threats."

She was mumbling, more talking to herself.

"Ryan," I said. She looked at me, or at least tried to.
"Why? Why did she do that?"

"Because," she said, leaning all her weight onto the left armrest, "I threw her *dolly* across the room."

"A doll? I don't believe it."

"Go ask Sherry! She was there—I'd ask her to come up, but she's no longer speaking to me because I'm nothing but a spineless fucking dyke—her words, not mine—I think I'm just a stupid fucking dyke." She slumped back and let the side of her face sink into the heel of her hand, squishing her cheek up to her eye socket. "She'd still have the baby if I hadn't talked her into going to Jan's."

"Ryan, that's—"

She held out a hand to silence me. "Don't. Just . . . don't." Then she bent over to pick up another bottle. "Probably just as well. It made Grace miserable."

She brought the mouth of the bottle up close to her eye to look down its empty throat. "I knew I should have just brought up the whole six-pack, but I was trying to be good."

I realized I wasn't going to get a straight story out of her when she was this drunk, so I stood up. "I'll go down and get you some more," I said, intending to bring her up coffee instead.

Her head fell back. "Awww. Would you do that? What a doll."

I left the garret feeling sick to my stomach. If it turned out my suspicions had just been the product of an overheated imagination, I'd never forgive myself. One flight down, I saw Sherry through a half-open door lying on a four-poster bed. Her left foot was bandaged and resting on top of a pillow, her left arm was in a cast, suspended in a sling. She was listening to music with earphones and her eyes closed. I pushed the door open another inch and knocked. She still didn't hear me. I entered and went over to her bed, and stood looking down at her a second. She was wearing jean shorts, and a sweatshirt with the arms cut off.

Without hair gel, her short red hair lay flat and parted on the side, like a little boy's. Her mouth was lax, but I could see her eyeballs dance to the beat of the music underneath her closed lids. Finally, she sensed my presence and opened them. They were puffy and raw-looking. She looked at me long enough to show she blamed me, and then closed them and her mouth, her lips pressed into a furious line.

"Sherry. Sherry, I need to talk to you." This close I could hear she was listening to Joan Osborne. "Sherry . . ."

Eyes still closed, she said, "I have nothing to say to you."

I reached out and turned the music off, and this made her rip off her earphones with her good hand.

"Who the hell do you think you are?"

"I wanted to say how sorry I am you lost the baby."

At the word *baby*, all the anger drained from her face. She laid her head back onto the pillow and covered her eyes with one hand and began to cry, silently. I sat down on the edge of the bed, unsure if I should touch her—if she'd welcome it. I placed my hand on her bandaged ankle. She didn't move her foot. A few moments later, she reached over and pulled a tissue from a box on the bedside table and blew her nose. She clutched the tissue to her chest as she rested her forearm across her forehead and stared up at the ceiling fan overhead, circling slowly.

"It was a boy. I thought that was so cool. Ryan and I were going to raise him to love women—to respect them."

I glanced around the room, which was surprisingly feminine for someone who came across so butch. Or at least tried to. Lavender curtains, a cedar chest with a crocheted coverlet, and lavender-skirted lamps. The only tough-looking articles in the room were their motorcycle jackets with the Iron Maiden logo on the back, hanging off a coatrack in the corner. She was still staring up at the fan.

"How did it happen?"

"She pushed me," she said, blinking slowly, setting a fresh run of tears down her cheeks.

"Who pushed you, Gail?" She shook her head no and bit her lip. "You don't mean Jan."

Her eyes lowered from the ceiling to me. "From the moment we showed up she was acting screwy. Like she was on something. It didn't faze her at all when Ryan told her about the ergot, and you'd think after telling her what you'd seen up in the room she'd at least follow us up and want to look for herself, but instead she goes and sits in a rocker in the nursery."

"And . . . you didn't see anything? Did you look down the dumbwaiter shaft?"

"Yes," she said sneeringly, "but maybe I should have shimmied down it, maybe then you'd be happy."

"Sherry, I really thought—"

"I don't care what you thought. It was stupid. I told Ryan that. But she doesn't think *right* when it comes to her sister. She treats her like she's some hothouse flower. It just encourages this learned helplessness of Jan's. If she wants to play mascot to the Guardian Angels, or not get sonograms or even cry over a broken doll, then that's her business, not ours."

I waited for her furious glare to cool to a more mild disdain. "So this really was over a doll."

Sherry adjusted her sling. "Jan was in the nursery, rocking with this doll in her arms. We come down from the upstairs room, and she won't even acknowledge us. She's just rocking and humming like some imbecile, but Ryan just can't let it go, so she pulls the doll out of her hands, a little too hard, and the doll hits the crib. She didn't mean to crack its head. It was an accident, but the way Jan is acting you'd think Ryan had bashed a live baby's head.

She was so hysterical it was almost funny. In fact, I thought she was joking until Ryan tries to say she's sorry and Jan reaches up and practically tears her larynx out."

The scratch was bad, but it could hardly be compared to the mauling of a wild animal.

"You know she didn't even care that her sister was bleeding? She was more concerned about the crack in the doll's face. At that point, I'd had it. While Ryan was in the bathroom trying to stop the bleeding, I told Jan even though her sister might let this go, I wasn't about to. I told her I was calling the cops because after what she'd just done she belonged in a nuthouse." She pressed the soggy tissue to her nose. "Next thing I know, I'm on my way down the stairs and I feel this push."

I looked down at the bandaged ankle. How could Jan push another pregnant woman down the stairs? It just didn't make sense. But then, I was still grappling with the fact that she'd attacked her sister over a doll. "Are you sure you didn't just trip?"

Sherry's thin nostrils flared as did her eyes. "Just like Ryan. Can't believe sweet little Jan would be capable of such a thing. Well, she's not my sister and far as I'm concerned, she's just a psychotic bitch. Like I told Ryan, if she doesn't bring charges against her, I sure as shit will."

I sat on the tiny stoop in front of their house, smoking a cigarette. It was now late afternoon and I felt tired and sad. Not just about Jan, or Ryan or Sherry's losing the baby, but about myself and the choices I'd made in my life. As a human being. As a woman. Just before I left the hospital my doctor had come in with the results of some tests, and told me that the septic infection had left me sterile. I would never be able to have children. "So much for pro-choice," I'd said, laughing. He was a mild-looking young man with a yarmulka on his balding head, and had looked at me with worry. "There are always alternatives," he said, thinking I was laughing on the outside, crying on the in. I told him thanks, I'd keep it in mind. However, when he left, I did cry. Not so much because I was upset I would never be able to have a child—I didn't desire one—but because it was no longer an option. A choice. It's true what they say: you never miss something until it's no longer there.

Grace was walking down the sidewalk, holding Fester in her hands. I crushed my cigarette out under the toe of my shoe, feeling a sudden sense of purpose.

"Hi, Aunt Annie," she said.

"Hi," I said, standing up. "I think it's time you took a bath."

In their green and pink bathroom, I held my hand under the water running out of the bathtub faucet to check the temperature. When it was the right degree, I pushed the plug into the drain.

Grace was sitting on the fluffy pink toilet seat cover, her arms crossed sulkily. "I *hate* taking baths."

"Too bad," I said, pouring a thick stream of Mr. Bubble into the water. "I'd just throw you into the laundry machine, but you might shrink."

I looked over my shoulder to see if I'd raised a smile, but she was looking at Fester. "Robin thought Fester was so cool. Are you going to keep him, Aunt Annie?"

"No."

"Why not?"

I sighed and stirred the bubbles with my hand. "Because it represents something that's . . ." The word *evil* came to mind, but I didn't feel that was right. I wasn't an evil person. "Something that's gone wrong."

"Oh. So you're just going to throw him away?"

"Yes."

"Why?"

"Well, if you get a bad report card, do you keep it around, or do you just put it away and decide to do better next time?"

It wasn't a very good comparison, but I wasn't a philosopher. I twisted around on my knees to face her.

"But I don't get bad report cards."

Hadn't thought about that. I guess I was using myself as an example. "Let's just leave it that it's not a good thing."

"Robin said it probably grew in you because the time that doctor in the *Zombie* picture did experiments on you."

The tub was full. I turned the water off. "Grace, I told you those movies were all fiction. None of that stuff really happens."

"I told Robin that. I told her about the exploding pigs and how they really didn't explode and the blood was cherry syrup."

"Would you do me a favor?" I asked as I wiped my hands on a pink terry cloth towel.

"What?"

"Would you promise me never to watch any of my movies again?"

Her little face looked dismayed. "Why?"

"Because . . ." I looked over at the monster—its hair, teeth, and bone—something that my body had tried to unsuccessfully piece together into a baby. "The movies are like Fester. They're wrong. And they make me very unhappy."

Grace slid off the toilet seat, looking at me as if I were a wounded puppy. She put her soft hand on my forearm. "I don't want you to be sad, Aunt Annie. You're my favorite aunt in the whole world. If you don't want me to watch those movies, then I promise, I won't."

I felt a painful pressure behind my eyes. I wasn't even her real aunt. I pulled her to me by the back of the neck and kissed her. "Thanks, sweet pea. I'd really like that." I let her go. "Now let's get those clothes off and get you clean."

CHAPTER 14

When I left Ryan's that morning, I felt like an English nanny in an old movie who comes and fixes everyone's messed-up life. I'd sobered Ryan up with four cups of coffee before she went to work; cleaned, fed, and put Grace to bed. I took a dinner tray up to Sherry and even helped her limp to the bathroom. By the time I left for the island, Grace was on her way to school in pressed clothes just as Ryan was coming home from the night shift. Sherry was still asleep, and I sat with Ryan in the kitchen drinking coffee while she drank chamomile so she could sleep. Not that it looked like she needed help. Her eyes and mouth drooped like a hound dog who'd been on a futile, all-night hunt.

She set her cup down. "Thanks for helping out. It really hasn't been as bad as you found us. Just that yesterday Sherry said she was leaving me."

"She's not leaving you."

She smoothed down her hair; it was sticking up where her nurse's cap had been hairpinned to her head. "Not if I press charges she won't."

"You didn't see it happen, did you?"

Her eyebrows raised along with her shoulders. "I

heard a scream and when I came out of the bathroom, Sherry was lying on the vestibule. Lucky it hadn't happened one flight down. That staircase is longer." She paused, looked down at her teacup, and blinked twice before continuing on in the same, tired voice. "Jan was in the hallway. I asked her what happened and she said she didn't know."

One of the guests came into the kitchen. She was my age but looked older. Not older, just more serious. I'd talked to her and her lover a short while after I'd put Grace to bed. They'd invited me out for a night-cap, but I declined. They were both professors and taught at the same university. I felt outclassed, and wasn't up for the condescending questions that in-evitably followed when I explained to "real people" what I did for a living.

"There's coffee, Pam. Help yourself," Ryan said. She did, as unobtrusively as possible, then left. Ryan's eyes followed her. "Can you believe she writes ro-mance novels? She's a professor of English literature so she writes under a pen name. Pretty famous too."

I shifted uncomfortably in my chair. "Ryan, doesn't it strike you as odd that Jan didn't want to see the room for herself?"

She squeezed her tea bag with her fingers over her cup as one side of her mouth pulled back in an ironic curl. "Annie, so many things strike me odd about my sister, I wouldn't know where to begin. You'll be happy to know Kevin's coming home. He's in Singa-pore but should be home in a few days. Soon as he is, he's going to get a court order."

"Eloise."

I didn't think I'd said it accusingly, but she threw the tea bag onto the table. "Look, what did you want me to do? I had to tell him. I got a job, a kid to take care of, and a relationship to mend. I just lost a *baby*."

I sat back, chastened. Through all of this, I'd lost

sight of that. Of course Sherry would feel that pain, but Ryan?

She lowered her eyes. "It's not the same as if, God forbid, anything ever happened to Grace, but I intended on taking care of it and loving it just as much as her one day." She picked up the tea bag and tore it in half. "That baby meant a lot to me and Sherry."

Mr. Green pulled up to the taxi stand. He got out of the car and opened the back door with a comically chivalrous bow and extended his arm for me to enter.

"Milady."

I laughed. "Mr. Green, I think we know each other well enough for me to sit in the front seat."

He shut the door. "Okay, but people might talk, seeing such a pretty young lady sitting next to me."

I smiled. "You never let me pay you for dropping my suitcase off at Jan's."

"Bah." He swatted the air. "It was on my way."

I went around to the other side of the car and got in the front seat. He followed suit.

"So," he asked, starting up the engine, "where to?"

I looked down at the gold horseshoe nestled in his gray chest-hair a moment, trying to decide if it was worth the trip. I looked out the windshield. It was a fine day, the end of the season, and the island was thinning out.

"How much would it cost to drive out to the Little Brown Schoolhouse?"

He turned his meter off. "You know, it's been such a good week businesswise, I think I deserve a little time off."

"Oh no, Mr. Green. I can't let you do that."

"Hey, like I said, it's not every day an old man like me gets to take a long drive with a beautiful woman."

As I buckled up, I felt my cheeks grow warm. It had been a long time since anybody had had a crush on me.

Mr. Green parked his taxi in the gravel pit that served as the Little Brown Schoolhouse's parking lot. It was the only car in the lot. He told me the school was set back in the woods, just follow the path.

"You're not coming?"

He winced uneasily. "Eh. Ginny and I . . . we got kind of a history. Years ago she wanted to date me, but she's not my type. You know what they say about a rebuffed woman. . . ."

"I think that's scorned."

"Scorned, rebuffed . . . all I know is she doesn't like me too much. I'll just wait out here and listen to the ball game on the radio."

I told him I'd try not to be long, and followed a signpost that pointed to a weed-choked path. The trees were so tall and close together their leaves strained the strong afternoon sun to glimmering flashes, and the path hadn't been cleared in some time; prickly burrs and rough plants scratched at my legs. Finally the woods opened up onto a clearing, and from the rundown state of the building I got the impression the Little Brown Schoolhouse wasn't exactly a must-see for tourists. Brown paint flaked off wooden clapboards, and the foliage was so overgrown and wild I almost didn't see the mannequin dressed up in Colonial duds in the corner of the sagging porch. She was poised in front of a butter churn that hadn't seen any action in some time; a spider had made its web using one of her fingers as an anchor. I wondered at the historic accuracy in butter being churned on a schoolhouse porch.

Posted beside the double-door entrance was the price of admission: two dollars for adults, one for children. Seemed like a good deal. I pushed through the wooden doors into a gloomy room. The plants outside the windows blocked out most of the sunlight. The place was small—only five rows of straight-backed pews. Out of the back of each of these a long slanted piece of wood jutted out, to serve as a kind of writing platform for the kids sitting in the row behind. At the front of the room was a desk with the proverbial apple on top, except this one was rotting, and behind the desk was a cracked blackboard on which was written in chalk *Silence is Golden.* I noticed a switch hanging from the wall next to a boy mannequin sitting on a stool in the corner. He was wearing overalls and a dunce cap. It was obvious his original purpose hadn't been to model dunce-wear. He was smiling and one arm was raised as if waving hello.

A small woman wearing a white Quaker-style bonnet stuck her head out of a doorway at the back of the room. A halo of cigarette smoke hovered over her. "The next school period starts in five minutes. Art thou by thyself or with a group?"

"Um, neither actually. Are you Ginny Hershel?"

From across the dark room, I thought the woman narrowed her eyes at me suspiciously. "And who might thou be?"

"My name is Annie Wojtoko. Anita at the library told me you're kind of like the local historian around here."

The woman came out of the room, taking a last drag on her cigarette before crushing it into an ashtray she was holding in the palm of her hand. "Yeah, I'm Ginny. Any friend of Anita's is a friend of mine," she said, coming over. "You'll have to forgive me, but I thought you might be someone from the board of ed. They've been trying to close me down for the last year."

I remembered Mr. Green had told me that Gail and she were somehow related, but up close, I had to wonder in what way. I guessed she was somewhere near Gail's age, but there was no resemblance at all. Her eyes were small and dark, and I could tell by the way her Quaker bonnet hugged her head her hair didn't have the thick coarseness of Gail's. After she dropped the Quaker accent I could tell she was more the "don't even try to feed me a line of shit" type, which I suppose was a good fit for the character she was portraying. The rest of her costume was just a plain, floor-length gray dress. She gestured to the front pew for me to sit and sat herself behind the desk, straight-backed, hands clasped in front of her but in close reach of a heavy-duty, knuckle-rapping ruler.

"What an interesting place," I said. "What kind of tour do you give?"

Ginny reached into her dress pocket and unwrapped a fresh pack of cigarettes. "Usually I give a lesson, just how someone like me would have given one in 1898. That's the last year this school was in use."

"Sounds like a great idea."

"I think so," she said. "But the board of ed complained it wasn't instructional in a 'positive' way," she said, making quotes with her fingers. "Just because I made some kid sit with a Dunce cap on his head. Now that right there wasn't historically correct, because a hundred years ago he would have gotten the switch for what he did." She indicated with a backward flick of her head to the one hanging on the wall. "Little shit carved his initials in the bench, but God help me if I'd done that. As it is, the idiot parents are suing for damage of self-esteem. Is it any wonder we have such nitwit kids today?"

She held the opened pack out to me.

"Thank you," I said, getting up to take one. After lighting mine, she lit her own and flapped her hand up and down in that exaggerated way some people feel they need to in order to put a tiny match out.

Then she unlocked the top drawer with a key around her neck and took out another ashtray and handed it to me.

"I have to keep this locked up. Once a nosey smarty-pants got into my desk and said, 'Ms. Hershel, I thought women weren't allowed to smoke back then,'" she said, mimicking a high voice, then laughed. "He sure had me good, and ever since then I lock everything up."

I smiled. There was an easy familiarity about her. I could imagine sharing a beer with Ginny at a local bar, or being on the same bowling league. And besides, we were both actors. Of a sort. She leaned forward on her elbows and took a long drag off her cigarette. It was an incongruous sight to see this birdlike woman, dressed as a turn-of-the-century Quaker with smoke curling from her mouth. "Anita's a nice gal. Too bad her son Carl's a dolt. A loaf of bread's got more sense than him. So, what can I do you for?"

"Well, I'm hoping you can explain a few things about the Clayton House to me."

She nodded knowingly. "The Clayton House. Better be good or Sybil Clayton will get you." I looked at her blankly and she laughed. "That's what mothers used to tell their children to get them to behave. These days, most people don't even realize what happened there, but when I was a kid you said a Hail Mary, crossed your heart, and ran like the wind whenever you had to pass by that house."

I took a drag off my cigarette. "Yes, I know about the tragedy. But what I really want to know is . . ." I cleared my throat, embarrassed. "Do women who can't conceive really become pregnant there?"

One of Ginny's eyebrows arched midpuff. "Honey, no one's ever told you how babies are come by?"

If I were truthful I'd say no; I'd "come by" the information myself. "Of course. *I* know it's not possible, but friends of mine, a married couple, live in the house and the woman, Jan, is convinced that's exactly what has happened thanks to the influence of . . . Gail Rusker."

As if from the script of one of my movies, the sun went behind a cloud and the foliage outside the windows filtered the darkening room to a gloomy, underwater green.

"Ah." Ginny nodded her head in grave appreciation. "Now that's a name that just *hearing* requires a drink," she said as she took her key and this time opened the bottom drawer of the desk. She pulled out a bottle of whiskey and two coffee cups, and I speculated on what else she had in there—the desk seemed to be a veritable treasure chest of vice.

"Don't think I'm a lush," she said, pouring the liquor. "It's just that it gets pretty lonely out here in the off-season."

She pushed one of the cups across the desk. I got up and murmured, "Of course not," before returning to the bench feeling as if I'd just retrieved an assignment. I felt bad Mr. Green wasn't on good terms with Ginny. He seemed the type to like a nip once in a while.

Ginny raised her mug. "Here's to the certainty that all babies are born of man and woman."

I lifted my cup. "Hear, hear!"

A wind kicked up outside, and as if nature were concurring the leaves on the trees rustled like millions of tiny hands rubbing together.

"At least real ones, anyway."

We took a sip. When she set her cup down, I asked, "What exactly did you mean by 'real ones'?"

"Real as opposed to imagined," she said, crushing her cigarette in the ashtray. "The three 'miracles'? Every one of them a hysterical pregnancy."

I felt my eyes stretch. "What?"

"You know, where the woman bloats up."

"I know what a hysterical pregnancy is, it's just

that . . . I felt Jan's baby. It kicked my hand," I said, holding my hand up as proof.

Ginny mugged. "Well, she has a husband, doesn't she?"

I had risen slightly at the surprise, and felt myself settle back into the pew. "Yes. Of course."

She chuckled. "Look, I'm sure your friend is having a real baby. This is something started by Gail Rusker, who, if you've noticed, is crazy."

"But three women who lived in that house did have babies under mysterious conditions."

Ginny leaned forward and rested her elbows on the desk as she bent back the left index finger with her right. "Okay, look. The first was Mary Prizewater. Fifty-five and claimed to be a virgin. Gail talks her into being her midwife, but she moves out around her fifth month and surprise, no more baby."

"Wait a minute. I'd heard she died in a car crash along with her baby."

She didn't miss a beat. "Adopted a year later. Number two," she said, her right index and middle finger joined to press back their left counterparts, "was Gillian Chance. Early thirties and rich as Croesus. Again, Gail is the midwife, but when she's rushed to the hospital for the delivery, no baby."

"But Kevin was told the baby was stillborn."

Ginny nodded in agreement. "Yes, and that's exactly what her family paid everyone to say. A friend of mine was one of them. They were embarrassed and rightfully so." She had one finger to go, and this time used her entire right hand to press the left three, as if they might put up resistance. "Now the third was a real interesting case. A local girl, fifteen-year-old Susan Lee Prince. She's a real troubled kid—sleeps around, father beats the mother, always telling tales to get attention—anyway, one day she runs away and everyone figures she's pregnant, which lo and behold, she is, but around this time Gail Rusker had started the Guardian Angels and helped her hide in the Clayton place, bringing her food and such until four months later Susan Lee shows up back home, terrified, telling a story that she saw a dead girl in a dumbwaiter in one of the rooms."

I almost spit out my whiskey. "Wait," I said, sliding forward, my breath catching in my throat. "Did you say a dead girl?"

"Yes. Ms. Wojtoko!"

She'd used her schoolteacher voice and I sat at attention.

"If you don't mind, please make sure your ashes make it into the ashtray. I work very hard keeping this place clean. This is still a schoolroom, let's respect it as such."

It seemed funny that here we were drinking whiskey and smoking and she was worried about ashes, but her stern look and firm voice took me back to the fifth grade when Sister Mary McCarthy chastised me for a similar offense: swiping my pencil shavings onto the floor.

"Yes, ma'am," I said meekly as I stubbed my cigarette out.

A sound like hail broke the tension as the wind sent the tree branches clattering against the side of the school. Ginny looked toward the window. "It's the season. The day starts out beautiful but can end with a hurricane."

"So," I started gingerly, "was Susan Lee's story checked out?"

She was still thinking about the storm. "Hmmm? Oh, sorry. I was just thinking the day's going to be a bust. Tourists don't come out in the rain." She took a sip of whiskey. "Of course. Especially since Sybil Clayton's girl drowned and they'd never found a body."

"And?"

"And no girl in the dumbwaiter. Plus, after a few days Susan Lee's stomach begins to go down like a balloon leaking air. When asked why she was no longer showing, she said, 'The girl took it back.' Everyone figured it was all just a ruse to draw attention from the fact that she'd gotten an abortion."

I stared down into my empty glass, unsure of what to make of all this. An unstable kid saw the dead girl; I found three strands of hair. Ginnie held up the bottle to ask if I wanted another, and I thought about the green drink Gail had been giving Jan.

I stretched my mug out to her. "Do you think Gail could have been giving the women something to make their stomachs expand like they were pregnant?"

Ginnie had poured herself another and was now screwing on the cap. "That, I have no idea about. My thought has always been she hypnotized them or something. They say under hypnosis people can be made to believe anything. If you could trick the mind into believing you're pregnant, why wouldn't the body follow?"

Raindrops began to patter the roof.

"I hope I put your mind at ease. See how all these things can be explained away?"

I looked over at the boy mannequin. The room had grown even darker, and he was swallowed up in shadow. "Maybe." Cautiously, I looked up at her. "Ms. Hershel, I heard that you're related to Gail."

A furious scowl broke over her face. "Now how in the hell did you hear that?"

"I . . . just heard."

"Oh yeah? Because the only one who'd know anything about that would be a son of a buzzard named James Green."

I smiled weakly. "All right. I asked if Gail had any family, and he said maybe you."

She shook her head and pursed her lips. "I'm sorry I ever laid eyes on that man."

"He said there was some history," I offered.

"Oh yeah? Did he say what kind?"

I felt myself shrink. "I . . . don't recall."

"That jerk. You watch it with him. He'll put the make on anything that moves. He still thinks he's forty-five. It's just pathetic."

I didn't want to hear any more. I'd rather think I was special. It was my weakness for older men.

"How did you get here?" she asked, a cunning glint in her eye. "Did he drive you?"

I didn't see the sense in lying. "As a matter of fact he did."

"Ha. Whatever you do, don't sit up in the front seat. The man might look like an old fossil, but his hands are as quick as a snakes' tongue."

I stood up and put my mug on the desk. "I'm sorry, I didn't mean to upset you."

"Oh, don't go."

My words had had the effect on her the way they used to have on a dog I once owned who loved to fetch ball. Whenever I held out her leash and said, "Let's go," she'd freeze and her eyes would grow mournful, begging me to stay. I felt sorry for this slightly eccentric woman. Alone out here with nothing but two mannequins to keep her company and an occasional busload of indifferent schoolkids. I sat back in my pew.

She returned to her stern, no bull-shit demeanor. "I'm sorry but I don't like people knowing I'm related to Gail." She poured herself another drink and raised her cup. "Here's to all lunatics that eventually die."

I raised mine too, heartily this time. When she set her cup down, she pulled out another cigarette and lit up. I noticed this time she didn't offer me one. She blew a long plume of gray smoke out into the increasingly damp air.

"Gail and I are half sisters. Same mother, different fathers. An older cousin had forced himself on my ma, but she couldn't bring herself to abort so she had Gail in the Clayton House, and left her there. I came along five years later, but by then my ma was happily married, and I was kept. It was just the luck of the draw, but Gail's hated me ever since. Especially since she was adopted by a floozy alcoholic, but I don't think she ever hated anyone as much as our mother. She made her life a living hell until the day she died. Some people just have no sense of gratitude," she said, shaking her head, eyes on the rotten apple.

"That's kind of hypocritical," I offered. "Especially since the Guardian Angels' mantra is adoption instead of abortion."

She looked out the window, which seemed to be melting it was now raining so hard. "Well, you know what they say, do as I say, not as I do. The thing she could never forgive was that my mother wouldn't take her even after Sybil's spree."

I sat forward. "What do you mean?"

"Gail was the only baby to survive."

I sat back, astonished, and now remembered reading in the *Vineyard Vine* that one of the babies had cholic and ended up sleeping with the nurse that night. "I guess in a way, it kind of explains her obsession with the house."

Ginny swirled her whiskey in her cup as her small piercing eyes wandered the room thoughtfully until they rested on the boy mannequin. "To tell you the truth, I kind of feel sorry for Gail. Years ago she came to our house. She'd just gotten out of Eloise, and demanded to know why Ma gave her up. My mother was a good woman who had to make hard choices. How was she going to tell this girl, who'd just tried to kill herself, that the reason she couldn't keep her was because she could never love a child begotten by rape?"

The sky crackled with thunder. "An unwelcome child," I said.

"What was that?"

"Nothing. I still don't understand what gain there is in convincing women they're having real babies when they're not."

Ginny stood up and went over to the corner, where a shawl was hanging. "Who knows why people do what they do?" She wrapped the shawl around herself. "Come on," she said, taking an umbrella from a stand. "We better go on home before real trouble starts."

Martha's Vineyard, 1922

Sarah sensed something was wrong when she saw her mother put the powdered sedative into the glasses of milk. It was usually Missy's job to deliver the guests their evening refreshment, but she was off tonight so Sarah was to take the drinks up to the women instead.

Her mother handed her the tray. "Don't leave until they drink it all."

Sarah took the tray and delivered the drinks. It was a cold winter night, and they welcomed the warm milk before going to bed. She did as her mother told her, and when she came back down into the drab, brown kitchen all four glasses were empty. Her mother was sitting at the table, reading one of her books, *The Unwelcome Child.* Sarah hated that book; she didn't believe children were damned because they were born out of wedlock, or from a lack of love, but her mother did, fervently. It was how she could do what she did, day after day. Sarah waited by the table to say good night, but her mother kept reading.

"Mother, may I go to bed now?"

Her mother turned a page. "Sarah, is there something you'd like to unburden yourself of? Something you'd like to tell me?"

Sarah stared down at the center part of her mother's gray head and swallowed hard. "No, Mother."

Her mother closed the book and looked up at this child she'd had late in life, at a time when a woman outlives her usefulness, and because of this, she loved her more than anything. She handed Sarah the book. "I'd like you to read this before you go to bed tonight."

Sarah looked down at it. "But I've read it."

Her mother folded her hands on the table. "I think you need to read it again. Tonight, before you go to bed."

Sarah knew better than to protest, but it was a short book, and could be read in under an hour.

"Yes, Mother," she said, turning to leave.

"Did you forget something, Daughter?"

Sarah came over and kissed her mother. Just as her lips pulled away from her mother's dry, papery cheek, her mother grabbed Sarah's chin and held it close to her face. Her mother's dark eyes were piercing and black like the eyes of a hawk, and her fingers were as strong as talons. She stared into Sarah's eyes, willing the girl to confess. But Sarah pulled back slightly, and just this small act of resistance told her mother all she needed to know. She released her daughter, and as if she couldn't bear to look at Sarah anymore, she turned her face away.

"Very well then. Go to bed."

Sarah sat at her desk, staring down at the book in the light of the lamp. Even though her mother would want an accounting of what she'd read tomorrow morning, she couldn't bring herself to read the horrible book. Not only did it repel every bit of her being, she was too nervous. Sarah had the feeling her mother knew, ever since she fired the groundsman, Peter McKenny, for no good reason other than that she no longer trusted him. And she'd remarked more than once she was looking "thick about the middle." But Sarah hoped that if she could hide her pregnancy up to the sixth month, her mother wouldn't be able to bring herself to "cleanse" her own daughter. She hoped that in the end, her mother would feel differently about her own blood. And besides, her mother wouldn't want to endanger her life; she rarely performed a cleansing past the fifth month. It was too dangerous.

Sarah looked down at her stomach, no longer held in from the bindings she kept tied tightly around her midriff.

"Just one more month to go," she whispered, as she stroked the top of her belly.

She woke up to see her mother standing over her, holding an oil lamp in her hand.

"Get up, Sarah," she commanded quietly.

Sarah hesitated, because in her nightgown she showed. "What's wrong?" she asked.

"There's a bird flying around in the room upstairs. Someone forgot to shut the window. I need you to help me catch it."

Sarah sat up and kept herself bent over as she slid on her slippers and kept turned away from her mother as she pulled on her robe. Her mother followed her out and up the stairs. The room where they did the cleansing was at the end of the hall. A lamp was lit, and as they walked down the corridor, Sarah prayed there really was a bird and this wasn't a trick. Her mother was good at tricking the girls. But the moment Sarah stepped into the room she knew there was no bird. Her mother's instruments were laid out on the table next to the bed, and the hypo was already filled. When she turned around, her mother was locking the door. She slipped the key into her pocket and faced Sarah. "Take off your clothes."

Sarah stood frozen. "I said take off your clothes!" her mother shrieked. She had no worry about waking anyone. The drugged milk would make sure everyone would be in a deep sleep well into the morning. With trembling fingers, Sarah undid the tie of her robe and took it off. She held it in front of her as she looked down at the floor.

"Everything," her mother said in a sharp whisper. Sarah looked up. Her mother was still holding the lamp up near her face even though the gaslights were on. The reflection of the flame turned her black eyes red. She undid the top buttons of her nightgown, and then looked up again at her mother.

"Mother, please," she whimpered.

"Everything!"

Her face burning, she pulled her nightgown up and over her head, then held it in front of herself, just below her protruding belly. The cold room made her skin prickle up, but she was hot all over with shame. She felt her mother's eyes on her stomach, and tried to hold it in. When she looked back up, she was surprised to see tears running down her mother's face. It was the first time she'd ever seen her mother cry. It gave Sarah hope that she wouldn't be able to bring herself to do it.

"But you're only fourteen," her mother whispered. "Has everything I've taught you fallen on deaf ears? Sarah, you're my daughter. How could you?"

"I wanted a baby," Sarah mumbled. "My own baby."

"Even though it would be damned?"

Sarah wiped her eyes with the back of her hand. "But it's not going to go to hell like it says in that book, because I want this baby. I *love* this baby."

Her mother set the lamp down on the shelf. "I'll not let an innocent soul go to hell."

"Please, Mother!" She grabbed her mother's forearm with one hand while she held up her gown with the other, and collapsed to her knees, trying to speak even while choking on tears. "Let me keep it."

Her mother looked down at her daughter's tear-filled eyes. Seeing her on her knees, begging, cut her so deeply that for a second she almost relented. But then she pulled away.

"Have you no sense of responsibility? Because of what I do, I'm despised. An outcast. You've seen how people clear away from us in town. Do you think I would have been able to endure such scorn all these years if I didn't believe with all my soul that what we do here is good and right? I love you more than life itself, Sarah, but if I let you have this baby it would be denying everything I've lived my life by."

She walked over to the table. "Now please, get up," she said with heaviness. She lifted the hypo up in her right hand and flicked it with her forefinger and thumb to check that there were no air bubbles. Sarah was still kneeling, rocking back and forth, crying as she pressed her hands to her stomach to feel her baby, worried that it could sense its mother's fear from her racing heartbeat, the sharp contractions of her diaphragm with each sob.

"Sarah."

Slowly, Sarah stood and walked toward the bed and its side table filled with murderous silverware. Still clutching her nightgown as if the cotton material were some kind of protective shield, she eyed the bucket at the foot of the bed. The bucket that would carry her baby down to the cellar where it would be thrown into the sewer. Her baby wouldn't even be given a final resting place, as Sarah had done with so many others. She stopped at the bucket and realized for the first time in her life how much she hated her mother. It was a hate so searing her insides felt molten. Yet it gave her the courage to pick up the bucket and swing it at her mother's head.

"Oh!"

Her mother staggered backward, a hand pressed to the side of her face as Sarah ran to the dumbwaiter. It was small, but she was sure she could just fit. She'd take it down and escape through the sewer if she had to.

"Sarah," her mother screamed, still stunned.

Sarah climbed up and pressed the button that would take her down to her escape. The machine groaned with her weight as she descended through the darkness. She heard her mother cry for her to stop. Her voice echoed down through the shaft, but Sarah knew her mother couldn't touch her. She hugged herself, happy that she'd saved her baby—her baby was safe.

CHAPTER 15

"We're here," Mr. Green said. I sat up in the back-seat as he pulled into the driveway. Ginny ended up sitting in the front after her car wouldn't start. The entire way to her house, she thundered as loudly as the thunder outside as she gave him "a piece of her mind," warning he better not try anything with me; I was a nice kid, and who the hell did he think he was anyway, telling me she was related to Gail Rusker? Last thing she wanted people to know was she was related to that lunatic, and if she ever heard him spreading it around again, she'd tell everyone the reason he always wore that stupid fool golf cap was that a hair transplant had gone wrong.

As Mr. Green got his umbrella out from under the seat, I tried to see the house but it was raining too hard. He opened my back door and helped me out. We hurried up the path through the torrential rain. At the front porch, we struggled with the wind to open the screen door. Once inside, I asked Mr. Green if he wanted a cup of coffee before he went home, but I think he was too embarrassed after the scene with Ginny. I thanked him for everything, and he went back to the car. I watched as he backed out of the driveway and then down Sea Thistle Road, the intermittent lightning causing his car to flash like a silverfish.

Once inside, I turned on a lamp and headed up the stairs, listening for any signs of life. In spite of the wind and rain, there was an oppressive silence, as if the house were wrapped in cellophane. At the second-floor vestibule, where Sherry had fallen, I turned on the overhead light to look at the ten steps, covered with a nailed-down carpet runner. It wasn't *impossible* that she'd slipped. Sherry resented Ryan and Jan's relationship. To me it was more believable that she'd lie to drive a wedge between the two sisters than that Jan pushed her down the stairs. Either way, I made sure I had a good grip on the banister as I climbed the rest of the way to Jan's room.

She was lying on her canopied bed in a thin white nightgown, sleeping deeply in spite of the driving rain coming through the blown-wide French doors. The curtains were soaked and a large puddle had formed on the wooden floor. I set my tote down and crossed the room to shut them. A towel was lying on a satin-covered stool, and I threw it over the puddle to sop up the water.

"Jan," I called out softly, coming over to the side of her bed. Her braid stretched out onto the pillow as perfectly as it had been placed, and clutched to her chest was that doll. When I'd first stepped on it, I'd thought it was the ugliest doll I'd ever seen, but now with its face cracked slantwise from the forehead down to the chin, the crevice splitting the red-painted mouth into a misshapen grin, it no longer seemed just ugly—it seemed evil. And according to Jan, it was the reason I'd lost my ovary. I'd taken something that belonged to *her*, and she in turn took something of mine. I took the doll from her hands and felt the middle section—it seemed the fetus was back in place.

For a moment I had the desire to wring its head off, but set it down on the bed instead.

I looked at Jan's face, and noticed it had filled out. She looked healthier. Or maybe it was just the rosy glow from one of her lamps, a ceramic figurine whose pink skirt served as a shade. As I was about to cover her up with the blanket, I paused and gazed down at her pregnant belly. Gently, I placed my hand on top. She shifted slightly and I pulled my hand back, but she sighed and her breathing remained slow and steady. I placed my hand on her stomach again. It felt warm and firm, and then I felt a faint thump against my hand, like that of a prisoner tapping against the walls of its cell. I smiled, relieved. There was a real baby in there.

I covered her up and headed to my room, but at the doorway remembered my tote. When I turned around, I noticed my reflection in the mirror across from her bed, in the full-length mirror in the corner, and even the one over the television set against the wall. In fact, it was damn near impossible not to see yourself no matter where you were in the room. I didn't remember seeing all these mirrors before. Had she gotten over her strange fear? She turned over onto her side, and as if her fingertips had eyes, her hand stretched across the bed to where I'd placed the doll and slowly drew it back in to her chest.

I went to my room, which was stuffy from being closed up, but the rain was too strong to open a window. I pressed my forehead against the cold windowpane and looked out at the black night. The ocean was tossing up high waves and throwing them against the huge boulders and rocky beach, evanescing the water into white foam. The wind rattled the pane, and I pulled my forehead away. Gail was somewhere in this house, but it had been a long day, and I was too tired to worry about her. Too tired to even undress. My sneakers were soggy. I kicked them off and almost threw my overnight tote down when I remembered Fester was still in there. I'd told Grace it was medical waste and needed to be disposed of properly, and intended to take it back to the hospital to destroy.

For now, I set him on the side table. As soon as I stretched out onto the bed, it seemed as if all the strange impressions of the day came rushing forward at once, like a riotous crowd that had just broken through a barricade—the mannequins at the bizarre schoolhouse, hearing that Gail had been the only baby to survive Sybil's insanity, the hysterical pregnancies, and then finally, Susan Lee's claim that she'd seen a dead girl in the dumbwaiter. Even if she were no longer there, the three long strands of hair proved to me that she had been at one time. The question was, why? I struggled to stay awake, but I felt myself give in to the exhaustion and worry I'd been fighting all day. As I closed my eyes and the sounds of the storm began to fade, I finally yielded to a sleep that promised to be as deep and enveloping as quicksand.

I opened my eyes. Jan was standing at the end of my bed, smiling. I blinked, trying to adjust my eyes to the light of the fan above. A medicinal smell filled the room.

"Jan, is anything wrong?" I asked, sitting up. My hand touched wetness.

She placed her hand over her mouth and giggled childishly. I pulled the covers back and saw Fester. "Jesus Christ," I yelled as I scrambled out of the bed. Then I whirled on her. "Why the fuck would you do something like that!"

Her hand dropped to her side, now looking unsure. "It's your baby."

"What?" I ripped off my shirt in a flurry of revulsion—

that monstrosity had actually touched my skin! I threw the shirt onto the floor and pointed at the bed. "It's a tumor, a mass of cells!"

Her face darkened. "It's your baby."

"Stop saying that! God, Jan. How can you equate a freak of nature with a baby?"

The formaldehyde was making me sick to my stomach. "Now how am I supposed to get that off my bed, pick it up with tongs?"

She tilted her head and looked at me as if I were the one behaving irrationally. Then she came over to the bed, and I watched as she wrapped a strip of gauze she'd had in her hand around the slimy ball, tucking the ends in just the way the tiny fetus's shroud had been tucked. I shrank back from her as she passed me on her way out of the room, holding the thing in both hands as if it were a precious object. I stood a moment, shivering uncontrollably in my bra and jeans, still too shaken to move. Finally, I snapped out of it and ran after her.

At the banister I looked over into the stairwell and just barely caught a shadowy glimpse of her, already descending the final flight. Jan was extremely cautious going up and down these stairs, but to cover three flights so fast she had to be moving at quite a clip. And with not much light—some feat for a pregnant woman in her eighth month. I flicked on the light switch that illuminated the stairwell and followed after her.

Downstairs, the kitchen doors were still swinging. I pushed through them and saw that the cellar door was open. I ran over and hesitated at the top of the stairs and called down into the darkness. "Jan?"

It was crazy for her to have gone down those stairs in the dark! I turned on the light switch, but grabbed a flashlight from a shelf and hurried down. At the bottom, the curtain of sheets were still swaying from where she'd passed through. I could barely hear the thunder down here. I shivered. It was cold, and all I had on was my bra and jeans. I held myself with one arm while I pushed the sheets aside with my flashlight.

"Damn it Jan," I cursed. "Where did you go?"

I flashed my torch around, and heard a thud come from the direction of the storage room. The door was open, and light spilled out. I was barefoot, and stepped carefully, trying to avoid any shattered glass from Kevin's ant farm that might still be lying around. At the storage room door, I stuck my head in and was amazed to see that a portion of the wooden shelves was actually a camouflaged doorway that opened into the interior of a hidden room. The faintest of light suddenly glowed from somewhere deep inside, and then Jan began to hum, the same tune I'd tried to sing for her that day. I knew I'd remember the strange yet beautiful melody again, its offkey strain seemingly random as if it had been composed by a deranged mind. I wiped the cold sweat from my forehead and stepped onto the creaking plank floor. As I made my way to the hidden room, I told myself it was silly to be afraid. After all, it was just Jan.

She had lit a candle, and was kneeling in front of a wooden bench. It reminded me of the old privies at the rest stops I used to see in rural areas whenever traveling as a kid: just a bench with a hole and cover. Next to this was a compartment, over which Jan was now hovering, engaged in some kind of activity. What, I couldn't see since her back was to me.

"What are you doing?"

She seemed oblivious of my presence and continued to hum softly to herself as I came up behind her and aimed my flashlight into the compartment. She was arranging packages similarly wrapped in dark, stiff cloth like the fetus I'd found in the doll, except they were all different sizes.

She moved one to the side, which was the size of a

full-term baby, and paused in her aria to lift Fester and nestle him in. "There. Even though he's messed up, he still deserves a proper place to rest in peace. Just like the others."

"What are you talking about? Whose are these, Gail's?"

She turned her face up into the glare of my flashlight, which I almost dropped when I saw that her right eye was sloping at a downward angle, as if lazy. I lowered the light away from her face and took several steps back as Jan returned to arranging her macabre casket. This wasn't happening. It wasn't. She was *not* possessed by a girl who had been dead almost a century.

I turned around and scanned the small chamber with my light. When I'd first come in, I hadn't paid much attention to anything else but Jan, but now I noticed a rocking chair up against a wall with a heavy throw hanging from its back and a small stool at its foot. It was set up as if someone came down here regularly to sit. Why? The only other thing in the room was a large washbasin underneath a curtained shelf on the other side of the room. I walked over and saw that a number of burned-down candles littered the inside of the basin.

"Jan, did you do this?" I asked, glancing over my shoulder. She was holding the candle in her hands, rocking back and forth and repeating something under her breath over and over. A prayer? I didn't know if I should just let her be or try to get her to snap out of it. I looked at the rocking chair, and realized that it was set up to face this basin. Or the shelf above it. I reached up and pulled the curtain back to reveal, not shelves, but a recessed nook and a door, just like the dumbwaiter upstairs, except that this one was iron instead of wood, and had a steel bolt instead of a latch. Just as I slid it aside and pulled the door open, Jan blew her candle out.

"My God."

I was staring at the remarkably preserved mummy of a little girl. She was curled up with her knees to her chest, pressed against her skeletonized arms that were still wrapped around her middle. Her skin was black and shiny as if it had been shellacked, and her lips had pulled from her teeth, but her light hair was still plaited into a braid. I calculated that the crown of her head, from which I must have plucked the three strands, stood at least five inches shy of the top of the carriage.

"She's beautiful, isn't she?"

I pointed my flash toward the door where Gail was standing. Her hair was undone, hanging down her back and front, and she was wearing a pink robe. I was still too shocked from the sight of this dead child, folded up in that small space, to speak. Gail walked over to the mummy with the unruffled dreaminess you usually see on the faces of either heroin addicts or the clinically out-of-touch.

"Sarah Clayton was a courageous girl. She died trying to stop her mother from aborting her baby, but her will to give life lived on. If I didn't think it would destroy the unique and precious aspect of the house, I'd expose her to the world and have her canonized as a martyr. But then, she wouldn't be having this baby. Isn't that right, Sarah?" she said, stretching her hand out to Jan, who was now standing and staring wide-eyed at the corpse.

"It's all right. Your mother can't hurt you any-more." Warily, Jan walked over. "It's finally going to happen," Gail said, taking Jan's hand. "We've both waited a long time for this, haven't we, dear?"

My voice, strangled by shock, finally broke free. "I want you to tell me what you've done to make her act this way!"

Gail's euphoria evaporated and she regarded me

with vexation. "I haven't done anything. As the time grows nearer, the true mother is getting stronger, that's all. Jan never would have been so weak if she'd not covered the mirrors, but like the others, she coveted what wasn't hers to begin with."

"Bullshit!"

Jan reached out and fingered the mummy's braid in a kind of awed wonder. She let go and was about to touch its face when the lights from the cellar, which had just been barely leaking into the storeroom, flickered and died. Everything went silent and dark, except for my flashlight.

"The storm must have knocked out the electricity," I said, and then grabbed Jan's arm. "Come on. I'm getting you to a hospital before it gets too bad to drive."

Jan pulled her arm from me. "No!" she cried, her face contorted into a snarl as she backed away. "You promised," she said, pointing at Gail. "You promised you wouldn't let anyone take me away!"

Gail held her hands up, placating. "No one is taking you anywhere. It's almost time."

Before I knew what was happening, Jan lunged for my flashlight and threw it across the room, smashing it against the wall. The impact must have knocked the batteries out, because we were now in complete darkness.

"Fuck!" I yelled as I went scrambling for the torch on all fours, feeling around the stone floor for the batteries. Gail was calling out for Sarah, but then she must have tripped over something; I heard the sharp slap of flesh against pavement followed by a cry of pain. My fingers touched upon the flashlight, and then a few feet away a battery. And then another. Gail was moaning. I was cursing as I tried to get the batteries into the flashlight the right way. Only Jan was silent. When the batteries were both in place, I swept the room with the light. She was gone, but Gail was on the floor, propped up against the wall cradling her wrist. She seemed dazed, but okay.

"Are you all right?"

"I . . . I think my wrist is broken," she said. She lifted it up with the other hand. Without the gold bracelets, I could see her scars fully. There hadn't been one clean swipe with a razor—the tissue was fissured and uneven. Her right wrist was swollen. Trying not to touch the scar, I flexed it back and forth, gently. She winced and drew her breath in through her teeth.

"I think it's just sprained. You'll be—"

With her good hand she grabbed me behind my neck and tried to pull me down, but I backed away quickly so that she fell forward onto her elbows.

"Shit," I hissed, feeling behind my neck with my free hand because her nails had scratched me as I'd pushed her away. I held my fingers up. No blood. I looked back down at her, wanting to hit her so badly I was shaking.

"You're lucky you're an old woman. Otherwise I'd knock the shit out of you."

"Annie, please," she said, her pupils so dilated her eyes were like two black disks. "Just wait. Just a little longer. It's almost time. Once Jan has the baby, then you can take her to the hospital, but don't take my Isabelle away. She'll die if you take her away," she said, her voice cracking as she bowed her head and began to cry. As I stared down at her, her body heaving with each sob, I realized this wasn't a scam to get the house. It had nothing to do with the pro-life movement or the Guardian Angels. It didn't even have anything to do with Jan. This woman really believed that this house, what had happened here, somehow had the power to bring back a baby she'd once lost. Seeing her at my feet like this, no longer the proud Guardian of the Unborn, warrior of the womb, but instead a sick, brokenhearted old woman, actually made me feel sorry for her.

"Gail, look at me." She lifted her head enough to look at my toes. Fine. I had no desire to see her tear-soaked eyes anyway. "You're going to stay down here while I take Jan to the hospital, but I promise I'm going to come back for you. There's a flashlight at the bottom of the stairs. You should be fine if you just sit quietly."

She tried to push herself up from the floor with her good wrist but collapsed again. "You can't," she sobbed. "You don't know what you're doing!"

I ran from the room. At the bottom of the stairs, I clicked on the extra flashlight and then jogged up the stairs as her cries followed me all the way to the top. Once I locked the door behind me, they became indistinguishable from the wailing storm outside.

CHAPTER 16

I found Jan upstairs in her room, standing in the doorway. She was clutching her stomach, looking down at her feet where a puddle had formed. The bottom half of her nightgown was soaked.

"What's wrong?"

She looked at me. "My water broke."

"What does that mean?"

Her eyes widened along with a smile. "It means it's time."

I bounded up the stairs. "What do you mean it's time?"

She leaned back against the doorjamb as her hands circled her belly. "I'm going to have my baby." She giggled stupidly.

"No," I said, shaking my head. "How can you? You have one month left!"

She nodded slowly, as if bliss were a heavy thing.

"I said *no!*" The smile dropped from her face. "Jan, I have to drive you to the hospital. That baby has no chance of living if it's born here."

"No," she said, backing away from me. "Gail told you. It'll die."

I went into her room and picked up the receiver on

the bedside table and listened for a dial tone, even though I knew it was futile. There was more electricity in the air than in the phone lines. I slammed it back down. "Fuck!"

She'd sidled all the way to the French doors where she was now cowering, gripping the handle poised to escape. I held my hand out as I walked over. "Come on. I'm driving you to the hospital."

She pressed up back against the doors. "Where's Gail? I want Gail!"

"Jan, please! Before it's too late."

"No! They'll kill it. Just like in my dream! I have to have the baby here. I have to!"

"Listen to me. . . ."

Her face contracted in pain and she folded over her stomach. "Oh! Oh my God." She began to crumple. I ran over and caught her before she hit the floor.

"Here," I said, guiding her over to the bed. "Lie down. Just lie down."

Her bony fingers were digging into my forearm. As I helped her into bed, my flashlight dropped out of my hand. "Goddamnit, we need light in here!" I picked it up off the floor and the beam skittered jumpily around the room. Thank God Jan was a candle freak. After lighting every candle I could find until it looked like a house of voodoo, I brought a large one back over to her bed and set it on the night table. She was wild-eyed, breathing shallowly.

"Look, I'm going to see if I can get a signal on my cell phone, okay?"

She gripped my arm. "Please don't leave me!"

"I'm not. I'll be right back. I'm just going down the hallway. I promise."

I pressed her hand back onto her stomach and ran out. My cell was in my tote and of course, there was no signal. I ran to the window. The backyard was flooding. The roads would be slick, if not flooded themselves. It didn't matter anyway—Jan was not going to leave this house. She cried for Gail, and I looked in the direction of the candlelight spilling out of her room into the hallway. A peal of thunder and lightning turned the sky an eye-blistering white. I dropped down onto the settee. What was I going to do? I'd have to go down and get Gail.

Jan yelled out.

"I'll be there in a minute," I yelled back, but I couldn't make myself move. There was no way I could let that deranged woman near Jan. Then I thought, how hard could it be to deliver a baby anyway? Women do it all the time. I was actually giving this serious thought as Jan lay down the hall, groaning, until I realized how many things *could* happen. Women can bleed to death, an umbilical cord can become a garrote. As disturbed as Gail was, I knew she'd at least never let anything happen to this baby. Especially if she thought it was Isabelle.

I ran out of my room, pausing at Jan's doorway just long enough to let her know I was going down to get Gail.

She looked up with her wet face shining in the candlelight. "Hurry."

The terror in her eyes confirmed that I was making the right decision.

"Gail!" I knocked on the cellar door to give her warning. "Jan's having her baby and I need your help." I knocked again. Either she couldn't hear me because of the storm or she was still in the little room communing with the mummy. I waited, but still no response. "Look, I'm unlocking the door, okay? You can come out."

I turned the lock and stood back, expecting her to charge me like a water buffalo, but the door remained closed. Cautiously, I opened it, afraid she might be standing behind the door waiting to bash me in the head with the flashlight, but she wasn't there. Then I saw that the railing had broken away. I aimed my flash into the cellar to see that she'd fallen to the floor below.

"Oh my God, oh my God, please don't let her be dead," I cried as I tripped down the stairs. When I reached her, I could see her white hair was soaked red with blood. Gently, I turned her onto her side, and saw that the right side of her skull was crushed. I placed my fingertips on the thick scar of her left wrist to feel if there was a pulse. Nothing.

I sat back on my heels and wondered why she had tried to climb the stairs without using the flashlight I'd left her, still beaming brightly at the bottom of the stairs. As I stared down at her one open eye, already turning milky with death, I realized I felt nothing. I should have felt panic, at least guilt, but it was as if my feelings had gone on the blink along with the electricity, and inside me there was just darkness. All I wanted to do was just stretch out on the floor and go to sleep. Instead, I reached out and closed Gail's eye, and then forced myself to get up.

Upstairs I stood in the center of the kitchen, trying to make myself focus on what had to be done, but my brain seemed like a quivering mass of gelatinous confusion. Every so often the lightning lit up my surroundings in explosions of silverish X-ray. I heard screaming, and looked in the direction of the cellar, but then realized it was Jan. Having her baby. *Think.* What needed to be done? Water needed to be boiled. For what reason, I had no idea except that they did it in the movies. I went to the cupboard and found a pot big enough to boil a turkey in and placed it in the sink. But as I watched it fill with water, all I could see was Gail, lying broken on the cellar floor like a doll that had been thrown down the stairs by a child in a fit of pique.

After the pot was filled, I carried it over to the stove and turned the burner on. The lightning illuminated the phone on the wall, and I picked the receiver up and pressed it to my ear in the futile hope that it might work. It was still dead. I pulled it away from the side of my head and stared down at the mouthpiece. This was my fault. Not just for locking a hysterical, injured old woman down in a dark cellar, but for being so arrogant in the first place to think *I* alone could save Jan. If I'd just stayed out of it, Kevin would have had no alternative but to put Jan in a sanitarium. He would be home right now, she'd be having her baby in a safe place, Sherry wouldn't have miscarried and I'd be back in New York shooting a Dr. Scholl's commercial.

As I tortured myself with these self-incriminating taunts, the storm outside had kicked up to a new level of anarchy. The wind became a screeching fury while the thunder ripped the sky as if the sound barrier itself were being torn in half. It takes only one lunatic in the asylum to set the others off in a frenzy, and I began to pound the receiver against the wall over and over again until my arm was rubber and the phone was nothing but a gutted shell, its wire entrails hanging out of its mouth in a stringy tangle. Then I slid down the wall into a heap of unrelieved sobbing as the zombielike flatness lifted. Something deep inside was opening up for the first time, like a newfound oil well gushing, spewing up the black ooze of dead creatures created over millennia of compression.

I don't know how long I stayed there, but Jan's screams were now coming in regular bursts of agony, as promised in Genesis. I looked up at the stove where the pot was boiling over. If I was going to do this, I had to get a hold of myself. I made myself stand up and turn the burner off. As the bubbles quieted, I stared down at them and took deep breaths. When my breathing finally slowed, I took the pot and headed back upstairs. For what purpose I was going to use this, I had no idea, except maybe to throw the kid in if it turned out to be anything other than human.

She gasped when she saw me in the doorway with the steaming pot of water in my hands. "Where's Gail?"

"She's . . . gone."

Her face grimaced in a mixture of fear and pain. "But it's coming!"

I set the pot down on the floor. "Aren't you supposed to be in labor for a long time?" A part of me was still hopeful I wouldn't have to go through with this, and I was praying that by the time the baby was ready to come the storm would be over and the electricity restored.

Jan shook her head wildly, then arched and grabbed fistfuls of sheet. "Gahhhh!"

I ran to her bathroom and got as many towels as I could carry along with a wet washcloth. When I came back out, she sobbed, "I'm going to die. I'm going to die."

"No, you're not," I said, stuffing the towels all around her. "You're not!" I began to wipe her brow with the washcloth. "We'll get through this. Women do this every day, right?"

Her eyes were frozen on me, bulging. She licked her lips and took my hand. "Please let me keep it. Please."

"Of course you're going to keep it!"

"Whatever happens, you won't take it away? Because she won't live, she won't live . . . Ahhhhh!" Another contraction racked her body. Wasn't she supposed to be pushing? Breathing rhythmically?

"Jan did Gail prepare you at all? Do you know what to do?"

Her eyes rolled up and her head rocked side to side on her pillow. "Uhhh," she groaned. Her hands, limp as rags, lifted to her mouth. She was muttering deliriously. I climbed on the wet bed and lifted her soaked nightgown. It was dark enough for me to be thankful I didn't have a clear picture. I was sure the sight of a baby's head emerging between Jan's legs would make me pass out, but there it was, just the crown. Jan's body bucked, her knee nearly knocking me in the chin, and screamed.

"Jan! I think you need to push! Next one you feel coming on, really push!"

She was crying, and still gibbering on, but on the next contraction when I yelled, "Push!" she did, but the baby's head didn't budge. Even though it was probably in reality only a matter of minutes, this seemed to go on forever, me crouching between her knees holding my hands like a catcher waiting for a fastball because I'd heard babies have been known to shoot out like bullets. The world was liquid—the rain outside, sweat pouring down both of us, the bed a swamp of fluid. When the head finally emerged, I screamed and laughed out of hysterical nervousness, and yelled over the thunder and pelting rain that this was a hell of a lot scarier than any movie I'd ever been in. Jan tried to laugh, but it turned into a whimpering cry as her head dropped back onto the pillow. For a moment I'd thought she'd fainted and I slapped her thighs begging her not to give up. All she needed was one last push and she was home.

Rallying herself one last time, she lifted herself back up onto her elbows. With teeth bared and eyes squeezed shut, she bore down with the grunting ferocity of a weight lifter hoisting three-hundred-pound barbells over his head and squeezed the baby out into the world and into my hands. Then she collapsed back onto the bed.

"It's a girl," I said, still crouching on my knees, too amazed to move. Strands of blood and viscous stuff that looked like egg white covered her flesh, which was wrinkled and loose as a suit two sizes too big. Otherwise, she seemed remarkably developed for a child one month premature. Jan was panting heavily. "Is she alive?" she asked, her voice pitched high with apprehension.

"I think so."

"Hit it."

I looked at her. "What?"

"Spank it," she yelled. "Hold her upside down by her feet and hit her bottom."

"Jan, I can't even lift a cat up by its collar!"

"Annie, please!" I held the baby upside down and gave it a gentle pat. "Harder," Jan shouted, her eyes bulging. "It's alive. Make her cry, Annie. Make her cry!"

I was scared I'd hurt it, but Jan looked like she was going to have a heart attack if this baby didn't wail. I thought of an old boyfriend I'd slapped across the face one time, and on the next try the baby let out a caterwaul worthy of the thunder outside. She was still tethered to Jan's uterus via an umbilical cord as long and curly as a telephone's, but I set her down on one of the clean towels and wrapped her in it, then handed her to Jan's waiting arms. Tears were streaming down her face along with beads of sweat. The baby was shaking her fists, red-faced and angry for getting a swat for no good reason, unlike the boyfriend for whom it had been a turn-on. I got off the bed and dipped the washcloth into the pot of water I'd boiled, now tepid, and handed it to Jan. As she wiped its face, she barely had the strength to lift her head to kiss it.

"My baby. My sweet, sweet baby," she murmured her voice raspy from screaming.

I watched this in dazed exhaustion, my body still quaking as if all my connective tissue had dissolved.

"Too bad Kevin's missed this," I mumbled. Either it didn't register, or she really no longer cared.

"Thank you, Annie," she said, her eyes slowly lifting to meet mine.

"Anytime. No! Strike that. Absolutely never again."

We smiled at each other. She seemed different. Herself. As if she were reading my mind, her eyes shifted to the bureau mirror across the room. "She's gone. I see me, now."

I turned my head, to see the both of us, looking exhausted and slimy as if we'd just spent the last hour Jell-O wrestling. "Where'd she go?"

Her gaze dropped back to the baby, who was making the torturous sounds a newborn makes—probably already sensing the good times were over.

"Here," she said, tenderly brushing her lips across the crown of its head.

After I cleaned the baby off, I went into the bathroom to wash up. I stared down at my hands, savoring the feel of the baby's body in my hands—its warmth, its lightness. The way its skin slid silkily back and forth over its tiny bones. Then I lifted my face to the mirror. The kid coming out of Jan's crotch looked better than I did right now. I looked like a madwoman. Jan's and the baby's blood was streaked all over my face, chest, and arms. My hair was matted down with sweat and God knows what else, and my facial muscles were still clenched, pulling my eyes open wide. It was the exact expression frozen on the replica of my decapitated head I'd brought home from my last movie.

"Annie," Jan called weakly. I went back into the bedroom.

"Yeah?" I said once I was by her side. The baby had quieted, she was at Jan's nipple, but Jan looked pale.

"You don't look so good."

"I think . . . I think something's wrong," she said, and then with great effort pulled back the blanket that I'd covered her up with. The white sheet had become solid red, almost black in the dim candlelight. A jelly-like sack was lying in the middle of a pool of blood.

"Oh my God. Oh my God! We have to get you to the hospital!"

"It's too late."

I pointed out the window. "Look, the storm's starting to die down. We can make it."

"We can't leave the baby."

"We'll take it with us!"

"No," she screamed so furiously she startled the baby and it began to cry. "Promise me, Annie, you won't take her out of this house. Promise me!"

I held my hands out, pleading. "Jan, it's all in your mind. The baby is real—nothing's going to happen to it. I promise. Please, we have to leave—"

"Promise me!" She was now clutching the child fiercely to her breast, so tightly I thought she'd crush it.

"All right, goddamn you, I promise! I promise! Are you happy now!" I collapsed onto the bed facing away and sobbed, along with the baby. A few seconds later, I felt her hand on my back. I turned around. She blinked once, and then her eyes stayed open and staring, the only light left in them coming from the reflection of the candles around the room.

By early morning, the storm was over. The sky was lightening from black to gray, and the candles had melted down to almost nothing. It had taken almost an hour for me to work up the courage, but I cut the umbilical cord from the afterbirth and tied it off with a shoelace, then wrapped the baby in a clean towel. Now we were both exhausted from crying, her from hunger, me from grief. I looked over at the baby, whose whole body was shivering in what seemed to me a soundless angst as she lay next to the body of her mother. Promise or not, I had to get this baby to the hospital.

I got up and pulled a shirt out of Kevin's closet and put it on, and was about to pick the baby up when I saw something sticking out from underneath Jan's pillow. It had been too dark to see before, but now I could clearly see two tiny feet. I reached under and pulled out her doll. Perhaps I was too emotionally numb, but for some reason I wasn't surprised to see her opened up once again, her stringy insides spilling out, except this time the fetus was gone. Probably lost somewhere in the bedding. I would have looked, but I no longer cared, and slipped the doll under the sheet next to Jan instead.

"I'm sorry," I said, then gathered the baby up into my arms and left.

Just as I set the baby in the front seat of Jan's red Mercedes, she began to all-out bawl again, like she knew I was betraying her mother. For a moment, I wavered. What if Jan was right? But I reminded myself she hadn't been in her right mind, not for some time, and though I may have failed Jan in many ways as a friend, this time I was going to come through. The Jan I knew would want me to get the baby she'd fought so hard to bring into this world safely to the hospital. I rubbed her belly gently. "It's going to be okay, kid. Just hang on."

I backed the car down the driveway, one hand on the wheel, the other on the baby's heaving chest. The storm had flooded and littered Sea Thistle Road with tree branches and debris. I maneuvered carefully around them as I drove through water as deep as the car's hubcaps. Right at the turnoff to the main road, the baby began to make strange, choking noises and when I looked down I saw her face was red. I pushed the towel away to give her breathing room, but her mouth kept puckering in and out as she gasped for air.

"Oh, come on," I said, shaking her gently as I scanned the neighborhood to see if anyone was around. The road was empty. I had to decide whether to go back to the house, or make a run for the hospital. I looked in the rearview mirror at the house looming up on the hill, and then back toward the direction of the hospital, where the sun was rising. The baby gurgled.

"God, please let me make it," I prayed, and pressed the pedal to the floor.

EPILOGUE

Seven years later, Martha's Vineyard

I sat on the bench waiting for Jimmy to pick me up from the ferry depot. It was a beautiful day and unusually warm for late September. The gingerbread homes were exactly the same as I'd remembered them from seven years ago, and so were the tourists taking a whirl around the island on their bikes, mopeds, or Rollerblades, one last time before the end of the season.

Jimmy's green Caddy pulled up. White lettering on the side spelled out Green Hornet Car Service followed by a phone number. He honked his horn and I waved.

"Jimmy!"

He got out of the car. Over the years he hadn't changed much. Maybe a few more lines around the eyes, and a little heavier in the jaw and waistline, but he still wore that golf cap and the gold horseshoe still hung around his neck. He'd changed the red satin windbreaker for a green one, the same color as his car. He'd come up with the idea a year ago because he needed to "stay competitive."

"Great to see you again, Annie."

He came up and we gave each other a long hug. Jimmy and I had stayed in touch over the years via holiday and birthday cards. When my dad passed away two years ago, he came to the funeral, and when his granddaughter got married, I went to the wedding.

With heartbreak on his face, he held me out at arm's length. "Aw, you cut your hair. You had such beautiful hair! Why'd you go and do that?"

I shrugged. "Long hair on a woman after forty looks like she's trying too hard," I said, but the real reason was that people didn't recognize me from my *Bloodfest* days as easily.

"Forty?" He waved his hand at me. "You don't look a day over twenty-five."

I swatted his compliment away yet giggled like a vain fool. "So," I said, resting my hand on the hood of the car, "how's it going with the Green Hornet?"

He leaned in and placed his hand beside his mouth. "Well, from what the ladies tell me, I still got that sting."

I rolled my eyes. "You old flirt."

"Ha." He slapped his thigh. "Come on. Climb on in and let me put your bag in the trunk."

I walked around the car. "Is Kevin's new house far?"

"It's maybe half an hour from the old place," he said, opening the trunk. "Wait till you see it—nothing like the other. All modern. He's got a Jacuzzi sundeck and a dock out back. Really something."

He slammed the trunk shut and I opened my door. "Well, Kevin always was the modern type. Jan was more Old World."

I was about to settle into the seat when he said, "If you like, we'll stop by the old place. Janette's party doesn't start until three."

I hesitated. I wasn't sure I wanted to see the house, now a must-see on every tourist's list of things to do on the Vineyard. When it came out in the news about Sarah Clayton's body being found in the dumbwaiter, the legend of the house, which until then had only been a local one, became internationally renowned. Kevin was inundated by reporters, parapsychologists, and kooks from all over. It got so bad he moved out and hired a caretaker to look after the house while it was on the market until he found out the guy was charging women a fee to stay overnight. Like a swarm of sterile locusts they had descended upon Sea Thistle Road, willing to pay any price in the hope that the house would work its magic on their dormant ovaries. Fed up, Kevin fired the caretaker and instructed the real estate agent to accept the next offer no matter how much below the asking price, and in an ironic twist of fate that must have had Gail tap-dancing in her coffin, a pro-life group bought it with the intention of turning it into a refuge for pregnant women.

That didn't last long. The problem was the women, usually indigent, strung-out junkies or young girls who'd run away from broken homes, tended not to like the busloads of tourists driving up the hill at all times of the day to gawk and take pictures as some loud-mouth on a megaphone shouted out the legend and events in gory, sensationalistic detail. So the pro-life group eventually sold it to a slick entrepreneur who turned it into its present incarnation, a kind of house of horrors. They hired Ginny Hershel to run the place, and just like at the Little Brown Schoolhouse, she dressed up in costume, except instead of portraying a turn-of-the- century Quaker schoolmistress, she now portrayed Sybil Clayton.

Jimmy said he doubted that the real-life Sybil Clayton was anywhere near as scary as Ginny's Sybil, and people loved it as she led them on a tour starting from the dumbwaiter room, showing them the instruments

Sybil used to abort babies with, then on to the nursery where she smothered the five newborns, then down to the unusually deep cellar, where little Sarah Clayton's body had been mummified in the dumbwaiter by the cold air. The tour concluded with a visit to the small shrine out back where the girl was interred in an aboveground tomb.

"Well," Jimmy prompted, "day's growing stale. I only mention it because Ginny said she'd love to see you."

"Okay," I said finally. "I'd be lying if I didn't admit I'm curious."

Jimmy's driving hadn't improved any, and I found myself gripping the armrest and the edge of the seat with white-knuckled nervousness as he swerved in and out of traffic and around slow-moving bicyclists.

"Hey, I saw your commercial," he yelled. He had a hearing aid in his right ear now, and tended to talk loud.

"Which one?"

"The one where that lady throws a bucket of water on you and you dissolve."

"Ah. The Floor Wax Witch."

"That's right. Boy, do I get a kick every time I see that! The boys down at the Clam Shak don't believe me when I tell them I'm your personal chauffeur whenever you're up here. You're going to have to give me an autograph or something so I can prove to them I know such a famous gal."

I smiled at the irony; I was a famous gal all right. Last time I talked to Peggy, she told me that the Floor Wax Witch was destined to be a classic. Right up there with the Maytag Repair Man and Charmin's Mr. Whipple.

"I got to say though, Annie, and I hope you don't take offense, but that stuff works like crap."

"Really?" I said, clenching my teeth at the near miss of the corner of an SUV's back bumper as Jimmy passed on its right, seemingly oblivious as the driver blasted his horn and flipped us the bird.

"My floor got all gummed up," he continued. "I can't take a step without the soles of my shoes sticking to the linoleum."

"Did you use water?"

"What?"

"I asked if you used water," I said, bringing my lips closer to his hearing aid.

"No," he shouted. "Am I supposed to use water?"

I laughed. "It helps. Otherwise it won't dissolve."

He laughed. "Oh, I get it. So that's why you dissolve. Hey, I get it now!"

We pulled up behind a purple tour bus sitting out in front of the house. Jimmy had warned me they'd changed it back to how it had looked when it was a hospital, but it was still a shock. Instead of yellow, it was now painted brown with beige trim. Jan's red and white rosebushes were gone, and the lawn that had been as springy as a sponge was now sandy and full of crabgrass. Even the picket fence was beginning to sag. I looked up at the widow's walk where a woman was taking snapshots of the landscape.

"I can't believe what they've done to Jan's beautiful house," I said.

"You know, if this is going to bother you we'll just drive on to the party. Ginny'll understand," Jimmy said.

I shook my head no. The reason I was up here was that although it was the anniversary of Jan's death, it was also Janette's birthday. Usually I preferred to spend the day alone, but when Kevin invited me, he reminded me I hadn't seen Janette since her baptism, a

THE UNWELCOME CHILD 297

lousy track record for a godmother. There's no adequate explanation as to why I've been such a reluctant participant in her life. It's true that he'd moved out West for the first five years of her life, but for the last two he's been back East, and whenever I've been invited to functions where there's no doubt Janette will be present, I've always come up with an excuse not to go. I've told myself it was because everyone else seemed to be moving on. Sherry and Ryan had another baby, Reese, Kevin was engaged, and soon Grace would be off to college. And as for myself? Although on the outside it looks like I've gotten on with my life (nice boyfriend, lucrative career), I've actually remained stuck in the past. It's not fair, but some part of me would rather mourn Jan's death than celebrate the life of the child that caused it, and that was exactly why I made myself come this time. As Kevin put it, it was time to let go.

I looked at Jimmy, who was watching me, his old eyes full of concern. "I think it'll be good for me to see the place. Kind of like putting old ghosts to rest, you know?"

He pulled his golf cap down low on his forehead. "Yes, I do."

On the porch, an enormously pregnant girl wearing a black smock over a gray dress was sitting in a chair in front of a small table. She was reading a Mary Higgins Clark novel propped on top of her stomach, which was obviously a pillow stuffed underneath her dress, and chewing gum. A sign said ten dollars for adults, six fifty for seniors. Children under twelve were not admitted. To the side of the table was a little stand of bouquets and a placard on which was written, *Flowers for Sarah's tomb—$12.*

"Hey there Tanya," Jimmy said. "This here is a friend of Ginny's. Mind if we just go on in?"

She flashed a smile. "Not at all. But she's down with a group in the cellar. She's just finishing up."

"Oh," I said, hitching my purse over my shoulder. "I really don't want to go down into the cellar."

"It's really cool," Tanya said.

Jimmy took my elbow. "We'll just sit in the parlor until she comes up."

The house inside was just as much changed as the outside. The silk-covered furniture had been replaced with polyester-covered replicas, and the crystal chandelier was now brass. A rubber runner ran all the way up the stairs to preserve the cheap carpeting that had replaced the rich wool that I remembered. But the light still streamed through the stained glass at the top of the house, fanning out into a colorful kaleidoscope onto the wooden floor below. I'd never forgotten Jan's words about the dust: *Right now, we're breathing in everyone who ever lived here.* I looked down at the reading table to my right. In a glass-covered case *The Unwelcome Child* was opened up to the underlined passage. Jimmy had taken a seat on a brown-and-white striped sofa.

"Jimmy, if you don't mind I'm going to go upstairs and look around."

He lifted himself up slightly. "You want me to come?"

"No no," I said, waving him back down. "I won't be long."

I bypassed the second floor and went on up to the third, straight to Jan and Kevin's old room, which was now "The Sybil Clayton Room." A rope across the threshold barred entrance, but even if there were no rope I wouldn't want to go in. Jan's light, airy sensibility had been replaced with Sybil's austere and cheerless personality. The curtains were heavy and the fourposter bed was plain and forbidding. Other than a cedar chest and a brown wooden armoire, the only other furniture was a small nightstand on which stood a portrait of Sarah and Sybil, the same one that had been in the *Vineyard Vine*.

I stepped back to read the glass-enclosed case just outside the doorway. In it was a picture of Jan, taken when she was still unpregnant and beautiful, and a blurb long enough to give a sketchy outline of what happened but short enough not to tax the relatively short attention span of the average visitor. In *Reader's Digest* simplicity, it told of her inability to get pregnant, her "odd" relationship with Gail Rusker, her "mysterious conception," the purported possession, and of course, her dramatic death, the details of which they'd gotten from the transcripts of my testimony at the inquest. The end was an epilogue that read like copy from a bad TV show.

Many people believe that if Jan Hostetter had not died, the child would have been prisoner of the house indefinitely, as the legacy was originally interpreted. Some even wonder, had Jan Hostetter, whose bleeding by all medical accounts should not have caused her death, had somehow intuited this and let go of her own life so her child could be free? Unfortunately, no one will ever really know whether she was truly possessed by a girl who'd died nearly a century ago, or by a disease of the mind. But if the former is true, then it proves what has been claimed about mothers since the beginning of time: Theirs is a love that has no bounds, by neither this world, nor another.

I leaned back against the wall. As angry as I was at Ginny for turning what had happened to Jan into such melodramatic tripe, I was grateful for the lie, because

Jan *did* bleed to death. Even though the coroner assured
me that her placenta had already been fragile, and
that I'd done the best that could be expected under the
circumstances, I could never really escape the guilt. It
was as if slivers of glass, imbedded in the skin of an accident victim, will keep finding their way to the surface
for years afterward, appearing as glistening and sharp
as when they first went in.

I crossed the hallway and peeked my head into the
nursery. Five cribs were lined up against the wall like
a barracks for babies, and in each crib was a doll. It was
a macabre sight, considering what had happened to the
real babies in those cribs. In the corner I saw what was
undoubtedly the influence of Ginny Hershel—sitting
with a doll on her lap in a rocking chair was the butter-
churning mannequin from the Little Brown Schoolhouse. I wondered where Dunce-boy was. As for the
mural, it was now covered with yellow wallpaper. There
was no way they could have known that the mural was
Gail's handiwork, or what *The Dead Child* motif symbol-
ized for her. As I headed to the staircase leading to the
top floor, I felt a secret satisfaction that they never
would.

I found the dumbwaiter room, a.k.a. "The Cleansing Room," occupied by what I judged to be three gen-
erations of the same family. A middle-aged woman
with orange lipstick and orange blush was ogling a case
where Sybil's obstetrical instruments were on display,
while an older woman with the same coloring and
blocky build was absorbed with the contents of a
medicine cabinet on the other side of the room.
Both were wearing Whale Watch T-shirts and had
teased red hair, although the older woman's appeared
to be a wig. The youngest generation was represented
by a scrawny, redheaded teenager sitting on a neatly
made hospital bed. On her T-shirt was an arrow

underneath the words *I'm Not With Them,* and if that didn't get the point across, her long face did, which gave the impression she'd rather be dead than here. Either that or it was seeing what plans her genes had in store for her in the persons of the two older women.

As I waited for them to leave, I stood in the hallway and pretended to be engrossed with a portrait of an actress from the turn of the century, supposedly one of the more frequent guests of the Clayton House.

"It says this here is tansy tea," the older woman said with a thick southern accent. "And that Sybil Clayton served it to the women to bring on a miscarriage. You know, Maybell," she said, turning to the middle-aged woman, "I could swear I saw this stuff when I was cleaning out Grandma Kay's house, sitting on the bottom shelf of her root cellar."

Maybell was too engrossed in Sybil Clayton's red leather abortion kit to look away. It was making her eyes pop so wide the tips of her false eyelashes almost touched her eyebrows.

"It sure does make the blood curdle, doesn't it?" she answered in a languid drawl. Then she glanced over at the teenager. "Marvalette, sit up straight. How many times have I told you slumping is bad for your digestion? What's the matter with you anyway? Ever since we got here you haven't shown one speck of interest."

"'Cause I'm *bored,*" the girl said, letting her head loll to the side as if she'd suddenly lost all muscle control.

"Bored! I'd like to see how *bored* you'd be if you lived back then and had to come and have this Sybil Clayton fix you up with these here tools," she said, tapping the glass with an orange fingernail. "You girls today just don't know how good you got it, right, Mama?" she asked the older woman.

The woman nodded her head, sending the safety chain on her purple-rimmed eyeglasses a-swinging.

"That's right, Marvalette. In my day, if a girl was un-married and pregnant, she might as well just jump in the Charleston River with a stone around her neck."

The girl crossed her arms but remained in a defi-ant slump. "Way-ell, I think abortion is no better than murder, and if I got pregnant tomorrow I'd *have* my baby, and no one could make me do any different."

"You'd have your baby," her mother scoffed. "Just wait and see how much you'd like it when you're stuck home with a screaming newborn instead of going out with your friends. Boy, won't you be singing a different tune then!"

"Maybell, don't listen to her," the older woman said. "At their age, they just like to provoke."

My patience had worn out and I entered. The mother of Marvelette checked her watch. "Well, I guess we better get going anyhow. Your daddy's waitin' on us for lunch and you know how irritable he gets when he's hungry."

They walked out, following one another like a string of red-haired ducks. Once they were gone, I stood very still in the center of the room, half expect-ing something bad to happen as it had every other time I'd been in it. Only nothing did, even as I ap-proached the dumbwaiter. It was open, but a screen was in place. I suppose to prevent anyone from falling in. A small card on the wall described Sarah's at-tempted escape from her mother "cleansing the un-welcome child from her womb." I wondered if they knew this for a fact, or like everything else were just taking dramatic license.

I crossed the room to the medicine cabinet. It was locked, but through the glass I could see the boxes of *Dr. Bronson's Female Pills* and *Belchem's Female Cure*, and the antique bottles of tansy tea, rue, and ergot, none of which turned up in Jan's autopsy report.

Nor anything else to account for her strange behavior. They even did a testing of the green stuff Gail had been having her drink, and it turned out to be exactly what Gail had said it was: just some herbs and oils.

I heard Ginny's voice, along with Jimmy's, coming up the stairs and a few moments later they appeared in the doorway. Ginny was wearing a black dress with a white smock and on her head was a gray wig parted down the middle. It was slightly askew, which made her look demented. I wondered if it was intentional. Either way, Jimmy was right—it was scary how much she resembled Sybil Clayton.

"Annie," she said, coming over. "How nice to see you." As we hugged, she patted me on the back as if she were trying to burp me. When we pulled apart, she looked around the room with a proud smile. "Well, what do you think?"

"What do I think?" I repeated, glancing over at the abortion instruments, then the medicine cabinet, and finally the dumbwaiter. "To be honest, I'm a little overwhelmed."

With an acquiescent nod, she placed her hands on her hips. "Some people think it's in bad taste, but the people who run the place are out to make a profit, and when they hired me I was told in no uncertain terms they didn't intend to have it sitting empty like the Little Brown Schoolhouse. If I didn't do it, someone else would, and they certainly wouldn't be doing it as accurately. I even went up to Eloise to search out Sybil's old records to get a better handle on her. And besides," she said defensively, "it's educational. I'm trying to get the board of ed to include a tour in their junior high sex education classes."

Her eyes landed on the rumpled coverlet that Marvalette had been sitting on. "Now will you look at that? There's a sign right there that asks you not to sit on the bed, but people just have no respect."

As she smoothed it back out, I told myself I couldn't very well sit in judgment of Ginny, considering what I used to do for a living. Besides, Jan wasn't anything to her, really, except the fourth finger to be ticked off on her hand, like she'd explained the first three troubled women to me that day in the schoolhouse. Still, I couldn't resist giving her a little dig.

"And Gail?" I asked. "Why isn't someone running around here playing Gail? She certainly was just as much a catalyst as Sybil. If not more."

"This is a guided tour, not interactive theater," Ginny said, standing up straight.

"Gail is here, in a way," Jimmy said. "When they buried the little mummy on the grounds, Ginny made arrangements to have Gail's ashes put in with her."

I looked at Ginny in surprise, who in turn was glaring at Jimmy as if she'd like to abort him right here on the spot.

"You did that?" I asked, astonished. "I thought you couldn't stand her."

She sighed as she took a pack of cigarettes out of her smock pocket. "What else was I supposed to do with her—set her on my mantelpiece?" She paused to offer me one, but I shook my head.

"No, thanks. I finally quit."

"Well then, how 'bout a shot of Wild Turkey?" she said with a wink.

"I'm up for that," Jimmy piped up, rubbing his hands together.

"I didn't ask you, you old fool," she said, going over to the medicine cabinet. "You certainly don't need to loosen up that big mouth of yours any more than it already is."

"I'd love one," I cut in before they started going at

each other. And frankly, right now I needed a shot. Of anything.

She unlocked the cabinet, took out one of the bottles and some tiny measuring cups. After she filled them all and they were in our hands, she turned to me. "Annie, you're the guest. What would you like to toast to?"

I looked down at my thimble-sized cup, and asked myself if I got what I wanted by coming here. I think in a way, I did. Perhaps turning the place into what it had once been was actually a blessing in disguise. In making it ugly again, they'd erased all traces of Jan—her beauty, her love of life. Women had come here to have their babies aborted, so it wasn't appropriate to have it look like something out of a fairy tale. A nightmare was more like it, and the depressing, spiritless feeling it now gave off was fitting. The only thing left of Jan was the aftermath. And since she was no longer a part of this house, everything that happened in it no longer had to be a part of me.

I held up my cup. "To Jan," I said. "And to letting go of the past."

"Here we are." Jimmy pulled onto a dirt road bordered with tall trees and scrubby bushes with pink flowers. The road went on about a half mile until it opened onto an inlet with a small island in its center. A number of homes were built along the edge, each with its own dock, to which small boats were moored. Privacy was evidently prized here. The houses were like faces peeking through the trees and thick vegetation. We circled around the perimeter of the inlet for about another quarter mile until we came to a tall two-story home. I don't know what style you'd call it. Ultramodern ugly? It was a square box, all natural wood and glass, while the property was landscaped with angular shrubbery, artfully placed rocks, and spiky, mean-looking plants that lined a flagstone path leading up to an entrance large enough for an NBA player to pass through comfortably.

"Well, it certainly is different from the other, isn't it?" I said, trying not to show my dismay.

"It's not to my taste," Mr. Green said. "I prefer more traditional, but the backyard leads down to the water and the sundeck gives you a great view of Lobsterville."

As we pulled into the driveway, Grace came through the sliding doors wearing a bikini top and cargo shorts. Even though she came down to visit me in New York a lot, it seemed like she was growing up so fast she was a different kid every time I saw her. At seventeen she already stood at five ten, three inches taller than myself, and as I'd predicted, she was growing into her mother's beauty. Her hair was a darker blond, but she had those glacier-blue eyes and a nose just long enough to save it from being pert. She played forward guard on her high school basketball team and hoped to get an athletic scholarship to B.U.

"Yo, Aunt Annie," she said, sauntering over to my side of the car. She ducked down and waved at Jimmy through my open window. "Jimmy."

I got out. As we hugged, I noticed a hickey on her neck. "Young lady, what is that?"

She grinned impishly and pulled her hair to the front. "I got bit by a really big mosquito."

"Um-hmm. I hope at least it was a really cute one too. How's it coming along?" I asked as I went around to the trunk from which Jimmy was already pulling my suitcase.

She stretched and yawned. "Mom and Sherry are fighting over a pinata in the backyard, and we're expecting Reese's bratty friends at the ferry any time now."

"Reese's friends? I thought this was Janette's party."

"I guess they were all busy," she said, taking my suitcase from Jimmy.

"What do you mean her friends are busy? They're eight-year-olds."

Grace shrugged. "I don't know. I think some other kid is having a party today also."

"Grace, tell your mom I'll be over later," Jimmy said, walking back around to his side of the car. "I got some errands I got to do."

I thanked him and he took off as Grace and I began to walk toward the house. "You know, Aunt Annie," she said, hooking her arm around mine, "I was thinking. Since you're going to be up here for the next few days, it's a shame to leave that nice apartment of yours empty. Don't you have plants that need watering or something?"

I patted her arm. "Nice try. But the only leafy green thing in my apartment is David's pot plant he brought back from Arizona, and he takes better care of that than me."

Grace made a face. "But I thought he was away for the summer."

"It's fall, he's back at Columbia, and even if he weren't the answer would still be no. Not only because your mother would kill me, but because I was once your age and know only too well what you'd be up to." I glanced at her hickey. "And if that's what you get from a mosquito, I'd hate to see what a cockroach would do."

She sighed as she opened the door. "Man, you're getting as farty as Mom in your old age."

Inside, Kevin was in the kitchen with his back to us washing dishes while Becka, his fiancée, was standing in the middle of a sunken living room giving out instructions to a short Latino woman in a maid's uniform. Becka was what you'd call "well maintained"—perfectly manicured, makeup like a mask, and nipped and tucked in all the right places. Right now her hair was in rollers and she was wearing a flowing blue silk robe and mules. The poor maid had that hammered-down look all people inevitably acquired once they'd spent any amount of time in Becka's presence.

"Now remember, as soon as the entertainers are finished, I want the children to stay down in the playroom. They're *not* to be running around while the adults are having their dinner."

"Yes, mees," the woman said.

"And please, *try* and do something with Janette's hair. Something other than braids for once. I'm tired of her looking like a milkmaid."

"But, mees, I cannot find her."

"What do you mean you can't find her?"

The maid shrugged. "She say she no want to come to party."

Becka became apoplectic. "What do you mean? It's her party! What little girl doesn't want to come to her own party?"

"I don't know, mees, but that what she say."

She waved the maid away with an imperious flip of her wrist. "I'm sure she's around, Consuelo. As soon as you find her, bring her to me and I'll have a talk with her."

"Becka," Kevin said, wiping his hands and turning around, "I think maybe it would be better if *I* talked to her." Then he saw us. "Annie!"

Becka feigned surprise even though we'd been standing there for five minutes. She stretched out her arms. "Annie, how nice to see you," she said with all the sincerity of the French welcoming Hitler.

The first time I'd met her, Kevin had stopped in to see me in New York. We'd gone out to dinner at an expensive restaurant to celebrate his making partner, and I remember the whole time she wouldn't look at me unless asked a direct question. She never once asked me about myself, and whenever the topic of Jan came up she always managed to change the subject. Even though I went out of my way to convey how glad I was Kevin was finally getting on with his life (although I neglected to say I was glad it was with her), I guess being the best friend of her fiancé's dead wife in some way threatened her.

We met in the middle of the living room and kissed the air on the side of each other's face. "So sorry," she said, patting her cheeks. "But my makeup is still setting."

Kevin came over and gave me a peck on each cheek, which I'm sure was due to Becka's standing right next to him. I looked at him closely, because not only were the streaks of gray no longer running through his red hair, the crow's-feet that had made great strides toward the outer reaches of his face over the years had mysteriously vanished without a trace.

"Are you taking Botox?" I asked, incredulous.

"No." He laughed, although the skin around his eyes didn't reflect his mirth. "You know what they say." He glanced over at Becka. "When you're in love, not only do you feel young, you look young too."

"Uh-huh," I said with an evil smirk.

"So," he said, sweeping his arm around the large room, "what do you think? Becka did the interior design," he said quickly, thereby heading off any tactless remark he knew I was only too capable of making.

I looked around at the unsightly modern art, all in shades of blue and gray, the white leather, chrome-trimmed furniture, and the mobile that looked like a car wreck gone through compaction hanging from the high ceiling.

"I can see that," I said.

"Well, I'd love to chat," Becka said, her mules already clicking in the direction of the staircase as she crossed the gray slate floor, "but my hair still needs to be done and I'm expecting the caterers any moment now." At the bottom of the stairs she whirled around and stretched her neck to address Grace, who was now sprawled out on the couch reading a magazine. "Oh, Gracie, darling, do you mind moving your motorcycle into the garage? I don't want our guests to think we're harboring any *gang* members here." Then she turned and, lifting the hem of her robe, ascended the stairs with such a queenly posture you'd think a throne awaited her at the top.

Grace tossed the magazine down and muttered, "Yeah, right. As if anyone would think she'd be cool enough for that."

"Grace," Kevin warned, and then picked up my suitcase.

"Caterers?" I glanced down at my overalls and espadrilles. "Was I supposed to *dress* for this?"

"Nah. Rebecca's just having a little 'soiree' after the kid's party. We'll just tell everyone you're a poor cousin from the Ozarks." He laughed, and I gave him the finger.

He took me up to a gray-paneled horror on the second floor with its very own glassed-in balcony that gave me a lush view of a bunch of leaves. He set my suitcase down. "I really appreciate you coming up. I know how busy you are."

"I'm looking forward to meeting Janette," I said, trying not to focus on a succession of prints on the wall behind him that looked like different versions of the same roadkill. "It sucks that some other kid is having a party today also."

He squinted as he looked out the sliding doors, even though the sun was so completely occluded by the trees it gave the room a cavelike gloom. "There's no other kid having a party. Becka just said that because of all the kids we invited, practically every one of them had an excuse."

I shook my head in disgust. "Kids are bastards."

"It's not the other kids, it's Janette," he said irritably. Then he sighed and thrust his hands into his pockets. "The truth is she'd rather stay up in her room with her dolls than be with other kids. Janette was never an outgoing child, but as she gets older it seems like she's becoming more and more withdrawn, living in her own world. I love her, she's my baby and all I have left of Jan, but even I have to admit something's . . . just not right with her."

The words caused him to bow his head with either shame or pain, I couldn't tell. He'd been so afraid that Janette might end up like his brother, Jan hadn't been in the ground a month before he had her tested for every conceivable mental disability. But to his delight, he found that no mental defect was lurking in his child's brain folds. If anything, she was a highly intelligent and normal little girl. At least that had been the general consensus until now.

I went over to him. There was an internal weariness dragging at him. I could see it in the downward turn of his mouth and the faded color of his normally emerald-green eyes. "Kevin, what's going on?"

He swallowed, sliding his Adam's apple up and down his throat. "Something happened between Becka and Janette that's making me think it might be best if we postponed the wedding . . . indefinitely."

There was a long pause, and I had the feeling whatever it was, this was the first time he'd spoken of it to anyone. I didn't want to push, but I was anxious to find out. "What? What is it?"

"The other night, I was working late and Becka was sleeping. When she woke up, she found Janette standing at the end of her bed. Becka thought she might want a glass of water or something, but when she turned on the light she saw that Janette had put one of her dolls on the bed next to her." His eyes lifted but only as high as the depression at the base of my throat. "It was split open."

"Jesus," I whispered. It was just too much a coincidence. I wanted to ask what did it look like? how was it torn? but I couldn't very well do that. Especially since I'd never revealed to anyone anything about the doll mutilations in the first place. Or about finding the little fetus inside. Perhaps because after Jan's body had been taken away, it had disappeared. When I looked back up at Kevin, I realized he was still waiting for my reaction.

"It sounds like she's . . . quite the practical joker," I said with a weak little laugh.

Kevin shook his head. "Janette would never mutilate one of her dolls as a joke. Especially this one. It's her favorite. It's such a . . . disturbed thing to do. I think she needs to see a psychiatrist. I'm hoping it's just a temporary reaction to my getting married and it can all be worked out."

"And what is Becka's reaction to all this?" I asked.

Kevin sighed and rubbed his eyes. "Ever since I suggested we postpone the wedding she's been on this campaign to win Janette over, which is only making Janette's life hell." His hands dropped to his sides. "That's what's behind this whole stupid party."

There was a knock at the door. I went over and opened it, to find Becka, her nostrils pinched together, looking directly past me.

"Kevin," she said, her voice an icy snap, "it's time to pick the children up from the ferry."

After he left, I sat down on the bed and took my mother's locket out from my blouse. Ryan had found it in Jan's jewel box, and thought I might want it back. As I traced my fingertip across the Virgin's carved face, I wondered if on some unconscious level I'd put off seeing Janette for so long for fear of this. Even though I'd made a toast earlier in the day to let go of the past, I couldn't stop wondering if the doll Janette had left in Becka's bed was the same one. I'd always figured one of the EMT workers took it, or it got caught up in the sheets and had been thrown away. Whatever the case, I was just relieved that I'd never have to see its ugly face again. I slipped the locket back into my blouse and stood up, thinking the room with a huge silver star on its door at the end of the hallway had to be Janette's.

Underneath the star, *Janette* was spelled out in pink, glittery letters. It was partly open. I knocked and stuck my head in, and immediately felt a little pain at the back of my throat, behind my eyes, because the room was filled with Jan's dolls. When she was alive, they'd always filled me with dread, but now that she was gone, I actually wanted to go over and hold one. Sort of. I entered the pinkest room I'd ever seen in my life. Pink furniture, pink carpet, pink-canopied bed with frilly pink pillows. I wondered which irked Becka more: Janette's strange behavior or all this pink in the midst of her gray-and-white scheme.

"An inch higher. No, that's too high, Ryan! I said an inch, not a foot!"

"Sherry, you want to do this, be my guest!"

I went over to the window and looked out to see Ryan standing on a ladder attempting to hang a pinata from a tree limb while Sherry stood below, directing her on the correct height and position with such fervor and exactitude you'd think she was in charge of hanging a Degas instead of a papier-mâché donkey. Ryan no longer lifted weights, and she was much smaller now, while Sherry had grown downright plump after she'd had Reese. I looked over to where Grace and Consuelo were tying pink balloons to a large festive picnic table, set up with party hats and pink plates. Another picnic table was set a ways down the sloping lawn, nearer the water, which I assumed was for the adults. Instead of paper cups and plates, there were wineglasses and china. Then I had the most peculiar feeling, as if I were being watched. But everyone down there was absorbed in their activity. I thought it was just my imagination, until I saw a little girl standing away from everyone else underneath a low-hanging apple tree, staring up at me.

For some reason, I pulled back out of sight behind the curtain. I placed my hand to my chest and realized my heart rate had shot up. It was absurd, the reaction I was having, but there was something about the way she'd been staring up at me . . . hiding there behind the tree like some small creature trying to camouflage itself. I told myself I was reacting this way because of the conversation I'd just had with Kevin, and all that it had brought up. I craned my neck around the curtain, but she was gone.

I looked around hurriedly for the doll, but didn't see her anywhere and was about to leave when I noticed Pippy, slumped over a baby piano with her face in the keys like a passed out drunk. I picked her up and stared at her freckled cheeks and snub nose, the two big black dots drawn in for her eyes. That bittersweet pain throbbed behind my eyes again and I pressed her to my chest. All day I'd been trying not to focus on how much I'd been missing Jan. *Annie, what are you doing to Pippy! Stop that!* I laughed, and for old times' sake took hold of her red braids and gave her a twirl.

"You shouldn't do that to her."

I looked over my shoulder, startled to see the little girl I'd just seen down in the backyard now standing in the doorway. Under her arm was the doll.

"You'll mess her hair up."

"I . . ." I was so disconcerted I couldn't speak. "I was just . . ."

As she walked over, I observed she was tall for her age. She had long blond hair pulled to the front in two braids, framing a face that had none of the delicacy of Jan's, nor the boldness of Kevin's. It was round and bland, but it was her gray eyes that I found disconcerting. As she looked up at me, there was no movement in them whatsoever. It was as if two gray stones had been pushed into a lump of clay.

"Her name's Pippy," she said. "I like her, but she's not my favorite so you can play with her, but only if you're nice to her and don't pull her hair."

I finally found my voice. "I'm sorry. You're right." She walked over to the doll-stuffed crib and began to take them out. "My name's Annie," I said. "We met a long time ago, but you probably don't remember. Your mom was my best friend in the whole world."

"I know who you are," she said, taking a doll from the crib and putting it aside. "You're the lady who took me out of my mommy's stomach."

"You remember that?" I asked, incredulous.

"Daddy told me," she said. I noticed she was taking the dolls from the crib one at a time with only one hand so she could hold on to the old doll.

"She used to be your mommy's favorite," I said, pointing to old crackhead. "What's her name?"

She paused to hold the doll out in front of her. "Betty. She's my favorite too."

"Really? How come?"

"Because she's so ugly the other dolls don't like her."

And she's been hurt, see?" She touched her finger to the crack in the face.

"Ah yes."

Janette stroked the doll's nose. "Poor Betty," she cooed. "No one wants you except me."

"May I see her?"

Janette hesitated, I guess trying to decide whether I was trustworthy or not. Finally she handed her to me. I looked down at the grisly mouth, those lifelike teeth. The paint on her nose was a shade off from the rest of her face, where Jan had mended it. Surreptitiously, I squeezed its middle. Something hard was inside. I looked at Janette, who was watching me as carefully as a mother cat watching its newborn kitten being handled.

I cleared my throat. "There's something inside her."

"That's her baby."

"Baby." It wasn't possible. After Jan's body had been taken away, I stripped that bed. How could it have gotten back into the doll? I looked back down at Betty, and it was everything I could do not to tear the damn thing open right then and there. But I could only imagine how that would look—a deranged woman disemboweling a child's beloved doll on her birthday. Almost as if she could read my mind, Janette took her from me.

"Janette, did you put the baby in there?"

She didn't answer. Instead, she placed the doll in the crib and covered it up with a blanket.

"Betty has to go to sleep now," she said, hinting she wanted me to leave. Then she began to rock the cradle. "Go to sleep, Betty. Go—"

I reached out and grabbed the crib. Now Janette stepped back, startled, and I felt a satisfaction at having ruffled her composure. "I'm sorry," I said. "But I'd like it if you answered my question."

Janette just stared at me, and as I looked into those gray eyes surrounded by all this pink, that unsettling sensation I'd had when I'd spied her down in the trees was even stronger now—a small creature camouflaging itself. I had no doubt that if I could look inside her, I'd find a soul as gray and cold as the color of her eyes. Then Consuelo appeared, and the spell, or whatever it was, broke.

"Mees Janette, it's time to dress for your party."

Janette looked over at Consuelo. "Okay, but first I have to rock Betty to sleep." Her eyes shifted back to me.

"Aiyiyi." Consuela laughed, and then said to me. "She do thees every time. Five minutes," Consuelo said, holding up five fingers.

As I got up, Janette returned to rocking the crib, but she never took her eyes off me. Even when I turned around in the doorway, she was still watching me. I told myself I was reading too much into it. Letting the past color the present. She was just a little girl. Odd, but still just that.

"Happy birthday, Janette," I said, forcing a smile. Consuelo shut the door behind us, and through it we heard Janette begin to sing her doll to sleep. But it wasn't until I was halfway down the hallway that I recognized it. I stopped short and had to steady myself by bracing my hand against the wall.

"Is something wrong, mees?" Consuela asked.

I turned and looked back in the direction of Janette's room. It was the melody that had haunted me over the years. Sometimes I'd wake from a deep sleep with the melancholy strain ringing in my ears, or I'd find myself cleaning, and humming it under my breath. But as soon as I became aware of what I was doing, it would dissipate like a ring of smoke gradually losing shape until there was nothing at all. And no matter how hard I tried, I could never recall it. It seemed to be a sly thing that only came to the surface when my guard was down.

Now, the half dirge, half lullaby was drawing me back in time to the house on Sea Thistle Hill. I've just given Jan my mother's locket, and we are standing in front of the mirror. I tell her to look in the mirror, to see how it looks on her. She doesn't want to, but I insist, and when she does she begins to hum this strange song. It's a song that "puts the little ones to sleep," she says, just as a young girl once sang the unwelcome children in her mother's nursery to sleep.

Just as her little girl is doing now.